Her Greek Millionaire

The wealth of Onassis, the body of Adonis…

Her Greek Millionaire

THE HUSBAND TEST
by
Helen Bianchin

THE KYRIAKIS BABY
by
Sara Wood

THE GREEK
TYCOON'S BRIDE
by
Helen Brooks

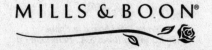

MILLS & BOON®

*MILLS & BOON and MILLS & BOON with the Rose Device
are registered trademarks of the publisher.*
Harlequin Mills & Boon Limited,
Eton House, 18-24 Paradise Road, Richmond, Surrey, TW9 1SR

HER GREEK MILLIONAIRE
© by Harlequin Enterprises II B.V., 2005

The Husband Test, The Kyriakis Baby and *The Greek Tycoon's Bride*
were first published in Great Britain by
Harlequin Mills & Boon Limited in separate, single volumes.

The Husband Test © Helen Bianchin 2001
The Kyriakis Baby © Sara Wood 2001
The Greek Tycoon's Bride © Helen Brooks 2002

ISBN 0 263 84475 7

05-0505

*Printed and bound in Spain
by Litografia Rosés S.A., Barcelona*

Helen Bianchin was born in New Zealand and travelled to Australia before marrying her Italian-born husband. After three years they moved, returned to New Zealand with their daughter, had two sons then resettled in Australia. Encouraged by friends to recount anecdotes of her years as a tobacco sharefarmer's wife living in an Italian community, Helen began setting words on paper and her first novel was published in 1975. An animal lover, she says her terrier and Persian cat regard her study as as much theirs as hers.

**Look out for the next passionate read
by Helen Bianchin:
THE GREEK'S BOUGHT WIFE
Coming in August 2005, in Modern Romance™!**

THE HUSBAND TEST
by
Helen Bianchin

CHAPTER ONE

KATRINA felt her breath hitch a little as her voice rose in disbelief. 'You're not serious?'

It was a joke. A tasteless, sick joke. Except lawyers didn't sink to this level of facetiousness during a professional consultation. 'Dear God,' she said irreverently. 'You *are* serious.'

The man seated behind the imposing mahogany desk shifted his shoulders, and eased into a well-rehearsed platitude. 'Your late father expressed concern at the difficulties you might incur.'

Difficulties didn't even begin to describe the shenanigans her extended dysfunctional family were heaping on her head.

Not that this was anything new. She had been *the favoured one* for as long as she could remember. Daddy's golden girl. His only child. A constant, immovable thorn in the side of his second and third wives and their child apiece from previous marriages.

No one could say her life hadn't been interesting, Katrina reflected. Three paternal divorces, two scheming ex-wives, and two equally devious stepsiblings.

During her formative years she'd been able to escape to boarding school. Except for holidays at home, most of which had been hell on wheels as she'd fought a battle in an ongoing war where reality had

5

been a seething sea of emotional and mental one-upmanship beneath the façade of pleasant inter-family relationships.

The time between each of her father's divorces had proved to be the lull before the next storm, and instead of bowing her down it had merely strengthened her desire to be a worthy successor to his extensive business interests.

Much to the delight of the man who'd sired her.

Now, that same man was intent on reaching out a hand from the grave to resurrect a part of her life she fought on a daily basis to forget.

Katrina cast the lawyer a penetrating look. 'He can't do this,' she refuted firmly as she attempted to hide the faint tide of panic that was slowly invading her body.

'Your father had your best interests at heart.'

'Making the terms of his will conditional on me effecting a reconciliation with my ex-husband?' she queried scathingly. It was ridiculous!

'I understand a divorce has not been formalised.'

Her level of desperation moved up a notch. She hadn't got around to it and, as no papers had been served on her, neither had Nicos.

'I have no intention of allowing Nicos Kasoulis back into my life.'

Greek-born, Nicos had emigrated to Australia at a young age with his parents. As a young adult he'd gained various degrees, then had entered the hi-tech industry, inheriting his father's extensive business interests when both parents died in an aircraft crash.

Katrina had met him at a party, their instant attraction mutual, and they'd married three months later.

'Kevin appointed Nicos Kasoulis an executor,' the lawyer relayed. 'Shortly before his death, your father also appointed him to the board of directors of Macbride.'

Why hadn't she been apprised of that? Dammit, she held a responsible position in the Macbride conglomerate. Choosing not to take her into his confidence was paternal manipulation at its worst.

Her chin lifted fractionally. 'I shall contest the will.' Dammit, he couldn't do this to her!

'The conditions are iron-clad,' the lawyer reiterated gently. 'Each of your father's ex-wives will receive a specified lump sum plus an annuity until such time as they remarry, sufficient to support a reasonable lifestyle in the principal residence they gained at the time of their divorce. There are a few bequests to charity, but the remainder of the estate passes in equal one-third shares to you and Nicos, with the remaining share being held in trust for your children. There is a stipulation,' he continued, 'making it conditional both you and Nicos Kasoulis refrain from filing for divorce, and reside in the same residence together for the minimum term of one year.'

Had Nicos Kasoulis known of these conditions when he'd attended her father's funeral less than a week ago?

Without doubt, Katrina decided grimly, recalling how he'd stood like a dark angel on the fringes, watchful, his touch cool, almost impersonal, as he'd taken her hand in his and had brushed his lips to her cheek.

He'd uttered a few words in condolence, politely declined to attend the wake held in Kevin Macbride's home, and had walked to his car, slid in behind the wheel, and driven away.

'And if I choose not to heed my late father's request?'

'Nicos Kasoulis retains control in the boardroom, and a financial interest in Macbride.'

She didn't believe him, *couldn't* accept Kevin had gone to such lengths to satisfy a whim to have his daughter reconcile with a man he had considered more than her equal.

'That's ridiculous,' Katrina refuted. *She* was the rightful heir to the Macbride business empire. Dammit, it wasn't about money...nor bricks and mortar, stocks and bonds.

It was what they represented. The sweat and toil of a young Irish lad from Tullamore who at the age of fifteen had worked his way to Australia to begin a new life in Sydney as a brickie's labourer. At twenty-one he'd formed his own company and made his first million. At thirty he'd become a legend, and had been fêted as such. With the pick of Sydney's society maidens to choose from, he'd acquired a wife, sired a babe, and had developed a roving eye. Something that had got him into trouble and out of marriage a few too many times. A lovable rogue, as Katrina's mother had referred to Kevin Macbride on a good day.

To Katrina he'd been a saint. A tall dark-haired man whose laugh had begun in his belly and had rolled out into the air as a full-blooded shout. Someone who'd swept her up into his arms, rubbed his sun-drenched cheek against her own fair one, told stories that would have charmed the fairies, and who'd loved her unconditionally.

From a young age she'd played pretend Monopoly with his kingdom, sitting on his knee, absorbing every business fact he'd imparted. During school holidays she'd accompanied him to building sites, had had her own hard hat, and had been able to cuss as well as any hardened labourer—mentally. For if Kevin had caught even a whisper of such language falling from her lips he'd never have allowed her on *any* site again.

Something that would have hurt far more than a paternal slap, for she'd inherited his love of creating something magnificent from bricks and mortar. Of siting the land, envisaging architectural design, selecting the materials, the glass, seeing it rise from the ground to finish as a masterpiece. Houses, buildings, office towers. In later years Kevin Macbride had delegated, but everything that bore his stamp had received his personal touch. It had been his Irish pride, and her own, to see that it was done.

To imagine conceding *any* of it to Nicos Kasoulis was unconscionable. She couldn't, *wouldn't* do it. Macbride belonged to a Macbride.

'You refuse?'

The lawyer's smooth tones intruded, and she lifted

her chin in a gesture of defiance. 'Nicos Kasoulis will not gain sole control of Macbride.'

Her eyes were the green of the fields of her father's homeland. Brilliant, lush. Emphasised by the pale cream texture of her skin, the deep auburn hair that fell in a river of dark red-gold silky curls down her back.

For all that Kevin Macbride had been a big man, his only child had inherited her mother's petite frame and slender curves, the hair and eyes from her paternal grandmother, and a temper to match.

Too much woman for many a man, the lawyer mused, who'd long been intrigued by the private life of one of the city's icons whose business interests had commanded large legal fees over the years.

'You will, therefore, adhere to your father's wishes as set out in his will?'

Live with Nicos Kasoulis? Share a home, her life, with him for one year? 'If that's what it takes,' Katrina vowed solemnly, and he was willing to swear he caught a hint of tensile steel that boded ill for any man hoping to bend her will.

Was Nicos Kasoulis that man? He would have thought so, given the look of him. Yet, despite the marriage, they'd separated after a few brief months, and rumour rarely held much basis for fact.

His business was to ensure Kevin Macbride's wishes were legally maintained. Not to wonder at the man's private life, nor that of his only child.

'I shall despatch formal notification of your willingness to comply.'

Katrina lifted one eyebrow, and her voice was dry and totally lacking in humour. 'Did my father specify a date for this reconciliation?'

'Within seven days of his passing.'

Kevin Macbride had never been one to waste time, but a week was over-zealous, surely?

She looked around the sumptuous furnishings, the expensive prints adorning the walls, the heavy plate-glass and caught the view out over the harbour.

Suddenly she wanted out of here, away from offi-cialdom and legalities. She needed to feel the fresh air on her face, to put the top down on her Porsche and drive, let the breeze toss her hair and bring colour to her cheeks. To be free to think, before she had to deal with Nicos.

With determined resolve she rose to her feet. 'I imagine we'll be in touch again before long.' There would be documents to sign, the due process of wind-ing up a deceased's estate. She extended her hand in a formal gesture that concluded the appointment, mur-mured a few polite words in parting, then she moved into the corridor leading to Reception.

The lawyer walked at her side, then stood as she passed through the double glass doors and stepped towards the lift.

There was no doubt Katrina Kasoulis was a beau-tiful young woman. Something about the way she held herself, her grace of movement, and that hair...

He hid a faint sigh, for she burned as a bright flame, and a man could get singed just from looking.

Katrina rode the lift down to the ground floor,

crossed the street to the adjacent car park, located the relevant floor, and slid in behind the wheel of her car.

It was almost five, the day's office hours reaching a close, and she eased the Porsche onto street level, then entered the stream of city traffic.

Katrina drove, negotiating the choked roadways until she'd covered distance and the traffic dissipated. Then she moved into a higher gear, heard the muted response of the finely tuned engine, and revelled in the speed.

It was almost six when she pulled to a halt on the grassy bank overlooking the beach. There was a tanker on the horizon, easing slowly down towards the inner harbour, and a few children frolicked in the shallows beneath the watchful eye of their parents.

Gulls crested low over the water, dipped, skidded along the surface and settled, only to move their wings in a graceful arc to skim onto the sand.

It was a peaceful scene, one she desperately needed to ease the ache of recent loss. There had been so much to organise, family to deal with.

And now there was Nicos.

It was over, done with. And she'd healed.

Liar.

She only had to think of him to remember how it had been between them. Not a day went past that her subconscious didn't force a memory. He invaded her mind, possessed her dreams, and became her worst nightmare.

All too frequently she woke in a sweat, his hands,

his mouth on her so real she could almost swear he'd been there with her.

Yet she'd always be alone, the security system intact, and she'd spend what remained of the night reading or watching a late movie on television in an attempt to dispel his haunting image.

Occasionally she bumped into him at social gatherings around the city, professional soirées where her presence was *de rigueur*. Then they greeted each other, exchanged polite conversation...and moved on. Except she was acutely conscious of him, his steady gaze, the latent power he exuded, and his sensual heat.

Even now her pulse quickened to a faster beat, and her skin warmed, the soft body hairs raising in awareness. Sensation unfurled deep inside, and spread through her body like a lick of flame, activating each pleasure pulse, every erotic zone.

This was crazy. She took a deep, steadying breath and held onto it, then slowly exhaled. Two, three times over.

Focus, she bade silently. Remember *why* you walked out on him.

Dear Lord, how could she *forget* Nicos's ex-mistress relaying news of a confirmed pregnancy and naming Nicos as the father of her unborn child?

Georgia Burton, a model whose slender beauty graced several magazine covers, had delighted in informing a conception date coinciding with a time when Nicos had been out of town on business.

Georgia's assurance her affair with Nicos hadn't

ended with his marriage was something Katrina couldn't condone, despite Nicos's adamant denial, and after one argument too many she'd simply packed up her things and moved into temporary accommodation.

Even now, several months later, the memory, the pain, was just as intense as it had been the day she had left him.

The peal of her cell phone sounded loud in the silence, interrupting the solitude, and she checked the caller ID, saw it was her mother, and took the call.

'Siobhan?'

'Darling, have you forgotten you're joining me for dinner and the theatre tonight?'

Katrina closed her eyes and stifled a curse. 'Can we skip dinner? I'll collect you at seven-thirty.' She could just about make it if she edged over the speed limit, took the quickest shower on record, and dressed.

'Seven forty-five. I have tickets, and valet parking will eliminate several minutes.'

She made it…just. Together they entered the auditorium and slid into their seats just as the curtain rose.

Katrina focussed on the stage, the actors, and blocked out everything else. It was a technique she'd learned at a young age, and now it served her well.

Between acts she gathered with her mother among patrons in the lobby, sipped a cool drink, and indulged in conversation. Siobhan owned a boutique in exclusive Double Bay, and had in the years since her divorce become an astute and extremely successful businesswoman.

'I've put something aside for you,' Siobhan relayed.

Her mother's taste in clothes was impeccable, and Katrina proffered a warm smile. 'Thanks. I'll write you a cheque.'

Siobhan pressed her hand on that of her daughter. 'A gift, darling.'

A prickle of awareness slithered down Katrina's spine, and she barely caught herself from shivering in reaction.

Only one man had this effect on her, and she turned slowly, forcing herself to skim the fellow patrons with casual interest.

A difficult feat when all her body's self-protective instincts were on full alert.

Nicos Kasoulis stood as part of a group, his head inclined towards a gorgeous blonde whose avid attention was almost sickening. Two men, two women. A cosy foursome.

Yet even as she was about to turn away he lifted his head and captured her glance, held it, those dark eyes steady, mesmeric, almost frightening.

He had the height, Katrina conceded, the breadth of shoulder, the stance, that drew attention.

Sculptured facial bone structure inherited from his Greek ancestors—wide cheekbones, strong jaw, not to mention a mouth that promised a thousand sensual delights and eyes as dark as sin—merely added another dimension to a man who wore an aura of power as comfortably as a second skin. Thick dark hair worn longer than was currently conventional added an individualistic tone to a man whose strength of will was equally admired as well as feared among his contemporaries.

If he thought to intimidate her, he was mistaken. Katrina lifted her chin, and her eyes flashed with green fire an instant before she deliberately turned her back on him.

At that moment the electronic buzzer sounded, heralding patrons to return to their seats.

Katrina's focus was shot to hell, and the final act passed in a blur of dialogue and action that held little consequence. Her entire train of thought was centred around escaping the auditorium without bumping into the man who'd stirred her to passionate heights, the mere thought of which caused her equilibrium to crash and burn.

An escape Nicos would contrive to allow, or not, as the mood took him.

Not, she perceived as they made their way through the lobby to the front entrance.

'Katrina. Siobhan.'

His voice was like black satin, dark and smoothly dangerous beneath the veneer of sophisticated politeness.

'Why, Nicos,' her mother breathed with delight as he bent to brush his lips to her cheek. 'How nice to see you.'

Traitor, Katrina accorded silently. Siobhan had

been one of Nicos's conquests from the beginning. Still was.

'Likewise.' He turned slightly and fixed Katrina with a deceptively mild gaze. 'Dinner tomorrow night. Seven?'

Bastard. The curse stopped in her throat as she caught her mother's surprise. Nicos, damn him, merely arched an eyebrow.

'Katrina hasn't told you?'

She wanted to hit him, and almost did. 'No.' The single word escaped as a furious negative.

Siobhan looked from her daughter to Nicos, who merely inclined his head in silent deference to Katrina.

Grr! She wanted to scratch his eyes out, and for a wild nanosecond she actually considered it.

He knew, darn it. She could tell from the faint musing gleam evident, the slight quirk at the edge of his mouth as he waited for her to pick up the ball and play.

There was no way around it, and better the truth than prevarication. 'Kevin, in his infinite wisdom,' she declared with heavy irony, 'has made it a condition of his will that I reside in the same house with Nicos for a year. If I don't, Nicos gains a majority control of Macbride.' She threw him a dark look that would have felled a lesser man. 'Something I absolutely refuse to let happen.'

'Oh, my,' Siobhan voiced faintly, her eyes clouding as she glimpsed her daughter's simmering temper.

Siobhan knew her ex-husband well. The iron will

beneath the soft, persuasive Irish charm. It had been a time ago, and she'd long forgiven him. For the one good thing to come out of their union had been Katrina.

'The man's a meddling fool,' she said quietly, and saw her daughter's wry smile. But a smart one. Oh, yes, Kevin Macbride had been nothing if not astute. And he'd developed an instant liking for the attractive Greek his daughter had wed. Maybe, just maybe, the father might achieve in death what he hadn't been able to achieve while he'd been alive.

Siobhan, how could you? Katrina seethed silently. While I'm capable of slaying my own dragons, I expected you to stand beside me, not welcome the enemy with grace and charm.

Nicos discerned each and every fleeting expression on his wife's features. She'd lost weight, her skin was pale, and at the moment she was a seething bundle of barely controlled fury. A bundle he was hard-pressed not to heft over one shoulder and carry kicking and cursing out to his car. And ultimately into his bed.

Katrina glimpsed the intent in those dark eyes, and wanted to *hit* him. 'Goodnight.'

The word was evinced as a cool dismissal. Icy, with a tinge of disdain meant to convey the edge of her temper.

She saw what he was going to do an instant before his head descended, and he anticipated her move, countered it, and captured her mouth with his own in a kiss that destroyed her carefully erected defences.

Brief, possessive, evocative, it brought a vivid reminder of what had been.

And would be again.

The purpose was there, a silent statement that was neither threat nor challenge. Merely fact.

Then he straightened, and his lips curved into a musing smile as he caught the unmistakable edge of anger in her glittering green gaze.

'Seven, Katrina,' he reminded her with deceptive quietness, and saw her chin tilt fractionally.

Cool, control. She'd had plenty of practice at displaying both emotions. 'Name the restaurant, and I'll meet you there.'

One eyebrow arched. A silent, faintly mocking gesture that put a serious dent in her bid for independence.

'The foyer of the Ritz-Carlton.'

An established, élite hotel situated a few blocks from her Double Bay apartment, negating the need to take her car.

She had no doubt it was a deliberate choice on his part, and she was sorely tempted to stamp her foot in childish repudiation. Instead, she offered him a cool glance and kept her voice neutral. 'Fine.'

Nicos inclined his head towards Siobhan, then he turned and began weaving his way through numerous patrons converging near the entrance.

'Don't say a word,' Katrina warned in caution as they gained the external pavement.

'Darling, I wouldn't dream of it,' her mother evinced with a soft chuckle.

CHAPTER TWO

THE evening was warm, the air like silk on a soft breeze whispering in from the sea as Katrina locked her car and set the alarm.

The hotel entrance lay ahead, its elegant façade attesting élite patronage in an established, moneyed inner-city suburb.

She'd dressed to kill, although only she knew how much time had been spent selecting and discarding one set of clothes after another in a quest to do battle and win.

Nicos viewed her entry into the lounge with veiled interest.

Business, he silently attested, noting the power suit in stylish black. The cut of the jacket, the mid-thigh length of the straight skirt, the sheer black hose showcasing shapely legs, slim ankles emphasised by stiletto-heeled black pumps. Jewellery confined to a diamond pendant on a slender gold chain, and a simple diamond stud worn in each earlobe.

Was she aware how well he could read her? The tiny signals that indicated her mood were evident in the sweep of her hair into a smooth, sophisticated French twist, the perfectly applied make-up, highlighting her eyes, the shape of her mouth. The tilt of her chin.

It was a façade, one he'd been able to dispense with easily. He retained a vivid memory of the way she melted beneath his touch. The spill of hair as he slid his fingers through its thick length and cupped her nape, angling her head so that soft, evocative mouth lifted to meet his own. The wild, untamed passion of her response as she met and matched him, treading a path to mutual satisfaction that was more, much more than he'd shared with any other woman in his lifetime.

He saw the moment she sighted him, and glimpsed the faint straightening of her shoulders, the way her fingers tightened over her evening purse. Her step didn't falter as she crossed towards him.

'Nicos.' Her greeting was polite, almost cool.

Take control, a tiny voice prompted. 'Shall we go through?'

Fire and ice, he mused. A combination that never failed to intrigue him. 'Eager to be done, Katrina?'

Her gaze met and held his. 'I'd prefer to keep this short,' she stated civilly, and caught the imperceptible lift of those broad shoulders.

'Such honesty,' he chided softly.

He made no attempt to touch her, but this close she was all too aware of his body heat, the faint tang of his exclusive cologne. Not to mention the aura of leashed power that was so much a part of him.

He was biding his time, she alluded with a tinge of bitterness. Tonight was a mere indulgence. A social formality in an attempt to create some form of mutual truce whereby they could co-exist for the next year.

Nicos had nothing to lose, while *she*…

Don't think about it, she chided silently as she entered the restaurant at Nicos's side.

Seated, she let him choose the wine while she perused the menu, ordering after scant deliberation a starter and a side salad.

'Not hungry?' Nicos posed as he watched her sip the excellent Chardonnay.

Katrina met his gaze with equanimity. 'Not particularly.' Her stomach felt as if it were attempting intricate somersaults, and the movement was not conducive to the easy digestion of food.

It irked that he could still have this effect. Worse, that all it took was one look at him and her pulse raced to a faster beat.

Was he aware of it? She hoped not. She'd spent a lifetime learning to mask her feelings. To smile, and pretend she was immune from the barbs two stepmothers and two stepsiblings had inflicted at every opportunity.

Adopting a façade wasn't difficult. She did it every day of her life. Professionally. Emotionally.

'Let's get this over with, shall we?'

'Why not finish your meal first?' Nicos countered silkily.

Katrina picked at her salad, then discarded it. 'I've lost my appetite.'

'Some more wine?'

'No. Thanks,' she added politely. The need for a clear head was essential.

Dammit, why did he have to be so blatantly male?

He savoured his food as he savoured a woman. With care, enjoyment, and satisfaction.

There was something incredibly sensual about the movement of his hands, and she had only to look at his mouth to imagine how it felt on her own. The devastation it could wreak as he pleasured her. He had the touch, the knowledge, to drive a woman wild.

Focus, she chided silently. This isn't about you. Or Nicos. It's about claiming a right to Macbride.

'We need to decide whose residence we'll share,' she began firmly.

He forked a succulent piece of fish, and followed it with a portion of salad. 'Naturally you'd prefer your apartment.'

It couldn't be this easy. 'Yes.'

He cast her a measured look. 'The Point Piper house is large. It would be more convenient for you to move in there.'

It surprised her that he hadn't sold the luxurious mansion they'd occupied for the few brief months of their ill-fated marriage. An architectural masterpiece built against sloping rock-face, it encompassed three levels of modern living, with terraced grounds, ornamental gardens, a swimming pool, and a magnificent harbour view.

It also housed too many memories. 'No, it wouldn't.'

Nicos replaced his cutlery and settled back comfortably in his chair. 'Afraid, Katrina?'

She looked at him carefully, noting his steady gaze, the seemingly relaxed expression. Deceptive to the unwary, she acknowledged silently, for Nicos Kasoulis possessed a razor-sharp mind and a killer instinct. Qualities that had gained him immense respect from both friend and foe. In the business arena, and among the socially élite.

It had been this ruthless streak that had appealed so much to Kevin Macbride, who'd seen in Nicos what he'd himself possessed: someone who knew what he wanted and went after it regardless of anything or anyone who stood in his way.

'Have I reason to be?'

His smile held a certain wryness. 'You must know I have your welfare at heart.'

'If that were so, you'd have stood down as executor of Kevin's will.'

'I gave him my word.'

'And that is everything.'

'Cynicism doesn't suit you.'

Katrina picked up her glass, and took a leisurely sip of wine. 'Forgive me,' she said without any hint of apology. 'I learned it at any early age.'

'Why not try a dessert?' Nicos queried blandly, and saw the fire bank beneath those brilliant green eyes.

She took a deep breath and sought to retain a semblance of calm. 'We need to arrive at some sort of compromise.'

Nicos slid a hand into the inside pocket of his jacket, extracted a bulky envelope, and tossed it down onto the table in front of her.

Katrina viewed it with suspicion. 'What's this?'

'A remote for the front gates, and keys to my home.'

He was far too sure of himself. 'Presumptuous, aren't you?'

'Practical,' he corrected.

'Arrogant,' she attested. 'What if I insist you move into my apartment?' she queried heatedly, hating him at that moment.

'Do you really want me in the next bedroom to yours?' Nicos queried mildly. 'Sharing the same living quarters, the same kitchen? In an apartment more suited to one person than two?'

'You know nothing about my apartment,' she retaliated, and saw the slight lift of his eyebrow.

'I was responsible for the gutting and rebuilding of the original homestead.'

She cast him a scathing look. 'Next you'll tell me you own it.'

Nicos inclined his head. 'Guilty.'

If she'd known, she'd never have bought it. Her eyes narrowed. Come to think of it, it had been her father who'd first drawn her attention to the penthouse apartment in the large, modernised, tri-level home. Less than a month after she'd walked out on Nicos.

Nicos watched the fleeting emotions chase across her expressive features before she successfully masked them.

'Mythos Investments is one of my companies.'

Of course. The name alone should have alerted her, but at the time she hadn't given much thought to anything other than finding a solitary haven of her own.

Suspicion ignited, and demanded answer. 'Did you employ a private detective to monitor my every move?' Katrina queried tightly.

An ex-military whose instructions were to observe, protect if necessary, and be unobtrusive at all times. A successful operation, Nicos acknowledged, for which the man had received a handsome remuneration.

His silence was more eloquent than mere words, and Katrina's mouth thinned. 'I see.'

Nicos's gaze speared hers. 'What do you see, *pedhi mou*?' His voice was dangerously quiet.

Too quiet. Like the calm before a storm. Something she chose to ignore.

'Two men bent on manipulating my life,' she retaliated fiercely. 'My father during his lifetime, and now *you*.' She picked up her water glass and momentarily toyed with the idea of throwing its contents in his face.

'Don't,' Nicos warned softly.

She was caught on the brink of violence. Aware of the acute satisfaction of such an action, and the folly of carrying it through. 'You read minds?'

'Yours.'

She took in a deep breath and released it slowly. 'The activity reports would have been incredibly repetitive,' she began tightly.

Work, social activities. A few male partners, none of whom had stayed overnight.

'How *dare* you?' The anger bubbled over. 'It was

an invasion of privacy. Harassment. I should file charges against you!'

His gaze didn't waver. 'It was protection.'

'Did Kevin know?' she demanded starkly.

'We discussed it.'

Traitors, both of them. 'Dear heaven,' she breathed with pious disregard. 'I'm twenty-seven, not seventeen!'

'You're the daughter of a very wealthy man, and—'

'The estranged wife of someone who is almost my father's equal,' Katrina finished bitterly.

'Yes.'

'I hate you.'

His shoulders lifted in an imperturbable shrug. 'So—hate me. At least it's an active emotion.'

She was steaming, her anger a palpable entity.

He caught the way her fingers curled into her palm, the whiteness of her knuckles as she sought control.

'If you leave now, you'll only delay the inevitable,' Nicos warned silkily. 'And invoke a repeat performance.'

It didn't help that he was right.

'I don't want this,' she vowed with unaccustomed vehemence. 'Any of it.'

'But you want Macbride.'

It was a statement she didn't, *couldn't* refute.

Why should sharing a residence for a year with her estranged husband pose any problems? They were both adults. They had extensive work obligations, separate interests. With luck, they'd hardly see each other much at all.

A tiny bubble of laughter rose and died in her throat. Who was she kidding?

Katrina looked at the bulky envelope, then lifted her head and met his enigmatic gaze. 'I won't share a bedroom with you.'

Their eyes clashed, brilliant green and dark brown. And held. She wasn't conscious of the way her breath hitched, or its slow release several long seconds later.

'I don't believe I asked you to.'

His voice was cool, almost ice, and she contained a slight shiver as it threatened to slither the length of her spine.

'Friday,' Katrina stated. The seventh day, thus fulfilling the first condition listed in Kevin's will. 'Evening,' she qualified.

'I won't be home until late.'

One eyebrow arched in disdain. 'I don't see that as a problem.'

Nicos inclined his head, signalled the waiter, and ordered coffee.

'Not for me.' She had to get out of here, away from the man who'd once held her heart, her world, in his hands.

Whatever needed to be faced, she'd face on Friday. But for now, she wanted to be as far away from Nicos Kasoulis as possible.

With unhurried movements she rose to her feet, collected her evening purse, barely stifling a startled gasp as Nicos unfolded his lengthy frame and caught hold of her wrist.

'What do you think you're doing?' she vented with an angry snap.

'I'd say it's obvious.'

The waiter appeared out of nowhere, accepted the cash Nicos handed him, beamed appreciatively at the size of the tip, and Katrina had little option but to allow Nicos to accompany her from the restaurant.

The instant they reached the foyer she tried to wrench her hand from his, and failed miserably. Short of an undignified struggle she was compelled to walk at his side through the elegant arcade to the street.

'If you don't let my hand go, I'll scream,' she threatened, *sotto voce*.

'Go ahead,' Nicos directed imperturbably. 'I imagine female histrionics will garner some attention.'

'You're the most impossible man I've ever met!'

His quiet laughter was the living end.

'Go to hell!'

'You don't want me to take you there,' Nicos warned with a dangerous silkiness that sent ice slithering down the length of her spine.

'I don't want you…*finis*.'

'Is that a challenge?'

'A statement.'

'A year, Katrina. Maybe we could attempt a truce of sorts?'

She spared him an angry glance. 'I doubt it's possible.'

'Try,' he suggested succinctly.

She reached into her evening purse, extracted a set of keys, and indicated the sleek white Porsche parked kerbside. 'My car.'

'Proving a point, Katrina?'

'Yes.'

'Perhaps I should follow your example.' He lowered his head and pulled her close in one easy movement.

She opened her mouth to protest, but no word escaped as he took possession in a manner that reached right down to her soul. And tugged at something long dormant. Evoking a vivid memory of how it used to be between them.

Of its own accord her body sank in against his, savouring for a brief few seconds the feeling of coming home. Of recognition at the most base level, and need.

The slow sweep of his tongue explored her own, tangled, then took her deep.

Dear Lord, how could she be this needy?

With a reluctant groan she tore her mouth away, and attempted to put some distance between them. Her own distress was evident, and she fought a mixture of anger and resentment as he brushed his knuckles along the edge of her jaw.

'Chemistry,' she dismissed with practised flippancy.

His eyes were dark, his expression unreadable, and she stifled a silent curse.

'You think so?' He took the keys from her hand,

deactivated the alarm, then he unlocked the door. He opened it, slid the key into the ignition, then stood to one side as she slipped in behind the wheel.

'Friday, Katrina.'

As if she needed reminding. With a deft twist of the wrist she gunned the engine into life, eased out of the parking space, then she sent the car forward at a quick pace.

She barely had time to shift through the gears before it was necessary to change down as she reached the driveway to her apartment.

Minutes later she'd garaged the Porsche and was safely indoors, choosing the lift instead of stairs to reach her apartment.

It wasn't late, only a few minutes past nine. Too early to go to bed. She toyed with the idea of phoning any one of several friends, suggesting she meet up with them and share a drink and chat a while. Except they would ask questions at such an impulsive action, and questions were something she'd prefer to avoid.

Instead, she undressed, pulled on an oversized tee shirt, removed her make-up, then she curled up in a comfortable armchair and changed channels on the television until she found something worth watching.

Katrina must have fallen asleep, for when she woke her neck felt stiff, one leg was numb, and a glance at her watch revealed it was long past midnight.

Minutes later she doused the lights and crawled into bed to lie awake haunted by the feel of Nicos's mouth on her own.

*   *   *

Choosing what to pack required minimum effort. A selection of clothes for the office, casual gear, and a few suitable outfits for the rare social occasion.

Katrina closed the zip on both suitcases, took one last look around the apartment, then she set the security alarm, closed the outer door, and summoned the lift down to the basement garage.

It was only a few kilometres from Double Bay to Point Piper, and no matter how she qualified the move it was impossible to control her nervous tension as she turned into the elegant street housing Nicos's home.

Katrina eased the car to a halt, engaged the remote control, waited as the high wrought-iron gate slid smoothly to one side, then she traversed the semicircular driveway towards a stylish tri-level home set in well-kept grounds. One of many in this tree-lined street where a mix of old and new residences provided an air of wealth in a harbour-front suburb.

The wide portico framed an impressive entry with ornate double doors protected by a sophisticated security system.

A married couple came in each weekday to clean and tend the grounds, but they would have left hours ago, Katrina reflected as she entered the lobby.

The house was silent, and it was impossible to shrug off a sense of *déjà vu*.

Late-afternoon sun hit the ornamental multi-paned leaded glass, sending prisms of soft pinks and greens across the cream marble-tiled floor, showcasing the high ceilings, the wide curved staircase leading to an oval balcony, an elegant chandelier.

To her right lay a large formal lounge and dining room, to her left a study, an informal sitting room, dining room and kitchen.

A spacious entertainment room, sauna, spa, gym, were situated on the lower floor, together with an indoor swimming pool with wide French doors leading out onto terraced gardens.

Five bedrooms, each with *en suite*, comprised the upper level of a beautifully furnished house with magnificent views out over the inner harbour.

For a brief few months it had been *home*. A place where she'd shared love, laughter, and great passion.

Don't go there, a tiny voice warned.

Discipline was something she'd mastered at a young age, yet she was helpless against the unwanted emotions invading her mind, her body.

Re-entering Nicos Kasoulis's space was a move fraught with tension. Yet what choice did she have?

None, if she wanted control of Macbride, Katrina reflected a trifle pensively as she ascended stairs to the upper floor.

Did Nicos occupy the master suite they'd once shared? Or had he moved into one of the other bedrooms?

The master suite, she determined minutes later. His clothes were there, and an array of masculine toiletries took up space on the marbled vanity.

She skimmed a glance over the large bed, and endeavoured to still her increased heartbeat. How could he bear to stay here? Occupy this room, this *bed*?

Pain clenched in her stomach, and she turned

abruptly away in an attempt to stifle a host of memories.

Control, she had it. But for how long? a devilish imp taunted as she chose a bedroom on the opposite side of the balcony.

There was, she saw at once, a small desk ideal for her laptop. A calculated guess on Nicos's part that she'd select this room, or sheer coincidence?

Second-guessing Nicos's motivation was a fruitless exercise.

Move your gear in, unpack, take a shower, check your e-mails, make a few calls, then have an early night, she prompted silently.

It was almost ten when hunger forced the realisation she'd missed dinner. Lunch had been a sandwich eaten at her desk, and breakfast had comprised orange juice and black coffee.

Hardly adequate sustenance, she decided as she made her way down to the kitchen to raid the refrigerator.

A ham sandwich and a cup of tea would suffice, and she'd almost finished both when she heard the front door close followed by the beep of the security alarm being set.

There was no way she could escape upstairs without detection, and she didn't bother to try. The slim hope she'd held that Nicos would simply ignore the array of lights on this level died as he entered the kitchen.

The mere look of him stirred her senses, and set her composure seriously awry.

A dramatic mesh of primitive sexuality and latent power that had a lethal effect on any woman's peace of mind. Especially hers.

It irked her unbearably that he knew, with just one look at her, no matter how she schooled her expression.

'A late-night snack, or did you miss dinner?' Nicos queried mildly as he crossed the room to stand a metre distant.

He took in the baggy tee shirt that reached her thighs, her bare legs and feet, and the hair she'd swept into a pony-tail. A look that was the antithesis of the corporate executive.

'You're back early.'

'You're evading the question.'

Katrina lifted the cup and took a sip of tea. 'Both,' she informed succinctly.

He loosened his tie and thrust both hands into his trouser pockets. She looked beat, and there were dark smudges beneath her eyes. At a guess she hadn't slept much in the past few nights.

Anxiety at their enforced living arrangements?

'Should we attempt polite conversation?' Katrina parried.

He looked vaguely dangerous. She tried to tell herself such a thought was the height of foolishness. But the feeling was there, in the look of him, his relaxed stance. Deceptive, she accorded warily, as all her fine body hairs rose up in protective self-defence.

Instinct warned she should tread carefully. Yet she

was prey to a devilish imp prompting her towards certain conflagration.

'How was your date—sorry, dinner?' she corrected deliberately.

One eyebrow rose with deliberate cynicism. 'Why assume my companion was female?'

'A calculated guess, given the increasing number of women in the business arena.'

'And my penchant for the company of women?' Nicos queried silkily.

'You have a certain reputation.' A statement that held a wealth of cynicism.

'I won't deny intimacy with previous partners,' he said with dangerous softness. 'The relationships were selective and meant something at the time.'

'But you don't offer fidelity. In or out of marriage.'

He didn't move, but she had the sensation he was suddenly standing much too close. 'You want me to reiterate something you refuse to believe?' he demanded silkily.

The air between them was electric. 'Why bother?' She held his gaze without fear. 'We did that to death at the time. It achieved nothing then. I don't see that it will now.'

His control was admirable, but his eyes were dark, almost chillingly still. 'If I were to offer the same query following your return from a business dinner, your answer would be?'

She didn't hesitate. 'Get stuffed.'

'An eloquent phrase.'

Katrina turned towards the sink and jettisoned the

remains of her tea. 'Forget *polite*.' She rinsed the cup and placed it in the dishwasher. 'Let's just stick with *good morning* and *goodnight*.'

'You think that will work?'

Why did she get the feeling he was at least one step ahead of her?

'The alternative is a war zone.'

'Battles won and lost?'

She gave him a long, considering look. 'It's not about whether you win or lose, but how you play the game.'

'An interesting analogy.'

'Isn't it?' She turned away from him and stepped towards the door. 'Goodnight.'

'Sleep well, *pedhaki mou*.'

His cynical drawl echoed in her mind as she ascended the stairs, and even in the relative safety of her bedroom the affectionate endearment recurred as a repetitive taunt.

Consequently sleep proved an elusive captive, until exhaustion overcame the many scenarios she plotted against him.

CHAPTER THREE

THERE was evidence Nicos had already eaten breakfast when Katrina entered the kitchen the next morning.

The aroma of freshly made coffee teased her nostrils, and she took down a cup and filled it from the cafetière, added sugar, slotted bread into the toaster, then sipped the excellent brew as she waited for the toast to pop.

A daily newspaper lay on the table, and she scanned the front-page headlines highlighting the latest criminal injustice, the fall of a major company, and touting plaudits for two councillors running in the upcoming elections.

When the toast was ready she spread it with conserve, topped her cup with coffee, then she pulled out a chair and dedicated fifteen minutes to acquiring an informative view of the day's reported journalism.

Until she reached the social pages, and found herself looking at a photograph of her and Nicos. Taken, she confirmed on closer examination, at a social function not long after their marriage. The caption read, *Together Again?*

An unidentified source confirms Nicos and Katrina Kasoulis have reunited to satisfy a condi-

*tion of Kevin Macbride's (of Macbride) will. Fact
or fallacy?*

Anger rose, and a sibilant curse escaped from her
lips.

Without pausing for thought she gathered up the
pertinent page and went in search of her errant husband.

She found him in the study, seated at his desk, his
attention focussed on the computer screen.

He glanced up as she entered, took one look at her
expression, and pressed the save key.

'Good morning.'

Katrina threw him a fulminating glare. 'Have you
seen this?' She cast the newspaper page down onto
the keyboard, and jabbed a finger at the caption.

Someone had been busy. Given her extended dysfunctional family, it narrowed the suspects down to
four. Any one of whom would take delight in presenting such facts to the press.

'You want to complain and request a retraction?'

She was so angry she could hardly speak. 'What
good would that do?'

'None whatsoever.'

Suspicion clouded logic. 'Were *you* responsible?'

Katrina saw his features harden and his eyes grow
cold. 'That doesn't even qualify for an answer.'

'*Who*, then?'

Nicos's silence was eloquent, and her anger took
on a new dimension.

'I need to make a few phone calls. Then,' she announced between clenched teeth, 'I'm going out.'

'I have an invitation to attend dinner this evening.'

'I wouldn't dream of stopping you.'

'For both of us.'

'You can go alone!'

'An action that would cause speculation, surely?' Nicos posed reasonably. 'Given our very recent reconciliation?'

'I have no intention of partnering you on the social circuit,' Katrina vowed tersely.

'Considering my attendance is minimal, it won't be a hardship.'

'And we haven't reconciled. We're merely sharing the same house!'

'So we are,' Nicos said with dangerous softness. 'However, for the duration of one year we partner each other whenever the necessity should arise.'

'That isn't a condition of Kevin's will.'

'Consider it one of my own,' he said hardily, and watched her green eyes fire with anger.

'Don't try to manipulate me,' she warned as she moved to the door, adding as a parting shot, 'I won't stand for it.'

'Be ready by six-fifteen,' Nicos relayed silkily.

Katrina didn't deign to answer, and barely restrained the temptation to slam the door behind her.

With carefully controlled movements she went upstairs, changed into tailored trousers, added a blouse, a jacket, slid her feet into heeled pumps, then collected her bag, caught up her car keys and went down to the garage.

Ten minutes later she drew to a halt adjacent a park, withdrew her cellphone, and made the first of several phone calls.

Whilst Andrea, Kevin's second wife, coveted wealth and a luxurious lifestyle, was self-orientated to the point of selfishness, she didn't possess a vicious bone in her body. Her daughter, Paula, by Andrea's first marriage, was overindulged and a snob, but an unlikely candidate to raise her stepsister's ire.

Which left Chloe, Kevin's third wife, and her son, Enrique, by a previous marriage. Each of whom would delight in causing Katrina grief.

Katrina had contacts, and she used them ruthlessly.

An hour later she had the answer she wanted. *Enrique.* Now, why didn't that surprise her?

Her stepbrother was a smooth charmer who made it no secret that in his opinion *he*, as the only male in a clutch of associated family females, should inherit a major share in Macbride. It mattered little that Kevin had insisted each of his successive wives sign a prenuptial agreement, and had made both Andrea and Chloe aware that Katrina was his successor.

Enrique was a young man who adored the high life, fast cars and beautiful women. He had also acquired an expensive habit in his teens, one that had seen him in a private clinic on more than one occasion during the few years Chloe had been Kevin's wife.

At least she knew her enemy, Katrina determined as she put the car in gear and headed towards Double

Bay. She intended checking out her apartment, reassessing her wardrobe; then she planned some retail therapy.

There were a few girlfriends she could phone to come join her and share lunch. Except the invitation would elicit questions she had no desire to answer, and while her heart ached for the loss of her father she knew he would hate her to grieve.

Life, he had always maintained, was a celebration. And he had celebrated it well.

Yet she missed his laughter, his love. He'd been her rock, her safe harbour. In a quirk of misplaced wisdom, he'd appointed Nicos in his place.

Katrina wanted to reiterate she didn't need or want Nicos's protection. Except Kevin had played his final card and had given her no choice.

It was well after five when she garaged the Porsche and entered Nicos's home with three evening gowns draped over her arm.

She reached the stairs as Nicos emerged into the lobby, and she paused, her expression one of controlled politeness.

'Formal, Katrina,' Nicos drawled as he reached her. He named the venue, the charity, and glimpsed her momentary disconcertion as they ascended the stairs.

How could she have forgotten? It was one of the city's prestigious social events, and one Kevin had unfailingly sponsored for as long as she could remember.

She had…how long? Forty-five minutes in which to shower, attend to her hair and make-up, then dress.

She made it with scant seconds to spare, and stood silent beneath Nicos's appraisal.

The crêpe georgette gown in jade-green with its bias-cut asymmetric flounces and figure-hugging lines accented her slim curves and highlighted her cream-textured skin. To save time she'd simply swept her hair into a careless chignon, had added diamond stud earrings and a matching pendant.

As to Nicos, the sight of him made the breath catch in her throat. He held his thirty-seven years superbly, his masculine frame attesting to a regular exercise regime. Attired in a black evening suit, white shirt and black bow tie, he looked every inch the wealthy sophisticate. Yet it was his innate sexuality and an intrinsic knowledge of the opposite sex that added another dimension. One any thinking woman couldn't fail to recognise.

A year ago she would have offered a teasing comment, brushed the edge of his jaw with her fingers and placed her mouth against his in a light kiss.

Now she did none of those things. Instead she crossed the lobby in silence at his side and slid into the car parked out front.

'Should we discuss the evening's role-play?' Katrina queried as Nicos cleared the gates and traversed the leafy street.

'In light of Enrique's link to a certain gossip columnist?'

'You knew?'

He cast her a quick, telling glance. 'Did you imagine I wouldn't make it my business to find out?'

She didn't answer. Instead she examined the passing scenery with detached interest. No matter where she'd travelled in the world, Sydney was *home*.

It was a beautiful city, with a picturesque harbour and buildings of varied architecture. Possessed of a relatively mild climate, the clear blue skies and sparkling waters of Port Jackson, with cliff-top mansions and numerous small craft anchored in the many bays and inlets, provided an endearing sense of familiarity evident as Nicos traversed the inner-city streets before easing the car to a halt adjacent the hotel's main entrance for valet parking.

Guests mingled in the large lobby adjoining the grand ballroom. Uniformed waiters circled the area proffering trays of drinks, and the buzz of conversational chatter abounded.

The social élite, Katrina mused, dressed in their finest, with the women collectively displaying sufficient jewellery to fund a year's aid to a Third-World country.

There were many guests present who would have sighted the photo of Katrina and Nicos Kasoulis and its teasing caption in the morning's newspaper gossip column. Circumspect interest was expected, and she forced herself to ignore the telling glances, the quiet asides as she stood at Nicos's side and sipped a mix of champagne and orange juice.

A few acquaintances made a point of extending their condolences for the loss of her father, others conveyed silent hand signals indicating they'd catch up through the evening.

Katrina sighted both of her stepmothers standing at opposite ends of the lobby, a presence that issued a silent statement of their individual importance on the social scene. Andrea had her man-of-the-moment in tow, while Chloe was partnered by none other than her son, Enrique.

It was a blessing that Siobhan, at least, didn't try to compete on any level, much preferring a less fashionably social existence.

Three of Kevin's ex-wives at one gathering would be too much to handle. It had been bad enough keeping the peace at her father's funeral, where a farce worthy of Hollywood had been played out for the benefit of those sufficiently intrigued to observe it. Of whom there had been several, Katrina reflected grimly.

Nicos watched the fleeting expressions chase across his wife's features, and caught the determined resolve evident as she mentally braced herself for an inevitable confrontation.

Andrea and Chloe's interest in Kevin's daughter could only be termed superficial, yet each woman painstakingly observed social etiquette. Enrique, on the other hand, was something else.

'You don't have to handle it alone.'

Katrina met Nicos's dark gaze, and forced her lips into a faint smile. 'Is that meant to be reassuring?'

'Count on it.'

'My bodyguard,' she stated with an attempt at cynicism.

'That, too,' he responded with light mockery.

'Katrina, darling.'

She turned at the sound of that soft, purring voice, and went into the air-kiss routine Andrea favoured.

'Nicos.' There was a degree of wariness beneath the superficial greeting before Andrea turned back to her stepdaughter. 'Kevin would be proud you made the effort to be here so soon after his passing.'

A compliment or condemnation? Katrina chose to take the words at face value. 'Thank you, Andrea.'

Five minutes after Andrea moved away, Chloe crossed the lobby to Katrina's side.

'We weren't sure you'd attend tonight.' Sleek, polished, and very self-assured, Kevin's third wife possessed the practised aloofness of a catwalk model.

'It's what Kevin would have wanted,' Katrina responded evenly before acknowledging her stepbrother. 'Enrique.'

A young man whose pretty-boy attractiveness was deceptive, during Chloe's marriage to Kevin he'd imagined that seducing Kevin's daughter would be a shoe-in…only to discover Katrina wasn't about to play. It hadn't stopped him from trying, and he'd never quite forgiven her for spoiling his plans of a dream ride through life on the Macbride fortunes.

His eyes gleamed briefly with something akin to bitter resignation as they raked her slender form. 'You look divine, sweetheart.'

'Doesn't she?' Nicos caught her hand and lifted it

to his lips, his eyes dark and unfathomable as he silently dared her to pull her fingers free from his grasp.

Her reaction to his touch was immediate and damning, for her pulse jumped to a quickened beat as warmth coursed through her veins. It felt as if her heart was working overtime, and it took considerable effort to appear unaffected.

'What do you think you're doing?' Katrina demanded quietly the instant Chloe and Enrique moved out of earshot.

'Damage control.'

'For whose benefit?' she queried with skepticism.

'Yours,' Nicos said silkily.

'I doubt playing charades will work.'

A hovering waiter took her empty glass and offered her another, which she declined.

It was something of a relief when the ballroom doors opened minutes later and the guests were instructed to take their seats.

The food had to be delectable, given the price per ticket, but Katrina merely forked a few mouthfuls from each course, sipped a glass of excellent Chardonnay, and conversed politely with fellow guests seated at their table.

The evening's entertainment was varied, and during a break she excused herself and threaded her way towards the powder room.

A headache was niggling away above her temple, and she'd have given anything to be able to leave and go home.

Except home was no longer her apartment, and the

term of her enforced sojourn with Nicos had only just begun.

There was a queue, and she had to wait to gain space in front of the long mirror in order to freshen her lipstick.

Was it design or coincidence that seconds after emerging the first person she saw was Enrique? Considering her stepbrother inevitably had a plan, she opted for the former, acknowledged his presence, and made to bypass him *en route* to the ballroom.

One glance at his expression determined he had a mission in mind and, unless she was mistaken, he was bent on ill intent.

'I wanted to see you alone,' he began without preamble.

She could almost pre-empt what he was going to say, but she remained silent, willing to admit she might be wrong.

'I need some money.'

'I don't have any on me.'

'But you can get it.'

They'd been this route before. In the beginning, she'd thought she could help, and had. Until she'd realised she was only feeding his habit. 'No.'

'Tomorrow. Meet me for lunch. Bring it then.'

She was past feeling sorry for him. 'What part of *no* don't you understand?'

'I'm begging you, dammit!' He pulled in his temper with effort. 'A thousand, Katrina. That's all.'

'Didn't playing news gossip informant pay well enough?'

His eyes hardened. 'I don't know what you're talking about.'

Her headache intensified. 'Even if I were to lend it to you, how long will that hold off the heavies, Enrique? A week? Then what will you do?'

'All I need is one win—'

'No.'

Katrina watched his features darken with dread. Enrique in a mean mood was something she'd prefer to avoid.

His hand caught her arm in a painful grip. 'Bitch!' he exclaimed with soft venom. 'You'll pay for this!'

'Let me go,' she said quietly, and clenched her teeth against a silent cry as his fingers twisted viciously on her skin.

'Do as Katrina says.' Nicos's voice was a chilling drawl. '*Now.*'

Enrique's hand fell to his side.

'I can't think of any good reason for you to threaten my wife,' Nicos said with dangerous softness. 'Touch her again, and I can promise you won't walk or talk for some considerable time.'

'You should be aware I've instructed my lawyer to contest Kevin's will,' Enrique declared vehemently.

'Something that will prove an exercise in futility,' Nicos advised with hard inflexibility. 'Each of Kevin's wives were well provided for in their divorce settlements,' Nicos continued with deceptive mildness. 'Neither you nor Paula have any reason to make a claim against Kevin's estate.'

'That's not how I see it!' Without a further word, Enrique turned and re-entered the ballroom.

Katrina cast Nicos a fulminating look, and almost died at the latent anger evident.

'I didn't need rescuing!'

His expression remained unchanged. 'No? From where I was standing, your charming stepbrother appeared to have the advantage.'

She could have told him Enrique had used a variety of bullying tactics in the past. And that Chloe's son felt his stepsister owed him by virtue of his mother's marriage to Kevin Macbride.

Her chin lifted fractionally, and her eyes were clear. 'I can handle him.'

A muscle clenched at the edge of his jaw. 'Verbally, without doubt,' Nicos acknowledged with an edge of cynicism.

Katrina barely restrained stamping her foot in angry frustration. 'Don't play the heavy, Nicos.'

'I'll take you home.'

'The hell you will.'

'Determined to thwart me at every turn, Katrina?'

She drew a deep, calming breath. 'If we don't go back in there, Enrique will imagine he's scored a point against me.'

'Fifteen minutes,' Nicos conceded. 'Then we leave.'

It was closer to an hour, and almost midnight when they entered the house. Together they ascended the stairs, and Katrina turned as they reached the landing.

'Goodnight.'

Nicos lifted a hand and caught hold of her chin, then his mouth closed over hers in an evocative kiss that was all too brief as his tongue skimmed hers, tasted, then retreated.

For a moment it left her wanting more, and she fought against the instinctive need to move in close and kiss him back.

Except that would be tantamount to an admission of sorts, and she'd spent too many months building up a barrier against him. To allow him to begin tearing it down would be the height of foolishness. Besides, she doubted she could bear the pain.

She pulled away from him, and he let her go.

Too easily, she reflected as she reached her room and closed the door behind her.

CHAPTER FOUR

SUNDAY dawned with grey skies and the imminent threat of rain. Katrina rose early, donned a sweatshirt, shorts and trainers, went downstairs to the kitchen, made up fresh orange juice, filled a glass and drank the contents, then traversed the spiral staircase to the gym.

The house was quiet, and she entered the large room, viewed the various equipment, crossed to the punching bag and swung a solid right into its centre. Something which bruised her knuckles, but gave infinite satisfaction.

'If you aim for a repeat, I suggest you don a boxing glove,' Nicos drawled as he entered the room, and she turned towards him with a glare that merely caused him to arch an eyebrow in silent query. 'Or perhaps you'd rather hit the quarry instead of making do with a substitute?'

Had he followed her down here? Doubtful, given time spent in the gym was part of his daily routine. She cursed herself for unintentionally choosing an early morning sojourn.

'Don't tempt me.'

She looked about seventeen, devoid of make-up and her hair caught in a pony-tail. Her eyes were stormy, her mouth soft and full. He had to curb the desire to cross the room and explore her mouth with his own, aware such an action would probably earn him a swift jab in the ribs and a diatribe worthy of a seasoned navvy.

Katrina crossed to the treadmill, adjusted the settings, and set it in motion, increasing the speed to a punishing pace, then followed it with time on the exercise bike.

She deliberately concentrated her energies on achieving a predetermined number of kilometres, and was unable to stem a heightened awareness of Nicos as he spent time with various weights, the bench press, and the treadmill.

Her fitness regime didn't come close to his, something that appeared clearly obvious as she picked up a towel and began to dab the sheen of sweat beading her forehead.

Katrina spared Nicos a surreptitious glance as she curled the towel round her neck. *He* could have been taking a walk in the park for all the effort it appeared to cost him.

The flex of well-honed muscle and sinew presented a dramatic mesh of strength and power, one that was impossible to ignore. For it brought images to mind she'd tried hard to forget.

It mattered little that she'd been unsuccessful. Or that being thrust back into his presence forced her to confront an ongoing battle with her emotions.

Anger and pain warred with a primitive alchemy. One she recognised, the other she condemned.

How could she feel anything for a man who had

not only kept his mistress after marriage, but had foolishly impregnated her without caution?

Why, then, had Nicos agreed to Kevin's ridiculous suggestion? Worse, what role did Georgia play in all of this?

Dammit, there was a child involved. A baby boy who must surely be only a matter of weeks old. What of him?

There were too many conflicting thoughts chasing through her mind for easy conjecture, and with a mental shake of her shoulders she contemplated entering the sauna, then the plunge pool. Except that would mean stripping off, and there was no way she intended to disrobe in his presence.

Besides, she really needed to put some space and distance between them, and she quietly exited the room. Breakfast, followed by a shower, then she'd don casual clothes and go out for the day.

Anywhere that would take her away from this house and the indomitable man who owned it.

Twenty minutes later she descended the stairs, *en route* to the garage, and encountered Nicos in the lobby.

He took in the bag slung over her shoulder, and car keys in her hand. 'Going out?'

'You object?' Katrina countered coolly.

'Now, why should I do that?'

She made to move past him. 'Don't wait up.'

A hand closed over her forearm. 'An observance of common courtesy wouldn't go astray.'

She cast his hand a telling glance, then lifted her

gaze to meet his. 'As to where I'll be, and the time of my return? Difficult, when I have no definite plans.'

'Except to escape.'

It irked that he knew her so well. *'Yes.'*

He let her go, and minutes later she eased her car through the gates, then headed towards the northern beaches.

She could have phoned a friend and organised to share the day, but she preferred solitude and a good book.

Choosing a relatively isolated beach, she spread out a towel, switched her mobile phone to message-bank, and opened the latest paperback release written by a favourite author.

Lunch was a sandwich bought from a nearby kiosk, plus bottled spring water, and she read for a few hours, then oddly restless she packed up her belongings and drove into the city where she browsed the shops at Darling Harbour.

It was easy to lose herself in the wandering crowd, and she paused to admire a silver bracelet displayed in a silversmith's window. Its intricate design was sufficiently unusual to warrant closer examination, and she was about to enter the shop when a familiar voice greeted her. 'Slumming, darling?'

Katrina turned to face a tall, slender blonde whose attractive features had, she knew, been cosmetically enhanced. The result was perfection, complemented by exquisite make-up, and her designer apparel emphasised sculptured curves and a physically toned body.

'Paula,' she acknowledged, aware her stepsister's smile was as superficial as her apparent warmth.

'Trying for incognito, Katrina? Or am I missing something, and *this*—' she indicated the shorts, shirt knotted at the midriff, and trainers '—is a new look?'

'It's called *casual*,' Katrina responded lightly, and witnessed Paula's faint moue.

'And where is the inimitable Nicos?'

'I left him at home.' That much was true. Although how long he remained there was another thing.

'So newly reconciled.' Her smile was the antithesis of sweet. 'Although everyone knows it's only to comply with dear Kevin's last wishes.'

'Everyone?'

'Why, yes, darling.' She appeared to sharpen her claws. 'You're the lead topic among the social set.'

Doubtlessly fuelled by erroneous speculation. So what else was new? 'Really?'

'Naturally, you're aware Enrique intends to contest the will.'

'As you do?'

'Oh, no, sweetie. I have it on authority it would be a lost cause.' Paula raked Katrina's slender frame. 'How does it feel to be an heiress, darling? You always were Daddy's pride and joy. You even married the prince, only to discover he had feet of clay.' Her smile held little warmth. 'Interesting coincidence his mistress is back in town.' Her eyes widened with false dismay. 'Oh, dear, you didn't know?'

She'd had a lifetime of experience in schooling her features. 'I should thank you for the advance warning.'

'My pleasure.'

Katrina didn't attempt to qualify a reason to leave. 'Bye, Paula.'

The practised pout didn't quite cut it. 'Just when we were beginning to catch up.'

Catching up with Paula was something Katrina preferred to avoid. A personality clash, Andrea had termed their animosity from the onset.

Friendship between the daughter of one partner and the daughter of another had never been an issue. Existing in superficial harmony required wit, wisdom, and an ever vigilant eye…for the barbed comment, the embellishment of truth, and the metaphorical stab in the back. It had been Paula's mission in life to discredit Kevin's *ewe-lamb*.

Andrea's stint as Katrina's stepmother hadn't lasted long, and just when Katrina had thought it could only get better, along had come Chloe and Enrique.

And that had been worse, much worse.

Katrina spared her watch a glance, ignored the temptation to ring Siobhan, and retraced her steps to the car park. She'd visit one of the large cinema complexes, take in a movie, grab something to eat, then go home.

Except there were too many choices, and she indulged the whim to see two movies, almost back to back, with time for a snack and coffee in between each scheduled session.

It was after ten when she garaged the car and let herself quietly into the house.

Nicos emerged into the lobby from his study as she was about to ascend the stairs. Did he possess X-ray vision? Or had he added a camera to his state-of-the-art security system?

His casual attire of jeans and a polo shirt emphasised his breadth of shoulder, lean waist, and long legs.

'Did you think to check your voice-mail?'

The silky query gave little indication of his mood, and she paused, meeting his level glance with equanimity.

'Not since mid-afternoon. Why?'

'Siobhan has rung twice. Enrique, ditto, stressing the need for an urgent response. And Harry, who assured you have his number.' His expression remained enigmatic, but she detected a hint of dangerous steel just beneath the surface. 'Each of whom revealed they'd tried and failed to reach you on your cell-phone.'

'You want I should apologise for inadvertently relegating you to message-taking?'

Nicos shifted slightly, a movement that seemed to bring him too close for comfort.

She kept her gaze steady, noticing the tiny lines fanning out from the corners of his eyes, before travelling down to encompass the set of his mouth, the firm line of his lips, the edge of his jaw.

He exuded an electric stillness that reminded her of a predator about to pounce. *Go*, a tiny voice prompted. Except she was primed to fight, and viewed escape as a negative option.

'I don't owe you an explanation,' Katrina cautioned, and watched the subtle flex of sinew and muscle as he thrust one hand into his trouser pocket.

'On that we differ.'

'Go to hell.' She turned to ascend the stairs, only to have Nicos spin her round to face him.

'Don't push it,' he warned with deadly softness.

His grip on her arm was deceptive, and she knew it would tighten measurably if she attempted to wrench free of him.

Katrina looked pointedly at her arm, then shifted her gaze to meet his. 'Forcible restraint, Nicos?'

'You want all out war?'

Apprehension slithered down the length of her spine. 'Polite harmony would be preferable.'

'Then, I suggest you work towards it.' His voice sounded like silk being rased by razor-sharp steel.

'Same goes.'

He released her arm, and she moved quickly upstairs, aware that he watched her ascent. Her bedroom resembled a sanctuary, and she closed the door, then crossed to sink down onto the bed.

With deft ease she activated her cellphone, replayed the recorded messages, then she rang her mother.

Dear, sweet Harry, who was contracted to redecorate two adjoining townhouses she'd recently bought as an investment.

'Colours, darling. We need to talk. You simply cannot have blue.'

So she'd ring him from the office, they'd argue, she'd relent and agree to his choice. Their token wrangling was viewed with the fondness of long friendship.

Enrique was something else. Arrogant, persistent, desperate. A dangerous combination, she perceived as she stripped off her clothes and made for the shower.

Later she lay in the darkness, staring at the ceiling. A few days down, with three hundred and sixty-two to go. How in heaven would she last the distance?

Katrina woke late with a headache, missed breakfast in her rush to get to the office on time, and from there on it was downhill all the way through the day.

Whatever could go wrong, did. She dealt with complaints in areas that usually ran smoothly, mediated and lost to a tyrannical subcontractor who bore an elephant-sized grudge, and was terse to the point of rudeness when Enrique insisted he take five minutes of her time.

Lunch was a non-event, and at two she sent out for sandwiches which she ate at her desk. At four o'clock she took a call from Kevin's lawyer informing Enrique intended to contest the will on the grounds he was entitled to a share of the estate.

Enrique's protest was merely a nuisance factor, but it was the lawyer's duty to apprise her of the development.

The headache, for which she'd taken painkillers

mid-morning and mid-afternoon, settled into a throbbing ache that left her feeling physically depleted.

It was almost six when she garaged her car and entered the house. All she wanted to do was indulge in a leisurely spa bath, take more painkillers, pull the shutters closed in her room, slip beneath the cool percale sheets, and shut out the rest of the world for as long as it took to lose the headache and regain her composure.

She almost made it. Would have, if she hadn't had to go downstairs to search for more painkillers, as all she had left was an empty blister pack.

Nicos found her in the kitchen, looking a whiter shade of pale, her slender form wrapped in a towelling robe, and her hair tumbling down her back.

'What in hell—?'

The words were barely audible, and quickly checked as he subjected her to an encompassing appraisal.

Katrina closed her eyes against the sight of him. The last thing she needed was a verbal inquisition.

'*Hell* works for me,' she said wearily. 'Where do you keep your supply of painkillers?'

He crossed to an expanse of inbuilt cupboards, opened one, and extracted a packet, then he filled a glass with water and handed both to her.

'Headache?'

'Yes.' She freed two tablets and swallowed them down with water.

She was hardly aware that he had moved to hook out a chair until he gently pushed her into it.

'What do you think you're doing?' Bed, all she wanted was to lie down and wait for the pain to go away.

He ignored her protest as he discarded his jacket, loosened his tie, and turned back the cuffs of his shirt.

'Be quiet, and relax.'

She opened her mouth, then closed it again as his hands began working the tense muscles at her neck, then her shoulders.

Oh, dear heaven, that felt good. So good. She let her lashes drift down, and just went with the flow as his fingers worked their magic.

No one had been this kind to her in a while. Not hands-on kind. Not since Kevin had fallen ill.

Unbidden, withheld emotions rose to the surface, and the tears welled then trickled silently down each cheek.

Nicos felt a plop of warm moisture hit his fingers as he used both thumbs to massage her neck, and he swore softly, then with simple expediency he lifted her from the chair and pulled her close in against him.

If he had said one word, she'd have jerked free, but the comfort he offered was too great, and for the first time since Kevin's death she quietly sobbed her heart out.

She was hardly aware that he rested his cheek against the top of her head, or that her arms crept round his waist as she held onto him.

After a while he swept an arm beneath her knees and carried her upstairs to her room. He turned back the covers, then lay down on the bed with her, all too aware that any minute she'd realise where she was and who was with her, and push him away.

Except she didn't. The shudders shaking her slender frame gradually lessened, and she fell still. Her breathing evened out and slipped to a steady beat as she slid into sleep.

Holding her reawakened a host of memories, each of them a torture to his libido, and after a while he attempted to slowly ease himself away, only to have her murmur in protest.

So he stayed. Aware he was all kinds of a fool. For enjoying the feel of her in his arms, her scent, the soft silkiness of her hair beneath his lips.

The evening air cooled, and he toed off his shoes, pulled up the covers, and eventually slept.

Katrina surfaced through the layers of wakefulness to an awareness that, while she was definitely in bed, she wasn't alone.

Not only not alone, but her head was cushioned against a male chest, a muscular arm kept her there, and her own arm lay linked around *his* waist.

Nicos. Realisation hit, and her first instinct was to scramble out of the bed and away from him.

Then several things registered. She was in her own room, Nicos was fully dressed, and she had instant memory recall.

Maybe if she slowly removed her arm… She attempted to dislodge it, only to have Nicos tighten his hold.

He slept like a cat, aware of her slightest move,

and he'd sensed the moment she'd woken, had felt the change in her breathing, the instant tension. He could almost hear her thinking.

What he wanted was to lean forward and brush his lips to her temple, to slip a hand beneath the gaping folds of her robe and caress her breasts. Nuzzle the vulnerable hollow at the edge of her neck, then trail lower to tease one tender peak as he let the fingers of one hand brush a path to the apex of her thighs.

Early morning lovemaking, he reflected, made for a wonderful way to begin the day.

Maybe… No, he dismissed. Not here, not now. When the time was right, there would be no hesitation. But he wanted her to need him, and for that he required time. Something, thanks to the terms of Kevin's will, he had plenty of. Wasn't there an analogy that those who waited got what they deserved? He thought grimly of his aroused body, the desire, and banked it down.

Half an hour in the gym, followed by a shower and breakfast, then he'd channel his energy into the corporate day ahead.

But first he'd indulge himself a little.

'Headache gone?'

Katrina's body tensed at the sound of his husky voice, and she cautiously lifted her head. 'Yes.' All her instincts screamed a warning to put some distance between them, fast.

'You slept well.'

It didn't appear that she'd moved much through the night. Or perhaps he hadn't allowed her to. For a moment she struggled with the need to thank him for offering support. A wave of embarrassment encompassed her body at the thought of the tears she'd shed in the comfort of his arms.

She slowly rose to a sitting position, caught his amused gleam, looked hurriedly down at her gaping robe, then quickly pulled the edges together.

With an easy, fluid movement Nicos swung his legs over the side of the bed and stood to his feet. His dark hair was slightly ruffled, and he combed his fingers through it, then he bent down to collect his shoes.

'Breakfast on the terrace at eight?' he slanted, enjoying her confusion. Without waiting for her to respond he moved towards the door, and Katrina was left gazing at the empty aperture.

For a few seconds she stood in stunned silence, then she quickly turned back the bed covers, gathered up fresh underwear and headed for the *en suite*.

Half an hour later she collected her briefcase and moved quickly down the stairs. She'd just set foot in the lobby when Nicos entered it via the passageway leading from the spiral staircase connecting to the gym.

Her heart executed a double flip at the sight of him in shorts and sweatshirt, a damp towel hugging his neck, and trainers. He looked disturbingly male, all bunched muscle, and the faint sheen of sweat leaving patches of damp on a tee shirt that clung to wide shoulders, a broad chest.

Nicos took in the briefcase, the business suit, the stiletto heels, and slanted an eyebrow.

'An early start?'

'Yes,' Katrina agreed evenly. She could put in some time on the computer before her secretary arrived and the day began in earnest.

He used the edge of the towel to blot moisture beading his forehead. 'Don't wait dinner. I'll be late.'

'So will I,' she responded without thought, and stepped towards the internal door leading to the garage.

What on earth had prompted her to say that, when she hadn't planned a thing? She could ring Siobhan and suggest they eat out, she contemplated as she fired the engine and eased her car towards the gates. Maybe take in an art gallery, or a foreign movie.

The day progressed with only a few minor irritations. She contacted Harry, and arranged to meet him in her lunch-hour at the townhouses where, in typical Harry-style, he overrode her suggestions with the air of *one who knows best*.

'Muted green carpet, a mix of pale apricot, peach and shades of cream for the paintwork and soft furnishings, darling.' He caught her hand and pressed her fingers to his lips, then drew a wide arc with one arm. 'It will be truly magnifica.'

'Not blue?' she teased, and caught his pained expression. 'Okay,' she capitulated with a warm smile. 'Suppose you tell me what colour scheme you've devised for the adjoining townhouse?'

Harry waxed lyrical, as only Harry could, and she wrangled a little, because he expected it, and they achieved a compromise with which each was quietly pleased.

She had a good eye for a bargain, a knack for being able to envisage the finished product, and the two adjoining townhouses numbered her third property purchase in the past year. Each one had been completely redecorated by Harry's team of contractors, and sold for a handsome profit. As she cut him a percentage of that profit, he had more than the usual interest in each project.

'I'm looking at something in Surrey Hills.' It was an older suburb, parts of which were becoming trendy among the 'double income, no kids' set.

Harry's eyes sharpened. 'A terrace house?'

'Three, actually.'

'Solid structure?' He fired off a number of questions, then requested the address. 'I'll go check them out, and get back to you.'

He would, she knew, make them a priority, and as she drove back into the city she wondered if his vision would match her own.

Three terrace houses might be a bit ambitious, but they were in a block of six, situated in a prime position, and formed part of a deceased estate which the family wanted sold.

The afternoon was busy. She left the office late, and went directly to meet Siobhan at the small, trendy restaurant a friend had recommended. New owners, a fresh decor and an appealing menu provided an excellent meal.

The film Katrina chose was a slick Spanish comedy

with English subtitles, containing wry, often black humour, and afterwards they shared coffee.

Her mother was great company, with an infectious wit, and very much her daughter's friend, for they shared an equality that dispensed with any generation gap.

'Are you coping okay?' Siobhan queried gently as she reached forward and caught hold of Katrina's hands, the touch warm, brief.

'Now, there's an ambiguous question.' She managed a smile. 'Care to define it?'

'Living with Nicos.'

The term held connotations Katrina didn't want to think about. 'Separate rooms, separate lives.'

A succinct summary that didn't come close to describing the electric tension apparent. It was a latent force, a constant reminder of what they'd once shared, and she rode an emotional see-saw trying to deal with it.

Siobhan wisely kept her own counsel. She knew her daughter well. Enough not to pursue a sensitive subject. 'More coffee, darling?'

Katrina shook her head. 'No, thanks.' She spared her watch a glance and saw that it was close to midnight. 'I really should get—' she faltered on the verge of saying home. 'Back.'

Nicos's Mercedes was in the garage when she drove in, and lights glowed in the house.

He appeared from the direction of the study as she entered the lobby. He'd discarded his jacket and tie, had loosened the two top shirt buttons, and had rolled up his sleeve cuffs.

'Interesting evening?'

She could prevaricate and almost did, except something in those dark eyes warned against defiance. 'Dinner and a movie with Siobhan,' she elucidated. 'We lingered over coffee.' If he could question her whereabouts, she could query his. 'Yours?'

'Dinner with a client.'

'Who won?' It was a facetious query, and one that brought a faint, humorous twist to the edge of his mouth.

'I achieved a narrow winning margin.'

Of course. Nicos didn't play to lose. 'Congratulations.'

He inclined his head. 'A business colleague has issued a dinner invitation for tomorrow evening.'

'How nice for you.'

'Naturally I expect you to accompany me.'

Naturally. 'What if I choose not to?'

'I thought we'd agreed to present a united front?'

'In that case, you won't object accompanying me to the ballet next Monday evening?' Katrina countered with a sweet smile. Nicos enjoyed the arts, but that did not include classical dance.

His gaze narrowed. 'You have tickets?'

'Of course.' A visiting Russian troupe had ensured a bookings sell-out, and she'd intended to invite a friend. Now she hastily revised her plans to include Nicos.

Her smile broadened. 'It's called negotiation. A term you're very familiar with.'

'Done.'

'In that case,' she said sweetly. 'I'll say goodnight.' Without a further word she turned and ascended the stairs.

CHAPTER FIVE

KATRINA dressed with care, choosing an elegant, fitted gown in cream ecru. The intricate small crystal and pearl beading made the top a work of art, extending to the hipline, where the beads fell in measured, loose strings to the hem to swing slightly with every move she made.

Tonight she sought a sophisticated image, and she pinned her hair into a sleek French twist, took time with her make-up, and added a diamond tennis bracelet with matching pendant and ear studs. Stiletto heels lent her added height.

She had wined and dined with some of the country's social élite, and could converse knowledgeably on any number of subjects.

So why should she be nervous about sharing an evening with a few of Nicos's associates and their wives?

Because what the tabloid press hadn't revealed, gossip and innuendo would have filled in the blanks…in spades.

The interest would be circumspect, the conversation polite. But without doubt, Nicos and Katrina Kasoulis would be the focus of attention.

'Ready?'

She turned and spared him a level glance, noting

the black evening suit—Armani? Cerruti? He favoured the impeccable tailoring of both designers. His
white shirt was of the finest cotton, the silk tie fault-
less.

However, it was the man wearing the clothes who
stirred her senses. The broad facial features, dark
piercing eyes, a mouth she had only to look at to
remember how it felt on her own.

He possessed a dangerous sensuality that drew
women like bees to a honey pot. Inherent charm and
an awareness of some indefinable primitiveness beneath a sophisticated façade. Add wealth and power,
and the combination was lethal.

She could understand how a woman would fight
for him.

As Georgia had?

Could *she* have gone to such lengths to have his
child and wreck a marriage?

Katrina mentally shook her head. A fair fight was
one thing. Employing devious underhand means was
something else.

'Have I suddenly acquired a few grey hairs?'

She registered Nicos's drawled query, and managed a quizzical response. 'Not to my knowledge.'

'Then, shall we leave?'

Their hosts resided in Woollahra, a gracious old
home set back from the road with a magnificent view.

Cars lined the illuminated driveway, and inside
guests mingled in a large formal lounge. Muted music
emitted from speakers, providing a pleasant back-

ground as Katrina moved at Nicos's side while their host performed introductions.

Nicos's hand rested against the small of her back. A proprietorial gesture, or reassurance?

Katrina accepted a flute of champagne and sipped the chilled liquid.

'I imagine we're supposed to project solidarity?' she inclined lightly, and caught the hint of amusement evident in the look he cast her.

'Advisable, wouldn't you say?'

'Just don't expect me to display adoring affection.'

His mouth curved into a warm smile. 'I'm disappointed. Adoring affection would make a pleasant change.'

'I'll save the animosity for when we're alone.'

'For which I'm incredibly grateful.'

'The animosity, or being alone?' It was almost fun to indulge in harmless banter.

'Both.'

'You enjoy our heated exchanges?'

Nicos lifted a hand and pressed a finger to her mouth. 'I enjoy watching your emotions at play.'

He was adept at discerning each and every one of them. Right now she was nervous, but determined to adopt a façade that only he could penetrate. It was evident in the slightly rapid beat of her pulse, the quick and almost too-ready smile, the depth of green in those beautiful emerald-green eyes.

His attempt to soothe was spontaneous, a light trail of his fingerpads across her shoulder blades, and he watched her eyes dilate in awareness of his touch.

'I think we should mingle, don't you?' Katrina murmured, and took a deliberate sip of champagne. This was madness. A simple gesture, and she had to control her body's natural instinct to lean into him. 'Thea and Rafe Richardson have not long arrived. Perhaps we could join them?'

It was a pleasant evening, the food superb. The table seating arrangements proved interesting, and while the conversation flowed, accompanied by scintillating laughter, Katrina was conscious of receiving circumspect attention…from several women, whose veiled curiosity searched for the slightest crack appearing in Nicos's or her own projected persona.

If anything, Nicos seemed bent on displaying an element of *tendresse*, much to her discomfort. It was evident in the touch of his hand on hers, albeit that it was fleeting. Whenever they spoke together, and it seemed it was often, he gave the impression each word held meaningful importance. His attentiveness was exemplary.

'You're in serious danger of overkill,' Katrina relayed in an undertone as he refilled her water glass.

'Taking care of you?'

She was willing to swear he wasn't talking about *food*. It brought forth a vivid memory of just *how* he'd taken care of her needs…in the bedroom, and out of it…and her frequently explosive reaction. He possessed the touch, the skill, the knowledge, to drive her wild.

By the time dessert was served, she'd had enough. If this was a game, it was only fair she began to play.

Without pause for thought she spooned a small quantity of superb *crème caramel* and offered it to Nicos. 'Taste this, darling.'

His gaze locked with hers, dark brown with emerald green, and the firm curve of his mouth parted to accept the morsel.

She refrained from repeating the gesture, and minutes later she laid a hand on his thigh. The sudden tightening of sinew beneath her fingers was encouraging, and she dug her nails in lightly, then slowly trailed her fingertips towards his groin.

'Payback, Katrina?'

'Yes.'

'Don't overstep the mark.'

'I wasn't aware any boundaries were set.'

'Retribution has a price.'

'Threat or challenge?'

His eyes darkened. 'It's your hand to play.'

A *double entendre* if ever there was one! Perhaps a retreat was advisable. Temporarily, she conceded, for she wasn't done yet.

With deliberate intent she turned to the guest next to her and began a conversation, the content of which she retained little memory within minutes of concluding it.

'I understand you're flying down to Melbourne tomorrow to examine two sites Kevin had under review,' said Nicos.

Katrina turned towards him and contained her surprise. Her lawyer knew of her intention, and had presumably seen it as his duty to relay the information to Nicos.

'Yes.'

'I'll accompany you.'

'Why?'

'It's in my interest as joint executor of Kevin's will and a member of the directorial board to sanction any decision you make regarding the sale of estate assets,' he evinced smoothly.

'I intend staying overnight.' An intention which should interfere with his business schedule.

'No problem. I imagine you've booked the early flight?'

She wanted to gnash her teeth, and barely restrained herself from doing so. He'd very cleverly manoeuvred her into something she could hardly get out of, given that it was a legitimate business trip. But it was the *overnight* bit that irked, for the invention had worked against her.

Coffee was served in the lounge, and she sank gracefully into a single cushioned chair. Here at least she was safe.

Wrong, she acknowledged minutes later. Nicos came to stand within touching distance, and his close proximity had a measured effect on her breathing. As well as other more intimate parts of her body.

What was wrong with her? They were each enacting a part. As soon as their car cleared the gates, it would herald a return to the status quo. Separate bedrooms, separate lives. Connecting only for the sake of appearances.

So why did she feel as if her body was a finely tuned instrument awaiting the master's touch? Every nerve was taut, each pleasure pulse acutely sensitised.

If he touched her, she'd go up in flames.

Did he know? Dear heaven, she hoped not! It would be a total humiliation. Hers.

She wanted the evening to end. To be able to go home, slip out of her clothes, remove her make-up, and crawl into bed. Alone.

Liar. You want to be with him. To experience once more what you once shared together. For the good times.

With Nicos, it had been more than sex. It had been intimacy, a physical expression of love between two people in tune with each other on every level.

All her protective instincts warned any attempt to revisit that special place would be akin to committing emotional suicide. And she was a survivor. She *had* to be.

It was after eleven when Nicos indicated they should leave, and she expressed her gratitude to their hosts, bade fellow guests goodnight, and walked at Nicos's side to the car.

Minutes later they cleared the gates and soon reached the arterial road leading towards Point Piper.

Street lights provided illumination, and the tree-lined avenues cast looming shadows. Many of the houses were in darkness, but every now and again a lit window revealed activity within.

'All talked out?'

Katrina turned slightly at the sound of that musing

drawl, and could determine nothing from his expression. In the shadowed interior, his features were all angles and planes.

'In recovery mode after playing charades,' she declared, and heard his throaty chuckle.

'That bad, hmm?'

In their hosts' home there had been security in numbers. Now they were alone, and effects of the game still lingered. Yet she was conscious of an elemental danger, aware that if she didn't tread very carefully she could unleash a situation she wasn't ready to deal with…now, or at any stage in the future.

Had Nicos's affectionate attention been entirely contrived? She told herself she didn't want to know. Except there was a part of her that reacted to his touch, and it irked unbearably that she hadn't been in total control of her emotions.

It didn't take long to traverse the distance between Woollahra and Point Piper, and Katrina slid from the car in one fluid movement, entering the lobby a few steps ahead of her inimitable husband.

The click of her heels on marble tiles sounded loud in the night's silence, and her steps were quick as she entered the spacious lobby and headed for the elegant staircase.

She was aware of Nicos resetting the alarm system, closing lights, and she fought against the instinctive need to run.

From what? a tiny voice demanded. *Yourself?*

She deigned not to answer, nor even give the

thought any credence as she reached the sanctuary of her room.

Nicos hadn't attempted to stop her.

So why did she harbour the intuitive feeling he had a strategy and a hidden agenda?

To seduce her?

Why? Except to prove he could?

And he had as much hope of achieving that as a snowflake's chance in hell, she vowed as she slipped off her heeled pumps and discarded the beaded gown.

Make-up removal came next, then she donned a nightshirt and slid into bed, all too aware that sleep was never more distant.

After an hour of tossing restlessly from one position to another she pulled on a wrap and made her way downstairs to the indoor pool adjacent the gym. There, she cast aside the wrap and dived neatly into the sparkling, crystal-clear water.

Katrina stroked several lengths, then changed style, enjoying the feel of cool water against her skin as she covered length after length.

It was mindless exercise, but one she welcomed in a bid to bring on a state of semi-exhaustion that would enable sleep.

Maybe then Nicos's image wouldn't haunt her, or invade her dreams.

Her muscles were beginning to tire, and her breathing was no longer smooth or even. Time to stop, she decided as she reached the tiled edge, then rested there for several long seconds as she caught her breath and smoothed excess water from her hair.

'Had enough?'

She gasped at the sound of that familiar male drawl, and went under as she'd inadvertently released her hold on the pool's edge.

Seconds later she rose to the surface, spluttering with indignation. 'You frightened the life out of me! How did you know I was down here?'

'Sensor security,' Nicos informed. 'A modem beeps beside my bed if lights are activated inside the house after the alarm is set.'

Katrina trod water as she tilted her head to look at him. It seemed a long way up! 'So you decided to investigate.' In the reflected pool lighting he resembled a dark angel, and his navy towelling robe made her supremely conscious she wasn't wearing so much as a stitch.

There were towels stacked in a nearby cupboard, but she'd have to emerge from the pool and walk several steps to reach one.

'Are you through expending excess energy?'

'Yes.' Please, God, he wouldn't guess *why* she'd chosen a midnight exercise stint.

He hunkered down and extended a hand. 'I'll help you out.'

'One way to help would be to fetch me a towel,' she declared dryly.

'Skinny-dipping?'

Suspicion darkened her eyes. 'Just how long have you been standing there?'

'A few minutes.'

She scooped up a handful of water and aimed it at him. 'You fiend!'

Nicos rose to his feet, loosened the tie on his robe, discarded it, and dived into the pool to emerge close beside her.

'Now we're on equal ground.'

Katrina lashed out a hand, and had it caught before it could connect. 'Let me go.'

His smile held a dangerous quirk that made her instantly wary.

'Please,' she added quietly, desperate to put some distance between them. He was too close, too physical, *too much*.

'Is it me you don't trust,' Nicos mused thoughtfully. 'Or yourself?'

She swallowed the faint lump that had risen in her throat. 'I won't play mouse to your cat.'

'Is that what you think I'm doing...playing?'

Her gaze was steady. 'I think you're deriving a certain amount of amusement from the situation.'

'And you'd like to escape?'

'I'd like to get out of the pool,' Katrina corrected.

'Then, go, *pedhi mou*,' he bade. 'I won't stop you.'

She watched as he moved away from her and stroked a leisurely pace towards the end of the pool.

With quick movements she levered her body onto the tiled surround, stood to her feet and quickly pulled on her discarded robe.

She should have felt cold, for the water had been cool, but instead heat flooded her veins and her heartbeat quickened measurably as she extracted a towel and wound it into a turban over her wet hair.

This wasn't the first time she'd shared the pool, naked, with Nicos. Except then… No, she determined resolutely, don't think about *then*.

Without a backward glance she quickly negotiated the two flights of stairs to her bedroom, showered and shampooed her hair before engaging the hair-drier, then she slid into bed.

A faint groan left her lips as she caught sight of the time. In too few hours her alarm would sound and she'd need to rise, change, pack an overnight bag, and leave for the airport.

CHAPTER SIX

MELBOURNE was a vast, cosmopolitan city with wide, tree-lined streets, electric trams, and changeable weather.

It was two years since Katrina had visited, and little seemed to have changed as the cab took a familiar route from the airport.

The hotel was a modern structure on the hill overlooking the city's heart, and within minutes of checking in Katrina and Nicos rode the glass-faceted lift to a high floor.

Their suite undoubtedly had a stunning view but, whilst there was a lounge area containing two deep-seated chairs, a coffee table, a desk with phone and fax machine, there was only one bedroom, not two, of which the focal point was a king-size bed.

'If you think I'm sharing that with you, you can think again,' Katrina declared as Nicos deposited their hand luggage.

'We share a house,' Nicos reminded her, slanting a hard glance.

'But not a room,' she argued. 'Especially not a bed.'

'Afraid of me, or yourself?'

She opened her mouth, then closed it again. 'That doesn't even qualify an answer.'

He unfolded two shirts and hung them in the wardrobe, took his toiletry bag through to the *en suite*.

Katrina mirrored his actions, shaking out the slither of uncrushable silk georgette she intended wearing to dinner and transferring it onto a hanger.

She was damned if she'd share the same bed with him. One of the comfortable chairs in the adjoining lounge area would suffice. Better, she could push the two together and arrange a makeshift bed with a pillow and extra blanket.

The niggle of irritation joined a deeper, more significant disturbance in the region of her heart as the reality of sharing this suite began to manifest itself.

Oh, get a grip, she admonished silently. They were here primarily for business purposes. They'd have lunch, attend the meeting, return to the hotel to shower and change, then enjoy dinner with Nicos's cousin, Stavros Kidas, and his wife, Eleni.

Lunch was pleasant, the food excellent in the hotel's exclusive à la carte restaurant, and Katrina began to relax a little.

They didn't linger long over coffee, and took a cab out to view the two adjoining sites.

Activity on two adjacent blocks merely confirmed Nicos's independent investigation, determining without doubt the intentions a major developer had for the entire block.

'They're going to rase everything,' Katrina opined, observing two old cottages that had stood for a century. They looked vacant, and soon to follow the fate of two equally old dwellings on their eastern boundary.

Kevin had negotiated to acquire the remaining ten cottages, with plans to remodel them into trendy boutiques, thus preserving the ambience of the surrounding area. Except a large multinational corporation had outbid him, and had offered Kevin an exorbitant sum for the corner site owned by Macbride.

'I liked Kevin's vision better,' she declared. 'The low-rise glass monstrosity already approved won't blend with its surroundings.'

Nicos threw her a calculating glance. 'You've decided not to sell?'

Her chin tilted a little, a gesture he knew well.

'They've already acquired most of the block, and if we retain the corner site it will depreciate in value.' Her eyes hardened, their purpose inflexible. 'We'll sell, but at a price. They'll pay, because it suits them.' She'd done her calculations. 'I figure it's worth another two hundred and fifty thousand.'

Nicos placed a hand on her shoulder. 'Kevin would be proud of you.'

Katrina hoped so. She desperately needed to establish credence in her father's business sector. As a woman, she knew it wouldn't be easy. Nor could she afford to make mistakes.

'Okay, let's go inspect the Toorak site.'

She turned back towards the cab, conscious that Nicos's hand had slid down to capture her own in a loose hold. She knew she should wrench free, but she indulged herself a few seconds of his touch, its warmth, and briefly wondered at her sanity.

Toorak was an exclusive suburb, an eclectic mix of old money and new, established elegant homes, tree-lined avenues, and a long bustling main street filled with trendy boutiques and equally trendy cafés.

It didn't take long to confirm extensive renovations would turn two adjoining properties into leased boutiques that would blend in beautifully with their surroundings.

'Keep these, and renovate,' Katrina stated, mentally transferring the profit from one site to this one. She liked the odds, knew it would work, and could hardly wait to set the plans in motion. She turned towards Nicos. 'What do you think?'

'Perhaps Siobhan might care to have a leasing interest with a Melbourne branch?'

He was good, very good, at reading her mind.

'The legal eagle we have a four o'clock appointment with is within walking distance from here?'

It took an hour of phone calls and intense negotiations, but Katrina emerged from the lawyer's office triumphant.

'We did it,' she said with satisfaction as she preceded Nicos onto the pavement.

Her eyes sparkled, and her smile reflected her elation.

'You did,' Nicos drawled in musing correction. 'I merely sat in and watched you play.'

So he had, but his presence made it easy, a backup she genuinely appreciated. She'd learned well beneath

Kevin's guidance, but not all men viewed a woman as having equal status in the business arena, and she held little doubt that she'd have had to battle harder if she'd come to this meeting alone.

'Thank you.'

'For what?'

'Being there.'

'My pleasure.'

Nicos hailed a cruising cab, and Katrina watched it swoop to a halt at the kerb. Seconds later the driver executed a U-turn and headed into the city to their hotel.

It was after five when they entered their suite, and Katrina slipped off her shoes and loosened her jacket.

'Do you want to take the shower first, or shall I?'

'We could share,' Nicos declared with musing indolence.

'No, we couldn't,' she refuted firmly, aware of tiny prickles of alarm slithering over the surface of her skin. She had no difficulty recalling how he looked *sans* clothes: the splendid musculature of his masculine frame, the breadth of his shoulders, the taut buttocks and powerful thighs. As to the instrument of his manhood...

Don't go there, she bade silently. Her heart began hammering at the memory of how it had been between them. His skilled touch, her reaction. Dear Lord, he'd never failed to send her up in flames.

Without a further word she gathered briefs and bra, caught up a complimentary bathrobe, and entered the *en suite*. For a few paralysing seconds she hesitated, then she quietly slid home the lock.

Twenty minutes later she emerged, the bathrobe securely tied, with her make-up bag in hand.

Nicos was seated on the edge of the bed, his attention taken by a documentary on television.

'Finished?'

Katrina wasn't conscious of holding her breath until she released it in a rush several seconds later when the bathroom door closed behind him.

By the time he re-entered the bedroom she was dressed, her make-up complete, and she was in the process of securing small diamond studs to her ears.

He had no inhibition at discarding his robe, and her eyes flicked over his frame, naked except for black hipster briefs, and her stomach did a backwards flip as she caught the fluid ripple of muscle and sinew as he reached for his trousers and pulled them on. A clean shirt came next, and she dragged her gaze away as he deftly attended to fastening buttons before tucking in his shirt and sliding the zip fastening home.

The thought of previously being held in those arms throughout the night was damning. But, oh, how she longed for the comfort they'd offered. The closeness, the caring…

What was she doing, for heaven's sake? She didn't, *couldn't* want anything from the man who had betrayed her.

Yet there was some intrinsic quality existent, an inherent knowledge that defied logic.

Sexual chemistry, she dismissed as she collected her evening purse.

'Shall we leave?'

'We're meeting Stavros and Eleni in the lounge bar,' Nicos indicated as they rode the lift down.

Katrina hadn't seen them since she'd left Nicos. Had he told them about their separation and reconciliation?

'No,' Nicos said quietly as they entered the lounge. 'Although I don't doubt they've heard.'

Was she that transparent?

There was no time to cogitate Nicos's keen ability to divine her thoughts as two people rose from their seats and moved forward to greet them.

'Lovely to see you again.' Eleni inclined with a warm smile as they settled into comfortable chairs.

Nicos beckoned the drinks waiter and ordered champagne.

'This is a celebration?' Eleni queried.

'Of a kind,' Nicos agreed, sparing Katrina a musing glance.

'I was sorry to hear about your father,' Stavros indicated. 'A sad loss.'

'Thank you.'

Stavros turned towards Nicos and began discussing a mutual business deal, while Eleni leaned towards Katrina.

'I can't begin to tell you how happy it makes me to see you both together again.'

What did she say to that? 'It's been a while,' Katrina agreed tentatively.

'Georgia is nothing but a troublemaker,' Eleni vowed quietly. 'She has put Nicos through *hell*.'

Really? On the few occasions Katrina had seen him during the months of their separation he'd looked perfectly fine.

'But then, of course you would know that,' Eleni confirmed.

Katrina didn't comment, although it was difficult to contain a smile as Eleni rolled her eyes with expressive distaste.

'The woman is a *witch*.' Eleni appeared to pull herself together and change the subject. 'So, you have been engaged in business matters all day. Now, it's time to celebrate.' Eleni's features softened. 'A celebration for us too. I am pregnant.'

'I'm so pleased for you.' Katrina's enthusiasm was genuine. A child was a beautiful gift, and Eleni had wanted babies from the day of her marriage.

Minutes later they gravitated towards the restaurant. The food was excellent, the service good, and the ensuing hours passed so quickly it was difficult to believe it was almost ten when Eleni indicated they should leave.

'My wife tires easily,' Stavros explained apologetically as Nicos settled the bill.

'One minute I'm fine,' Eleni said with amusement. 'The next I can hardly keep my eyes open.'

They walked towards the exit through the hotel lobby and Stavros organised for the concierge to fetch their car.

'We will see you again soon, yes?' Eleni embraced

Nicos, then turned towards Katrina. 'Take care, Katrina.'

Their car arrived, courtesy of a porter, and within a few brief minutes they were gone.

'Would you like to have a drink in the lounge?' Nicos queried as they re-entered the lobby.

'Okay.' Anything to delay taking the lift back up to their suite.

Nicos ordered coffee, and Katrina sipped hers slowly as she indulged in the idle pleasure of people-watching. Couples, singles, young and old.

'Penny for them?'

She looked at Nicos, and was unable to gain much from his expression. 'It's been a successful day.'

'Yes, it has.'

'Can I take it as joint executor, you approve my decisions?'

'I have no doubt as to your ability to make them,' Nicos said evenly.

'Thank you,' she responded solemnly.

'I believe you've been looking at property.'

Katrina's eyes sharpened. 'I'm using my own personal funds, which gives you absolutely no reason to question me.'

One eyebrow slanted. 'I was making an observation.'

'You want addresses? So *you* can check them out?' She could feel the anger begin to rise. 'Or has your source of information already given you a full report?'

'You use Kevin's lawyer for your own affairs,' he reminded silkily.

'He contravened client confidentiality privilege?' she queried, scandalised.

'Not at all, and only in respect of commenting on your business acumen,' Nicos said smoothly.

Katrina took in a deep breath and released it slowly. 'I enjoy restoring property.'

'The terrace houses are a good investment.'

'You know about them—*how*?'

He held her gaze. 'I'm negotiating to buy the remaining three in the same block. The agent rang me this morning and mentioned my wife's expression of interest.'

Another breach of confidentiality? Or had the agent simply assumed a husband and wife were aware of each other's financial investments?

'You intend to outbid me?'

'No. I had in mind we could collaborate.'

Her interest was piqued. 'Harry would be delighted.' She hastened to explain. 'The interior decorator I use. He's very good.'

'Have him ring me.'

A waiter hovered with a cafetière of steaming hot black coffee and offered to refill their cups, which they each declined.

Katrina stifled a yawn, then rose to her feet. 'I'm going up to bed.' She was tired, and they were due to take the morning flight to Sydney.

Nicos unfolded his length and walked with her to the lift, summoned it, and within minutes they entered their suite.

CHAPTER SEVEN

'WHAT do you think you're doing?'

'Organising a makeshift bed,' Katrina informed him as she took down a blanket and snagged a spare pillow.

'The bed is large,' Nicos said with dangerous softness.

Katrina met his gaze with open defiance. 'I'm not sharing it with you.'

'Is it me you don't trust? Or yourself?'

'You,' she responded succinctly, and stepped through to the lounge.

She pulled two chairs together, facing each other, and decided it should be quite comfortable if she adopted a foetal position.

Seconds later she extracted a long cotton tee shirt from her bag and retreated to the *en suite* to change.

Hmm, not so comfortable, she admitted to herself within minutes of settling herself down. She doused the lamp, and the suite was shrouded in darkness.

Katrina reflected on the events of the day, ruminated the prospect of Siobhan's enthusiasm at opening a Melbourne branch of her Double Bay boutique...and shifted position on the chairs.

To no avail, for one hip soon became numb from

the hard upholstering. Damn. Maybe if she lay on her back with her knees bent.

How long did it take for her to decide the chairs were a no-go sleeping situation? Half an hour? She had no idea of the passage of time when she carefully manoeuvred herself free and spread one half of the blanket on the carpet.

She leaned forward to collect the pillow and knocked her elbow. A faint groan escaped her lips. Hell, that hurt.

Was Nicos asleep? She stifled the temptation to take the pillow and bat him over the head with it.

She should have insisted on two separate suites. Dammit, why hadn't she?

At that precise moment the bedroom lamp went on, and in the next instant Nicos stood towering in the archway that separated the small lounge and bedroom.

Without a word he moved forward and scooped her into his arms.

'Put me down!' Katrina vented in fury.

He did. On the side of the bed he occupied. 'Stay there,' he warned in a voice that sent shivers scudding down the length of her spine.

She bounced back onto her feet and watched as he crossed round to the opposite side of the bed. 'The hell I will!'

He threw her a dark lethal glance. 'If you want to fight, I'll oblige.' He waited a beat. 'Just be aware how it will end.'

'I'm shaking!'

'You will, if you don't get back into bed.'

She didn't move, and her eyes burned emerald-bright with rage. 'Since when did you become such a dictatorial tyrant?'

'Ten seconds, Katrina,' Nicos warned silkily.

Her eyes went to the telephone on the bedside pedestal. 'Reception can find me another suite.' She picked up the receiver, but she didn't even manage to punch one digit before Nicos cut the connection.

'Don't even think about it.'

She rounded on him in fury. 'How dare you?'

'Easily.'

Without thought she snatched up a pillow and threw it at him, only to watch as he deflected it onto the bed.

His anger was a palpable entity. The bedside lamp cast shadows in the room, and his frame seemed to loom large, his features all angles and planes.

'Three nights ago we shared a bed half this size.'

'That was different.'

He moved with the grace of a cat, his speed indolently deceptive as he skirted the bed.

Katrina took one look and scrambled across the mattress to the other side. She couldn't win, there was nowhere to go, and she fought like a wild thing as he caught hold of her, stilling her flailing arms with galling ease.

In a moment of madness she bit him, hard, connecting just above one male nipple, and registered his intake of breath an instant before she was pushed down onto the mattress.

She bucked, trying vainly to free herself, and gave

a startled cry as he straddled her hips and pinned her wrists above her head.

'Get off me!'

He held her securely, his knees trapping her thighs, yet still she arched against him, twisting her body as she attempted to wrench her arms free.

'Stop it. You'll hurt yourself.'

'Dammit, let me go!'

Her eyes were a brilliant green, dilated with a mixture of outrage and anger, her hair a mass of tumbled curls.

She made one desperate last-ditch effort, only to concede defeat. Her chest heaved, and her breath escaped in short, furious gasps. If looks could kill, he'd be dead.

He waited, watching as her breathing steadied, and his eyes were impossibly dark. There was a stillness apparent in those strong, masculine features, a leashed savagery that caused the breath to hitch in her throat.

No. It was a silent scream that didn't find voice.

The room faded from the periphery of her vision. There was only the man, the latent, magnetic intensity evident.

Primitive awareness eased the sudden knot in her stomach, and she battled the slow heat warming the blood in her veins.

A faint whimper escaped her lips, part groan, part despair. What was happening to her? It seemed as if everything had coalesced and Nicos had become her total focus.

Her body had a memory of its own, and she was

powerless to stop the treacherous awakening as passion flared.

Damn you, Nicos. The silent curse didn't find voice. *Don't.*

Except it was way too late.

Slowly he lowered his head, and his mouth brushed hers, the touch feather-light in an evocative, teasing gesture that wasn't nearly enough.

He felt the faint quiver of her body, sensed the heat, and he nibbled on her lower lip, then nipped the full centre, soothing it with the tip of his tongue before tracing the soft contours.

The strength of his arousal was a potent force nestled against the most vulnerable part of her anatomy, and sensation throbbed, primitive, urgent, libidinous.

She parted her mouth, wanting more, much more than this gentle seduction, and she moaned an entreaty as his lips savoured the line of her throat, then nuzzled the sensitive hollow at the edge of her neck.

I should stop this, *now*, before it's too late, she groaned silently.

Except she was powerless to still the deep need, the mesmeric, erotic witchery of his seduction.

When his mouth found hers again, she kissed him with possessive hunger, angling her head for closer purchase.

Her whole body was on fire, and the breath hissed between her teeth as he freed her wrists and dispensed with her long cotton tee shirt.

A swift tugging movement divested his briefs, and

she cried out as he sought her breast, teasing a tender peak before suckling shamelessly.

Her hands slid over his shoulders, caressed his spine, then she dug her fingers into his buttocks.

Now. Her breath came in ragged gasps as he sought the moistness, his touch finding the acutely sensitised nub with unerring accuracy.

She went up in flames, then cried out as he sent her higher, and she wasn't conscious of pleading with him, or begging his possession.

Nicos took her with one deep thrust, and heard her faint intake of breath as silken muscles stretched to accommodate him. He stilled, enjoying the enclosure, the tightness as she gripped and held him, then he began to move, slowly, almost withdrawing completely before surging in to the hilt.

Again and again he repeated the action, increasing the movement until she met and matched his rhythm in a tumultuous ride that left them both slick with sensual sweat.

Katrina waited for her breathing to steady, convinced she was unable to move so much as a muscle. Dear heaven. She closed her eyes, too enervated to do anything, and she groaned out loud as he gathered her close and rolled onto his back.

His hands brushed over her skin in a soothing gesture, and she felt his lips at her temple, the soft hollow beneath her ear.

It felt so good, like coming home after conquering the stormy sea.

Slowly she lifted her body, arching it gracefully as

she rose above him. She lifted a hand and tucked her hair behind one ear, then the other, then she touched the tip of her finger to his chest and traced a teasing pattern through the dark hair, pausing to tug a little before following the line arrowing down to his waist.

She felt him harden, his length expanding as she brushed a teasing path back and forth at the juncture of their connection, only to have him replace her fingers with his own.

Her pleasure was immediate, the wild surge of exquisite sensation almost more than she could bear, and this time it was she who rode him on the path to mutual ecstasy.

Yet it was Nicos who held her at the brink, then tipped her over in a mutual, spellbinding free fall.

Katrina fell asleep curled close in Nicos's arms, her head pillowed against his chest.

Throughout the night they reached for each other, satisfying needs that were alternately urgent, then slow and magically sweet.

There was a part of her that never wanted the sensual dreams of the night to end. How many times had she imagined such a night, relived it again and again, only to wake alone with an emptiness that was all too real?

But as the first light of dawn crept over the horizon she responded to the trail of fingers caressing the curve of her waist, exulted in their intimate touch, and melted into her lover's body, fitting so well it was as if they were two halves of a whole.

It was late when they rose from the bed and shared

a shower. Even later when they sat down to room-service breakfast, lingering over coffee before dressing and checking out.

The late morning flight landed in Sydney after midday, and Nicos collected his car, stowed their overnight bags in the boot, then dropped Katrina outside her office building before traversing inner-city traffic to his own.

She should have been tired, but instead she felt energised, and she rode the lift to her office, checked with her secretary, ordered in lunch, and got to work.

Nicos phoned at four to say he'd be delayed, and Katrina indicated she needed to bring work home.

'Don't wait dinner.'

'You want to ring Marie, or shall I?' Katrina queried, only to have him respond he'd already done so.

It was after six when she entered the house, and she checked the refrigerator, saw the delicious salad Marie had left for her, then ran lightly upstairs to change and fill the spa bath.

Her solo dinner could wait for half an hour while she relaxed in the pulsating water.

Not such a good idea, she reflected, as the memory of Nicos's lovemaking came vividly to mind. Even the thought of what they'd shared caused sensation to spiral through her body, and she groaned out loud as she recollected her hungry response.

Nothing had changed, she determined, then closed her eyes in frustrated resignation. Who was she kidding? *Everything* had changed.

It was almost seven when she donned jeans, a cotton top, and went downstairs to the kitchen.

The salad was delicious, and after she'd eaten it she curled up in a chair in the sitting room and used the remote to switch on the television.

She must have dozed, for she came awake at the touch of hands sliding beneath her thighs.

'Nicos?'

'Who were you expecting?' he drawled musingly.

'I can walk,' Katrina declared. 'Put me down.'

He reached the stairs and began to ascend them. 'You doubt my ability to carry you?'

She weighed little more than a child, and he wasn't even breathing heavily when he reached the landing.

'For heaven's sake, put me down!'

He let her slide down to her feet, and she moved a few paces, then turned towards her room.

'Goodnight.'

'Where do you think you're going?'

The query was quietly spoken, yet beneath the softness there was a hint of steel, and Katrina looked at him in silent askance.

'My room.'

'No.'

'What do you mean—*no*?'

'Last night—'

'Was a mistake.'

'The hell it was.'

'We…' she paused fractionally '…got carried away,' she qualified. Words, they were only words.

None of which even began to describe the extent of her emotional involvement or her reaction.

Nicos's eyes darkened. 'Is that how you describe it? *Carried away?*'

She met his gaze and held it. 'What else would you call it?'

'We share the same room, the same bed.' He stilled her protest by pressing a finger to her lips. 'It isn't an option.'

Her eyes sparked green fire. 'Since when did you get to call the shots?'

The palm of his hand slid to cup the edge of her jaw. 'From the moment we made love last night.'

She felt her insides begin to liquify. 'We had sex.'

'So we did, *pedhi mou.*'

He sounded amused, and she fought against her body's response. She didn't want to succumb to his seduction, didn't need to do battle for her own self-preservation. It had taken *months* to build up a resistance to him. Yet in one night he'd managed to tear it down as if that invisible wall had never existed.

'I'm tired.' Katrina offered the excuse in desperation. 'All I want to do is slip into bed. *My* bed. *Alone.*'

He smoothed the tip of his thumb over the soft fullness of her lower lip. 'So you shall,' he said gently, and let his hand fall to his side. 'But it won't be alone.'

With that, he turned and walked towards his room without a backward glance.

Dammit, couldn't he see she needed time to assimilate what had happened between them? That she was at war with herself, and in a constant state of flux at having succumbed to the dictates of her flesh?

In the light of day, all she could focus on was her own weakness. This man had betrayed her with another woman. Worse, that woman had borne his child.

At the time she'd dealt with it. But now, the very structure she'd carefully built was falling down around her ears.

She wanted to hate him, and told herself she did. But she hated herself more.

Katrina reached her room and closed the door behind her. There was no lock, and unless she dragged heavy furniture to bar the door, there was nothing she could do to keep him out.

She cast the double bed a pensive glance. She was darned if she'd just slip between the sheets and lie *waiting* for Nicos to join her.

There was little doubt that he *would*.

She could, however, make a silent statement. There were three other bedrooms upstairs. She'd occupy one of those in the hope it would add emphasis to her intention not to sleep with him.

Katrina chose a bedroom, selected linen and made up the bed, then slid wearily between the covers.

She should have been asleep within seconds of her head touching the pillow. Instead she lay staring into the darkness for what seemed an age, her limbs and mind as tense as a tightly stretched wire.

She told herself she didn't, couldn't, want him. Yet her body was a mass of contradictions as memory persisted in providing a vivid replay of what they'd shared the previous night.

It would be so easy to adopt a rational mindset where she simply enjoyed the intimacy of sex. *Why not?* a silent voice demanded. Just enjoy the intense pleasure of physical contact throughout the year she was forced to stay with Nicos, then walk away. Heart whole, with no regrets.

Impossible. She'd gifted him her heart, her soul, almost from the first moment they'd met. For months she'd thought she'd reclaimed them, but last night had proved beyond doubt they were his. Always would be.

She hated herself for it. Hated him.

A shaft of light pierced the darkness as the bedroom door opened, and her tense body became rigid as Nicos stood silhouetted in the aperture.

Katrina's lashes fanned down. Maybe if she lay perfectly still he'd assume she was asleep.

She should have known better. Within seconds she felt the bed covers move, followed by the faint depression of the mattress as he slid in beside her.

How long before he reached for her? Five seconds, ten?

Minutes later she was still counting, and it took concentration to keep her breathing steady.

'What do you plan?' Nicos drawled. 'A game of musical beds?'

Had he known she was awake? Or was he simply taking a calculated guess?

'Don't sulk.'

'I've never sulked in my life,' Katrina vented as she turned her head towards him, then wished she hadn't, for he lay facing her, an elbow propped on the pillow.

With a fluid movement he reached out and snapped on the bedside lamp.

The light illuminated his features, and his dark gleaming gaze held a tinge of humour...and something else she didn't care to define.

'I'm *trying* to sleep.'

'Without success.'

'You don't know that.'

He brushed the back of his hand against her cheek, then let it trail down to the edge of her mouth.

'Don't do that.'

Her eyes were dark, the hollows smudged through lack of sleep, and she was pale. He felt her lips quiver beneath his touch, and saw the pulse jump at the base of her throat.

'Tired?'

Heat began to flare in the region of her stomach, curling in an upward spiral, and she swallowed compulsively. 'Yes.'

He leaned towards her and placed his mouth against the soft curve at the edge of her own. 'Want me to do all the work?'

His hand trailed a path to her navel, paused, then travelled low to begin an intimate exploration.

'You don't play fair.' Her voice was little more than a whisper.

'Is that a *yes* or a *no*?'

He possessed a skilled knowledge that brought forth a strangled gasp as she arched against him.

Nicos swept his tongue in an erotic dance with her own, nibbled at her lower lip, and absorbed the groan that rose from her throat.

He took it slowly, seducing her with a gentle touch, so that she simply held on and allowed him to lead a path to total conflagration. *Hers.*

Afterwards he held her close, his lips against her hair as he brushed light fingers back and forth along her spine.

CHAPTER EIGHT

SPRING was the traditional timing of the springtime gala dinner, hosted by one the city's prominent fundraising associations and headed by a media-conscious doyenne who utilised all her people skills to provide a glittering social occasion.

With so many worthy charities abounding, it was possible for the socialites to lunch and dine out with repetitive frequency, and many did. Others were more selective, choosing to grace only certain events with their presence.

Tonight's soirée numbered high on the scale of *de rigueur* attendances, Katrina acknowledged as she entered the grand ballroom of an inner city hotel at Nicos's side.

It also entailed some tactful juggling between Siobhan, Andrea and Chloe, who would each be seated at different tables with their individual coterie of friends. Somewhere in that equation would be Paula and Enrique, who retained an intense dislike for each other, but who would for the sake of social etiquette concede to present a united front…whilst doing their best to avoid each other like the plague.

Add general interest by fellow guests as to the state of Katrina and Nicos Kasoulis's reconciliation, and the evening resembled something akin to a trial by fire.

Years of practice as Kevin's daughter ensured she chose a stunning gown in pale mist-grey with a bias-cut overlay in pale blue polyester chiffon. It moulded her slender curves like a second skin, flaring out from the knee to swirl at her ankles. Tiny beaded straps were a token gesture holding the bodice in place, and her jewellery was confined to a delicate diamond necklace, ear studs, and matching bracelet. Stiletto-heeled pumps completed the outfit. She'd swept the length of her hair into an elegant twist.

Time spent perfecting her make-up ensured her *armour* was in place.

Smile, Katrina bade silently. Facial muscle strain was a small price to pay for surviving the evening.

'Preparing to do battle?' Nicos murmured as he led her towards their designated table.

'Can you doubt it?' Katrina conceded. 'There's Siobhan,' she indicated, and felt the brush of his hand at the back of her waist.

'Andrea and Chloe are seated on opposite sides of the room.'

She offered him a winsome smile. 'Then let's go do the greeting thing in order of priority.'

It was a while before they took seats at their own table, and she had the feeling as the evening progressed that they were merely players on a social stage, each performing a scripted part.

Did that encompass Nicos's solicitous attention? The touch of his hand, the slow musing smile that sent tiny lines fanning out from the corner of his eyes?

There was a part of her that wanted it to be genuine, while another part was afraid to deal with it if it was.

She had only to look at him to *see* the man beneath the sophisticated façade. The impeccable tailoring sheathed a male body in superb physical condition, which exuded an aura that was sexually primitive and intensely sensual.

Those eyes, that mouth... Oh, for heaven's sake, she chided silently. Control yourself!

The meal comprised three courses, skilfully broken up by brief speeches, and entertainment. It was while dessert was being served that Katrina took the opportunity to glance around the large room.

And felt her heart jolt at the sight of a familiar sleek dark head. The height, the stance...

It couldn't be, could it?

Even as she watched, the woman slowly turned, and Katrina sensed the blood drain from her face.

Georgia.

What was she doing here? Not so much in Sydney, but *here*, attending an invitation-only event...

Then she saw her stepbrother hand Georgia a drink, and everything fell into place.

Enrique, enraged at her repeated refusal to lend him money, had chosen to cause trouble in the most diabolical way he knew how.

Dear heaven, *why* did her life seem filled with fraught situations?

Her first instinct was to escape. Except that would play right into Enrique's hands, and she was darned if she'd give him the satisfaction.

Had Nicos sighted Georgia? Somehow she doubted it. He was deep in conversation with a colleague and, unless she was mistaken, Georgia and Enrique were beyond his peripheral vision.

Katrina sensed the moment Nicos saw her step-brother and recognised his companion. He didn't appear to move, but she was willing to swear most of his body muscles reassembled from relaxed mode to full alert beneath the fine tailoring of his evening suit.

Almost on cue, Georgia turned slightly and, with a smile and a word to Enrique, she excused herself and began threading her way towards them.

'Now, *this* will be interesting,' Katrina declared, *sotto voce*.

'Behave,' Nicos warned, and she threw him a stunning smile.

'Why, Nicos,' she chastised sweetly, 'I intend to be politeness itself.'

There would be avid eyes watching every move, every nuance in her expressive features, she perceived.

The separation of Katrina and Nicos Kasoulis had garnered press at the time. Just as their reconciliation was gaining undue attention now.

The appearance of Nicos Kasoulis's former mistress provided a reason for titillating gossip, and it didn't take much imagination to realise the phone lines would be running hot with conjecture over Georgia Burton's arrival in town.

'Nicos.' The name emerged from Georgia's lips as a sultry purr, while at the same time her eyes devoured him. 'I was hoping to see you here tonight.'

Sure. I just bet you planned it right down to the finest detail, Katrina thought silently as she inclined her head in acknowledgement. 'Georgia.'

Georgia's practised pout held just the right degree of regret. 'You haven't returned my calls.'

'I had no reason to,' Nicos informed her with an iciness that sent shivers down Katrina's spine.

'Not even for old times' sake? We go back a long way.'

'It's over. It has been for some time.'

Her expression was mildly calculating. 'How can you say that when we have a child together?'

'*You* have a child,' Nicos conceded, 'whom we both know is not mine.'

'Still in denial, Nicos?'

'Perjury is a punishable offence.'

'So is refusing to take responsibility for one's child,' Georgia retaliated.

'Your bravado veers towards the incredible,' Nicos stated grimly.

'*Incredible* aptly describes your sexual skills.' Georgia shifted her gaze to Katrina. 'Surely you agree?'

'I'm not into ego-stroking,' Katrina proffered with pseudo sweetness.

'And you think I am?'

Katrina didn't bother to answer, and watched as Georgia offered a practised smile, then turned and melted into the milling guests.

'That went down well.'

Nicos spared her a dark glance. 'She's courting trouble.'

'And you won't stand for it?' Katrina queried, feeling the anger stir beneath a veneer of social politeness.

'No.'

'I think I need to go visit the powder room.'

'Effecting a temporary escape?'

'Right first time.'

She'd learned from an early age to pin a smile on her face and hold her head high… Years of practice meant ease in acquiring a social façade. It was a game, a pretense, and she did it well.

It helped her greet a few acquaintances as she threaded her way through the fellow guests, to pause and converse briefly with a one or two.

The powder room was relatively empty, and Katrina smoothed a hand over her hair, took time to freshen her lipstick, and was about to retreat when the inner door swung open and Georgia entered the room.

Coincidence? Unlikely. This was a deliberate move on the model's part to initiate a one-on-one confrontation.

She could escape, but why, when Georgia was determined to have her say?

'I imagine there's a purpose to you following me here?'

'Of course.'

'So why don't you get it over with?'

'The terms of your late father's will must be a terrible trial to you.' Georgia inclined with practised languidness.

The game was about to commence. It took two to play, and she was determined not to lose. 'In what way?'

'Why…sharing the same house with Nicos, of course.'

Attack was better than defence. 'After he betrayed me?'

'Difficult, darling. Surely?'

'We agreed to compromise,' Katrina said steadily.

'Oh?'

'And enjoy the fringe benefits.'

'Such as?'

'Sex.' She even managed to effect a secretive smile. 'Nicos does the sex thing superbly well.'

Georgia's eyes narrowed. One to Katrina. But how long before the model evened the score?

'Agreed, darling. But can you be sure it's *you* he's thinking of at that…ah…' she paused for effect '…intense moment,' she concluded with delicate emphasis.

Too soon, Katrina acknowledged.

'How can you compete,' Georgia continued archly, pitilessly, 'when I have his son?'

'Has that been proven conclusively?'

'Why else would our individual lawyers be in the throes of hammering out a settlement and child support?'

Not so good, she conceded, aware just how the odds were stacked against her. 'And where *is* your son, Georgia? Isn't he a little young to leave with a sitter?'

'My mother flew in from Brisbane with me. Naturally I have a nanny.'

Naturally. Whatever happened to hands-on motherhood?

'If you're so important to Nicos,' she said carefully, 'why didn't he initiate divorce proceedings as soon as I left him?'

'How can you be so sure he didn't?' Georgia countered. 'A legal separation doesn't require documentation, other than a noting of the date both parties live apart. The Australian legal system recognises a decree nisi application one year after the date of separation.'

'In which case, our reconciliation has thrown a spanner in the works.'

Georgia mentally sharpened her claws and aimed for the kill. 'Not really, darling. A year isn't long in the scheme of things. I'm prepared to let him have you for a while.' Her smile was pure feline. 'After all, I'll get to keep him for a lifetime.'

'You're that confident?'

'Determined,' the model assured.

Katrina felt sickened. 'What makes you think I'll give him up so easily?'

'You did before. Why should this time be any different?' A soft laugh slipped from her carefully painted mouth. 'Oh, darling,' she chastised with pitying candour, 'you're not going to fight for him, are you? It would be such a demeaning exercise.'

'Demeaning to *whom*?'

There was a telling silence, then Georgia pursued softly, 'I play to win.'

'So do I.'

The model took a deliberate minute to check out her mirrored reflection before meeting Katrina's unwavering gaze. 'Then, we shall see who takes the prize.'

As an exit line it was a doozey.

It was several long seconds before Katrina felt calm enough to leave the relative sanctuary of the powder room and re-enter the ballroom lobby.

Nicos was standing close to one of the main doors, one of a remaining few guests, as most had already entered and were in the process of being seated.

He watched her cross the floor towards him, his eyes narrowing as he caught sight of her carefully composed features.

She was a spunky lady in many ways, but grief for Kevin was taking its toll. Georgia with her insidious innuendo was an abomination, and Enrique was again trolling for cash.

He experienced angry exasperation at the hand fate had dealt him, and impatience at being forced to wait for the resolution. Yet it was the end that justified the means.

'Georgia ensured a confrontation.'

Katrina lifted her chin and met his dark gaze with equanimity. 'Ah, you noticed.'

'There's very little I don't notice about you.'

'Well, now, there's the thing,' she commented with unaccustomed flippancy. 'I'm sure I should be flattered.'

'She upset you.' It wasn't a query, merely a statement.

'Observant, too. Please don't ask me for a word-by-word replay.'

'Katrina—'

'Let's go enter the social fray, shall we?'

'It'll keep.'

There were friends present whom they needed to connect with, acquaintances to acknowledge, and it was almost midnight before they could slip away.

Katrina sat quietly in the car as Nicos traversed city traffic and headed towards the eastern suburbs.

'Want to talk about it?'

She transferred her attention from the brightly lit street and could define little from his shadowy profile.

He'd been so chillingly cool with Georgia…for her benefit? She returned her gaze to the scene beyond the windscreen. Even *looking* at him hurt.

'Not particularly.'

As soon as they reached home she slid out from the car and moved through to the lobby ahead of him, mounting the stairs at a quickened pace, almost as if she was intent on putting as much distance between them as possible.

Which was ridiculous, she admitted silently as she reached the landing and made her way towards the bedroom.

Nicos followed, watching as she stepped out of her shoes, then she removed her jewellery before freeing the zip fastening on her gown.

'I had no idea Georgia would be there tonight.'

Her fingers stilled for a few seconds, then she slid the straps free from her shoulders and carefully slipped the gown down over her hips.

All she wore were thong briefs, and he wondered if she had any idea how provocative she appeared. Pale, satin-textured skin, slender, toned curves, and firm breasts which fitted perfectly into his palms.

He wanted to skim his hands over her hips, then slide up to cup each breast, teasing the peaks with the tips of his thumbs, then replace his hands with his mouth.

'I don't really care.' It was as well her face was hidden from him, otherwise he'd have seen through the fabrication in a heartbeat.

Then he was there, his hands turning her towards him, and he dealt with her token struggle as easily as if he were restraining a child.

There was little she could do to prevent him capturing her chin and tilting it so she had little option but to look at him.

'Yes, you do.'

His voice was a soft drawl, and she fought against swallowing compulsively, afraid the gesture would give hint to her fragile emotions.

'Don't.' The single word was a desperate plea as his head lowered down to hers, and she closed her

mouth against him, only to have her lips part invol-
untarily at the first, slow sweep of his tongue.

It was a kiss to die for, gentle, evocative, pervasive,
and she ignored the taunting little voice in her head
that warned he was merely embarking on a skilled
seduction.

A faint groan sighed in her throat as he reached for
the pins in her hair, slipping them free with practised
ease, then he threaded his fingers through its length
and held fast her head, angling his own as he deepened the kiss to something that was almost an oral
duplication of the sexual act itself.

Then it was too late, and she was unaware of him
removing his clothes, only that he had, and she
reached for him, drowning in his touch as he tumbled
her down onto the bed, the magic his mouth was able
to evoke, and her own unbridled response.

It was only later, much later that she rolled away
from him, angry with herself for her own weakness
and with him for what she perceived as his ability to
take advantage of it.

'Deny what we share, if you can,' Nicos said hardily.

Her eyes assumed a fiery sparkle. 'And that's supposed to make me feel okay? You think I don't hate
myself for this…addiction to—'

'Sex?'

'*You.*'

'Thank you, *agape mou*,' he acknowledged silkily,
'for the distinction.'

Katrina burst into angry speech. 'I shouldn't be

able to feel like this. It's—' words momentarily failed her '—disgusting!'

His expression hardened, and she glimpsed a muscle tense at the edge of his jaw. 'I can think of many apt descriptions,' he said with deceptive quietness. '*Disgusting* isn't one of them.'

'What would you call it, then?' she demanded.

'Sensual magic. Primitive passion. Raw desire. Meshing into something unique…for both of us.'

Dear God. In the beginning it had been all of that, and more. Much more. She closed her eyes, then opened them again. Even now, after everything that had split them apart, the emotional intensity was just as fierce. A primeval force demanding recognition.

A year ago she would have vowed it was *love*. But how could she call it that now in the face of his infidelity? It didn't make sense.

'Yet three months after our marriage…*three* months,' she emphasised, 'your obviously not-so-ex-mistress delights in revealing she's pregnant and names you the father.' Her eyes sparked green fire. 'A fact by anyone's calculation that lays the proof of infidelity squarely at your door.'

Anger moved up a notch or two. 'Hell, you must have gone straight from our nuptial bed to hers within days of returning from our honeymoon!' It didn't help to remember the idyllic, carefree few weeks they'd spent on Maui. Lazy days and long, love-filled nights.

'At the time you took Georgia's word over mine.' Nicos wanted to *shake* her. 'Did you pause to consider how that made *me* feel?' His hands fisted, and he controlled the urgent need to smash something. Soon, he would have the proof he needed. But for now all he had was words.

'Did it never at any time occur to you that Georgia deliberately set out to destroy our marriage? You, *me*?'

'Yes.' It was an honest admission, one that had been her first thought. A woman scorned could prove a dangerous threat. 'But she provided dates, places…hotels.' Receipts as confirmation. The horror of being presented with such proof came flooding back, the memory leaving her features pale, her eyes too large, too dark with remembered pain.

'I wasn't with her.'

'Dammit, she was *pregnant*,' Katrina vented. 'She had medical proof.' Her breath hitched, and she sought control. 'She showed me a copy of the ultrasound.' A video delivered to her apartment weeks later by special messenger. Vivid, cruel evidence she'd only been able to view for seconds before being physically ill.

It was too much. To think she'd behaved shamelessly and wantonly in his arms sickened her.

With a groan that was part despair, part self-loathing, she rolled to the edge of the mattress, only to have any form of escape felled before her feet could touch the carpet.

'Let me go.'

His grasp was firm, with a hint of steel should she attempt to struggle. 'No.'

She turned on him, like an angry, spitting feline.

'What do you want to prove, Nicos? Superior male strength?' Her eyes speared his, darkly luminous, and totally without fear. 'Sensual expertise?'

Something moved in his eyes, and she banked down the sudden apprehension that clenched in her stomach.

He didn't say a word. The silence stretched between them, like a taut wire on the verge of breaking. She could see the tension, *feel* it, as if it was a throbbing, palpable entity.

Then he moved, tumbling her down on top of him, anchoring her there with an arm whose hand splayed over her buttocks, while the other fisted in her hair as he dragged her head down to his.

He ravaged her mouth, conquering it in a manner that left her stunned and unable to breathe. It was a total ravishment that gave no quarter as he used the edge of his teeth, his tongue, and plundered at will.

She heard someone whimper, and was unaware the sounds came from her own throat.

It was possession. Absolute, total *possession*. Savage in its intensity, devouring, devastating. Almost barbaric.

A man teetering on the edge of controlling his emotions, bent on imprinting his image on her soul.

Something stirred deep within, an answering, compelling need that rose of its own accord, dispensing her shocked passivity and replacing it with active response.

Katrina was hardly aware of the change, only that she was meeting and matching his passion, greedily intent on giving what he'd taken, and with equal fervour.

Hard and fast, with no preliminaries. She wanted, needed the force of it, the intense, animalistic coupling with no holds barred.

She used her hands to push against his shoulders, her voice little more than a guttural plea as she arched against him, rising to cushion the moist folds of her femininity against the base of his arousal.

With a deliberate intention to tease, she rocked against him, gently at first, then slowly traversed the length of his shaft and back again, creating a tactile slide that brought a deep, husky groan.

Heat pulsated fast, heady, magnetising, as it washed in vibrating waves through her body, and she rose up, tantalising him further for several heart-stopping seconds before she took him deep inside in an achingly slow movement that tested his control as much as it did her own.

Unleashed passion flared, raw and libidinous, as they took a ride that lasted long and left them both breathless and slick with sensual sweat.

Katrina subsided against him, and sighed as his fingers traced a lazy pattern along the edge of her spine.

This...*this*, was everything and more. A special time before problems and doubt could intrude.

The lingering aftermath of erotic, riveting love-making, where every sensual pleasure-pulse had become acutely heightened in sexual intimacy.

What they'd just shared was more than just sex. More than the slaking of mutual desire.

At this precise moment Katrina was loath to put a name to it.

Nicos nuzzled a sensitive ear lobe, then took the soft flesh between his teeth and bit gently before moving to caress the curving slope of her neck, following it inch by inch to settle in the hollow at the base of her throat.

A faint moan escaped her lips as his mouth found hers, initiating a gentle exploration with a slow, evocative sweep of his tongue that stirred the lingering warmth to renewed life.

With a fluid movement he rose into a sitting position and held her loosely in his arms as he trailed a path down to her breast.

The darkened peak invited his touch, and he circled the aureole with his tongue, savouring it, before taking the peak into his mouth.

Katrina felt her body give an involuntary shudder as he began to suckle, and she cried out as he grazed the tender nipple with his teeth. Seconds later he sought the soft flesh beneath the peak, bestowing a gentle bite before moving to render a similar salutation to its twin.

She had a need of her own, and her fingers sought the dark whorls of hair on his chest, tugging a little as she trailed his midriff and followed the narrowed line of hair to his navel, caressing it before tracing a path to tangle in the soft curling triangle of hair at his groin.

His reaction was immediate as he swelled deep within her, and she touched where they joined, feather-light, tantalising, and heard his groan as he lowered her down onto the mattress.

This time he took it slowly. Building the intensity with loving care as he sought the highly sensitised nub and stroked until the pleasure mounted and her soft, throaty murmurs begged him to ease the ache deep within.

Then she did cry out as he shifted, leaving her bereft, only to settle his mouth over her navel and trail slowly down to gift her the most intimate kiss of all.

Could you die and go to heaven, and still be mortal? she thought. At what point did pain become pleasure? And vice versa?

Katrina didn't know. She was aware that it could be both. A pleasure so intense it hovered close to pain and the need for fulfilment. The sense that she could never know its equal, the acuteness so erotically evocative she wanted it go on and never stop.

Was it *she* who cried out? She, who begged, *pleaded* with the man whose skilled touch came close to destroying her?

When he entered her, it was almost a relief, and she welcomed him, willing the intensity to lessen, only to have it rebuild and escalate as he took her to the heights, and beyond.

This time she wasn't alone, and she heard his exultant groan as he reached his own climax, and she savoured the moment, loving his passion and the joy of sharing it.

Afterwards she might analyse and dissect, but for now she was content to live for the moment.

And that was Nicos. Held in his arms, her cheek buried against the curve of his shoulder, she heard the strong, steady beat of his heart, felt the strength of his large muscled body, and savoured the comforting warmth of his breath as it stirred her hair. A stray hand skimmed lightly over her waist and settled possessively on her hip.

She loved his scent, the faint muskiness of his skin. The flex of muscle and sinew beneath the satin smoothness of its olive texture. The subtle tang of his exclusive cologne that always seemed to linger, the result of layering the same expensive brand with matching soap and deodorant.

There was something in the way he cupped his hand…beneath her elbow, her chin, curving over her shoulder. A light possessive touch that claimed her as his own.

And the simmering passion evident in his dark eyes. The look that made mere words fade into inadequate comprehension.

Once, in the beginning, she had only to meet his gaze to *know*. To nurture that need, to be aware when they were alone the night really began…a long night of loving, pleasuring each other until sleep claimed them and they woke to a new day's dawn.

Could it ever be that way again?

Complete and utter trust. Total fidelity. Because together, they were twin halves of a whole. Two hearts beating together. One soul, one love.

At the time, she'd thought nothing could come between them. *No one* could ever tear what they had asunder.

Yet someone had, and the spectre that was Georgia remained.

CHAPTER NINE

'RISE and shine.'

Katrina heard the words, lifted her head and groaned, then rolled onto her stomach and buried her head beneath the pillow.

'It's the middle of the night,' she protested in a muffled voice.

'Nine o'clock,' Nicos informed her with amusement. 'You get to have breakfast in bed, then we're driving into the Blue Mountains for a picnic.'

She wasn't sure which surprised her the most...breakfast in bed, or— 'A picnic?' she queried as she removed the pillow and turned to look at him. 'Are you mad?' It might be spring, but it was still cool. And several degrees cooler in the mountains comprising the Great Dividing Range.

The mattress depressed as he sank into it, and the aroma of freshly brewed coffee, toast, and...was that bacon?

Orange juice, too. She levered her body into a sitting position and bunched a pillow behind her back.

'This is decadent,' Katrina began as she plucked a glass of juice from the tray and took half the contents in one long swallow. She cast him a suspicious glance. 'What do you want?'

He swung long legs onto the bed, copied her action

with the pillow, then began to do justice to a plate of eggs, bacon and toast. 'I couldn't prepare breakfast and serve it in bed out of the goodness of my heart?'

He had already showered and dressed, and she silently cursed him for appearing so refreshed and vital at this hour of the morning, while she felt like something the cat had dragged in. Hair a riotous tumble, naked, and needing, she admitted silently, at least another hour's sleep.

'No,' Katrina declared with stunning succinctness.

'You malign me. I remember a few occasions when I brought you breakfast in bed.'

'Yes,' she agreed. 'Except you were contriving to keep me in bed, not persuade me to get out of it.'

'I thought we could get away for the day, take in the scenery, pick up some lunch, and have a break.'

She finished the juice, and forked some bacon into her mouth. Was it possible to maintain light-hearted camaraderie? To cast aside lingering animosity and—uppermost—attempt to dismiss Georgia for a day?

'No phones, no interruptions, no pressures,' he continued.

'We each have a cellphone,' she reminded him cynically.

'So, we have any calls go to message-bank.'

'It'll be cold in the mountains.'

'I could be persuaded to change my mind if you prefer to stay in bed.'

'A picnic sounds great,' she capitulated with alacrity, and heard his amused chuckle.

What was the alternative? A repeat of last Sunday?

Or did she contact a friend and organise time spent exploring The Rocks with its many craft shops and food stalls? Maybe arrange time on the court at a private tennis club? Or did she bury herself in work on the laptop?

There were many choices, none of which held much appeal.

Besides, an entire day spent in Nicos's company could help put their enforced relationship in perspective.

What perspective? Katrina mentally derided as she showered, then dressed in jeans and a rib-knit top.

It was nine days since she'd moved back into his home, and already she was sharing the same room, the same bed. Despite her voiced avowal to the contrary.

So what did that say about her? That she was weak-willed and malleable? Or merely enjoying the fringe benefits of their relationship?

Neither was true, she dismissed, as she pulled on socks and slid her feet into trainers.

There was a part of her that wanted to block out the turmoil Georgia's reappearance had caused. The woman's timing was masterful. Contrived to destroy any chance of what she perceived could lead to a genuine reconciliation?

Was that Georgia's aim?

Dear heaven. Was the woman desperate enough to resort to deliberate subterfuge?

Katrina didn't like the way various scenarios were swirling through her brain, and she resolutely put them on hold as she slung a sweater over her shoulders and knotted the sleeves together in front.

She intended to seize the day, and enjoy it as best she could…without introspection or censure.

Nicos took the Great Western Highway to Katoomba, passing through various small towns which often seemed to merge. There they picked up filled rolls, fruit, bottled water, and drove on through precipitous valleys, taking a turn-off leading to a picturesque waterfall where they stopped to have lunch.

Nicos took a rug from the car and spread it on the grassy verge. They sank down comfortably, and began eating in companionable silence.

It was cool, much cooler than Sydney, the peace and tranquillity a direct contrast to city living. It was possible to almost *hear* the silence beyond the soft rush of water spilling down the rock face.

The isolation was complete, and it wasn't difficult to imagine another time when life was reduced to carving out an existence, rising with the dawn to take from the day as much as humanly possible.

The evolution of man had advanced into the twenty-first century, but the beauty of nature abounded, often stark, frequently simple…a pertinent reminder of a primitive power.

Katrina finished her ham and salad roll, and bit into an apple.

'Thanks,' she said quietly.

'For bringing you here?'

'Yes.' She could feel the tension of the past few weeks begin to ease, and a sense of peace invade her being. The city seemed far distant, as did the stress of everyday living, Enrique's demands...*Georgia*. Even her aggression with Nicos temporarily ceased to exist.

He capped his bottled water, and stretched out. His jeans were a soft denim that moulded his legs and clung lovingly to his hips. A thick sweater covered his polo shirt, accentuating his breadth of shoulder, the depth of his chest.

Katrina finished her apple, then rose to her feet, only to have Nicos capture her hand.

'There's no rush.' He tugged her down beside him. 'Rest for a while.'

She *was* tired, and perhaps if she closed her eyes for half an hour...

'Time to leave. It's going to rain very soon.'

She opened her eyes, saw the overcast sky, registered the rug draped over her incumbent form, and stood to her feet. 'What time is it?'

Much later than she thought. She'd slept for more than an hour.

A light, misty rain could be seen shrouding the ranges, and soon after Nicos set the car in motion rain began splattering the windscreen. The green foliage took on a dark blueish-green tinge, and once they'd traversed the mountain and reached the valley below the mist cleared and there was sunshine.

For some reason Katrina felt reluctant to have the day end and return home.

'How do you feel about strolling round The Rocks and eating pizza alfresco?' he asked.

She turned towards him as they entered the city fringes. 'Done,' she agreed with an impish smile.

It became a pleasurable few hours as they examined the many craft and novelty shops, the restaurants and outdoor cafés abounding at the popular Rocks area, topped by the best pizza she'd ever tasted washed down with a glass of wine and followed by strong, sweet black coffee.

There was a sense of anticipation, an expectancy of how the evening would end as Nicos garaged the car, and Katrina entered the house at his side, then ascended the stairs to their room.

By tacit agreement they showered together, taking their time then, both towelled dry, Nicos led her to the bed, tumbling her down onto it with him. A husky chuckle emerged from his throat as she rolled on top of him.

Tonight was his, to pleasure and gift him the ultimate in sensual arousal. His skin tasted of soap and male muskiness as she trailed her lips from the edge of his mouth down the column of his neck, laving each nipple before travelling low…to tantalise the most vulnerable part of his anatomy with her lips, tracing his shaft with the tip of her tongue, and rendering a trail of soft kisses from groin to its acutely sensitive tip.

Nicos's groan urged her on to take an even greater liberty, and she embarked on a sensual tasting that drove him almost to the edge of control.

Then it was she who cried out as he returned the favour, lingering until she went wild and begged his possession.

Long afterwards they lay together, limbs tangled, her head pillowed against the curve of his shoulder as he buried his lips in her hair.

It was late morning before Katrina checked her voicemail for messages: Siobhan, suggesting lunch one day through the week; Enrique, demanding she return his call urgently, followed by a second call with a similar request; Harry, who waxed eloquently about soft furnishings and request he discuss them with her over lunch the next day; and messages from two friends suggesting lunch.

She returned each of them, then got on with the day. Allocating, delegating, deferring, with an efficiency that had earned Kevin's respect. Estimates had been faxed through regarding her plans for the Melbourne site, and she tended to those, checking details and figures with close scrutiny.

For once she managed to leave the office at five, although there appeared little advantage as she sat stationary in stalled traffic, a delay which meant she didn't reach Point Piper until almost six.

Consequently there wasn't time for the leisurely shower she'd planned, and choosing something to wear to dinner and the ballet didn't permit much deliberation.

A bias-cut gown in three layered lengths of red, cyclamen and pink...colours which should have been at variance with her auburn hair, but contrarily complimented it.

Make-up complete, she caught up an evening purse and emerged to find Nicos waiting for her, looking his attractive best in a dark evening suit, white shirt and black bow tie.

The mere sight of him sent a jolt of sensual electricity through her body, and his slow smile made her ache for his touch.

Dinner was a hurried meal eaten at a Double Bay restaurant, and they waived a starter, settled on a main course, and declined dessert in order to reach the theatre before the first act began.

Swan Lake was a graceful, classical style, the music hauntingly beautiful as the dancers completed their practised moves to a level of breathtaking perfection.

One act followed another, each performed with superb artistry, and Katrina experienced a sense of disappointment when the curtain came down at the close of the final act.

Clearing the theatre and reaching their car took a while, and afterwards Nicos drove to Double Bay where they lingered over lattes and watched the social set at play.

Katrina mused that she and Nicos had sat at this particular sidewalk café during their brief courtship, and after their marriage.

It had been a favoured way to end an evening out. Almost as if they were deliberately lengthening the anticipation of what was to come. All it used to take was a look, Nicos would settle the bill, and together they'd stroll hand-in-hand to the car. Lovemaking had been a delight, for their shared intimacy had been borne out of *love*, rarely lust…although she'd exulted in the occasions Nicos had barely held onto control.

'Pleasant thoughts?'

Nicos's voice intruded, and she cast him a solemn glance. 'Varied,' she responded succinctly, and watched the edges of his mouth curve into a warm smile.

'Shall we leave?'

It was close to midnight when they arrived home, and Katrina made little protest as Nicos undressed her, then took her into his arms.

Their lovemaking was slow, almost gentle, and afterwards she curled in against him and slept until morning.

Nicos had already left when Katrina woke, and she showered, dressed, then ate a light breakfast before driving into the city office of Macbride.

She booted up the computer and got to work, frowning with vexation as the phone provided a constant interruption to the data she was intent on checking.

Consequently when it rang again she automatically reached for the receiver and intoned her usual businesslike greeting.

'We should do lunch.'

Katrina heard the words, recognised her stepbrother's voice, and cut straight to the chase. 'There would be no point in it,' she refuted evenly. 'Besides,

I have an appointment to lunch with a colleague.' A slight stretch of the truth, and one Harry would adore.

'I have some interesting information regarding Nicos,' Enrique revealed.

'Which you'll divulge for a price?'

'You know me well.'

Too well. 'If I wanted an account of Nicos's movements, I'd hire a private detective.'

'Why hire a professional when you have me, darling,' he responded smoothly.

'Goodbye, Enrique,' she concluded with resignation.

'Nicos is in Brisbane with Georgia.'

Did a heart stop beating, then race into overdrive? She was willing to swear hers did. Nicos had said nothing at breakfast about flying interstate. Nor had he intimated he'd be late home for dinner.

'Ring his office, if you don't believe me.'

'I don't have time for this.'

'But you're curious.'

Curious was too tame for what she was feeling right now. *Angry* came close.

'You have my cellphone number,' Enrique taunted.

She ended the call, and endeavoured to focus her attention on a compilation of figures on the computer screen.

It didn't work. Her concentration was shot, and after making a third mistake she pressed the save key and dialled Nicos's private line, only to hear a recorded message refer the caller to his cellphone.

Which could, Katrina rationalised, simply mean

that he was in an important meeting or out of the office.

With an effort she returned her attention to the work at hand, only to redial the number half an hour later and receive the same response.

Dammit, this was ridiculous. *Phone him*, then get on with the day!

Nicos answered on the second ring, and his caller ID negated the need for verbal identification.

'Katrina. Something wrong?'

Considering she never rang him, it was a reasonable assumption.

'Enrique is negotiating information,' she said without preamble.

'And you opted to go straight to the source.'

His voice was a cynical drawl that sent a shivery sensation slithering the length of her spine.

'Yes.'

'I took the late morning flight to Brisbane with my lawyer to personally expedite certain legal matters.'

Her stomach tightened painfully. 'With Georgia.' She didn't even voice it as a query.

'Yes.'

Had she expected him to lie to her? 'Thank you for the clarification,' she said with icy politeness, and cut the connection.

Seconds later the phone rang, and she refused to answer.

With cold-hearted determination she finished the day's work, cleared her desk, caught up her laptop, and left the office ahead of her usual time, amazed that she felt so calm.

Katrina took her car up to street level, then headed towards Double Bay and checked into the Ritz-Carlton hotel.

One night alone wouldn't contravene the terms of Kevin's will, she concluded as she glanced around the luxuriously fitted suite. There was everything at her fingertips. She could work from her laptop, order in a meal, and screen any incoming calls on her cell-phone.

There was a certain pleasure in calculating the time it would take Nicos to arrive home and discover her absence. How long before he made the first call? Seven o'clock?

Fifteen minutes past, Katrina saw with a degree of satisfaction. She'd changed out of her clothes, phoned her mother, taken a shower, donned the hotel's courtesy bathrobe, and had eaten a light meal delivered by room service.

She ignored the insistent peal before the call switched to message-bank. His voice when she played it back was curt and controlled.

Half an hour later he called again, and this time there was a degree of anger evident.

By now he would have rung her apartment, and probably Siobhan, who on strict instructions from her daughter, would deny any knowledge of Katrina's whereabouts.

At what point would he give up?

Not easily, she determined, as she checked the digital screen on her cellphone before taking a call from her mother.

'Darling,' Siobhan chided gently. 'This is most unwise of you.'

'A temporary lack in wisdom isn't that big a deal,' Katrina assured her, and heard her mother's sigh.

'Nicos doesn't know where you are, and you're not answering your phone.' There was a brief pause. 'At least let him know you're safe.'

Siobhan had a point. 'If he rings again,' she agreed in capitulation.

'He isn't a man with whom any sensible woman plays games,' her mother warned.

'I'm not feeling particularly *sensible* right now.'

'Take care, Katrina.'

As an exit line it held connotations she didn't want to examine, and for the first time in several hours she felt the first prickle of unease.

Something that seemed to magnify when her cellphone pealed fifteen minutes later.

Nicos.

She activated the call, and forced her voice to remain cool, steady, as she relayed, 'I'm fine. I'll be home tomorrow night.' And cut the connection.

When it rang again, she didn't answer.

She attempted work on her laptop, then gave it up after a frustrating half hour, opting instead to check the television programs.

Choosing an in-house movie, she adjusted the pillows and slid into bed.

The stark realism of the action theme suited her

mood, and superb acting added another dimension, capturing her attention almost to the exclusion of all else.

The sudden double knock on the door startled her, and she banked down a momentary stab of fear.

Then common sense overrode apprehension. This was a first-class hotel with tight security.

The assurance didn't do much for her composure, and she crossed to the door, checked the safety latch was in place, and demanded identification.

'Room service, ma'am.'

Katrina opened the door a crack to see a uniformed waiter bearing a tray. 'I didn't order anything.'

'As you didn't use the dining room this evening, ma'am, complimentary evening tea is provided.'

She welcomed the service. 'Just a moment.' It only took seconds to release the latch, then pull open the door.

Big mistake. Nicos materialised behind the waiter, looming like a dark angel bent on castigation.

It was too late to slam the door. One glance at Nicos's expression was enough to realise he wouldn't allow something as simple as a locked door stand in his way. He'd bribed the hotel staff to organise a waiter to deliver tea. To have a porter, or even the hotel manager, request entry for one valid reason or another wouldn't present much of a problem.

The waiter, undoubtedly *au fait* with almost *any* situation, didn't so much as blink as he entered the suite and placed the tray on a table before retreating with decorous speed.

Katrina waited until the door closed behind him before turning towards Nicos.

'What in *hell* do you think you're doing here?'

Her face was scrubbed free of make-up, her hair a mass of curls tumbling to her shoulders, and her eyes were sparking green fury.

The complimentary towelling robe was too big, too long, and looked incongruous on her slender, petite frame.

Given another occasion, he might have been amused. Now, he was treading a fine line between anger and rage.

He advanced into the room, and stood regarding her with ruthless appraisal. 'I might ask you the same question.'

His voice was quiet, controlled, and much too dangerous for her peace of mind.

'I wanted a night alone,' Katrina qualified.

'Let's take this home, shall we?'

'I'm not going anywhere.'

Nicos didn't move, but she felt his presence had suddenly become an ominous threat.

'We can do this in a civilised manner. Or I can carry you kicking and screaming down to the car.'

Her hands closed into fists. 'You wouldn't dare.'

'Try me.'

'I'll call hotel security.'

He indicated the phone resting on the bedside pedestal. 'Go ahead.'

'Nicos—'

'Five minutes, Katrina. Change into your clothes or remain as you are. The choice is yours.'

'No.'

'It's not open to negotiation.'

She swore, and saw one eyebrow lift as speculative amusement temporarily overrode anger.

'Four and a half minutes…and counting,' he relayed coolly.

He could count as much as he wanted, but she had no intention of moving an inch.

They faced each other, like two opposing warriors bent on conquest. Who would win was a foregone conclusion. He had the height and the strength to overcome her with minimum effort.

Which he did, when the time was up. Gathering up her laptop and bag, he collected her business suit, shoes, and flimsy underwear in one hand, then he hauled her over one shoulder as if she weighed little more than a child.

It didn't prevent her from balling her fists against his back, nor attempting to kick any part of his anatomy where she could connect.

'You *fiend*! Put me down!'

He turned towards the door, and she hit him again for good measure. 'If you *dare* to walk out of here like this, I'll kill you,' Katrina vented furiously.

'You had your chance to leave with dignity.'

Dear heaven. *'Nicos—'*

Except it was too late.

Please God, don't let anyone be in the corridor, or the lift.

The corridor was empty, but the lift was not.

'Oh, my,' a feminine voice said quietly, while the man at her side spared a faint chuckle.

'He's a wolf in sheep's clothing,' Katrina accused vehemently, landing a hard fist against Nicos's ribs for good measure.

Was there no end to her humiliation?

'Some wolf. Some fantasy.'

Did she detect *envy* in the woman's tone?

The lift slid to a gentle halt, and Katrina was carried unceremoniously to where Nicos had parked the Mercedes.

'I have my own car.'

'You imagine I'll let you drive it?' He released the alarm and opened the passenger door. 'I'll arrange to have it picked up in the morning.'

'I'll need it to go to work.'

He tossed her clothes onto the back seat along with her bag, then placed the laptop on the floor before sliding her down onto the cushioned leather.

'So, I'll drive you.' He released the seat belt and leaned over her to clip it in place. Then he closed the door and crossed round to slip in behind the wheel.

'You're the most arrogant, *impossible* man I've ever met!'

He fired the engine, then speared her a dark glance. 'Save the name-calling until we get home and I can deal with it.'

Katrina retreated into silence, and didn't offer a word when Nicos drew the car to a halt in the garage.

With considerable dignity she exited the front seat,

collected her gear, and strode into the house ahead of him.

Savoir-faire was difficult, given the towelling bathrobe's hem trailed the floor, the folded-back sleeves had long become unfolded and hung down past her fingertips, and the cross-over front edges were in danger of parting. As to the waist tie…forget it!

She discarded the laptop on one of the wall tables in the lobby, aware Nicos was right behind her.

'Let's take it in the lounge, shall we?'

Katrina halted mid-step, and turned to face him. 'What's wrong with right here?' She dropped her bag, placed her clothes down beside it, then tugged the edges of the robe into place, and fastened the tie belt.

She resembled a belligerent child playing dressing up, he mused, fighting a need to verbally flay her for giving him a few of the worst hours in his life.

'Suppose you explain why you hung up on me, refused to take my calls, didn't bother leaving a message, weren't home, and left me to conduct a wild-goose chase in order to track you down?'

A hand lifted and she began counting off each query in turn with an angry indignance that grew by the second.

'It should be self-explanatory! You declined to tell me you were flying to Brisbane, presumably with the express purpose of seeing Georgia *and* your son.' Her eyes glittered with fury. 'I had to be informed of it by Enrique…a fact you confirmed. How do you think I felt?'

'So you decided to run away.'

'I did not *run away!*'

'What else would you call booking into a hotel and leaving me no word of where you were?'

'Dammit, I was so angry, I wanted to *hit* you!' she cried, wanting to rail her fists against him. For hurting her afresh.

'If you'd taken one of my calls—'

'You could have explained?'

'Yes.'

Her chin tilted. 'Told me what you thought I wanted to hear?'

'The truth.'

'Which is?'

'Months of legal dialogue are about to reach a conclusion.' His eyes darkened measurably. 'Georgia won a reprieve during her pregnancy against DNA testing to prove paternity. With the birth, that reprieve has been negated.' Frustration became evident, and he banked it down. 'There was a delay in the results being given to my legal representative. Today's meeting between both lawyers was an effort to expedite the release of that information.' He waited a beat. 'I went along in the hope of adding some weight to legal argument.'

'And were you successful?'

'It may take a few more days.'

'At the time you asked me to believe Georgia was a psychotic whose jealousy got so out of hand she became pregnant by someone else and named you as the father in a deliberate attempt to break up our marriage,' Katrina relayed, vividly recalling the photos, dates, that Georgia had presented as proof of her affair with Nicos. 'I didn't buy that story at the time...' she took a deep breath and let it out slowly '...any more than I buy it now.'

'Your trust in me is heart-warming.'

All the anger and pain rose to the surface. 'Damn you, Nicos. She was your mistress for more than a year!'

'A relationship that was over long before I met you.' He paused, his gaze lancing hers. 'If, as she claims, she was the love of my life...why did I marry *you*?'

'My prospective inheritance?'

His eyes darkened with glittering rage, and for one brief second she thought he might strike her. A muscle tensed at the edge of his jaw as he sought control.

'Get out of my sight before I do something regrettable,' Nicos demanded in a tight bitter voice that caused her stomach to knot with apprehension.

For a heart-stopping second she hesitated, and he ground out, 'Go. Or, by the living God, you'll wish you'd never been born.'

Katrina remained where she was. It was a matter of strength. *Hers*. Mentally, emotionally. And she refused to slink away from him in fear.

'*Fool*,' he said with chilling softness.

In one swift movement he lifted her over one shoulder and strode upstairs. Restrained violence emanated from his taut frame, and his hands were hard on her soft flesh as he released her unceremoniously down onto the large bed they shared.

He discarded his jacket, tore off his tie, and she watched in mesmerised fascination as his shoes and trousers followed. Then his shirt, and lastly his briefs.

A naked, gloriously aroused male, slim-hipped, superb musculature, he resembled a powerful force as he followed her down onto the bed.

His hands reached for her robe and dragged the edges apart, then he lowered his head and feasted on her breasts in a manner that caused her to whimper as he crossed the line between pleasure and pain.

There were no preliminaries as he took her in one powerful thrust, and she cried out as he plunged deep, then withdrew to plunge even deeper. Repeating the action again and again.

This…this was an annihilation, a primitive, no-holds-barred mating that spared no thought to seduction or pleasure. Only the need to slake a raw, barbarous hunger.

He roused in her a matching anger, and she reared up and sank her teeth into the muscle surrounding one male nipple…and heard his husky growl: his revenge was merciless, and she was repaying it in kind.

It was her only victory as he straddled her and pushed her arms above her head. Helpless, powerless, she tossed her head from side to side as he held her captive and branded her his own.

With each grazing bite, her muscles tightened around him, the spasms increasing in intensity until they merged as one.

It was more than she could bear, and she began to plead, then beg, willing him to stop. He did, emptying himself into her in a shuddering climax, then in one fluid movement he rolled onto his back, taking her with him.

She wanted to disengage and scramble to the outer edge of the bed, except he pulled her down against him and held her close.

His breathing was equally rapid as her own, and she lay still, her eyes closed against the sight of him, her mind blanking out the ravaged, almost savage, sex.

Nicos held her throughout the night, and when she thought he slept she slowly shifted her body, only to have him anchor her in close against him.

CHAPTER TEN

KATRINA woke to find she was alone, and for a moment she lay still as images of the previous night emerged, haunting her with their pagan intensity.

Nicos's hunger had been wild, unprincipled…without consequence or thought except to assuage a primeval need.

His controlled anger was infinitely more formidable than if he'd raised his voice or had resorted to smashing an inanimate object. Of which there were a few exquisite antique pieces positioned on beautiful rosewood chests flanking the lobby.

She shifted position, tentatively stretching her body…and felt the slight pull of ill-used muscles. There was an ache deep within, a remnant of his possession, and she was conscious of the sensation with each move she made.

What time was it? She rolled onto her side to check the digital clock, then sat upright in shocked surprise. *Eight?*

That left her thirty minutes in which to shower, dress, and fight traffic in order to arrive at the office on time.

She made it downstairs, caught up her laptop, her bag, and turned towards the front door…only to come to a faltering stop as Nicos emerged into the lobby.

For a moment she stood completely still, her gaze trapped in his as he closed the distance between them.

When he almost reached her, her defence mechanism kicked into place and she found her voice.

'I'm already late.'

'In which case, a few more minutes won't make any difference,' he ventured silkily.

She wanted out of here, with space between them and time caught up with the mundane routine of business to occupy her mind. 'I have to leave.'

'No,' Nicos countered quietly. 'You don't.' He lifted a hand and caught hold of her chin, tilting it to examine her features.

He doubted she'd slept any better than he had. How many times had he soothed her restless form through the night, while battling his own demons?

It mattered little that she'd provided provocation. His reaction to it was inexcusable.

'What do you want?'

Now there was a question to which he could find no single answer. Uppermost was the most important one by far. He stroked the tip of his thumb over the full curve of her lower lip. 'Are you all right?'

'Do you care?' The retaliatory words were out before she could stop them.

'Yes.'

She was powerless to prevent the faint quivering sensation that shook her slim frame. 'I don't have time for a post-mortem.'

Nicos dropped his hand. 'Tonight.'

Katrina stepped back a pace, then skirted his tall

frame. 'Before, during, or after we've attended the art exhibition?' She saw his eyes darken, and was unable to resist querying sweetly, 'You can't have forgotten?'

'No. I've already checked the day's diary.'

She turned as she reached the passageway leading through to the garage. 'I could be late.'

It became the day from hell. Traffic was backed up due to an accident, trebling the usual time it took to reach the city. Consequently it was after nine when she walked into her office.

To discover the computer network was down, and several irate messages from a client company whose head honcho wanted Macbride to supply top quality work for a cleverly worded contract worth peanuts.

There were, Katrina fumed, still men who imagined they could slip anything by a colleague simply because of her gender. She made the call, confounded him with figures and logic, then icily informed him Macbride was not interested in dealing with him, only to have pithy invective heaped on her head.

Just when she thought the day couldn't get any worse, her secretary relayed,

'Georgia Burton is in reception.'

Katrina felt her stomach twist at the announcement. It would be easy to insist Georgia make an appointment, with no advantage except to delay the confrontation.

'Show her in.' Nerves had her smoothing a hand over her hair and repairing her lipstick. She'd just tossed the capped tube into her drawer when a discreet knock at the door preceded Georgia's entrance.

The model looked a million dollars in a pale silk suit, an artfully draped scarf, stiletto heels, and perfectly applied make-up.

Katrina indicated one of three comfortable chairs. 'Please, take a seat.' In a calculated movement she checked her watch. 'I have to attend a scheduled meeting in ten minutes.'

'Darling, five minutes will do.' Georgia crossed to the plate-glass window and took a few valuable seconds to look out over the city before turning towards Katrina.

'Nicos and I have struck a deal.'

Don't let her get to you. 'Indeed?'

'I thought you'd be interested.'

'Why would you think that?'

'Doesn't it bother you that Nicos still continues to see me?'

'Should it?'

'Yes, considering you're an obstacle that prevents him being a father to his son.'

'An obstacle you intend to remove?'

'I'm glad you get the drift.'

'That this is a last-ditch effort on your part?' she queried with deadly softness. 'How long, Georgia, before due legal process forces the release of your son's DNA results?' Her gaze didn't falter as she mentally sharpened her claws. 'A day, hours, before your elaborate scheme falls apart?'

'Nikki is Nicos's son!'

'I'm sure you wish that were true.' Katrina aimed for the kill, and played the biggest gamble of her life. 'But it's not, is it?' Dear Lord, what if she was wrong?

Georgia's eyes narrowed. 'Two days ago Nicos was in Brisbane with me.'

'A meeting which took place in a lawyer's office.'

'Is that what he told you?'

'What if I told you I have a private detective's report tabling Nicos's every move?' She didn't, but Georgia wasn't to know that.

'Then, you have precise details of each liaison.'

Stay calm, Katrina bade silently. She's merely calling your bluff. Or was she? *Don't go there.*

Summoning icy control Katrina stood to her feet and crossed to the door. 'You'll have to excuse me.'

Georgia's features were composed, her voice dripping with pseudo sympathy. 'He may remain married to you, darling, but he'll always be mine.'

She swept out the door with the sort of smile that made Katrina want to smash something.

Déjà vu, she reflected grimly as she crossed back to her desk.

Nine months ago she'd stood in this office shattered beyond belief at the news Georgia was pregnant with Nicos's child.

Had she been wrong? Could Georgia have contrived evidence that, while appearing irrefutable, was in fact erroneous?

Nicos had asserted his innocence from the beginning. *What if he was right?*

There was nothing she could do, but wait for the DNA results to be released.

Lunch wasn't even an option, and by mid-afternoon she was punchy. Make that *very* punchy, she determined after taking a call from her wayward and very persistent stepbrother.

She couldn't even threaten to expose him to Chloe, for his mother was well aware of his habitual need for money and *why*. It was, Chloe had explained languidly, a phase. As far as Katrina was concerned, Enrique had long outgrown this *phase* and was several steps down the path to addiction.

It was five-thirty when she left the office, and she joined the commuter trail of bumper-to-bumper vehicles clogging the city's arterial routes leading to suburbs on all compass points.

Nicos's car was already in the garage when she parked the Boxster close by, and he was there in the lobby when she entered it.

Katrina threw him a fulminating glare as she by-passed him and made for the stairs. 'Don't even ask.' And she missed the way his eyebrow slanted with cynical bemusement as he viewed her ascending.

When she reached the landing she deftly removed one heeled pump, then the other, and by the time she reached the bedroom she'd unbuttoned her jacket, had loosened the camisole she wore beneath it, and was working on the zip fastening of her skirt.

A minute later she walked naked into the *en suite*, cast the spa-bath a covetous glance, longing to sink into the capacious tub and have the numerous jets work magic on her tense muscles...except she couldn't afford the luxury of unlimited time.

The shower beckoned, and she twisted the dial, adjusted the temperature, then stepped beneath the cascading water, collected the rose-scented soap and began lathering her skin.

She felt tired and emotionally wrung out and, dammit, she hurt in places she didn't even want to think about.

A slight sound alerted her attention, and she turned, gasping out loud as Nicos stepped naked into the shower stall with her.

'What in hell do you think you're doing?'

He took the soap from her nerveless fingers. 'I'd think it was obvious.'

'Oh, no, you don't,' Katrina said with a growl as he smoothed the soap over her shoulder. She made to grab it from him, and failed. 'Give me that!'

'Why don't you just relax?'

Relax? She was about as relaxed as a tightly coiled spring. *'Don't.'*

His hands were effecting a soothing massage at the edge of her neck, and she gave a silent groan that was part pleasure, part despair as his fingers eased out the kinks, then shifted down her back, inch by blissful inch, then they began working their way up again.

It felt so good, she forgot her anger, the tension of the day, and she simply closed her eyes and relaxed beneath his touch.

He soaped every inch of her skin, slowly, and she

sighed as his fingers trailed the contours of her breast, then travelled low over her hips.

'We don't have time for this.'

'Yes, we do.'

His fingers slid towards her navel, then slipped down to tease the soft curling hair at the apex of her thighs...and stroked with unerring expertise.

'We shouldn't arrive late.' She groaned as sensation began a slow spiral through her body.

'No,' Nicos murmured in agreement, shifting his hands to bring her close against him.

He lowered his mouth over hers, gently brushing his lips against her own, then he slid his tongue between her teeth and initiated a slow, sensual exploration that heated her blood and sent her pulse thudding to a quickened beat.

She slid her hands to his shoulders and clung as he deepened the kiss to something so incredibly erotic she lost track of time and place. There was just the two of them, and the magic that was theirs alone.

Nicos eased back from the brink of passion, softening his mouth as he trailed his lips over hers, pressing light kisses to each corner, the slightly swollen lower curve, before burying his mouth into the vulnerable hollow at the base of her neck.

How long did they remain like that? Five minutes? Ten? *More?*

Katrina felt wonderfully mellow, and filled with a lazy warmth that crept towards wanting more.

'We should get out of here,' she began to say tentatively, and felt his lips trail up to settle against her temple.

'Uh-huh.'

She leaned forward and closed the water dial while Nicos snagged a towel, handing it to her before catching up another for himself.

The temptation to linger was great. Even greater was the need to stay in and not venture from the bedroom at all.

'Later,' Nicos promised, his eyes dark with slumbering passion as he pressed a finger to her lips.

The art exhibition was held in a city gallery, featuring up-and-coming artists among whom two were gaining coveted acclaim.

Katrina wandered among the strategically placed paintings, and gravitated towards one that had caught her eye.

There was something in the use of colours that reminded her of Monet and the garden theme he so loved to depict on canvas. Beautifully framed, it reminded her of the French countryside with its fresh fields and flowers.

'Like it?'

'Yes, I do.' It would look perfect in her apartment. Or better yet, hanging on a wall in her office.

She moved on, aware Nicos had become caught up in conversation with a fellow business associate.

'Dear Katrina, we do seem to garner invitations to the same events.'

'Enrique.' She acknowledged. 'Why am I not surprised to see you here?'

'I have contacts, connections,' he relayed with a glib smile. 'Schmoozing is the name of the game, and I excel at working a room.'

'Alone?'

'Young, budding artists aren't Chloe's thing. Have you thought about my offer?'

'I don't need to think. The answer, as always, is the same.'

'Katrina,' Enrique chastised, shaking his head. 'I'm willing to trade information to your advantage.'

'No.'

'*No?*' He waited a beat. 'Aren't you in the least curious to hear some interesting facts about Georgia's love-child? Facts Nicos can substantiate?'

A cold hand clenched round her heart. 'That's old news.'

'It made good copy at the time.'

'Is there anything you won't do for money?' she demanded fiercely.

'I have an expensive habit, darling, which needs constant feeding.' His smile reminded her of a shark baring its teeth. 'It matters little whether the newspaper pays me, or you do.'

'Go to hell.'

'I take it that's a *no*?'

'A very definite and permanent refusal to your demands, now or at any time in the future,' Nicos said in a dangerously quiet voice. 'Take heed, Enrique. If you contact Katrina again, I'll have a restraining order served on you before you can blink.'

'You can't threaten me!'

Belligerence tempered with false bravado didn't augur well with a man of Nicos's calibre. 'I've stated facts.' His voice was hard, almost deadly with intent. 'It's your choice whether you comply or not.'

Enrique cast Katrina a look that was filled with animosity. 'You owe me. Kevin owes me.'

'Harassment is a punishable offence,' Nicos reminded him with chilling softness.

Enrique swore. 'I hope you both rot in hell.' He turned and began threading his way through the milling guests.

'Charming.'

Nicos inclined his head. 'Indeed.'

'I think I'll go check out some of the exhibits.'

He fell into step beside her, and they hadn't moved far when a guest signalled his attention. Katrina offered a polite greeting, then left the two men to talk.

'Something to drink, ma'am?'

Katrina smiled at the hovering waiter, and selected a flute of champagne from a proffered tray, then she browsed among the exhibits, returning to the painting she'd admired. It held a discreet sold sticker, and she felt a stab of disappointment, mentally cursing herself for not seeking out the gallery owner and negotiating a price.

'I think,' Nicos drawled as he rejoined her, 'we've provided sufficient patronage. Shall we leave?'

There were a few acquaintances present among the guests, and it took long minutes to observe the social niceties before they were able to escape the gallery.

'Hungry?'

She cast him a solemn glance as he eased the car out of its parking bay. 'Are you offering me food?'

'Did you manage lunch?'

She hadn't managed breakfast either, and had subsisted on fruit, a sandwich her secretary had sent out for, and coffee, tea and juice throughout the day.

Somehow finger food comprising canapés, miniature vol-au-vents and crackers with cheese proffered at the gallery were no substitute for a meal.

'Not as such,' she admitted, observing the short distance the car travelled before sliding to the kerb adjacent to a trendy pavement café in Double Bay.

The menu was a mix of exotic-sounding dishes, and she chose a prawn risotto with bruschetta, followed by black coffee. Nicos ordered the same, and they sipped iced mineral water as they waited for the food to arrive.

Katrina was supremely conscious of him, aware the fine clothes were merely the sophisticated trappings of a man whose heart moved to a primitive beat. It was evident in the way he held himself, his eyes reflecting an innate strength, a power that combined a dramatic mesh of elemental ruthlessness with indomitable will. Add latent sensuality, and it became something lethal, mesmeric.

Rarely had she seen him exert due force, or resort to anger. Except for last night. It had been like unleashing a tiger, and she shivered slightly at the memory.

'Cold?'

She'd worn elegant evening trousers, with a matching camisole and jacket, and the night was mild. 'No.'

A waiter presented their food, and they ate with leisurely ease, then lingered over coffee.

It was after eleven when Nicos garaged the car and they made their way indoors. The events of the past few days were beginning to have their effect, and all she wanted to do was remove her clothes and crawl into bed.

'Let me do that.'

Katrina shot him a startled glance as his fingers took care of the buttons on her jacket. The camisole came next, followed by the trousers, which he slid gently down over her hips, and she stepped out of them, then toed off her stiletto-heeled pumps.

She murmured in protest when his hands reached for her bra clip, and she stilled as he began easing free her bikini briefs.

'Nicos—'

He stilled anything further she might have said by placing a finger over her mouth, and she stood helplessly as he divested his own clothes.

In one fluid movement he placed an arm beneath her knees and carried her into bed with him.

'Now, where were we?'

His fingertips drifted to her waist, explored one hip, then trailed to settle at the apex between her thighs.

A sound that was part groan, half sigh, whispered from her lips, and her mouth parted beneath his own as he took her down a path towards sensual ecstasy.

Last night had been in anger, and there was a need

to make amends for the intensity of his emotions, the loss of control.

Tonight was for her, and he took it slowly, employing such incredible gentleness she was on the verge of tears when he slid into her.

Afterwards, he held her close, his lips buried in her hair as she drifted to sleep.

CHAPTER ELEVEN

NICOS had already left when Katrina entered the kitchen, and she popped bread into the toaster, poured coffee, then she balanced a cup and a plate, tucked the daily newspaper beneath her arm and opted to eat breakfast on the terrace.

The sun's warmth was enticing, the air still…a perfect spring morning. Tiny buds were beginning to emerge along the garden borders. Soon, multicoloured impatiens would burst into new life, and the lattice along the back wall would display a tapestry of multicoloured sweet peas.

Peace and tranquillity, Katrina mused. She bit into her toast, then sipped the hot, sweet black coffee as she skimmed the daily headlines.

Until she reached the gossip column.

Which prominent Sydney businessman, recently reconciled with his heiress wife, has been exonerated of fatherhood by DNA testing? The ploy by an ex-mistress to provide herself with a meal ticket has failed due to the success of medical science.

Nicos? Katrina's stomach twisted into a painful knot. Following Enrique's directive yesterday, the reference held too many coincidences for it not to be.

163

Dear heaven. She felt sickened as the implications began to sink in.

She looked blindly out over the landscape, not seeing the superb view, the terraced pool. Her mind was a kaleidoscope of remembered images.

The nine months between then and now disappeared in a flash. She felt the pain as if it were yesterday.

Georgia informing her she was pregnant with Nicos's child. Nicos's disavowal. Her own disbelief. The arguments. The chilling silences. Followed by Katrina's decision to leave.

In seeming slow motion she caught up her plate and cup, the newspaper, and carried them into the kitchen. With automatic movements she rinsed and stacked the dishwasher, then dressed for work.

She called her office, said she was delayed, and half an hour later she entered the elegant suite of offices Nicos occupied downtown.

Getting past reception took only the necessary time for the girl behind the desk to buzz his secretary, only to have her offer her personal regrets that Nicos was engaged in an important meeting.

'It's a matter of urgency.' Her urgency to discover the truth.

'I've been instructed not to disturb Mr Kasoulis under any circumstances.'

'I'll take the blame,' Katrina said coolly.

The boss, or the boss's wife? Each were irretrievably linked, and she sensed the secretary's dilemma.

'I'll tell him you're here,' his secretary conceded

after a few seconds' silence, and crossing to the desk she picked up the phone and made the call. Seconds later she replaced the handset. Her expression was carefully composed as she turned back to her boss's wife. 'I'll show you through to Mr Kasoulis's office. He'll join you in a few minutes.'

It was a large corner office, with magnificent views of Port Jackson harbour. Antique furniture, leather buttoned chairs, genuine oil paintings on the walls.

Katrina crossed to the tinted, floor-to-ceiling plate-glass window, and stood watching a passenger ferry as it headed towards the Manly terminal. A huge tanker lay anchored in the entrance, awaiting a tug-boat to guide it into a designated berth. A peaceful scene that was totally at variance with the turmoil seething beneath the surface of her control.

The almost silent click of the door closing caused her to turn, and she wore Nicos's raking appraisal as he closed the distance between them.

'What is it?'

Katrina felt the knot in her stomach tighten as he reached her side. Oh, hell, just cut to the chase. She slid the newspaper clipping from her jacket pocket, and handed it to him. 'Read this.'

He was good, she conceded. There was no change in his physical expression as he scanned the news-print. Then he crunched it into a ball and tossed it in the direction of a waste-paper basket. 'For that, you pulled me out of a meeting?'

'I consider it important.'

Nicos cast her a long, level look that was impossible to read. 'Of such urgency it couldn't wait until this evening?'

'No.'

'You want me to confirm it?'

'Yes,' she stated simply.

'Let me guess,' Nicos began with marked indolence. 'Georgia confided in Enrique, who then sold the information to a newspaper contact?'

'*Yes*,' Katrina reiterated. Her eyes flashed with long withheld anger. 'Dammit, you could have told me yourself instead of leaving me to discover facts from a newspaper!'

'*When* would you have had me confide my intention to have Georgia provide tissue samples for DNA testing, Katrina?' His voice was pure silk. 'Should I have introduced it as idle conversation during the few social functions where we accidentally happened to attend at the same time? As Kevin lay dying in hospital? At his funeral?'

Katrina's gaze sharpened. 'You *knew* Kevin had redrawn his will, incorporating the condition stipulating my control of Macbride.' The anger began to build, gaining momentum. 'So you waited. Both of you making the decision to take advantage of a bad situation.'

'Yes.'

Her eyes sparked green fire. 'You didn't have that right!'

'The least I could do for him, and you, was to allow him your total focus, unclouded by other issues which could be resolved—'

'At a later date.' A cold hand closed around her heart. 'And if Kevin's health hadn't been in jeopardy?'

His gaze was hard, inflexible, almost dangerous. 'You doubt I would have told you?'

She couldn't be sure. She wanted to be. Desperately, with all her heart.

Nicos read the momentary indecision, the aching intensity of her emotions. Yet still he waited.

'Do you know what I went through when Georgia confronted me with her pregnancy and named you as the father of her unborn child?' she demanded.

'At the time, I distinctly recall stating my relationship with Georgia was over long before I met you.'

She'd chosen not to believe him. 'You have to admit the evidence seemed weighted against you.' Dear heaven, the barbs, the innuendo had been very cleverly orchestrated. 'Georgia provided dates, places, that coincided with your absence.'

'Even given there was any truth in it, do you think I would have been sufficiently foolish not to take precautions against a possible pregnancy?' he continued relentlessly.

'Prophylactic protection has been known to break.'

Nicos wanted to wring her slender neck. 'I gave you my word. It should have been enough.'

Kevin had believed in him. Why hadn't she?

Because Georgia had pressed all the right buttons, she perceived silently. Shock, disbelief, anger had done the rest.

Anger flared. 'What did you expect, Nicos? That

I'd turn a blind eye? Dammit, my heart felt as if it had been ripped from my body!'

'Did you spare a thought for my reaction?' His voice dropped to a dangerous softness. 'Have you tried beating your head against a brick wall, yet make no impression?'

She was temporarily bereft of speech.

'Do you know how long it took for me to get proof of my innocence? How many legal battles I fought to have Georgia submit to DNA testing during her pregnancy? And failed?' His features assumed an angry mask. 'How the legal system forced me to wait until the child was born, *and* go through the process of a court order to have DNA tissue testing carried out on the child?'

'Just *how long* have you known the result of the DNA test?' she demanded.

'Since late yesterday afternoon.'

He thrust his fists into his trouser pockets in an attempt at control. 'Georgia's intention was to latch onto me for child support, and acquire a meal ticket for life. She didn't care who got in the way. Or who she hurt.' His eyes were hard, his expression inflexible. 'It seems the father of the child is a charming playboy living far beyond his means. They set up the scenario together.'

Her expressive features conveyed more than mere words, unaware he read every emotion.

'You doubt I would leave any stone unturned?' he queried hardily.

Katrina stood silent for several seemingly long seconds.

'I have copies of court documents, reports from private detectives, and now the DNA result,' Nicos explained.

Nine months of anguish, broken dreams, lonely nights. They had each experienced their own individual hell, caused by a woman whose wicked inability to let go of an ex-lover had damaged their lives and had almost wrecked their marriage.

To think how close Georgia came to achieving her goal… It made Katrina shudder to even contemplate it.

'I owe you an apology.' Her voice was stiff, the words almost disjointed.

His gaze held hers. 'Are you offering one?'

A whole gamut of emotions crowded for release. 'Yes, dammit!' Oh, hell, she wouldn't cry. That would be the final humiliation. Her chin tilted as she fought for control. 'You're right. Here, now, isn't the time or place for this.'

She turned away from him and took two steps towards the door, only to have a hand close over her arm as he pulled her back towards him.

'Oh, no,' Nicos said with lethal softness. 'You aren't going to walk away this time.'

Her eyes shimmered with unshed tears. 'What do you want?'

Her voice broke, and it almost undid him.

'You hold me to blame for using the terms of Kevin's will?' he demanded quietly. 'Taking the opportunity to repair what Georgia had torn apart?' He waited a few seconds, then pursued her, saying, 'Proving to you that what we shared was too special to cast aside?' He released her arm and thrust hands into his trouser pockets so as not to catch hold of her shoulders and shake her.

'I needed for you to *see*, to *feel* you're the only woman in my life. Each time we came together, you had to *know* it was an act of love. Not just physical sex to scratch an itch.'

Dear God, she had known. Deep down in a subconscious level, there had been recognition. She should have listened to her instincts, instead of allowing Georgia's vicious innuendo to take root.

'Except once,' Nicos revealed darkly. 'When I hauled you back from the hotel.' He smote a fist into the palm of his hand, and the explosive sound echoed starkly round the room. 'I was so angry at yet another legal delay; then to arrive home and discover you gone... I was so close, yet still not close enough to a resolution. To have you openly defy me attacked the barriers of my control.' He lifted a hand and pushed fingers through his hair. 'I lost it. And shocked you.'

'No, you overwhelmed me,' Katrina corrected. '*You* were always the one in control of your emotions. To have you display such a degree of unleashed passion was exciting. Mind-blowing,' she added. There was nothing left. Not even pride. 'I loved you so much.' It was all she had. Words. Yet they came from the depths of her soul.

Something moved in his eyes, fleetingly, then it was gone. He lifted a hand and brushed his knuckles over her cheek. 'And now?'

'It never changed,' she admitted simply.

'Thank you.' He knew what it cost her to say it.

He touched the tip of his thumb to her lips, felt them quiver, and offered a faint smile. 'Was that so hard?'

'Yes.'

Such honesty, so hard-won. His fingers slid down her throat, caressed the hollow there, then slipped to cup her nape.

Her mouth was soft, tremulous beneath his own, and he savoured it gently, then took her deep, with such passionate intensity there could be no room for doubt.

He felt the breath sigh from her throat, caught it, and pulled her in against him until the softness of her body melded to the hardness of his own.

His hand slid down her back, shaped the firm buttocks, then paused on her thigh, aware of its line, before shifting beneath her skirt.

The heat of her flesh drove him almost to the edge, and he had no other thought but to divest her clothes, his own, and ravish her here, now, uncaring of time or place.

He explored the moistness, sent her up and over, then caressed with an expertise that drove her wild.

It was almost more than she could bear, and her fingers tore at the buttons on his shirt, found the skin she so desperately sought, and moved lower in a feverish craving to touch him as he was stroking her. Until he was past need, beyond hunger.

Dear heaven, it wasn't enough. Not nearly enough.

His mouth left hers, trailed the slim column of her neck, then grazed her throat, nibbling the swollen softness of her lower lip before plundering at will.

Katrina became lost, so caught up with him, she was hardly aware he had dragged his mouth from hers until she registered the insistent buzz of the in-house phone.

'Kasoulis.' His voice was hard, inflexible, and she swayed slightly, then moved back a step.

Only to have him circle her wrist and hold her still.

His eyes never left hers, and she felt her own widen as she took in his dishevelled clothes, the state of her usually immaculate business suit.

'Reschedule, please. Tomorrow afternoon.'

Katrina could imagine his secretary's response.

'I don't give a damn what excuse you offer.'

Nicos listened, then cut in, 'The deal is more important to them than it is to me. They'll concede.' He cut the connection.

Katrina tried for calm, and failed miserably. 'I should go.'

'We are.' He brushed light fingers over her breasts, lingered, then reluctantly tended to the buttons on her blouse.

With deft movements he redid his own buttons, tucked his shirt back into his trousers, and straightened his tie.

His mouth curved into a lazy smile. 'Somewhere with no interruptions.'

'But you have an important meeting—'

'I just cancelled.'

A witching glimmer of humour danced in her eyes. 'So you did.'

He kissed her briefly, a swift, evocative gesture that didn't begin to satisfy.

Katrina watched as Nicos negotiated the traffic, aware of him to a heightened degree. His male scent, the faint tang of his cologne.

He possessed an elemental sexuality that stirred her senses to fever pitch. Primitive, raw, and wholly mesmeric, it had the power to turn her into a willing wanton woman, shameless, libidinous, and totally *his*.

'A hotel?'

'You want to shock Sofia and Andre?'

She shot him a mischievous smile. 'I guess not.'

Katrina slid from the passenger seat as Nicos handed the car over to a porter, and she entered the spacious lobby, admired a magnificent floral arrangement as Nicos checked in, then entered the lift at his side.

Could the other occupants sense the shimmering passion? It was all she could do not to reach out and touch him.

There were words she longed to say, but they could wait. What they wanted, needed, from each other, could not.

Nicos drew her into the suite, fixed the do-not-disturb sign, locked the door, then drew her into his arms.

His mouth closed over hers with a hunger she met and matched, their hands busy as they discarded each layer of clothing, until there was the warmth and intimacy of skin on skin.

Heat and passion, desire and hunger. Wild ravaging need.

Now.

It was a silent language two lovers shared, and a groan escaped her throat as he lifted her high, then slid into her with one powerful thrust, his hands caging her hips.

Katrina flung back her head, exultant in his possession, and she simply held on as he captured her breast, teasing the tender peak until she cried out for mercy. Only to have him ravish its twin.

Her hands slid to his shoulders, then moved up to hold fast his head as she brought it to her own in a kiss that mirrored the sexual act itself.

It was a turbulent coupling, and she gasped as he took her deep, only to withdraw and take her again, long slow movements to maximise her pleasure.

She sensed the moment he was at the brink of losing control, and she joined him as they tipped over the edge, his husky groan mingling with her own in a climax that left them both shuddering their release.

He held her close, nuzzling the sensitive skin at the edge of her neck until the raggedness of their breathing slowed and evened out.

Then he carried her into the bathroom, filled the

spa-bath, and lifted her into the pulsating water before retreating to the bar fridge for champagne.

Katrina sipped the chilled contents of her flute as he stepped in to sit facing her.

'*Salute.*' He touched the rim of her flute with his own, and her lips parted in a winsome smile.

She felt almost in awe of the entire gamut of emotions invading her senses. There was love, its strength and tenure overwhelming. An intense awareness there could be no one else, ever, capable of taking his place in her heart.

It was a knowledge imprinted in her soul. Inviolate.

Nicos lifted a hand and trailed light fingers across her cheek, watched her eyes dilate as he traced the outline of her generous mouth.

Her lips parted, soft and slightly swollen beneath his touch.

'Thank you.'

One eyebrow lifted slightly. 'For what, precisely?'

Her eyes were the darkest green, and incredibly eloquent. '*You*,' she said simply. His tenacity, everything that made him the man he was. To consider, even for a moment, that he might have let her walk away filled her with pain.

'You're mine,' Nicos said gently. 'No other woman comes close to you.'

It hurt unbearably that she had doubted him. Yet the purported facts had been damning, at the time his denial beyond proof. And Georgia had been very convincing. Such incredible lengths Nicos's former mistress had gone to destroy a marriage.

A faint shiver slithered down her spine. That Georgia had almost succeeded—

'Don't go there.'

He read her so well. Too well, she attested silently.

Nicos caught her close and savoured the sweet curve of her shoulder. His hands soothed, brushing lightly over water-slicked skin, pausing to render supplication to vulnerable pleasure pulses before drifting low in an evocative trail that stirred her senses anew.

A soft sigh left her lips as his fingers caressed the sensitised nub, taking her high with a skilled ease that left her breathless.

'Nicos.' His name was both plea and protest.

'Hmm?' His voice was a teasing murmur at her temple.

'If you plan taking this further, I should tell you I skipped lunch.'

His husky laughter was almost her undoing. 'I thought I had your undivided attention.'

Katrina placed her lips against his in a brief teasing kiss. 'You do.' Believe me, you do, she added silently.

He rose to his feet in one fluid movement, lifted her effortlessly onto the tiled floor, then wrapped a towel round her slim form before fixing another at his hips.

'Let's go check out room service.'

It was later, after a leisurely meal and what remained of the champagne, that Katrina caught hold of his hand and pulled him towards her.

'Do you have plans for this evening?'

He gave a faint smile. 'We could go home.'

The word had a nice sound to it. 'Hmm,' she teased, pretending to consider their choices. 'Or we could get dressed.' She fingered his complimentary towelling robe, one of which she also wore. 'And take in a nightclub.'

So she wanted to play. He was willing to join in the game. 'Or a movie.'

Katrina traced a finger down the deep V of his robe. 'It would be a shame to waste the suite.'

He stood still, content to let her have control, for now. 'A shame.'

She teased the dark hairs arrowing down to his waist. 'Do we have any wine?'

'Red, or white?'

Her faint smile held a wicked tinge. 'It doesn't matter.'

'Want me to check?'

Her fingers were busy, and far too close to a vulnerable part of his anatomy.

'Uh-huh.'

Nicos moved a few paces, retrieved a small bottle of wine, popped the cork, part-filled two goblets and handed her one.

Katrina dipped a forefinger into the light-coloured liquid, traced a pattern along the edge of his collar bone, then she leaned forward and slowly followed the same path with her tongue.

With one hand she undid the tie fastening his robe and pushed it off one shoulder, then the other, letting it fall to the floor in a heap.

His eyes were dark, and she saw the pulse leap at his throat as she circled one male nipple.

Minutes later his breath hissed through his teeth, and firm fingers closed over her wrist, stilling the evocative trail. 'Dear God,' he ground out. 'Are you done?'

She tilted her head, and her lips curved into a provocative smile. 'Had enough?'

A muscle clenched at the edge of his jaw. 'Be warned, I intend to reciprocate.'

A light laugh escaped her throat. 'I'm counting on it.'

Later, much later, it was she who groaned out loud. She who pleaded, then begged as he took her on a mercilessly provocative journey that explored the senses until she shattered, fragmenting into a thousand, exquisite pieces.

Katrina lay supine, seriously doubting her ability to move. Even lifting a hand seemed to require too much effort. She was barely aware when Nicos pulled up the bed covers, and drew her in close against him.

She slept, waking to the light brush of Nicos's fingers as he traced a line along the edge of her waist to her hip, then her thigh. His lips teased the soft hollow at the base of her throat, and she moved close to nuzzle his chest.

It was a wonderful way to begin the day. Slow, lazy seduction, and equally slow sex.

Lovemaking, she qualified, glorying in the feel and the taste of him.

Afterwards they hit the shower together, then

dressed, they ordered in breakfast and ate it out on the terrace, watching the city come alive as ferries crossed the harbour and road traffic began to build.

A new day, Katrina mused as she sipped the aromatic coffee. The sky was a clear blue, with hardly a cloud in sight, and the sun lent the promise of warmth.

There was a sense of timelessness, and a need to encapsulate the moment and store it somewhere safe.

Nicos studied her profile, the fine bone structure. She possessed a beauty of soul and spirit, an intrinsic quality that was uncontrived.

He felt his body harden remembering the degree of intimacy they'd shared. Two minds so finely attuned, he knew her thoughts, her innermost secrets.

Katrina's skin prickled, and she turned slightly, met his gaze, and felt her insides begin to melt at what she saw in those dark depths.

'Time to go,' she said gently as she rose to her feet and offered him her hand.

Together they took the lift down to reception and collected the car. Ten minutes later Nicos double-parked outside the towering steel and glass structure which housed the corporate offices of Macbride.

Katrina kissed her fingers and touched them briefly to his lips. 'Until tonight.'

He watched her disappear through the revolving glass doors, then he eased the car into the flow of traffic.

There was a place in the Greek Islands where the sun kissed the translucent waters, vines grew on the gentle slopes, and white-washed villas dotted the hillside. He had an urge to take her there, to relax and enjoy the simple pleasures of life for a while. He'd have his secretary make the arrangements.

Within minutes of reaching his office he picked up the phone, issued specific instructions, and got on with the day.

Across town Katrina viewed the rectangular-shaped package the courier had just delivered, and removed the protective wrapping to reveal the painting she had admired at the art gallery.

She picked up the phone, dialled Nicos's number, and responded as soon as he answered.

'Thank you. It's beautiful.'

'My pleasure.'

His voice was warm, and sent tingles down her spine.

Minutes later there was another delivery, and she opened the slender florist box to discover a single long-stemmed red rose nestling in a swathe of tissue. The card read, '*Katrina, agape mou. Nicos.*'

My love. She lifted the rose to her cheek, savoured the velvety texture on her skin, then gently inhaled the delicate perfume.

Katrina had a plan of her own, and she implemented the arrangements, rang Siobhan with the invitation, then sank back into her chair with a warm smile.

'*A private dinner*,' Katrina declared as she rose from the bed next morning. 'In celebration,' she added, teasing gently, 'We get to dress up, for each other.'

'I gather this is something special?' Nicos queried as he joined her in the shower, and caught her nod in assent.

And it was. Very special. Her gift to him.

Had he guessed? she mused as she led him out into the gardens just before dusk. There, beneath the spreading branches of a beautiful jacaranda, stood a celebrant with Siobhan at his side.

'A reaffirmation of our wedding vows.'

Nicos drew her into his arms, settled his mouth over hers in a kiss that lasted long and took her breath away.

'You get to do that *after* the ceremony,' the celebrant teased gently.

'Count on it.'

Siobhan brushed a tear away as the celebrant intoned the words Katrina had requested. With joy for her daughter's newfound happiness, and the man who so obviously cherished her.

The meal Katrina had Marie prepare was a simple repast served in the candle-lit dining room. Chilled champagne and a single-tiered miniature wedding cake added an unexpected touch.

Afterwards Nicos drew Katrina into the study and slid a diamond-studded ring onto her finger.

'Eternity. Ours,' he said gently, watching her beautiful eyes coalesce with emotion. 'There's just one other thing.' He unlocked a desk drawer and handed her a document. 'Read it.'

Legalese, gifting her the one-third share bequest in Macbride originally assigned to him by Kevin Macbride.

'It was always yours,' Nicos relayed quietly. 'Now it's official.'

Words momentarily failed her, and she dashed the sudden tears that sprang to her eyes. 'I love you.' Tremulously spoken words that came straight from the heart. 'It never stopped.'

Nicos lifted both hands and gently cupped her face. 'I know.' He kissed her with lingering passion, then carried her upstairs to bed.

CHAPTER TWELVE

KATRINA repositioned herself on the low-set lounger and let the warm Aegean sun caress her bikini-clad body. Dark lenses protected her eyes, and she tipped the large straw hat over her face.

It had taken Nicos a few phone calls to delegate, book a flight to Athens, and organise hire of this elegant cruiser.

They'd been here a week. Lovely lazy days and long nights filled with lovemaking. Idyllic, she thought as she closed her eyes and let her mind drift.

All the doubts and turmoil, the insecurities, had vanished. A trial by fire, she reflected, wincing slightly as Georgia's spiteful image sprang vividly to mind.

'Don't,' Nicos cautioned gently. He was so keenly attuned to her that he sensed the slight tension evident, divined and sought to alleviate it as he brushed the pads of his fingers across her midriff in a soothing gesture.

Her skin was a light honey-gold, its texture silky smooth beneath his touch, and he took pleasure in the caress as he explored the line of Lycra stretching low across her hips.

The slight hitch in her breathing brought forth a faint smile, and he traced lower, witnessed the way her stomach muscles tightened, then he leaned towards her and bestowed a kiss on her navel.

'You're in danger of shocking the natives,' Katrina said in a husky drawl, and heard his soft laughter.

'There's not a soul in sight.'

'Binoculars, paparazzi and long-range-zoom camera lenses,' she reminded him indolently, not wanting to move.

He had the touch, the skill, that took her from warmth to heat in a few seconds flat. Desire and passion followed in equal time.

'Want to take this down below?'

A soft chuckle of laughter emerged from her throat, and she lifted a hand, tilted her hat so she could look at him. 'Are you serious?'

His answering grin held a wolfish quality. 'You're not?'

She pretended to consider her options. 'I guess I could be persuaded.' Remembering just how good he was at persuasion had her heartbeat moving up a notch.

His fingers pressed a vulnerable nub, so lightly she almost groaned in need of more.

'If you need to think about it…'

A hand snaked out and managed a grip onto his chest hair, tightened a little. 'Don't toy with me.'

Her husky growl was quickly silenced as his mouth took possession of hers in a kiss that promised flagrant seduction.

When he lifted his head she ran the edge of her

tongue over the slightly swollen contours of her mouth.

'Well, then. That settles it.' She lifted a hand and pressed fingers to his lips, felt them move in a gentle caress, then she rose to her feet in a single, fluid movement, tugging him upright.

The cruiser was large, the galley and bedroom spacious.

Nicos pulled her in close and rested his cheek against her head.

He took it slowly. They had all the time in the world, and he instigated a leisurely tasting, savouring each shudder, each hitch of her breath.

She was *his*. The most important thing in his life. Always had been, even when they'd been apart. There could never be anyone else to take her place in his heart.

He said the words, in soft, guttural Greek, then in English, and she felt the moisture well in her eyes at the depth of emotion evident.

She captured his head, let her hands slide to frame his face, searched his beloved features, and saw what she knew in her heart, the depths of her soul. The unconditional love of a man for one woman. Beyond boundaries, forever true. It was an infinitely precious gift. One she would treasure for the rest of her life.

'Promise me something,' Katrina began to say gently, and saw his smile.

'You have to ask?'

'Let's work at making every day special.'

'That's a given.'

'There's just one more thing.' She reached up and kissed him, a fleeting touch. 'You have my love, my trust.' Her mouth shook a little. 'Always.'

'As you have mine, *agape mou*,' he whispered softly, and proceeded to show her a depth of passion that surpassed anything they'd previously shared.

Childhood in Portsmouth meant grubby knees, flying pigtails and happiness for **Sara Wood**. Poverty drove her from typist and seaside landlady to teacher, till writing finally gave her the freedom her romantic blood craved. Happily married, she has two handsome sons: Richard is married, calm, dependable, drives tankers; Simon is a roamer – silversmith, roofer, welder, always with beautiful girls. Sara lives in the Cornish countryside. Her glamorous writing life alternates with her passion for gardening which allows her to be carefree and grubby again!

THE KYRIAKIS BABY
by
Sara Wood

PROLOGUE

EMMA sat staring into space, her eyes huge with fear. Her solicitor would come, she told herself. He'd have the answer. He must.

The question wouldn't go away. It was driving her mad. Over and over again it hammered into her aching head.

Where is my baby?

She broke her numb silence with a whimpering moan of despair, a thin, poignant figure drawn in on herself, a woman lost in her own dark world.

Only two weeks ago, she'd stood petrified with fear in the dock and had heard the foreman of the jury pronounce her guilty. It had all been a blur from then on. At Leyton Women's Prison, a note had been handed to her from her brother-in-law, Leon. It had been brutal in its simplicity. 'I have your child.'

She'd heard nothing since. Her baby, Alexandra, had vanished off the face of the earth.

From that moment on, life had been suspended for Emma. Perhaps she had eaten at some time—she wouldn't know. And sleep had come only when her exhausted body could take no more of the waking hell. Even then she'd been plagued by nightmares from which she'd woken sobbing, and drenched in a cold sweat.

That morning, preparing for visiting time, she'd noticed with sudden shock that the months of stress had etched a network of fine lines around her mouth. Furrows scoured her high forehead and a deep notch had been excavated between her brows.

Leon had done this to her.

In the cheap mirror she'd seen that her blonde hair was

5

now lank instead of thick and lustrous. Emma had grimaced, had scraped the lifeless hanks back into a severe pony-tail and had fastened them carelessly with a rubber band, unconcerned that spikes of hair stuck out at all angles.

She looked awful. So what? Who was there to see? She just didn't care. Nothing mattered any more. How could it? Alexandra was her baby and she'd been spirited away. And she was just *six months old*.

Her baby. The focus of her entire existence. Something miraculous, salvaged from a terrible marriage to Taki. Sweet, dimpled little Lexi, whose chuckles and sunny nature could make her smile despite her worries and who'd roused in her such a fierce and tender passion that she'd been shaken by its profundity.

And now Lexi had disappeared. Sitting disconsolately at her appointed place, she took a dog-eared photo from her pocket and stared at it with empty eyes.

Her thoughts tortured her. What happened, she wondered miserably, when a baby was abruptly parted from its mother? Would she eat? Would her child be bewildered and upset— or would anyone's arms, anyone's smile be acceptable? She thought of Lexi, sick from crying, and groaned.

'Oh, my baby!'

She lifted a frail hand to stifle a sob. The action made her vaguely aware that people were stirring around her, their voices rising above the normal subdued mutter that was normally adopted in the large visitors' hall.

Dragged from her inner torment, she lifted her head and gloomily followed the source of interest. And instantly she froze, transfixed by the man who stood in the distant doorway.

Not her solicitor. Someone tall, dark and broad and undeniably Greek, his sharply tailored city suit and impeccable grooming quite incongruous amid the plethora of T-shirts, jogging pants and designer trainers.

Leon. The unfeeling brute who'd abducted her baby.

The pain in her chest intensified as a harsh protest scraped its way from her throat. He'd come to gloat! To read her the riot act, to talk about her lack of morals and his right to take Alexandra.

Right! she seethed. What about her right to justice? Her rights of motherhood? Why had she automatically lost *her* rights as a human being?

Battle-ready, Emma drew her weary body upright, her eyes glittering with anger. She'd have him arrested! He was a fool to have come...

The thudding of her heart seemed to trip and falter as logic poured cold water on her impetuous thoughts. Leon was no fool. If he was here, it was to say something important. What could that be?

Her fevered imagination quickly provided answers. Her baby was dead. A cot death. An accident. An unidentified sickness...

She gasped, and somehow she was on her feet, catapulted by an unknown force that had flung her chair violently to the ground. Leon's eyes swerved to meet hers and he recoiled in shock, as if her appearance appalled him. But Emma was way beyond personal pride.

'*Is she dead?*' she yelled hysterically across the vast hall.

Aghast, he shook his head and mouthed one word. 'No!'

She swayed, her whole body sagging in relief. A warder roughly ordered her to sit but her knees were already giving way beneath her and if a fellow prisoner hadn't righted her chair Emma would have collapsed in a crumpled heap onto the floor.

Her baby was alive. *Alive!* 'Thank you, God. Thank you,' she whispered emotionally.

She trembled all over, her knees juddering against the low metal table. Hands as shaky as a drug addict's covered her eyes. She knew she couldn't take much more.

I must stay calm, she thought in panic. To be more controlled and rational. OK, maybe restraint had seldom featured in her impulsive and passionate nature and her life had been splattered with spectacular foot-in-mouth mistakes—but she had to find some semblance of control. Leon must be persuaded to surrender Lexi.

All her instincts were urging her to hurl abuse and accusations at Leon, to repeat the terrible things she'd privately called him over the past nightmare days. After that, she thought grimly, it would be a nice twist to get him thrown in jail.

But a rare caution warned her against this. He held the welfare of her baby in his hands. Perhaps only he knew where Lexi was. If she annoyed him, she might never see her daughter again.

Her bitter scowl of disappointment would have unnerved him if he hadn't been engrossed in talking to a warder. She glared. Surrounded by grey and depressed people, he looked indecently fit and vigorous as he finished his conversation and threaded his way carefully between the seated prisoners and their visitors.

It seemed to Emma that his whole manner suggested he was concerned that any contact with them might contaminate him irrevocably with some vile disease.

Yes, she thought, near to choking with indignation, this place is a terrible dump! The atmosphere is rank, the bare walls are grimmer than Alcatraz and the clank of keys and clang of gates are two of the most chilling sounds on earth! And she, sweet heaven, she would have to suffer it every wretched day of her life for the next five years!

The injustice made her head spin. She was innocent. *Innocent!*

Aching with anger she tortured herself with the milestones she could miss in five years of little Lexi's life. Her baby's first words, her first steps, the momentous day when she'd start school. And daily cuddles. Smiles, gurgles, small loving arms...

She gave a shuddering sob. Those joys were her right as

a mother! This was her baby, her very flesh and blood, and the person she cared for above all others. How dared he play hide-and-seek with her child!

Resolutions scattered. Uncontainable fury brought her to her feet again when he had come to a mere yard or two's distance of her trembling figure.

'Where is my baby? What have you done with her?' she demanded fiercely.

'Sit down.' Leon snapped.

His outstretched hand gave an imperious wave and, to her amazement, it halted the two frowning warders bearing down on her. Authority, she thought with glowering resentment. He has it in spades. Well, not with me!

'Answer my question, damn you!' she insisted grimly, remaining on her feet out of sheer cussedness.

Tense, and smouldering with a volcanic ferocity, Leon slid into the seat at her table. And yet even there he still managed to dominate the room, perhaps because when seated his height and breadth seemed more than that of the average man. Emma scowled. Nothing about the handsome Leon could ever be remotely termed average.

The blue-black of his hair was more intense, the density of his dark and expressive eyes more mesmerising than any she'd ever seen. The people who met him were always disturbed, intimidated or attracted, depending on their sex and their connection with him. But no one ever forgot the charismatic Leon Kyriakis.

And nor had she. Not one moment of their lovemaking. Despite everything, she felt his inexorable sexual pull now and wilted at the sheer strength of his strong-boned and finely chiselled face, and the curl of his electrifyingly sensual mouth that once she'd kissed and tasted so avidly, so lovingly. Until his utterly callous betrayal.

The furnace in her loins fuelled her loathing as his burning eyes captured her gaze. For a second or two a crackling hostility shot between them, heating up the atmosphere till she felt her skin too must be on fire. And then his ink-black eyes silvered with lethal contempt.

'Sit down, Emma,' he repeated harshly, 'or you'll be back in your cell with your knitting and your mug of cocoa and I'll be halfway to the airport.'

Alarmed, she promptly obeyed, her head lowered in anger while she curbed a wealth of tart answers. She could have kicked herself. She'd *known* she had to handle him carefully. And yet she'd stupidly waded in with all guns blazing. Not much of a kid-gloves approach, was it?

Calm. Restraint. Operate brain before mouth. But how, when violent emotions constantly erupted within her? She missed her baby desperately and her greatest fear was that Lexi might be pining too. No one else knew her little ways. Nobody could understand her baby as she could.

Tears suddenly blurred her vision. Knuckling them away miserably, she looked up with dead, hopeless eyes, all the agony in her heart showing plainly on her ashen face.

'I can't bear this any longer! If you have a shred of pity, you must tell me! Where is my baby?' she implored.

Leon immediately edged his chair back, frowning down at the table. 'Safe.'

He cleared his throat and fiddled with his cuff, apparently annoyed that it was showing a centimetre less than its twin.

'Thank God,' she whispered.

She swallowed ineffectively. There was a solid lump blocking her throat and she gagged on it, desperate to clear it so she could speak. Seeing this, he pushed a glass of water towards her and she stared, oddly surprised at the contrast between their two hands.

His was tanned, broad and virtually pulsing with life. Hers looked a ghastly white, just skin and bone, as if, she thought deliriously, she was in a living death.

She clasped the glass as if grabbing a lifeline but her hand shook too much when she raised it and she abruptly put it back on the table. No histrionics. Reasoned argument. For her baby's sake...

The hard lump eased a little and she could swallow. 'How...how is she?'

Her voice quavered and his mouth immediately contracted into a hard line. What had she said to annoy him? Emma felt awash with terror in case he lost his not inconsiderable temper and refused to listen to her.

'Don't do this to me. I must know,' she begged wretchedly.

'Alexandra is well and happy.'

He spoke in a stiff undertone and she leaned far across the table, frantic to hear every word he uttered. Leon seemed to shrink back as if she was invading his space. He loathed her, she thought dully. How was she to win him round?

She bit her soft lower lip intently, anxious to hear about her beloved baby. 'Is she very upset? Does she...cry much?' she said jerkily.

'No.'

Her eyes widened. 'Don't lie to me!' She flung the words at him. 'She must!'

'If I say she doesn't, then it's true,' he answered irritably. 'She'll cry for a while when she's tired or hungry or needing comfort but she soon stops. Otherwise she's content. I am not a liar. I come from an honest people,' he pointed out, forcing the words fiercely through his tightly clenched teeth.

'I'm honest too. I don't deserve to be in prison, accused of fraud,' she hurled.

'Such injustice.' He tutted, his expression cynical and disbelieving.

Emma realised that it was no use trying to persuade him that she was whiter than snow. He had her down as a criminal and that was that.

'Lexi's OK, then?' she persisted in a plaintive tone. 'She's eating properly?'

'How many times do I have to tell you?' he said irritably.

'She's absolutely fine. Use your common sense. Why would I allow any harm to come to her?'

Emma paused to consider this. In her experience Greeks loved children and had a way with them. Lexi was probably being spoiled rotten.

A twinge, as sharp as a knife, twisted in her breast with such force that her hand lifted to ease it. For her daughter's sake she felt relieved that all was well, but she felt more bereft than ever.

Maybe she wasn't necessary to Lexi's well-being at all. Her child could exist without her. But could she exist without her child? Her heart went cold and she shuddered, sliding her thin arms around her shivering body, consoling herself with the fact that only she knew all the tiny things that made Lexi truly content.

'She does have her teddy bear, doesn't she?' she began shakily. 'And I don't suppose you realise that she needs her yellow blanket—'

'It's with her as we speak. I removed everything from your house which looked remotely as if it belonged to Lexi,' he retorted.

Emma gaped, astounded at his thoroughness. 'You planned this!' she accused hotly. 'You knew exactly what you would do if the jury pronounced me guilty—'

'Of course I did. I couldn't allow my late brother's child to remain in the care of a stranger,' he snapped.

'She's my neighbour. Lexi knows her. It was only temporary, anyway,' she argued. 'I fully expected to be free—'

'And what did you organise if not?' he asked sardonically.

'If there was a problem, my neighbour was to bring her to the mother-and-baby unit here.'

He still hadn't answered the question. Where was her daughter? Suddenly she had a flash of fear, picturing her baby abandoned outside in a car, or in her buggy by the prison entrance where anyone could abduct her… She drew in a choking breath.

'And what about *your* babysitting arrangements? If you're here,' she said jerkily, her voice rising in panic, 'who's looking after Lexi now?'

His eyes flickered. 'Marina. My—'

But she'd got there before him. 'Your *wife*!' she said breathily.

Emma sat stunned. Of course. Who else? she thought dully. And then she noticed something strange. There was a sliver of pain knifing across the dark depths of his eyes and bitterness had drawn his mouth into a hard line.

He wasn't happy, she realised with a shock. Pangs of half-remembered love touched her shuttered heart. She'd adored him once. They'd been students together and he'd been everything to her. But one day, totally out of the blue, she'd seen him emerging from a local restaurant with a drop-dead gorgeous blonde on his arm. Her world had disintegrated rapidly.

'An engagement party,' the obliging Greek waiter had said, his apron stuffed with tips from the affluent, laughing crowd.

The lintel above the entrance where they were posing for photographs had born a banner with the elaborately printed legend, Leon and Marina. It had been emblazoned with hearts and love knots. The waiter picked up a discarded menu with the same design and the appalled Emma had known that this must have been planned for some time.

Tears of rage and misery had rendered her speechless. He'd been organising his wedding while vowing he loved her…even while he was sleeping with her!

'Leon!' she'd cried rawly.

He'd looked directly at her and turned a deathly white. *'Emma!'*

All eyes had been upon her then. Clearly appalled that she'd found him out, he'd spoken to a younger man at his side who'd come over and introduced himself as Leon's brother, Taki.

'He's the Kyriakis heir, she's the Christofides heiress,' Taki had explained gently as he'd driven her home. 'Our families have been linked for generations. Don't take this personally,' he'd said soothingly, when she'd continued to sob. 'It's how we do things. We need sex so we find a woman who is amenable. Then we marry a more suitable virgin.'

The humiliating words dug deep. She'd been used as a whore! Bought presents, taken out to dinner…and in return he'd pillaged her heart and soul and body!

Broken-hearted, her self-esteem at rock bottom, she'd relied increasingly on the attentive, kind Taki. His respect for her had been deeply touching. Eventually she'd succumbed to Taki's charm offensive and married him, unaware of his fatal need to outdo his rival brother.

She gave a grimace. Incredibly, Taki had believed that Leon would be jealous of his marriage to her. But why, when she had nothing—and the elegant, shopaholic Marina had breeding, wealth and social position?

Her heart thudded in alarm. This was the woman who was now looking after her child! What, she thought with uncharacteristic sourness, did a clothes-horse on legs know about such things?

Her brows beetled together in a fierce scowl. 'Your wife had better be the Mary Poppins of child care—or you'll have me to reckon with!' she muttered.

'Marina has a daughter of her own,' he drawled crushingly.

She felt she'd been stabbed in the lungs. Leon had a child. 'Bully for you both,' she cried, finding her breath again. 'Then, you don't need mine.'

'Damn right, I don't.'

Her mouth opened in astonishment. He didn't even want her darling Lexi. 'Then, why take her?' she asked, aghast.

He looked down his patrician nose at her. 'I had no choice.'

'No…*choice*?' She spluttered the words incoherently.

Leon looked grim. 'She needs a home. She needs us.'

'Me. She needs *me*. I'm her mother,' she quavered.

'Not much of one.'

'I'm terrific.'

'Matter of opinion.'

'I'll get out on appeal—'

'I think not. The evidence was clear-cut and damning. Get used to this situation, Emma,' he said sharply. 'Serve your time—'

'I will if I must, unfair though it is. I could bear anything if I had my baby back.'

'Out of the question.'

Incensed, she banged the table and knocked over the glass of water which spilled onto her lap. Leon produced a handkerchief but she refused it, too caught up in her bid for her child to care that her dress was wet through.

'If you're a father,' she said, hoarse with emotion, 'then think how you'd feel if your child was taken from you.'

Astonishingly, his gaze became cynical, as if that wouldn't be hard to bear. He has no heart, she thought bleakly. Her beloved baby wasn't even wanted. How could he feel like that? The only Greek in the world who didn't like children and he had to snatch her baby.

'It's happening all the time,' he observed obliquely. 'People split up, children end up with one of the parents—'

'But I'm the *remaining* parent,' she pointed out, barely clinging to sanity. Why couldn't he understand what Lexi meant to her? She had no one else in the world. 'You have no right to abduct my child. I could have you arrested.'

'That would be extremely unwise,' he said with quiet menace.

She tensed in alarm. 'Why?'

'It wouldn't get your child back.'

'Maybe not,' she muttered bitterly, giving her wet dress a shake, 'but it would bring a big grin to my face and play merry hell with your social life.'

His breath hissed in and he fixed her with eyes as cold as

charity. 'You'd do that to score points off me?' he enquired softly.

Her desolation intensified. Of course not. She'd gain nothing—other than a useless, petty satisfaction—by giving Leon grief. And she'd ruin her chances of finding Lexi.

Her chest seemed to tighten with despair. 'I'd do anything, anything to get my own child back where she rightfully belongs,' she declared jerkily.

There was a lift of a black-winged eyebrow. 'You're at a slight disadvantage being in prison,' he observed.

She flushed, a hectic colour burning two scarlet spots on her pale, bony cheeks.

'Have you no heart? No soul? She should be with me—'

'Alexandra might be legally yours but that's as far as it goes,' he said sternly. 'You just aren't fit to be her mother.'

'That's not fair,' she seethed, outraged at the slur.

'*Fair?* You dare to speak of fairness?' he rasped, his voice shaking with barely contained fury as he struggled to keep the volume down. 'How can you sit there claiming to be as innocent as a Madonna? You systematically defrauded members of my family *and* our lifelong friends and business acquaintances, and left them penniless,' he hissed.

His big fists clenched on the table and she stared at them, suddenly frightened of his intense passion.

'But that's the point—I didn't,' she protested, her voice wobbling alarmingly. 'It…it wasn't me—'

'You disgust me!' he scathed. 'Have you any idea of the consequences of your crime in our close-knit society? Our family bank here in London was seen as the safest place this side of Fort Knox. People relied on us. *Trusted* us. No wonder Taki got drunk! His own wife had destroyed his family business, his family honour and innocent lives. He'd lost his job and his own honour—'

'Honour!' she choked.

'Yes! Ever heard of the word?' he taunted.

'You *hypocrite*!' she said breathily, forgetting Taki's dishonesty and attacking Leon's instead. 'How can you sit there and talk of honour when you forgot to mention your engagement to another woman while we were together?'

That went home. He recoiled as if she'd slapped him, his skin suddenly taut and sickly pale.

'That *was* a matter of honour—'

'Yes, I know. Honouring some long-standing family arrangement,' she said scornfully. 'You used me for sex—and you talk of *honour*.'

'Don't try to wriggle out of this,' Leon retorted, white-lipped. 'The truth is that Taki was appalled at what you'd done. And he got so paralytic that some bastard mugged him and left him to die in the gutter. Your actions caused his death.'

Frozen in horror at Leon's twisted interpretation of the facts, she tried to speak. But his accusation had stunned her with its cruelty and all she could do was to slur helplessly, 'It's a lie! I'm…I'm…'

'Guilty on all counts,' Leon finished in disgust. 'Now, I hope you understand that I feel I owe you no sympathy. My family means everything to me and you ripped it apart with your evil scheming. You destroyed my only brother—'

'No—'

'Are you denying,' he went on relentlessly, 'that you cold-bloodedly married him out of petty revenge—?'

'I loved him—'

'Liar! He said you'd asked for a divorce.'

Emma bit her lip hard. She hadn't wanted to split her family up. But she'd had no choice. Leon knew nothing of the agonising that had gone before her painful decision.

'Y-yes, but—'

'Don't bother to find excuses,' Leon said, growling. 'Taki had served his purpose. You'd seen a way to make me pay for marrying Marina and you took it. Well, congratulations. You succeeded in making my life hell.' His eyes glittered. 'Forgive me,' he ground out through his teeth, 'if I return the compliment.'

She gave a low moan and buried her face in her hands, all

hope virtually abandoned. His Greek heritage made him proud and hot-blooded and deeply devoted to his family. In his eyes, she'd harmed that family. And so he wanted to destroy her. And how better than to take away the baby she adored?

Panic and despair filled her head as defeat stared back at her. But she knew she had to rouse herself and make one last attempt to convince Leon that he'd jumped to all the wrong conclusions.

'You must listen to me,' she begged. 'You've got it all wrong. I've done nothing to be ashamed of. I'm truly innocent—'

'Sure. You, and everyone in here,' he mocked.

'No, I am—'

'You knew what was happening,' he said snarling. 'You were the financial director—'

'That's the point, I wasn't, it was in name only I *swear*—'

'Stop it!' he snapped furiously. 'You've perjured yourself enough.'

'Leon,' she mumbled, 'you're not giving me a chance—'

'Did you give Taki a chance? Or those people who are now living on pittances instead of healthy pensions? My family will have to pull out all the stops to ensure they don't suffer, thanks to you. It could take us years.'

It was hopeless. He was implacable. 'How can we have become such enemies?' she asked miserably. 'Once…'

The rest of her words died in her throat. His eyes blazed with such an intense hatred that every muscle in her body turned to water, her hands feebly clawing at the table for support as she struggled to stay in her seat and not slide to the floor in a boneless heap.

Leon's face suddenly loomed close to hers and she found herself pinned in place by the anguish that ripped at his face.

'Once! Once we were lovers,' he said in a terrible, raw whisper. 'My passion matched yours, my hands caressed your body. My lips knew yours, our bodies pulsed together—'

'Leon—' she said, breathily brokenly, unable to bear any more.

He touched her face, his fingers trembling with a barely contained passion. She assumed it to be a shuddering anger and shrank back in distress.

Leon's nostrils flared. 'I'd never have come within a mile of you if I'd realised the depths of your viciousness—that you could blame Taki for the fraud.'

'It was him,' she insisted hopelessly.

'Pity the jury didn't agree with you,' he countered.

There was a sudden silence between them. They were at deadlock. Emma gave up. Her late husband's betrayal was no longer important.

Alexandra's future *was*. The next few moments could affect her child's life for ever. Sick and weak, she rallied the last drop of energy in her body.

'Shun me,' she declared, her voice shaking with emotion. 'Hate me, think what you like. Forget I ever lived if that pleases you.' Panic rose within her like an uncontrollable flood and she raised a tearful face in one last passionate plea. 'But let me have the child I love.'

'Not in a million years,' he replied coldly. 'I won't let Taki's daughter be brought up in an English prison by a callous, cold-blooded female. She's out of your reach now...not even in this country.'

Abruptly he rose to go. Emma couldn't speak, could barely think for shock. Her beloved Lexi was in Greece! A cracked sound filtered through her trembling lips as the reality hit her like a stone. Her mouth quivered as a terrible emptiness enveloped her. She hadn't a hope of getting her baby back.

The nausea rose to her throat and sweat beaded her forehead. Hardly aware of her surroundings, she struggled for control, afraid that she'd be sick, then and there.

'You're...a *monster*!' she whispered in horror.

'Am I?' he said curtly. 'And what kind of mother are you? Did you once think of Lexi while you were plotting your criminal activities? Did you ever wonder what would happen to her if your fraud was discovered? Were you so wrapped up in your own selfish need for vengeance that it didn't *matter* what happened to any of the people who had the misfortune to be involved in your life?'

Emma gazed at him tearfully. 'But…I love her,' she mumbled.

'And I have her best interests at heart,' he countered grimly. 'She will remain with me. I came to put your mind at rest. Lexi is safe and content and will be well cared for. She will be taught to be honourable, well-mannered and honest.'

It sounded so dutiful. So utterly empty of warmth and affection. This was her baby he was talking about! A child who needed cuddles and affection, a mother's love… 'Is that all?' she said jerkily.

'More than you would have provided,' he said coldly.

'Leon!' she said choking, tears spilling unchecked down her unhappy face as she was forced to accept the unthinkable.

There would be another woman mothering her baby, someone else reading bedtime stories, comforting Lexi, watching her grow up…snuggling into that baby-scented skin…

She gave a shuddering moan. 'Oh, Leon, what about *love*?'

He had half-turned to leave. Taut in every line of his body, he jerked his head around and looked her full in the eyes. Now she was sure of his unhappiness, of some deep pain he suffered.

Her limpid gaze pleaded with him for compassion and understanding. The silence and the tension between them intensified and she knew they were both thinking of the past when they had been wildly happy together and without a care in the world.

'Love,' he rasped with a glacial contempt, 'is a fool's *illusion*.'

CHAPTER ONE

SECURE within the walled grounds of Leon's country mansion, the two-and-a-half-year-old Alexandra slept contentedly in Leon's arms while he laid plans for her to inherit his domain. When, he reminded himself grimly, he'd dealt with the problem of his ex-wife and her child.

He returned to more pleasant thoughts, planning for the day when he'd tell Lexi how his family had been rewarded with land for outstanding bravery. Like his father before him, he'd show his niece the hill where a lookout had spotted the Saracen pirates who'd roamed the seas of Greece in the sixteenth century, and who'd threatened to capture the entire island of Zakynthos.

And they'd walk from the beach where Kyriakis ships had set out for the decisive battle, to the shady, vine-covered terrace where he now sat. There, he would tell her, in his late father's words, that the land would be hers, all the way from the coast, across the fertile plain and to the hills beyond.

She murmured in her sleep and burrowed deeper, her wilful little face soft with dreams. Smiling down at her, he stroked the silky blonde curls and had a sudden, sharply painful recollection of caressing Emma's shining hair long, long in the past.

The rosy image was brutally replaced by Emma's shocking appearance more than two years ago, when he'd confronted her in that unspeakable prison. He shifted, uncomfortable with the memory. In a moment of weakness he'd almost given in to her, his intentions shaken by Emma's distress and her alarming physical deterioration.

But she had shown no penitence and he couldn't ignore the facts. Lexi's moral welfare had been threatened. It had been his duty to protect his brother's child in accordance with his promise to his ailing father.

He looked down as Lexi stirred, her eyes opening to show the same cerulean blue as those of her mother. He smiled fondly. Reluctant to take on another child, he'd nevertheless been enchanted by her.

'Mama,' she whimpered, her face crumpling in bewilderment.

He winced as if from a body blow. 'It's OK. I'm here, sweet pea,' he said softly, holding the tiny body close.

He knew she wasn't properly awake and was likely to sleep for another twenty minutes or so. She was dreaming. At her tender age she couldn't have any memory of a mother who'd last held her when she was still a baby. Could she?

Alexandra curled up grumpily and her eyes closed again, soothed by his stroking hands. But Leon felt disturbed and unsettled.

When she seemed to be safely asleep again he headed for his study where he placed her carefully on a wide sofa at the far end of the room, protecting her with a barricade of pillows.

The house slumbered, silent and hushed. Marina, who was sharing the big house with him still, insisted everyone took a siesta after lunch and he'd often had cause to be grateful for the respite it afforded him.

Frowning hard, he strode up and down, thinking. The moment he'd dreaded was almost upon him. Lexi would soon ask questions about her mother. He needed to know what to say. Or…what to show her.

His eyes slewed to the locked drawer in his desk. Something other than his own will compelled him to stride over and slip the key in the lock. His fingers shook with impatience. Nothing could stop him now, not even the need to protect his own bruised heart.

With his pulses pounding loudly in his ears, he removed the home video from the drawer and slotted it into the machine. After a quick glance at the sleeping Lexi, he pulled up a leather armchair and focussed tensely on the unfolding pictures.

A slow hiss escaped his lips. He'd forgotten how beautiful Emma had been when they'd gone out together. She'd been twenty, studying economics on day-release at the college where he was taking a postgraduate course.

Her sense of fun and *joie de vivre* lit the screen and Leon found himself on the edge of his seat watching avidly as her supple and voluptuous body dipped and swayed in a laughing parody of a belly dancer. Sex oozed from every pore of her body, heating him, tugging at his loins.

Giggling, she ruined the profoundly erotic effect by whooping and turning a series of exuberant cartwheels.

'Mama!'

'*Lex!*'

Leon jerked around, poleaxed. Alexandra was sitting up and staring wide-eyed at the screen. His heart pounded hard as the hairs stood up on the back of his neck. She didn't know what she was saying.

Cursing himself for being careless, he hit the off button. Lexi scrambled over the cushions and ran to him. Before he knew what she was doing she had reached across his knee and switched the video on again.

'Mama,' she said in firm defiance when he snapped it off for the second time.

He stopped breathing. It was a coincidence. She was copying Marina's child who was always yelling for her mother. Only the other day Lexi had called his ex-wife Mama and had been quickly corrected, only to repeat the word again and again until the edgy Marina had screamed in exasperation.

He smiled wryly, remembering how secretly amused he'd been by his bolshie little niece. Lexi was strong-willed; as stubborn and as determined as any Kyriakis male.

And, he acknowledged, with the added advantage of devastatingly female weapons. Already she'd climbed onto his lap and her arms were twining around his neck pleadingly.

'Lexi see,' she coaxed, showering his face with kisses.

Melting already, he considered this. The damage—if any—had been done. If not, they could both enjoy the remainder of the video. And he wanted to, very much.

Brushing aside the danger to his peace of mind, he nodded. 'All right,' he conceded.

'Thank you very much,' she chanted solemnly, remembering her manners.

He grinned and hugged her. 'Minx,' he murmured fondly, curling up with her to watch.

He could see that Lexi was enraptured by Emma's virtuoso performance for the camcorder. As always, Emma went too far—this time, one cartwheel too many—and to the little girl's delight Emma rolled helplessly into a nearby duck pond before emerging hooting with laughter, her eyes sparkling, pearly teeth glistening and her hair festooned with pondweed.

'Finished,' he announced tautly, when the screen went blank.

His memory furnished the rest. He'd put down the camcorder and dragged Emma into his arms. He'd kissed her till she couldn't breathe. Oh, God, he remembered so well!

Seven years later he could still smell and taste the pondweed and feel the indescribable warmth and softness of her welcoming, laughing mouth as she'd lured him into the woodland beyond.

Grimly he swung Lexi into his arms and suggested a swim, relieved that she had asked no questions. He wasn't ready to supply answers.

As she tugged him along excitedly, he reflected that he would have to decide how he should handle the question of Emma. Did he tell his niece the truth one day about her jailbird mother? Or should he give a sanitised version? And should he ever reveal who the woman in the video was?

His brow furrowed deeply. If he did the latter, Lexi would

be captivated. She'd want to meet her mother—whereas he intended to keep them apart as long as possible.

He felt a chill steal over him despite the heat of the early afternoon. Emma would be released in a couple of years or so. And then Lexi would no longer be safe from harm.

He looked at her sweet face as she sang happily to herself, absorbed in 'helping' her to wriggle into a bathing costume which sported a large daisy cutely adorning her small bottom. His heart lurched. Ever the attentive, doting uncle, he swept her curls up and expertly fastened them with a scrunchie.

He loved this little scrap. From day one she'd wormed her way into his frozen heart and with every flutter of her lashes and big, gummy smile she had set about thoroughly defrosting it. Now she meant everything to him—and life without her would be untenable.

He made a silent pledge. Emma would never get her daughter back. Not while there was still breath in his body.

'And…Mrs Kyriakis,' murmured the smooth, young immigration officer, 'what are your plans now you are on Zakynthos?'

Emma remained composed, even though her heart and stomach seemed to have shot down an elevator into her trainers and were now sending alarm signals through her entire system.

She'd had a lot of practice in self-control over the past two years—and getting into the country was far more important than some of the things she'd silently borne in prison. Consequently she managed to flash a warm smile.

'Simple. I'm going to get a tan!' she announced airily.

With a show of cheerfulness she indicated the sun cream, lodged precariously on top of her belongings which had been tipped unceremoniously out of her case.

'I see. Staying…where?' enquired the officer idly, scanning a list.

She craned her neck. It looked like the names of people.

Her dramatically fertile imagination provided details. Drug dealers and terrorists. Rapists. Paedophiles, whatever. Her heart leapt back into her chest with an unnerving suddenness and sat there palpitating. Maybe she was on that list as an undesirable!

'Your hotel?' prompted her interrogator.

Emma forced another broad smile. 'Hotel! I wish. I'm looking for something cheap. A friend of mine said it was easy to find rooms to rent,' she confided. 'Can you recommend anywhere?'

He studied her thoughtfully and ignored her attempt to disarm him. 'You have a Greek name.'

She'd been ready for that one. Nodding slowly, she gave herself time to calm her leaping nerves and to steady her voice. 'My husband…' she frowned at the shaky delivery but plunged on '…he…he died in England more than two years ago.'

Unfazed by her apparent agitation, the officer gave her a calculating stare. She recognised in him the same detachment as that adopted by the prison officers. They'd heard too many lies and too many sob stories to be anything but suspicious of emotion.

'He has family here?'

Emma tensed. Her solicitor had said there were many people in the phone book with the name Kyriakis and her arrival shouldn't provoke comment. She hoped this officer was merely bored and was using her to hone his interviewing technique.

'My late husband lived and worked in England. His family—wherever they are,' she said, suggesting a vagueness as to the Kyriakis whereabouts, 'were opposed to our marriage. They never came to the wedding.' She allowed a puzzled frown to ripple her forehead. 'What is this? Everything's in order, isn't it? All I want is a holiday in the sun. I've had an operation. I need rest and no hassle—'

'Ah. The pills.'

Emma watched as he curiously fingered the homoeopathic remedies for sickness and exhaustion. Her prison sentence had been cut short on compassionate grounds because she'd been so ill. She had her solicitor to thank for that. Dear John! Bless him for his support. She glanced at her watch and bit her lip. He'd be waiting for her, wondering where she was…

'Someone meeting you?'

She blinked. He was good! Someone ought to promote him to head inquisitor, she thought wearily.

'I've never been here before,' she said, evading the question with a politician's skill.

'You looked at your watch.'

'Yes. I need to eat at regular intervals and take my pills at certain times. With the two-hour time difference, I was anxious not to get in a muddle.'

'Really.'

This man would have made an angel edgy, she thought sourly. She felt suddenly weak and passed a hand over her hot forehead.

'I need to sit down,' she muttered. Without waiting for permission she went to a bench against the wall and sank onto it, leaning her back against the cold stone, terrified of failure. 'I don't understand the problem,' she said quietly. 'I can't be the only person who arrives without any definite accommodation. I don't have enough money or clothes to stay here for long, you can see that. I'm not carrying drugs, or anything else illegal. I'm just an ordinary woman hoping for some sun, sea and sand to help me become well.'

Indifferent to her evident frailty, the officer turned over the contents of her case with a desultory hand.

'I see. Would you wait here?' he asked politely.

As if she had any choice! Patiently she waited. An hour. Two. Exhausted from her four a.m. start, she curled up on the hard bench and promptly went to sleep.

'Mrs Kyriakis?' The officer was shaking her shoulder. 'You can go. Enjoy your holiday.'

Relief brought her fully awake. She was free! A joyful smile began its journey across her face but she lowered her sparkling eyes hastily and tried to think how an ordinary holiday-maker would feel.

'About time,' she grumbled. Getting up stiffly, she saw that she'd slept for nearly an hour. 'Some welcome!'

The officer gave an only-doing-my-duty shrug and she continued her show of irritation as she repacked her case then trudged out of the room.

She couldn't believe it. She was here. Really here. And not far away was little Lexi. Soon she'd be holding her baby in her arms again. Excited, Emma thought blissfully of the moment when Lexi would call her Mummy.

'*Wonderful!*' She breathed ecstatically.

Back in his office, the officer punched numbers on his mobile. 'She's on her way,' he warned.

Leon thanked the officer, tucked his mobile into the pocket of his linen jacket and waited tensely beneath the shade of the tamarisk and pine trees opposite the airport entrance.

The first call, some two hours earlier, had come out of the blue. For a moment he'd thought the officer had made a mistake but the name, the age and the description had been spot on. If this *was* Emma, then the young man's alertness had possibly prevented an attempted abduction.

Leon thrust his shaking hands into his pockets and forced back the flash of fear. A tiny child's happiness depended on his ability to handle this situation. Caught off guard by the unexpectedness of Emma's arrival, he'd had only a short time to decide his plan of action. But he must make no mistake in its execution.

He stiffened, every muscle in his body creaking with strain. His heart raced. It was Emma.

Like a butterfly spreading its wings, she drew herself up, took a deep breath and flung her head back to absorb the sunshine, her whole body language exuding uninhibited joy.

'Entirely misplaced,' he muttered.

If she thought she was free to snatch her daughter, she was wrong! He'd watch her every step of the way. She might be devious and driven by revenge to cause him the maximum amount of trouble, but he was on his home ground and had a whole raft of people looking out for his best interests.

And Lexi's. God keep her safe. How could Emma drag a child away from the only home she'd ever known? Her lawyer, John Sefton, had hinted something like this might happen but he'd never believed she could ignore her daughter's needs so ruthlessly.

Emma set off as if she knew where she was going. Interesting. He kept his distance as she headed for the taxi rank—which she ignored. The drivers didn't ignore her though, and he didn't blame them for staring in admiration.

'*Poli oraya*,' they murmured, seeking his agreement as he drew level to them.

Yes, she was strikingly attractive, he acknowledged grudgingly. Prison had obviously been no hardship and the gaunt, sick woman had become a beauty again.

Her long-legged stride was fluid, giving an impression of suppleness and energy. Leon's mind, perhaps overwhelmed by those lushly swaying hips, translated that vigour into Technicolor visions of athletic sex.

'Forget it. You're celibate,' he muttered under his breath, reluctantly amused by his astonishing arousal.

But he couldn't. She'd gained weight—though not the plumpness of her youth. To Leon's hot appraisal her figure was more spectacular than ever before: full breasted, yet slim, and with a tiny waist above those eye-catchingly seductive hips.

She wore a blindingly blue sundress the same colour as her eyes and her blonde hair swung around her shoulders in a thick and glossy cloud. Her skirt was being whipped by the wind around her long, bare legs and afforded breathtaking glimpses of firm and shapely thighs.

Leon tried to normalise his thudding pulses as she stopped and looked about her—clearly waiting for someone. Caught between desiring and despising her, he allowed himself the brief luxury of letting his sexual imagination run riot.

He wished he hadn't. His libido seemed to be making up for lost time and it was taking over his mind as well as his body.

With hazy eyes, he saw a car come to a stop alongside her. A man clambered out. Emma opened her arms in welcome, her face wreathed in smiles.

Leon's vision sharpened. John Sefton, Emma's lawyer. He knew him well from the custody discussions they'd had over the past two years. And that was no proper greeting between a professional man and his client, he thought darkly. Too much hugging. Too much delight.

Spurred by an anger which had come from nowhere, Leon noted the stubby male fingers gravitating slowly towards Emma's highly touchable rear and strode forwards before the roving hand reached its target.

His heart pounded like a trip hammer in his chest and he had to concentrate hard on containing the overwhelming emotions which battled for supremacy in his seething brain.

'Well! They're letting jailbirds into my country now!' he drawled.

Emma gasped at the venom-laced voice, detached herself from John's enthusiastic embrace and whirled around.

'*You!*' she said stupidly.

Leon's cynical eyes lingered mockingly on her parted lips and she felt a flush creeping up her body as he began to investigate the rest of her with breathtaking thoroughness.

'Yes, me. I live here,' he observed when his tour had climbed to her cleavage. 'What's your excuse?'

She bristled, wanting to shout, My child, dammit! What do you think? Instead, she summoned her new and remarkable self-control, raised an eyebrow and with cool composure murmured, 'I've come to arrange access.'

Custody was out of the question. John had fought for that on her behalf ever since she'd been sent to prison and he'd hit a brick wall. Access was a different matter—though she intended to remove Lexi from the island, once they had got to know one another well.

'I was going to call you. I wanted time with Emma first,' John said to Leon, looking flustered.

'Oh, yes?' Leon drawled coldly and turned to Emma. 'I've got half an hour free. We'll discuss it. Without your boyfriend.'

Emma let her mouth tighten with irritation. 'You've met John several times. You're perfectly aware that he's my legal adviser—'

'And hopes for more,' Leon murmured, his gaze challenging John's.

'Don't be ridiculous—' she protested indignantly.

'Ask him,' drawled Leon.

'My relationship with my client is her own business,' John said rather pompously.

And, she felt, defensively. She looked up at him with different eyes. Could Leon be right? And then she frowned. Of course not! It would suit Leon to cause trouble between herself and John, who'd become her friend and ally.

'John has worked long and hard on my case. He's good and kind and worth ten of you,' she declared loyally. 'Without him I'd have been alone in the world.' Her face flushed when she thought of those terrible, heart-breaking days and her voice faltered. 'John was there for me. He stood by me and encouraged me when I was desperate. And he never gave up fighting for my early release.'

'How dedicated. And, I trust, well-paid?' Leon said purring.

But the look he gave her lawyer was one of pure menace and she felt John shrink back in apprehension. That bothered her. She needed her lawyer to be more than a match for Leon.

'That's none of your business,' she replied. Selling her

house had been a price worth paying. 'The sun is too hot for me. Can we find some shade?' she suggested and slipped in a crafty, 'Or perhaps we could go to your home now?'

Leon's dark eyes considered her for a moment. She met them boldly at first, confident of her hard-won protective shell. But slowly his eyes seemed to melt and she felt as if she was floundering in fathoms-deep water. A silky sensation seemed to be flowing up her body, softening her tense muscles and turning her brain to treacle.

The heat. It was melting her as though she were an ice cream. She licked her dry lips and lifted her hair from her damp neck.

'I will talk to you and you alone,' Leon said, his voice low and rolling through her unnervingly. 'Otherwise... nothing.'

'That's not on, Emma!' John began in protest.

She gave him a particularly dreamy smile, partly because of the warm liquidity of her body and partly because her friendship with John seemed to annoy Leon.

'What does it matter? It's what we want and I'll come to no harm,' she said affectionately. John didn't look too sure. Amused, she rested her hand on his arm and fondly kissed his cheek. 'I'll see you later. I've got your number. I ought to speak to Leon if I'm to visit Lexi before...' she gave him a conspiratorial smile '...before I return to England.'

'I don't like it. Don't make any decisions. Don't agree to anything. Remember his agenda,' John advised sullenly.

'Of course,' she said soothingly. 'I'll—'

'Can we get on?' interrupted Leon irritably.

'We have a man in a hurry!' She smiled at John. 'See you later.'

Leon pointedly opened the door of her lawyer's car but his bad temper didn't disturb her at all. As John drove grumpily away she reflected that this was more than they'd hoped.

Leon's intransigence had been so deeply rooted that she'd thought he'd refuse even to see her. She and John had consequently planned on resorting to the courts for access and they had been resigned to a lengthy legal battle.

In preparation two weeks previously, John had brought in everything she'd need: extra clothes and medication, the dwindling remainder of the money from the sale of the house where she and Taki had lived—and a selection of toys and clothes for Lexi.

But now Leon was agreeing to talk to her! Unable to hide her delight, she turned starry eyes on him.

'I'm grateful for your time, Leon.' Longingly she added, 'How is she?'

Hard eyes sliced into her delight, reminding her that she had a long way to go before she got what she wanted.

'Very well.'

She hesitated, needing to know more. 'Happy?' she asked lightly.

'I'm delirious, thank you,' he mocked, looking nothing of the sort.

Emma bit back her irritation. She'd be able to judge Lexi's state of mind soon enough. Leon might do everything in his power to restrict access, but surely no court would support him? A mother must count for something out here.

'I wondered,' she asked hesitantly, 'do you have any photos?'

The need in her voice was more than obvious. Let him know how much she cared, she thought, wondering why he didn't answer straight away. Leon ought to know how badly she wanted to see Lexi. He might then realise that the courts would recognise that too—and therefore be persuaded that Lexi's life would be enhanced by visits from her birth mother.

She held her breath when his hand slipped into the inner pocket of his jacket. Without a word he handed over a slim leather case. Emma's fingers shook as she slid the photos out and looked at her daughter for the first time in two long years.

'Oh!' she said breathily.

Still a sunny-faced child. Sturdy, laughing, obviously happy. In cute bathing costumes or sweet dresses, with her hair up in delightful bunches or dancing on her shoulders. On a boat, in a pool, surrounded by presents…

So many photos, she thought in wonder, blinking through her tears. Her heart somersaulted. Bleakly she realised that Leon must adore his niece. And…Lexi…would she adore him?

A pain scythed right through her. She fought back a moan. Perhaps she was making a mistake! Horrified, she raised her head to meet his devil-dark stare, her eyes huge with distress.

'Yes, Emma. She's happy. So why smash a child's care-free life?' he asked quietly.

She couldn't answer. A lump sat hard and hurting in her throat. She blinked at him in acute misery as her carefully constructed plans began to tumble down on her head.

John had insisted that Leon always spoke of Lexi as a chattel. Never with love. She knew that Leon had talked about doing his duty in looking after Lexi, and honouring a promise he'd made to his father.

Based on the fact that he'd told her he'd never wanted to assume responsibility for his niece, Emma had assumed that his interest in Lexi was minimal. Naturally she'd believed that Leon's own child must be the favourite and that little Lexi came a very poor second-best.

Whereas the opposite seemed to be true. Leon apparently kept the contents of a photo album on him, every picture depicting Lexi. Her mouth trembled and she touched her injured breast with a faltering hand. Briefly a flash of something indefinable flickered in Leon's eyes. A glint of… triumph?

'Go home,' he murmured softly. 'Save yourself grief. And Lexi. Think of her feelings if you suddenly appear on the scene. The upheaval, the shock…'

He sounded confident, utterly sure that she'd accept the wisdom of his words. She frowned, trying to iron out the discrepancy between John's report and the lovingly collected photographs kept close to Leon's heart.

John wouldn't lie—he had her own best interests at heart. Whereas Leon would do anything to dissuade her. So what was the truth of the matter? How could she be sure that she wasn't about to tear her daughter's life apart?

Her heart cramped. If she ever thought she'd damage Lexi, she'd abandon all plans of abduction. Maybe, she thought in dismay, her journey had been all for nothing!

CHAPTER TWO

EMMA struggled to unravel the truth. Leon couldn't be trusted. It would suit him very well if she gave up and went home, abandoning her child for ever.

She frowned. Something was nagging at the back of her mind. To do with the photos. What could it be? There were a lot. And… Her head lifted as it dawned on her what was wrong. Lexi had been alone in every shot.

'Is she in any other photos you've got? Could you have a look?' she asked, pretending to be dispirited in the hope she'd catch Leon off guard.

'You've seen them all. These are the only ones I have on me.' He purred, sure it seemed, of success.

'Just the ones of Lexi.'

'My beloved niece,' he said with surprisingly believable sincerity, piling on the sentiment.

She could have hit him. That confirmed her theory! Every knotted up muscle in her body relaxed and she stared at him with cold blue eyes.

'How extraordinary! It's a strange father who carries a dozen or so snaps of his niece but none of his own child.' She gave him a sugary smile, seeing that he looked totally disconcerted. Her eyes gleamed. 'Might there be a reason for that?' she murmured.

'What reason could there be?' He growled, an extraordinary tautness bringing his cheekbones into high relief.

'Deception,' she retorted, lashing him with a scathing glance. 'I think that you knew I'd be here and so you deliberately collected the photos to show me—'

'A kind gesture, surely?' He frowned at her.

'Not under the circumstances, no.' she replied, lifting a

36

challenging chin. 'You've made it clear that you don't want me to meet my daughter. Why, then, would you whet my appetite by showing photos of her? To tease me? I think not. You wouldn't risk increasing my desire to see her.'

His eyes blackened. 'How about pride?' he said bitingly. 'To show you how well she is cared for—'

'You don't fool me!' she scoffed. 'John's told me about your indifference to Lexi—'

'Has he, now?' Leon muttered grimly. 'Has he indeed?'

'Yes. And it broke my heart to know she wasn't important to you.'

'She is—'

'Oh, maybe as a Kyriakis, as your brother's child, but not because you feel any love for her. I got the impression she was a nuisance. My *daughter*! That's what's hurt me so much. She's with you because of your wretched pride and because you think you're better than me—'

'That last part is certainly true.'

'We'll see about that!' she said flaring, beside herself with anger. 'Lexi needs me. I'm here to bring some love into my daughter's life.' She choked.

'You'll bring confusion and uncertainty—'

'No, I won't,' she insisted hotly. 'I can't believe you almost succeeded in deterring me. How could I have been so stupid as to doubt my own instincts? You cynically assembled those photos to imply that Lexi is the most important person in your life—'

'She is!' Leon declared furiously, his hands balling into tight fists.

'Pull the other one!' she scorned. Her head was up, her hair flying about her face as she shook with indescribable anger. 'Common sense says that your wife and your own daughter must be dearer to you. You may well flinch. I've sussed you out, haven't I? You're *despicable*, Leon, attempting to prevent her from seeing the one person who can give her real love. I know you begrudge looking after her—and

I'm going to prove it. I can't *believe* you staged this farcical show of devotion!'

'You're wrong about my feelings for Lexi,' he said, his voice vibrating with passion. His eyes glittered. 'And I would warn you to be wary of what Sefton says. He has ulterior motives—'

'Yes. He *cares*!'

'But who for? Just consider carefully everything he says,' Leon said shortly.

'He told me you were sly,' she shot. 'I think that's pretty accurate. Meeting me here *wasn't* a coincidence, was it? I suppose the immigration officer tipped you off so I had to sit about cooling my heels while you ransacked your house for photos of my child.'

'Staphos called me, yes,' he conceded. 'We're fishing buddies. He had a hunch you must be Taki's widow. But I always carry these photos.' He contemplated her thoughtfully. 'I wasn't expecting to see you for another couple of years.' A sardonic curl deepened the etched arches of his mouth. 'Are you on the run?'

She glared. 'Of course not. I was released six months ago.'

'Six months!' he exclaimed with exaggerated surprise. 'And you were so desperate to see your beloved daughter that you dawdled straight here!'

'I've been ill.' She flung the words at him, seething at the injustice of his remark. 'That's why my sentence was reduced.'

'You've recovered remarkably well,' he observed with heavy sarcasm.

'Good nutrition, a healthy lifestyle and a clear conscience!'

'I can believe two out of three,' he mocked.

She couldn't fence with him any more. She felt emotionally drained. Anger and anxiety weren't good for her and she tried to avoid it. Unfortunately there was something about Leon that made her blood boil. Whatever had happened to her self-control? she wondered gloomily. One snarl from Leon and it ran away with its tail between its legs.

'This isn't getting us anywhere,' she said wearily. 'We must come to some arrangement. And I'd rather we talked where I can sit down out of the sun. I'm not fully fit and this heat saps my strength.' Longingly she thought of a long drink in a frosted glass with ice in it. 'Perhaps we can find a taverna.'

Leon shrugged and picked up her case. 'My car's over there. If you insist on wasting your time…'

'Being reunited with my child is hardly a waste of time,' she rebuked icily.

She trudged behind Leon feeling as battered as if she'd gone twenty rounds in a boxing ring. Maybe she'd beaten him in the first battle of wits, but there would be more difficulties put in her way and she must rally her energies and be on full alert.

'Staying long?' He flung the words curtly over his shoulder.

She hurried to catch up, conscious that every taxi driver was watching their progress with interest. Tired of hedging, she decided to be frank.

'As long as it takes.'

He glanced down at her defiant face, his mouth creaking up in a faintly mocking smile.

'Then we'd better find you a home you can grow old and grey in.'

With a groan, Emma slapped her hand to her forehead in dismay. 'I forgot. I've got one. A home, I mean.'

'Where?' he enquired quickly.

She frowned. 'That's the trouble—I don't know. I should have got the address from John before he left. He's found me some cheap rooms to rent in the town.'

'He usually stays at the Hotel Zantos,' Leon commented drily. 'Five star. Two pools. Sauna—'

Emma hardly heard. She was concentrating on staying upright. She'd taken on too much, she realised gloomily. She wasn't fit enough yet for all this hassle. She was dead on her feet and had nowhere to go for a good bath and an extended collapse.

'I've got to call him,' she said wearily. She closed her eyes and gave a heavy sigh. 'Do you have a phone?' she asked in a small voice. 'Please, Leon,' she whispered, on the edge of exhaustion.

He studied her uplifted face, tension stretching the skin over his taut jaw.

'Let's get across the road to the shade of the trees,' he said quietly, as taxis, hire-cars and coaches roared into life, heralding the arrival of another planeload of tourists.

Too feeble, too close to tears to reply, she allowed his proprietorial hand to descend on the small of her back while he shepherded her through the mêlée. His palm burned its imprint into her flesh and when she stumbled in confusion his arm slipped more securely around her waist.

Its instant comfort baffled her even more. He was her adversary and she should cringe from his touch. But then, it had been a long time since a man had held her close, years since she'd felt safe and protected.

Her eyes grew huge. That last occasion had been when she and Leon had been together. He'd kissed her goodbye the night before his engagement to Marina. She remembered it well. Lingering. Loving.

She winced. The wonderful strength and pressure of Leon's arm was a false security. He'd have thrown her to the lions if he could have found some lurking near the hire-cars.

'All right?' he asked quietly when they reached the other side.

His head was bent to hers in query. The soft hairs on her cheek tingled from the drift of his breath. Something warm and disturbing was coiling in her stomach and sharpening her senses even while weakening her body. And then he had dropped the case and was turning her to him with a surprising gentleness.

Without any effort on her part, her eyes closed in response. His breath came warm and quick on her sensitised mouth. She felt like putty in his hands, too tired to fight his hypnotic appeal. It was both wonderful and frightening. She had to get away. Fast.

She opened her eyes a fraction. 'I...I don't feel too good,' she whispered miserably, her heart sinking as she realised that she was too fatigued to successfully plead her case for access.

'In that case, let's forget the taverna and cheap digs and get an upgrade,' he murmured soothingly.

'I just want John,' she said in panic. And to sleep for a hundred years... Her eyes met his and were misted with longing.

'Touching. But you can make do with me.' Tight-lipped again, Leon pushed her resisting body into the car. 'Relax. You'll snap tendons, screwed up like that. What are you worried about? As sure as hell I'm not in a mood for abduction.'

'Once was enough, was it?' she flashed, obstinately remaining stiff as a board in the seat.

'More than.'

Simmering darkly, he leaned across, intent on fastening the seat belt for her. Emma swallowed as first his beautifully smooth golden jaw and then the ever-kissable nape of his neck came to within a hair's breadth of her breathless mouth. Incapable of stopping herself, she inhaled, her senses reeling from the clean, fresh maleness of him.

And she was too weak to protest, too shattered by the journey and, perhaps, the emotional excitement, to prevent him from invading her space and protesting that she was perfectly capable of fastening her own seat belt. Because she wasn't.

Unaccountably panic-stricken, she stared out of the window. It was the upsurge of memories, she thought. Her brain was playing tricks with her body, reminding her of love and tenderness…

Her eyes widened as she saw that her case had been abandoned some distance away. 'My case! It'll be stolen!' she cried in agitation.

He paused, turning to look at her. This close, his eyes seemed as black as newly hacked coal. Suddenly Emma couldn't get her breath, and sat stunned by the impact of the electrical charge that leapt across the gap between them both and which wrenched fiercely at her pained heart.

The man was married. He ought to keep himself switched in neutral, she thought crossly.

'Your case is safe. We're *honest* on this island,' he snapped.

She winced as his words seemed to slide like a cruel knife into her ribs. The seat belt finally slotted into place. Leon moved back with a tantalising waft of lemony soap and a blur of glossy dark hair and polished skin. His hair still curled defiantly at the nape, she saw, remembering his efforts to keep it strictly in check.

Her door slammed. She watched him retrieve the case and stride back, grim-faced. For a moment or two she could breathe again. It was a long time since she'd felt so limp and short of oxygen. Presumably anxiety and the heat had affected her.

Emma groaned. This was bad news. Over the next few days she *must* be able to cope with whatever Leon threw at her. The way things were going, she could well have a court case to cope with.

After that, if she eventually won access, she'd need to be at her physical peak if she was to respond to Lexi's needs.

Emma let out a deep sigh. She'd intended to hire a car and take her daughter to the beach. There they could make sandcastles, play in the water and generally have a good time.

However long it took, she meant to forge a strong and loving relationship with Lexi. She knew she could do that.

Her love for her child had survived despite the long separation. Her illness had intensified the knowledge that only one
thing in the world mattered: being with her emotion-starved
daughter and showing her what it was like to be truly loved.

She leaned back, worried. There was so much to do before
Lexi was safe in England. There would be the hazardous
journey with Lexi and John: boat-hopping up the chain of
Ionian Islands, a secret landing on the Greek coast and then
the long drive across Europe.

Throughout the trip she'd have to be focussed exclusively
on Lexi, playing games to pass the time, keeping her amused
and happy so that it all seemed great fun.

It had sounded perfectly feasible back in England. The
route had been mapped, John had returned from his recce
with an optimistic report on secluded coves and rarely used
roads. But… She bit her lip. If she wasn't strong enough—
if she fell ill…

Horribly daunted by what lay ahead, she passed a shaking
hand over her forehead as Leon slid into the driver's seat.
Doubts multiplied. If she lacked energy she'd never cope.
Lexi would feel abandoned and bewildered.

Her breath caught in a choking anguish in her throat. The
thought of failure made her feel sick.

'You look shot to pieces. I think you need cheap digs like
a hole in the head,' he commented shrewdly, starting up the
car.

'A luxury hotel would be preferable, but beyond my
funds,' she retorted, wallowing crossly in the ambitious
thought of a soft bed, room service and an *en suite* bathroom.

'Wait and see what I can come up with,' he said, sounding
smug. 'If you don't like where I take you, we'll ring your
lawyer and get you to his rat-infested hovel instead.'

'Promise,' she mumbled, almost past caring about rats as
long as there was a mattress to rest her weary body.

She let out a long and whispering sigh and felt his dark
glance on her parted lips.

'On my father's head,' he said softly. 'Take a break for now,' he added, as if soothing a fractious child. 'Sleep. I'll wake you when we arrive.'

Emma did her best to disobey but felt her heavy lids closing like shutters. Yet Leon's image stayed to torment her remorselessly: the classic Greek profile, thick lashes concealing liquid black eyes, patrician nose and achingly sensual mouth. Before getting into the car he'd removed his jacket, his open-necked cream shirt moulding to his muscular back and torso.

Her breath quickened. He was dangerously attractive. Tension hung in the air so thickly she could feel it. Even from a short distance away his magnetism poured over her like a relentless tide till she felt she might drown beneath it.

But why was he being considerate? It would amuse him to see her living in the hovel he'd so mockingly described. She racked her brains to determine why he was going out of his way to find her decent accommodation. And could only come up with one answer. For some reason, as yet unknown to her, it suited him.

And therefore his offer should be rejected. Hovel it was, then, she thought glumly.

Music filtered drowsily into her subconscious. Gentle zithers, a haunting refrain. She felt herself relaxing and began to surrender to desperately needed sleep.

Lexi was close, she thought dreamily. Almost in her arms. Another huge sigh of pleasure was expelled from her soft lips and, although she slept, her hands unconsciously sought refuge at her wounded left breast.

Leon shook his head to clear it. He'd be fine if he kept remembering that there was vengeance in her soul. She'd do anything to hurt him. And Lexi was the weapon she'd choose.

He knew he couldn't keep mother and daughter apart. Eventually the court would be faced with Emma's doting mother act and grant access. His only hope was if he could convince them she was not a reformed character.

He glanced at her then scowled at the road ahead, trying to eradicate the sight of her lush breasts swelling beneath her dress. He ached from wanting her. But that was out of the question.

He dragged his mind back to the problem. Emma would visit Lexi and one day make an abduction attempt. He thought of the vulnerable little Lexi being hauled across Europe with two strangers and his chest expanded with uncontainable rage. Sefton was a creep. He didn't trust him an inch.

He had to keep Emma away. And to do that, he needed clear evidence that she wasn't fit to go near his niece and that any contact would be harmful.

His pulses quickened. An idea was forming in his mind. One that would kill two birds with one stone.

He too had a weapon. Sex.

CHAPTER THREE

'IT's lovely,' Emma said longingly, wandering around the villa's elegant sitting area in awe. Quality floor tiles. Stunning traditional furniture, heavily carved, the sofas invitingly squishy and with huge cushions she could picture herself sinking into... She groaned. Heaven. 'But I can't possibly stay...'

'Let me make you some tea,' called Leon from the kitchen area beyond. 'Then I'll explain the set-up.'

'Tea!' She sighed, instantly seduced by the sound of a kettle being filled. 'OK. Then I must call John,' she insisted, being ruthless with herself. And very annoyed by the wistful note that had crept into her voice.

She paused, even more irritated to be disconcerted by the breadth of Leon's tautly muscled back as he stretched up to one of the blue-painted units. It was a back. Gorgeous, granted, but nothing to quiver about.

'I expect there's some chocolate cake somewhere,' he mused, bending to search in one of the lower cupboards.

In doing so he provided her with an unwanted but riveting view of his neat and muscular rear beneath the straining material of his linen trousers. She primmed her mouth in exasperation.

His body had been spectacular. Still was. She really must get out more. Appalled at her rampaging pulses, she did an about turn and concentrated on her suspicions.

'Just where and what is this place? I doubt I can afford it,' she remarked coolly, parking herself at the stylish marble dining table adorned with blue china pots of all shapes and sizes. She picked one up. It was Chinese. 'Leon!' she cried, breathless with hope and abandoning her assumed indifference. 'Is this your house?'

He glanced amiably at her, the dazzle of his beautiful smile raising her blood pressure a few notches. She glared it back down again where it belonged.

'It's mine,' he replied. 'But not where I live.'

What did that mean? she wondered, while he put a temptingly rich dark cake and two plates on the table in front of her. He seemed very much at home, very familiar with the place.

Leon pulled out one of the wrought iron chairs opposite her and sat down on the comfortable linen cushion, his muscular arms resting on the table. Emma dragged her fascinated gaze away from their tanned strength and obliterated all thought of being held by those arms.

But her treacherous body had remembered the fluttering of her heart when he'd escorted her across the road earlier, and the almost intimate pressure of his firm hand. And so she found her voice stupidly husky when she asked what had just occurred to her.

'I hope this isn't a secret hideaway for your mistress?'

His eyes glowed. 'My...mistress?' he said slowly.

It was crazy, but she had the distinct impression that he was thinking of her in that role. Perhaps he remembered how good they'd been... Her breath rasped in, every bone and sinew in her body back in memory lane. Blue eyes locked with brown. He was remembering too, she realised in panic, shaken by his blatant hunger.

'Leon!' she said croakingly and furiously cleared her throat. 'I don't know why you've brought me here, but if it's to...to...'

'To what?' He smiled beguilingly. 'Why don't you indulge?'

She blinked, eyes wide and alarmed. 'In...what?'

'Cake,' he said, purring, with the charming, lopsided smile

which had weakened her knees on countless occasions before. 'What did you imagine I meant?'

She blushed. But she wasn't mistaken. She knew desire when she saw it. Knowing Leon's arrogant assumption that all women would come running if he snapped his fingers, knowing how little he respected her in particular, she was sure he was expecting her to say, Yes, please, and, Thank you, when he made a move on her.

He probably assumed that because she'd been deprived of male company for some time, she was up for grabs. And, she remembered grimly, he'd used her purely for sexual pleasure before.

'I'm not hungry,' she said haughtily. He could make of that what he liked.

'I am.'

She flashed a sharp glance at him. His teeth were biting into the chocolate cake, but his tone had been laden with throaty sexuality. That was why she was here, then. For a bit of slap and tickle.

Misery washed over her, far out of proportion to her disappointment in his motives. For a brief moment she had thought that he was being nice to her in finding somewhere for her to stay. But he did want to use her again. She felt like crying.

'You eat away, then,' she said. 'While I call John. Where's the phone?'

His hand caught her arm in a gentle but inescapable grip. 'Hold on a moment. You can't turn down a chance like this. You want somewhere to stay, don't you?'

She shivered. Something hot and fierce ricocheted between them, ripping through her tense body and cutting her legs from beneath her. Incapable of staying on her feet, she collapsed into the chair again. But, as she did so, his fingers slithered up the softness of her arm.

Before she could stop herself, she let out a gasp. The sensation had been electrifying, every cell in her body responding as if they had been individually charged. Appalled, she wrenched herself free, her mouth tight with disapproval. She knew his game. And would resist.

'Not with strings attached. I'll take the hovel and its rats rather than your love nest and you.'

'This has never been a love nest,' he said, his voice soft and low. It vibrated deeply into her fractured nerves, soothing them. And alarming her even more. 'It's just one of four villas I've had built for the holiday trade. Diversification.'

She wasn't convinced. Too much valuable china. Sensationally beautiful drapes at the windows. Kitchen equipment to die for. Terracotta busts in niches. Murano glass lampshades and hand-carved furniture. Holiday trade!

'Luxury market, presumably?' she scorned in disbelief.

'Of course.'

'So where are the occupants? The designer-label buckets and spades?'

'It's not quite finished and nobody's used it yet,' he explained, his mouth quirking up in amusement.

'Except for whoever's partial to tea and chocolate cake,' she muttered.

'My…designer used this as a base.'

'Ah. I understand. Female, blonde and beautiful?' she asked sourly before she could stop herself.

His eyes seemed to bore into her skull. 'The description fits her.' He smiled faintly. 'Does that bother you, Emma?'

'It ought to bother your wife,' she pointed out, hating herself for minding. He was dangerous. A womaniser with an overactive sex drive. And, she thought indignantly, her daughter was in his care!

'Ex-wife,' he corrected softly.

Her eyes widened in astonishment. 'Oh. I didn't know…' Emma tried to interpret his expression but it was unreadable. She remembered only too vividly how her own marriage had disintegrated, leaving scars and recriminations behind. And now…yes, there was a hint of pain in his eyes. Her face softened in sympathy. 'I am sorry, Leon. It's—'

'I don't want to talk about it.'

'No. Of course not…'

Extraordinarily, Emma wanted to comfort him. He seemed…tense, perhaps caught up in his own grief.

'Stay,' he urged.

She didn't dare. He was fancy-free and twice as dangerous. Loathe to drag herself out again, she raised her hands in a helpless gesture.

'I can't let John down. He's gone to all that trouble—'

'Not *very* much trouble, I imagine,' Leon said cynically.

'I said I'd phone him—'

'But this is so much more convenient than somewhere in town, twenty minutes away,' he argued. And temptingly he added, 'We're actually on my land, Emma. My house is the other side of the olive grove.'

Her eyes rounded in a wildly revived hope. What was he implying? He wouldn't let her come this close to his house if he didn't intend to let her see Lexi, would he? Or was this a cruel joke, to tease her with, before letting her down—the so-near-and-yet-so-far trick?

'It sounds too perfect. Why bring me here?' she asked suspiciously.

'Simple.' He threw her one of his devastating smiles. 'I thought that if you're to be on the island then you might as well be somewhere I can keep an eye on you.'

She glared. 'I'm to be spied on!'

He shrugged. 'You're not doing anything you shouldn't, are you?' He waited for her to comment but she just stared doggedly, refusing to be drawn. She watched him dig deep into his range of smiles and select one that was utterly persuasive and suspiciously benign. 'It's rent-free and near your daughter,' he informed her. 'Can you afford to turn my offer down?'

'Depends who I share with,' she said warily, very much tempted.

'No one. Other than whoever you invite.' He reached across the table, his fingers almost touching hers. But not quite. She looked at them, dazed, every nerve in her body tingling as she waited for his hand to inch a little closer. 'You'd like to be close to Lexi, wouldn't you?' he coaxed.

Brute! She stared helplessly, her heart lurching as she imagined little tea parties with Lexi here... A walk to the nearby village—if there was one—for ice creams...

'Yes...' She choked. How could she trust him? 'But—'

'I'll make the tea while you think about it,' he said with warm understanding.

Too warm. He was up to something. 'I've thought. I don't want to be spied on,' she said reluctantly, common sense overruling her yearning heart.

He brought over a blue and white teapot and pulled his chair even closer to hers, studying her with an expression of concern.

'But, Emma, you're tired. You don't feel well.' His voice did its stroking act on her, evoking a dangerous need for sympathy and a shoulder to lean on. 'Surely,' he murmured, 'you don't want to go charging across the countryside to find Sefton's nasty little rented room?'

No. She didn't. But she'd have to. The thought of it made her feel weak. 'So you're Sir Galahad now, are you?' she muttered.

He gave a small chuckle that made him seem eminently harmless and friendly. But she knew better.

'Hardly. But see it from my point of view. Supposing you're taken ill in some backstreet dump in Zante town? How would that look? There'd be a scandal when it gets out what our relationship is.'

'Oh. Your precious reputation!' she snapped waspishly.

'Absolutely.' He leaned forwards earnest-faced, apparently unaware of her sarcasm. 'It would be unforgivable if I did not offer hospitality to my late brother's wife, whatever I think of her, whatever she has done.'

Thoughtfully she picked up a slice of cake. 'That makes sense,' she remarked, nibbling off the layer of chocolate icing reflectively. She saw him smiling to see her eating despite her declaration that she wasn't hungry. And went for the kill. 'You can't afford to have the courts thinking you're vindictive.'

'Courts?' he asked, raising his brows. His smile was pure charm as he turned her gibe back on her. 'I hope we can come to an arrangement without their involvement.'

Her heart thudded with excitement. But she kept her head.

'You were worried about Lexi's welfare earlier on,' she declared. 'What's changed your mind?'

He raised expressive shoulders and poured out the tea. 'You. I did everything I could to dissuade you but obviously you're determined to see her, come hell or high water. I can't stop you. You *are* her mother. If I forbid you to see her and you put in a complaint then tongues would wag—'

'Bad for your reputation,' she suggested, seeing that this could work in her favour.

'My honour would be tarnished. No one would understand that my motives were purely in Lexi's interests. I don't like this, Emma. But providing we go about this sensitively, I don't see how I can decently refuse.'

Her eyes shone as his words sank into her tired brain. 'Oh, *Leon*!' she gasped, overwhelmed.

He pushed the crumbs around his plate with his forefinger. 'Don't imagine you're having things all your own way. Having conceded the *possibility* of access, I want to hammer out the when and how and what with *you*—and not some lawyer.' His voice lowered. 'She's too important to be stuck in the middle of an unpleasant legal tussle. And I prefer to have some say in what happens to her. So we do this on my terms. Understood?'

Emma stared. She could hardly believe that he was actually acknowledging her rights at last. And if they could do this amicably then it would save time—and thousands of pounds in fees. She would be spending time with Lexi—with Leon's blessing—and her daughter would be back in England sooner than she'd ever imagined.

Her smile grew in magnitude till it irradiated her face. 'Thank you,' she said breathily. 'I agree. I don't want her upset either. I just want to see her, Leon.'

'So you'll stay here in this villa,' he said quietly.

'Yes! Yes!'

She was crying and laughing. He didn't know what to do. She sat there, tears trickling down her cheeks, obviously trying to control herself. And failing. The point of her tongue slid out to capture each silvery droplet and Leon felt an extraordinary lurch of sentiment and compassion before he realised these were probably tears of exhaustion.

And that he could use this moment to his advantage.

He felt a brief sense of distaste but something else—perhaps sympathy, perhaps desire—drove him to push back his chair and bend over her.

He'd had to concede more than he'd wanted. But she was on his land, under his eyes, subject to his demands. It could have been worse. Under Sefton's guidance, she would have gone to the courts and perhaps won unsupervised access. She might have told Lexi immediately who she was. And that wasn't in his plan at all.

Gently he wiped her eyes, steeling himself to ignore her startled look and the appealing flutter of her wet lashes. With great care he dabbed at her face and leaned close to wipe her mouth.

It took great self-control not to kiss her. It was too soon.

'Now we've got that out of the way, why don't you drink your tea and I'll show you around?' he suggested, far too huskily for his liking. He mustn't frighten her away.

'Oh, Leon!' she said breathily, almost ruining his plan by

turning starry eyes on him. 'I'm so glad we're not at daggers drawn any longer!'

He had to move away. And hide his shamed face. He hated this but he didn't see any other way. Deception wasn't in his nature and it went against everything he stood for. But he'd do this for Lexi. She had to be protected from Emma.

'Come and see the view. It's worth staying for alone,' he said, managing to sound hearty, and he flung open the back door.

'*Oh-h-h!*'

Tears forgotten, Emma jumped up, enchanted. Framed by the doorway was a sunken terrace surrounding a swimming pool, its water an invitingly clear aquamarine. Flowers tumbled in profusion from Ali Baba pots around it and already she could smell the scented breeze that ruffled the leaves of the orange and lemon trees shading one end of the terrace.

Stretching across the skyline she could see a range of green undulating hills. And from their wooded slopes, to the citrus orchard beyond the pool lay a fertile valley filled with silvery olives and vines and the tall, pencil-slim shapes of dark cypress trees. One lone and magnificent cypress had been planted strategically by the pool, and it soared like a malachite rocket into the bright blue sky.

'You like?' Leon enquired close by.

She'd drifted to the doorway to gape without knowing it. The view was affecting her strangely. She felt calm and at peace, almost as if she was responding emotionally to the timeless beauty of the landscape. Perhaps because she was so keyed up.

But it *was* stunning. She could spend hours drinking it in, smelling the scents on the warm breeze, feeling the sun on her tired body.

'I like,' she murmured with quiet fervour, her eyes dreamy.

'You can swim any time, night or day. It's quite private,' Leon said.

She saw herself in the turquoise water, letting it ripple over her skin. Her eyes glazed, her thoughts racing. She'd buy one of those blow-up chairs for the pool. A ball. She could see herself and her daughter; laughing, splashing, cuddling…

'Does Lexi like the water?' she asked, suddenly horribly aware that she knew nothing about her child. Her nerves began to jangle. This wouldn't be easy…

'Swims like a fish. She'll love it here,' he assured her. 'Better than a hovel?'

She grinned. 'I'm sure John chose somewhere utterly charming and cosy,' she defended.

Leon took her elbow. 'Forget him. Come and explore. There's a ground-floor bedroom this way, with its own terrace and bathroom,' he said, guiding her through to the living room end.

'I'm not quite sure what's happened. You were so hostile when we met,' she mused, reluctant to believe in his conversion. 'I was somewhere to the left of Satan's auntie.'

He chuckled, smiling down at her and she wished he wouldn't. His hand slid casually up her arm and his fingers absently stroked her sensitised skin. It was all she could do not to let out a gasp but she kept it lodged in her chest, hard and hurting.

'I know. Can you blame me? I have to protect Lexi's interests.' He smiled again, less certainly, but the warmth in his eyes melted her doubts. 'But I realise now that I have no choice. For Lexi's sake we must try to be civil to one another.'

Emma released her breath and smiled back, deliriously happy. In these surroundings, away from Leon's interference, she could spend long hours with Lexi. Picnics. Reading stories. Learning about her child. She felt dizzy with excitement.

'When can I see her, Leon?' she asked eagerly.

'Bath, shower and so on through there, bedroom here…' he went on, urging her forward as if he hadn't heard. A light came on in the darkened room. 'What do you think?'

Spectacular. His designer had an enviable style. She couldn't believe her luck.

She glanced around the spacious bedroom with its cool tiles and beautifully carved four-poster. Leon had detached himself and was drawing back the two sets of fine lawn drapes—royal blue and a contrasting white to tone in with the colour scheme in the room. He lifted the latch of the full-length shutters and the room was instantly bright with sunshine.

'Terrace.' His arm swept out in an invitation.

Emma pushed aside the fluttering drapes and went out. She murmured something complimentary about the fabulous roses and persevered.

'I'd like to meet Lexi tomorrow,' she said firmly.

'Of course. Come upstairs.'

She was dumbfounded. Ecstatic! Had it really been that easy? 'Leon!' she cried in glee, hurrying after his retreating figure. 'Do you really mean that?'

At the top of the stairs he turned and she, lost in her world of dreams and delight, almost bumped into him.

'Whoa!' he said, amused.

His hands steadied her and the dancing light in his eyes clouded. Emma could feel the heavy pulses in his thumbs where they pressed into the soft flesh of her arms. She wilted beneath his silence, the intensity of his gaze liquefying her bones and driving all sense out of her head.

'Leon…'

She felt him quiver. His name had been but a whisper from her dry throat. The sexual tension held her as his captive, and she found her head tipping back so that her hair flowed down her back like ribbons of honey. A gesture of surrender.

Bewildered, she tried in vain to say something banal to hide her overwhelming desire to be kissed by those laughing, edible lips. But all she could do was to stare into his eyes, her mouth ready and her entire body waiting, hoping.

'I think,' he muttered brusquely, suddenly whisking away

and collecting her case, 'you're overtired. I'll put this in the downstairs bedroom for you and then I'll leave you in peace—'

'Yes,' she croaked hastily, horrified and shame-faced at her shocking reaction. She *was* tired. Emotionally muddled. That was it. Mortified, she realised that Leon must have interpreted the message in her eyes—in her explicit body language. And yet he'd rejected the chance to kiss her.

She stood in the middle of the room, scarlet to the roots of her hair. Clearly, she'd been wrong about him. Maybe he had flirted. Or perhaps he couldn't help projecting sex appeal. Or she'd wanted… Yes, she had to admit—shaming though it was—that she found him intensely attractive.

It was perfectly possible then that she'd read all the wrong things in the way he'd looked at her. It was the only explanation. Because when she'd let her hunger surface, he'd been horrified because he genuinely despised her.

Was that it? Her mind was so befuddled and tired she couldn't think straight. She had to explain…

He was already in the bedroom, slamming down her case. In a temper, it seemed—annoyed that he'd got himself trapped with a sex-starved wimp. She inhaled several times to calm herself. She'd almost made a disastrous mistake.

'I'm so exhausted I hardly know what I'm doing,' she called, her voice genuinely shaky.

'Thought so. You'll need food. I'll have some things delivered.'

Nerves jangling, she waited till he emerged, avoiding her eyes. Her brain was beginning to function again. He'd said he was leaving… She felt a stab of fear when she realised that she didn't know where she was.

'You…you haven't dumped me somewhere inaccessible?' she asked anxiously as he strode purposefully to the door and opened it. For all she knew, his house was miles away. And she had no transport. She was virtually a prisoner… 'Leon, don't leave me!' she began in panic.

His burning gaze flicked to meet hers. He said nothing, but he didn't have to. She knew shock when she saw it. Emma's hand flew to her mouth.

'I meant… I—meant…' she stammered incoherently.

'Later,' he said thickly. And marched out.

Later, she thought. Later…what? Had he said, See you later, and she'd missed the first part? He had mumbled.

She stood with her eyes closed, waiting for the waves of warmth to stop running in her veins and directing her leaping pulses to settle down. Foolishly she thought of him and instantly the sensations returned: the hammering heartbeat, the sense of reckless abandon, the terrible desire to melt into his arms.

The past was not done with. Because he'd left her so abruptly all those years ago, she had never really wiped him from her memory. Taki had accused her of that once, when she'd refused his drunken attentions.

'It's him!' he'd screamed, totally losing control. 'You think of him when we make love. You speak his name in your sleep!'

She'd been horrified. Because it was true—she *had* thought of Leon and his tender, passionate and sensitive love-making. It had been the only way to cope with Taki's rough and coarse approach. And her silence had fuelled Taki's anger.

He had taken her then, brutally stifling her cries with a crushing hand. But he'd never touched her again.

She shuddered. Her knowledge of men was minimal. Just the two brothers. One who'd taken her beyond herself, to the outermost reaches of pleasure. The other had kept her too close to harsh reality, the discomfort, the ugliness, the baseness of sex.

So, she mused, she had mistakenly put Leon and his ability to arouse her in a category he didn't deserve. All these years, despite her hatred of him, she'd thought of him as a great lover. And now she was face to face with him again, that myth was being perpetuated in her stupid brain.

Idiot. He couldn't be the only man in the world who took his time and was unselfish! It was just technique. Nothing more. And she *had* missed sex, and was very much in her prime, so all she had to do was to keep her distance from him and concentrate on Lexi.

She heaved a huge sigh and forced herself to begin unpacking. Halfway through, she realised she was shaking with fatigue, her strength sapped by the long and tension-filled day. Wearily she stripped off her clothes and showered, then closed the bedroom shutters to exclude the light. Fumbling in the darkness, she slid thankfully into bed.

Maybe she had no idea where she was on the island. But in a few hours she'd be seeing her child. She felt a lurch of apprehension in her chest and tried not to think about it yet. Her instincts would direct her.

Two years was a long time. So much had happened! In the warm darkness her fingers tentatively touched the deep scar on her breast, with its pinpoint tattoo marks which had guided the radiographer.

She'd been lucky. She might have died if the lump hadn't been discovered in time. And she was almost well again. The skin wasn't red there any more and the soreness had gone— the nausea too. Only the tiredness persisted and soon that would go too.

When the lump in her breast was diagnosed as malignant, she'd had just one reaction. Not fear for her own life, not regret or anger, but, *I want to see my child if I am to die.*

Well, she'd cheated death. In fact, she had a normal life-expectation. The future stretched ahead invitingly and she counted her blessings every single day. Every hour, she had vowed, would be lived to the full. She wouldn't waste the precious gift of life.

The thought of dying prematurely had stripped her world to the bone. Some things were important, most were trivial.

It didn't matter if it rained. She was there to see it, to feel and smell it. It didn't matter if a bus or a train was late. She was there to catch the next one.

But Lexi…she *was* important. Emma felt the passion fill her heart. She must have her child back, for both their sakes. Leon didn't care for anything other than his precious honour and reputation. Only she, Emma, would devote herself utterly to Lexi. Only she could truly love her child.

Leon would also realise that after a short while, she mused. He'd see her with Lexi and… Her heart thundered as her thoughts leapt ahead. Perhaps he'd even surrender Lexi willingly and she could forget the idea of abduction! The thought of going through with that terrified her now. But she would, if she had to.

Deeply happy, she conjured up the image of her daughter, now burned indelibly into her mind from the photographs she'd seen. Lexi was gorgeous. Emma's eyes glistened with tears. And she couldn't *wait* to see her in reality.

'Tomorrow, sweetheart!' she promised, as she curled up in the big, comfortable bed. 'The first day of our lives together.'

No more pain. No heartbreak. Just Lexi.

She'd never been happier. Everything she wanted lay within her grasp. Life was good again. Emma let out a deep, satisfied sigh. And let sleep enfold her.

CHAPTER FOUR

WHEN she woke it was a moment or two before she remembered where she was. By then she was aware of noises in the living room. She clutched the sheet to her chest, listening in alarm.

Leon had a key. The designer-blonde, presumably. Who else?

Wary of being surprised by a drug-crazed burglar whilst still stark naked, she slipped her feet to the floor and felt her way to where she'd left her clothes.

'Bother!' she said, yelping, when her fumbling hand knocked her small glass pill pots and her camera to the tiled floor.

'Emma? Are you all right?'

Leon, she registered in relief. But she couldn't find the pills. Didn't know if they'd spilled out... Worse, if anyone on the island stocked the unusual remedies...

'Emma,' bellowed the voice, right by the door.

'No, I'm not all right,' she yelled, still grovelling. At least it was only Leon. *Only!* 'Yes, I'm fine.' she cried, locating the tiny pots—intact. 'Don't come in,' she squealed in panic. 'Where's the light? Oh, darn it, where—?'

'I'm coming in!'

She heard the door handle turning. '*No!* I'm not *dressed*!'

There was a silence. The handle creaked back into place again and she grabbed the sheet, twisting it around her body securely before heading for the direction of the door. For a moment she hesitated then eased it open to find Leon apparently frozen to the spot on the other side.

'I knocked something over,' she explained with rather

61

breathless dignity, as his startled gaze flicked over her mummified figure. 'I couldn't find the light switch.'

He drew in a long, slow breath. 'Left of door.'

'Thanks.' She located it but decided to leave herself in relative shadow. She frowned, and broke the stiff silence. 'What exactly are you doing here?'

Leon seemed to be interested in the space just above her head. 'I brought your groceries. Supper. Breakfast.'

'Supper?' Startled, she looked at her watch. It was nine-thirty. Presumably, since the light was on in the living room, it was evening rather than morning. 'Oh. That's really kind of you, but…' This was awkward. Uncertain as to the etiquette of such a situation, she decided on a graceful retreat and a regrouping. 'Stay there. I'll be out in a minute.'

Closing the door she flicked on the light and hastily unwound the sheet. Supper. Was he staying? Her pulses began their remorseless tattoo and she gritted her teeth to outwit them. But she couldn't ignore her tingling, naked body and stomped to the wardrobe to find something to wear.

For some reason she was sorting through her clothes and tossing up between her only two decent outfits. A flirty red dress with a cleavage-displaying bodice and short skirt which she'd bought from a second-hand shop when she'd been several pounds thinner, and a green halter-neck top whose matching skirt slunk closely over her hips to the floor.

Or there was always a nice, safe shirt and jeans.

She smiled ruefully. Who was she kidding? She'd seen Leon. He'd been wearing a long-sleeved cream shirt with a toffee-coloured tie and beautifully cut trousers in a dark honey shade. With toning shoes.

Green, she decided impetuously, wriggling into the top. At least most of her was covered, except for her back which was hardly an erogenous zone.

She, too, could look groomed and expensive. She, too, was worthy to be a Kyriakis. Leon couldn't complain that she wasn't good enough for Lexi in this, she thought, reaching back to knot the ties securely.

'Sure you're OK?'

She flung up her tousled head. 'Yes. Coming.' And grabbed the skirt. Her fingers stilled as an awful realisation dawned. No bra—because of the low back. Mini briefs because of visible panty line. Help! How unwise could she be?

'I've put the potatoes on.'

'What?'

'Do you want aubergine salad or feta for starters?'

Starters? 'Aubergine,' she shouted. 'But—'

Her fingers dithered. She could wear the top with jeans— '*Stifado*, OK?'

Muttering under her breath, she hauled the skirt up and fastened its zip hastily. He was safe. He'd proved that earlier. She wanted to look her best. And she was starving.

'Depends what that is,' she said uncertainly, walking barefoot to where Leon stood, chopping and stirring.

'Beef. Red wine, garlic, onions, tomatoes and bay…'

He looked. And looked away fast, ruthlessly attacking the garlic innocently waiting for the pestle. Something had happened to his breathing system.

'Leon,' she said, unnervingly close. About two feet away, he reckoned. He'd have preferred twenty. Or the next village. 'I—I don't like to be difficult, but…I only eat organic food. It might sound cranky, but I don't want my body to deal with pesticides—'

'This is from my land,' he told her. 'It's completely organic, so there aren't any chemicals or pesticides and I don't think it's cranky at all. I think people should make up their own minds about what they eat. But it makes sense to play safe with children. I keep an eye on the things Lexi eats.'

She beamed, impressed and surprised. 'I'm really pleased. That means so much to me.' She surveyed his preparations. 'Leon, this is totally unexpected. You're being unnecessarily generous,' she said warmly.

He could see her bare arm out of the corner of his eye. It was smooth and golden and he wanted to touch it. Melt his mouth along it. Now.

The garlic suffered a ferocious pulverising.

'The main course was virtually cooked. My supper from home. You needed to eat and so did I. And we had to talk before you met up with Lexi.'

Frowning, he mixed the garlic with the lemon juice and herbs, wishing he could beat the hell out of it with a hand whisk and get rid of his tightly suppressed physical energy.

He'd thought he could handle this, that his desire to kiss her could be mastered. It was vital that it didn't look as if he was taking the initiative. But she was tearing into his self-control with every breath she took and every glance from those soft blue eyes.

She drifted somewhere behind him and the hairs rose on the back of his neck. And that wasn't all. He gritted his teeth, knowing he must get a grip of himself.

The seduction *must* seem to be her idea. Then he could go to the courts and block her attempts to see Lexi again, on the grounds that she was amoral. If he was going to huff and pant like an adolescent male over centrefolds then his plan wouldn't work.

'Leon.' She touched his arm and he jumped.

'What?'

'You *are* engrossed in the cooking.' She laughed, her face, her smile, her beautiful body right next to him. 'I said, who's looking after Lexi?'

He moved away and slammed a pan on for the rice. 'Marina.'

'Your ex-wife.' There was a chilly pause. 'You're on friendly terms with her, then?' she asked, but it was clear from her dubious tone that she didn't like the arrangement.

What did he tell her? At least, he thought ruefully, the mere mention of Marina had sent his hormones into hiding.

He felt able to face the green goddess without revealing his intentions.

'We still live together in the same house.'

'Good grief!' she cried, not unnaturally stunned.

'It's a large house.'

'Are you together for the sake of your daughter?' she asked, her eyes still wide with surprise.

'Yes,' he said in a low tone. 'For Soula's sake.'

Emma absorbed this for a moment. 'And how does Lexi fit into this?'

She was beautiful. No make-up but perfect skin, tousled hair straight from bed, making him think—

'Oh, dear. What's wrong?' she asked anxiously, noting his eyes were fixed intently upon her.

'Your hair. Not wrong…' His voice petered out.

She had raised her hands to her sexily tumbling waves, the action lifting her breasts to high, hard-tipped globes beneath the clinging material. She was near-naked, he thought, his throat drying.

'Bother. Sort of ruins my attempt at looking half decent. You mentioned food and out I rushed without brushing my hair.' She sighed. 'Tells you my priorities. I'll go and—'

'Don't. Leave it. It's only me,' he muttered, turning abruptly to weigh the rice.

His hands were shaking so much that he spilt half of it all over the tiled floor. Laughing, Emma searched the cupboards for a dustpan and he found himself having to cope with the sight of her slim, curvy rear outlined far too temptingly for any man to resist.

But he did his best to keep his hands to himself. What, however, was *she* doing? Seducing *him?* The dress… Her smiles… He sawed in a harsh breath. This was perfect.

He stared at the rice and couldn't remember if he'd weighed it or not. So he started all over again. Perhaps they'd be making love very soon, he thought, and was startled by his elation.

Emma was glad to be scrabbling on the floor. Leon seemed distracted. Almost curt. Perhaps he thought she'd jump him. Better put his mind at rest. And there was nothing better, she decided, than to talk about another man in warm and glowing terms.

'John's a good cook,' she offered, standing up flushed from her exertions.

A dark look. 'Oh, yes?'

'He makes the definitive spag. bol.,' she said with feeling, remembering how delicious it had been.

'I imagine a few Italians might disagree with you.'

Emma giggled at his dry comment. Then she continued with her paeans of praise, to make Leon think that she had a particular interest in John.

'I rate him very highly,' she said with genuine fondness and a faraway look in her eyes. He had been wonderful. Her rock. 'Not many lawyers would be so dedicated to their clients. I think I told you that I owe my freedom to him.'

Leon snorted. She was losing him, his attention directed to preparing the meal. Providing supper was evidently an attempt to meet her halfway, but his heart wasn't in it. That was understandable, she thought. He didn't want Lexi to be hurt.

Well, she'd have to coax him round. Make him see that she wasn't a monster but sensitive and caring. She'd pull out all the stops. That should do it.

She tipped the rice into the bin and washed her hands. 'Anything I can do to help?' she asked amiably.

'It's all done. Meat's heating up. Waiting for the rice and potatoes.'

'Then,' she said eagerly, grabbing an opened bottle of red wine and a couple of glasses, 'let's sit down and talk strategy.'

He seemed reluctant but after checking the oven he joined her and grudgingly accepted the glass of wine. Worried about the rigidity of his muscles, she decided to loosen him up a little and kicked off by curling up on the settee.

'Cheers,' she said merrily, hoping he'd be softened by her winning smile.

'Giamas.' He raised his glass, drank, and put it on the table beside him.

His mouth was moist with wine. She realised she was the one who was softening. 'Yammas,' she repeated throatily.

He looked at her, his eyes dark and glowing. She drew in a shuddery little breath, shaken by the bolt of heat which had hurled itself at her defenceless body.

Her wineglass slipped from her numb fingers and like lightning Leon sprang forward to save it, his left hand splaying out to shield her dress from splashes as he caught the glass in mid-air. Sitting in a state of paralysis, she could feel the heel of his hand pressing into the upper swell of her breast, burning, *burning*.

He didn't move a muscle. She stared at him, her eyes huge with confusion and he stared back. It was as if she were drugged, her lashes lowering drowsily, lips parting as she gasped for snatches of air. It was happening again, she thought helplessly, and could do nothing to stop it.

Their mouths were inches apart. She could feel the very heat of his body, was breathing his breath, being drawn by his magnetism closer, closer...

His hand lifted its pressure from her breast. It seemed he tore his gaze from hers. She blinked, high spots of colour reddening her cheekbones as he put her glass next to his and used his clean handkerchief to dab at the few splashes of wine on her bare shoulder.

'Woops,' she said in a feeble croak.

Leon slanted her a sideways glance and her pulses went haywire again. 'It was water last time,' he said huskily.

'Nerves.' She'd said too much.

Balanced on his haunches, far too near for her sanity, he

wiped the wine droplets from his own hand and studied her for a paralysing second or two.

'Why would you be nervous, Emma?'

She swallowed. Because something crazy was going on. A madness had possessed her. And she didn't like it, didn't want it, was terrified...

He put a tentative hand on hers. 'About Lexi?' he suggested softly.

'Yes,' she said squeakily.

That too. She lifted agonised eyes to his.

'I'll check the rice.'

He rose, taking her glass and his magnetism with him. Emma allowed herself a sigh of relief and tried to understand what and why she couldn't master her feelings, why she felt hopelessly drawn to him. Drawn! It was more like tumbling headlong into a warm and silky sea and allowing it to blot out the past, the present and future and not even caring.

She passed a shaking hand over her face.

'Here's a clean glass,' he murmured.

Her mouth stretched into a parody of a smile and she took it with great care. The wine hit her stomach quickly and revived her.

'I'm a renowned "dropper",' she told him brightly, as he strode back to the kitchen area.

'Remind me to provide plastic beakers when you come visiting,' he drawled. 'The *melijanosalata's* ready. Come and eat.'

Hugging that word 'visiting' to herself, Emma unwound her legs and slid them to the floor, quickly tugging her dress down where it had become rucked up. It didn't matter. Leon hadn't noticed. He was trying to light the candelabra on the table, the flickering light intensifying the planes and hollows of his face. His beauty made her stomach contract.

'It all looks wonderful,' she said huskily, glad to get her weakening body into a chair again.

'My pleasure. Enjoy.'

Her fork carried a neat stack of the aubergine salad to her mouth and she widened her eyes in surprise when she tasted it. 'Mmm! Gorgeous! I—' Her voice wavered. It seemed impossible for her to meet his eyes and not drown. 'Thanks for the food,' she babbled. 'For the gesture. For this. You must let me know what I owe you—'

Leon's eyes flickered. 'On the house.' He smiled, his eyes crinkling in the appealing way that had always sent her heart lurching. 'I need your co-operation, you see.'

She might have known. She hid her peculiar disappointment by eating. 'Go on,' she mumbled warily, between mouthfuls.

He took a deep breath. 'There is a slight problem about you seeing Lexi.'

She felt immediately sick. 'No,' she whispered.

'Please, Emma,' he said earnestly, 'it's nothing insurmountable. The trouble is, that Lexi knows nothing about you.'

'Oh. Is that all? Well, you can fill her in, and so can I. I've got a picture of me somewhere, I brought it specially—'

'No.' There was something about his manner that made her clutch at her throat. 'I mean,' he said quietly, 'that she doesn't know you even exist.'

She gave a horrified gasp. '*Leon!* How could you do this to her? To me?'

'What was I to say? That her mother was away? She has no concept of time—I couldn't tell her that you'd turn up in a few years. Besides,' he admitted, 'I hoped you wouldn't.'

'She would have asked about me at some stage,' Emma cried.

'I know. But initially it seemed simpler if she spent her first few years just being with me—and Marina and Soula— as if that was the norm. She doesn't really know how other families function.'

Daggers of pain were zigzagging across her chest. 'She...calls Marina, Mummy?'

He hesitated and she held her breath, aching. 'No,' he said eventually. 'Emma, she's been too young for explanations up to now. I was working up to telling her in due course, but you turned up sooner than I'd imagined. I wasn't expecting you. She's just a baby still, Emma, only just out of nappies. The last thing I want is for her to be disturbed by your arrival. I'm sure you feel that way too and would want to ease your way in gently.'

Her eyes were huge with dismay. This was awful. She'd have a lot of groundwork to do before Lexi felt comfortable with her. It looked as if she'd be staying for some considerable time, because she would not take Lexi back to England until her daughter had grown to love and trust her.

'What are you suggesting?' she asked, searching his face for an answer.

He did seem concerned. His jaw was tight with strain. Perhaps he did care about Lexi. She bit her lip, suddenly on uncertain ground. A false step and her child would be lost to her for ever. She put her fork down with a clatter, misery tugging down the corners of her mouth.

'Emma,' Leon said soothingly. 'I understand how you feel—'

'Do you?' she muttered, flicking up a sullen glance at him.

'I can imagine what it would be like to have a child, who I'd watched over as a baby, asking who I was...'

His voice had cracked. Her quick appraisal told her that his mouth had compressed and that he was valiantly trying to hide a private pain.

Her eyes softened. 'It happened to you, didn't it?' she said gently. 'You were estranged from your own daughter.'

'It...was a different situation.' He growled, apparently more interested in eating.

But Emma could see that swallowing was a problem and she knew herself what that meant. She couldn't eat when emotion had constricted her throat. She felt very tender and protective towards him.

'And how did you resolve it?' she asked softly.

'Who said it was resolved?' The bitterness in his tone was unmistakable. He abandoned his efforts to finish his starter and took a gulp of wine instead. His eyes were raw with anguish. 'I made a mistake, Emma. In my ignorance, I imagined I could walk back into Soula's life and everything would be fine. I couldn't, and it wasn't.' He leaned towards her, his expression fierce. 'I know what happened to that child. So Lexi isn't going to be messed up, not by you or anybody. She's happy and carefree and I will go to hell and back to keep her that way.'

Emma stared in dismay. There were pitfalls in her path that she never knew had existed. 'You know what went wrong with Soula,' she said jerkily. 'So you can make it right, this time.'

'I can.' He removed their plates and carried dishes to the table, waving aside her offer of help. 'This is how we'll do it. I want you to come to the house and be introduced to Lexi as someone her daddy used to know.'

'But...' She stared at him helplessly. He was absorbed in lifting the lid of the casserole dish. An aroma of spices and herbs wafted enticingly in the air but she ignored it. 'You're robbing me of the moment I've dreamed of. She's my *child*—'

'I know.' His hand reached across the table to hers in a consoling gesture but his expression was determined. 'That's why you'll do this.'

'No. I won't—'

'Your needs or hers? You have to choose,' he said fiercely. 'This needs very delicate handling. First you both need to make friends. I don't want you telling her that you are her mother until she's ready.'

He became blurred. She rubbed her eyes till they cleared. 'I don't think I can agree,' she whispered. 'All these years I've waited to hear her call me Mummy.' Her voice shattered.

'I'd look at her with longing and pain,' she said brokenly, 'and everyone would see—'

'I'd be there,' he said quietly. 'No one else.'

'Marina—'

'Is hardly ever around.'

'Soula—'

'Wouldn't notice. She's too concerned with her own problems to be aware of anyone else's.' His hand curled around hers properly, tightly, and she realised how passionately he felt about this. '*Try* it. For Lexi. I'm giving a lot here, Emma. I could fight you over this and force you to apply to the courts and to hell with my reputation. I don't want that. Lexi will be harmed. Come tomorrow. You've waited a long time, I know, to be acknowledged as Lexi's mother. A little while longer won't hurt.'

It would. It would. Her lip trembled. 'Leon, you don't know what you're ask-ask…' Tears backed up in her throat. She looked at him in mute appeal.

His hand slid from hers and stroked the side of her face, stopping her sobs altogether. A rush of longing engulfed her like a tidal wave.

And then they were both staring at his mobile phone, which seemed to be buzzing and jerking around at the far end of the table. Leon said something short and pithy in Greek and stretched out for it.

'*Ne?*' he snapped. His brows zapped together furiously as he listened. 'She's here.' Leon held out the phone. 'Sefton.'

It was a moment before Emma had gathered herself sufficiently to sound vaguely normal. She opted for, 'Hi,' deciding that any more syllables would betray her shakiness.

'I've been going crazy wondering how you are,' complained John petulantly.

'I'm sorry—' she began, immediately contrite.

'Where are you? Do you know what time it is? If you don't get to your digs—'

'I—I've got somewhere to stay,' she mumbled, feeling

horribly guilty. 'John, I totally forgot! I arrived here and fell asleep—'

'Where's here? And what's *he* doing there?'

She could almost hear his lower lip jutting out. 'Leon's let me use a house on his estate,' she explained in a remorseful rush. 'I'm seeing Lexi tomorrow, isn't that wonderful?' She accepted the plate of beef from Leon and nodded her thanks.

'Where? I ought to be there. And where exactly is this house?' John demanded truculently.

'I've no idea. Where are you? Hotel…Zantos.' Hearing Leon's amused snort, she glanced up at him and found herself smiling. 'I'll ring you,' she said drily.

'Let me know when and where to pick you up,' he ordered.

She took a deep breath. 'No, we'll meet later and I'll report on my progress. I'll explain why, when I see you. I have to do this on my own, John. I don't want to rock the boat. Leon's been very accommodating.' Absently she helped herself to rice and vegetables. 'I must go,' she said, cutting across John's protests. 'We're discussing the arrangements. *John.* Listen to me,' she begged. 'Please don't do this to me. It's just that I don't need you for this stage of—'

She blinked and slowly lowered the phone. 'He rang off!' she exclaimed in astonishment.

'He would. Potatoes?' Leon offered politely.

She dug into the crunchy roasted potato slices and added them to her heaped plate. 'I don't understand it,' she said with a frown. 'We've never disagreed before.'

'Maybe,' Leon murmured, sipping his wine reflectively, 'you've always gone along with what he's said. Look, don't worry about it now. We have more pressing things to discuss. Do you accept my suggestion? In the morning, you can walk through the olive grove to my house and we'll have coffee. Lexi will be playing in the garden. Then I'll suggest we go to the beach together. My land runs to the sea and we have a small beach house. It's a very beautiful spot. You'd like to see her swimming, wouldn't you?' he said persuasively.

Unfair, she thought. 'If I say no?'

'Then my gates will be locked to you, and you won't get near her. You will have to take the legal way out. And if you are granted access, I will not make your meetings with Lexi easy.'

It was a grim prospect and the pictures he'd painted were vivid in her head. Watching her daughter playing, seeing her run and laugh…spending the better part of the day with her, larking about in the sea…

She let out a little, quivery breath. His solution couldn't be faulted. And she'd see Lexi in the morning.

'Yes,' she whispered, her face soft with quiet joy. 'I agree.'

The warmth of the food and the wine—had she drunk too much?—was making her feel very mellow and relaxed. Nothing mattered. Only her child.

'Thank you,' he said huskily. 'I knew you'd do what's best for her. To tomorrow.'

'Tomorrow.' she said, her voice low with passion. 'Tomorrow.'

CHAPTER FIVE

HE TOLD her about the island while they ate, his melodious voice and deep love for his homeland slipping effortlessly into her mind, like the heady wine.

'Coffee and brandy outside?' he murmured, when they'd finished the rich, sweet filo pudding. 'Bit of pudding—corner of your mouth,' he added.

Her finger found the sticky blob and her tongue enjoyed the last taste of cinnamon-flavoured honey and walnut.

'Thanks. And outside would be lovely,' she said with a sigh.

Her mind swirled deliciously with magical names: Zeus and Apollo and Aphrodite, Troy, Odysseus and Homer. But it was his own story that had captured her imagination. And she wanted more information about him.

When he opened the door to the garden, the colour of the pool took her breath away for the second time. But now it was lit by underwater lamps and its delicate aquamarine contrasted dramatically with the velvety darkness, which was broken only by the thick scattering of twinkling stars above.

Stepping down to the terrace was like moving into another world. There seemed to be an intense silence over everything, almost weighting the air. And nothing ruffled the extraordinary stillness other than an occasional whirring from a few diffident cicadas or the rustle of a lizard as it moved in the undergrowth.

'It's very peaceful,' she said in a hushed whisper, as they pulled their chairs around to enjoy the view.

'A little different from London,' he replied softly.

Smiling, she sat there, her senses swimming from the incredibly powerful perfume of the roses and thought of everything he'd said, remembering every detail of his impassioned words.

Long ago the Venetians had called Zakynthos the flower of the east, the island of love. In rich and fervent tones Leon had painted pictures for her: the rich greens of the landscape, the olive, pine and cypress trees, the carpets of spring flowers and crystal-clear seas.

He'd spoken of the warm sense of community, the age-old values of courtesy, respect, and hospitality. She could see in her mind's eye the old men sitting over a game of chess in the *kafenion*—the café—and dark-eyed boys herding goats in the mountains. And she looked forward to visiting Zante town and seeing the busy port he'd described with its fishing boats and island ferries chugging back and forth across the sparkling sea.

Even more fascinating, he'd told her how once the beaches in the south had been black with loggerhead turtles, which hauled themselves up to lay over a hundred eggs apiece in the sand, digging shafts with their rear flippers. In answer to her eager questioning, he said that many still came to the beaches where they'd been born and the hatchlings—as small as a child's hand—emerged at night in a helter-skelter dash for the sea. She would like to see that.

Yes. It was different from London. Given time, her soul could recover here, as well as her body, she thought wistfully.

'The tourists who come to this island and this villa will never want to leave,' she mused, feeling envious.

'Then, they will show remarkable good taste,' he said huskily.

Idly she mused that it would be wonderful to live on the island. But that was impossible as far as she was concerned. If she wanted Lexi, she'd have to live in England, out of Leon's clutches.

'You have it all,' she said, lifting her head to inhale the scented breeze.

'No one has it all.'

'John thinks you have,' she said slowly.

Leon grunted. 'He's blind. Beware his advice—'

'You keep denigrating him,' she complained mildly. 'Don't spoil this pleasant evening.' It was more than pleasant, she thought. For the first time in years she felt at ease. And happy. That was because she was close to her goal. 'John's been unbelievably kind to me. I don't know why.'

'Because you're beautiful.'

Astonished, she turned her head to look him full in the face. In the soft lamplight he seemed deadly serious. Her heart bumped unevenly. And she couldn't prevent herself from saying breathlessly, 'Am I?'

'Stunning.'

With an effort he looked elsewhere. He wanted to drink her up: her wide, solemn eyes with their fringe of impossibly long lashes which so often closed in ecstasy; the fine-boned face and its satin skin which he could still feel warm and vibrant beneath his fingers from where he'd dared to touch her earlier; her mass of rich gold hair heaping in scented drifts about her shoulders...

He sucked in a breath. Those silky smooth shoulders! The perfect back, naked to his startled eyes when she'd first turned around. The high mounds of her lush breasts...

There was a tremendous pressure within his chest. She was leaning forwards, her dress falling away from her long, glossy legs. Leon knew he was in trouble when he couldn't locate his brandy glass. Things were happening too rapidly. She was far too sexy and he too hungry.

'Oh, look, Leon,' she whispered furtively, her hand descending on his knee. 'Bats,' she said in breathy excitement.

Bats! Flitting over the pool, dipping like tiny black scimitars to drink... While flames roared inside him, fires consumed him, his head was near to exploding...

And now their gazes had meshed. Electricity shot between them and every muscle and sinew in her body contracted as his did. His arms were around her though how they'd got there he didn't know. Amazingly, her hands were curving around the nape of his neck, drawing him close.

He could manage only the shallowest of breaths, high in his throat. For a second or two they remained frozen in a tense and expectant tableau, postponing the moment their lips met—as surely they would.

But the waiting was delicious, so tormentingly exciting, and he could enjoy the perfection, the fragrance of her skin and hair, the heat of desire leaping from her sultry eyes.

Imperceptibly he inclined his head and her lips parted with a tortured moan. Knowing her as he did, remembering the madness that had descended on them both when they had made love, he closed his eyes briefly and groaned too.

With deceptive gentleness—because his animal instincts were driving him to rip her clothes off and make hot, passionate love to her without pausing for breath—he tipped up her chin.

His finger slipped erotically along the line of her jaw. They looked into one another's eyes and did not speak but their eyes and their bodies spoke for them. Closer and closer his mouth came until it was almost on hers.

Never in the whole of his life had he felt like this. His whole world had become focussed on a woman's lips: lush and full, pouting and trembling, the whiteness of her even teeth startling in the hushed stillness of the night.

A faint touch of her lips. Satin, he thought, and then slowly, thoroughly, he moved his mouth over hers without pressure, reminding himself of its plush curves…

He smiled affectionately. A little stickiness. The tip of his tongue darted out. Honey. He sucked gently at her lower lip, knowing with a growing triumph that she was trembling in his arms as if demons were shaking her.

Up, up to the peaked arch of her upper lip, down and then up again. Sweeping along to tantalise the corner with his tongue. Nothing sweeter.

He rose fluidly and she slithered up his body with him

while his mouth wandered the contours of her slender jaw, his hands cupping her face so that soon his lips could feel the length of that smooth throat where her pulse beat so rapidly.

Still he was gentle, as if hardly daring to unleash his passion. But she was restless and impatient, her hands digging in his hair, tugging his head towards her so that his kisses deepened. She nibbled at his mouth. Began to devour him.

Her body moved lightly against his in a sinuous motion and, as the sleek voluptuousness beneath the thin dress began to make itself known, he found himself close to forgetting everything he'd planned.

She *had* intended seduction, he thought hazily. And then, before he could ask why, his mind fractured as the heat of her loins suddenly flared against the pounding throb of his body.

'Emma,' he breathed helplessly.

'Kiss me. *Hard*,' she moaned.

He cried out in anguish, his voice hoarse and thick, cracking with the choking passion that commanded his senses. With a rough moment, his hand splayed over her tight buttocks and jerked her into him while his mouth descended on hers in a ruthlessly driving kiss that obliterated everything from his mind but their two bodies and the explosive longing which would not be denied.

Yes, this was how it used to be. Her sighs, her eagerness, the drowsy flutter of her curling lashes, the instinctive lure of her wickedly enticing mouth. The feel of her hands on his chest and shoulders as if they were loving the shape of him, and which made him feel a giant among men. The rising tension between them, driven by demanding hands and lips, the desperation, oh, the sweet desperation to taste and touch and know every inch of one another's bodies…

Her fingers tugged at his shirt buttons, then his impatient, impulsive and passionate Emma, her face beautiful in its frustrated anger, gripped both edges and ripped the shirt open to her avid greed.

He felt her soft cheek rest on his chest, looked down with dazed eyes, saw the gentle curve of her face against his bronzed skin and then watched with mounting, sweet agony as her mouth began to explore.

Shaking, he reached around to her back, letting memories return. Vaguely he registered that the strong rope of muscles on either side of her spine was less pronounced now but her skin was still flawless to his trailing caress.

The tie at her waist came undone easily. Just up to her nape now and when that bow was undone he'd have her breasts in his trembling hands.

'*No!*'

Emma wriggled in his grasp, cold reality suddenly descending. She couldn't. Wanted to, yes. *Yes!* But...

'No, Leon,' she rasped, when he continued to tussle with the tie at her neck.

She put her hands up. Peeled off a surprised finger or two. Met his bewildered, hazy eyes and wanted to weep. Her body screamed at her, wanting, starving for his magic touch.

It had been so good, she mourned. No...more than that, it had seemed as if her heart was being healed.

'No,' she moaned.

His hands fell away. He stood there thrusting shaking fingers through his tousled hair, the dark curls dancing angrily on his frowning forehead. She took a step back and then another, her eyes averted from that smooth and golden torso which her hands had caressed only a few wonderful moments ago.

'Why?' he said gratingly.

She bit her lip and found it was trembling. Because there was an ugly dent in her breast, a savage scar. She feared his disgust and that was something she wasn't strong enough to bear yet.

Suddenly he was walking away, back up the steps to the

villa, each stride thundering his anger. You don't do this to men, she thought miserably. They never forgive you.

'Leon, please…'

He paused, waiting for her explanation, his body language explicit in its tense fury. Then, when she struggled for an excuse, he whirled, his eyes slashing like swords in the darkness of his face.

'A game, was it?' he rasped. 'Get me excited, lure me on, push me away, get me in your power… Oh, come on, Emma,' he yelled, beyond anger, almost out of control, 'I'm not a kid you can play around with. This isn't Taki, or Sefton, hanging on your every word, turning somersaults to please you—'

'I—I'm sorry, I didn't mean… It got out of…hand—' She choked.

He erupted, cursed in Greek, the words hurtling through his teeth. And then he smashed his fist into the palm of his hand as if furious with himself. She could see the effort it was costing him to rein in his temper. The line of his mouth was hard and vicious, his jaw rock-solid.

With scant regard for his shirt, he almost punched it back into place. She saw the absence of buttons and dropped her eyes guiltily, horrified by the violence of her passion.

'I don't like being teased,' he growled dangerously.

She gulped. 'It wasn't like that.'

'How was it then?' He shot the words vehemently.

For the life of her, she didn't know. Other than frightening in its intensity, the terrible loss of conscious thought, the way she'd lurched headlong into a seething cauldron of lust and sensation.

'I've no idea,' she croaked, her eyes glistening.

For long, painful seconds, which ticked by in an agony of suspense, he glowered at her as if promising a murderous revenge. And then he turned on his heel again and ran up the steps.

He couldn't comprehend what had happened, only that he

had to get away before he said any more. She'd been close to surrender, his goal almost within his grasp, and then…

Heaven help him. He paused, standing stock still in appalled silence. He'd forgotten why he'd broken his self-imposed celibacy. And if Emma wasn't intending to succumb and prove herself to be unsuitably loose, then he had to come up with some other way of protecting Lexi.

His brain wouldn't function. All he could think of was the devastating sense of loss when she'd drawn back and refused him. He stared bleakly at the door, paralysed as he relived her erotic caresses, feeling the tautness in his body as every nerve sprang to life again and tortured him with what might have been.

He hated her. He hated himself.

For several seconds, Emma remained in stunned silence, horrified by the destruction she'd caused by letting go of her inhibitions. Her brain only jerked into operation again when the back door slammed in the breeze behind her.

In panic, she raced after Leon, skidding across the marble floor in her desperation to head him off before he stormed out.

'Leon!' Gasping for breath, she flung herself bruisingly against the front door, her arms outstretched to bar his way. 'What about Lexi?' she wailed wretchedly.

'Oh, now you think of her, do you? Yourself first, her somewhere far down your order of priorities… My God, Emma,' he said exploding, 'you really are selfish, aren't you? All you think about are your own needs, your own games of power play. It didn't occur to your scheming little mind that I might take offence at being dangled on the end of a line, and refuse to let you see her.'

'No,' she moaned, limp with despair. Her tormented eyes begged. She caught his arm but he flung her hand off as if it had scalded him. 'Don't do this to me—'

'There are several things I'd like to do to you,' he said icily, 'all of them unspeakable.'

He reached out, his expression menacing, and pulled her to his body, crushing her against him so firmly that she could feel his hard, taut muscles and the pulse of his arousal against her pelvis. She dragged in a strangled breath and he gave a mocking smile then lowered his mouth to take hers in a punishing display of contempt.

Then he let her go. And, insultingly, wiped the back of his hand across his mouth.

They were panting hard and fast, shocked by where their passions had taken them, hating, wanting, prevented from fully releasing the dangerous emotions that had been ignited.

She knew that. He knew that. It scared them both, this uncontrollable hunger that took no account of its consequences.

She could hardly stand. Her fist was at her stinging mouth, holding back the screech within her.

'Move aside,' he hissed, dark and feral and more menacing than anyone or anything she'd ever known.

'But…Lexi,' she whispered brokenly. It stuck in her throat to beg. But beg she must. 'Tell me I can still…' She cringed. His eyes had blazed with fury. 'Let me see her,' she whimpered in a small, tinny voice.

He seemed to be thinking rapidly but it was several nerve-racking seconds before he came to some conclusion and by then her mind was in shreds.

'Why not?' He bit out the words, to her utter surprise. He took a stride forward and had caught her jaw in one hand before she could blink. 'But the situation is different now,' he said, growling softly, his breath hot and harsh on her face.

And she flinched as if it scalded her. 'D-d-different?' she stammered.

'You will see her. You will see more than you would wish. You will learn how happy she is, how this island is her home and that she would die of misery anywhere else. You will see how much she loves me and you will suffer, Emma. You will suffer because you will realise that she doesn't need you and doesn't want you and that her life will be all the better if you never tell her who you are, if she never knows for the rest of her life that she is your daughter!'

Released, she crumpled to the floor, all the bones in her body useless. The door closed very quietly behind Leon and as she lay curled in a despairing heap, she heard his car driving away.

The pain made her double up. Holding her lurching stomach, she tried to find the strength to stand but could only manage to crawl towards the nearest chair.

Sobs racked her body. She had made a terrible mistake and her longed-for meeting with Lexi had been ruined, perhaps with fatal results.

Her mouth tightened. OK. She'd tell him why she'd refused him. Let him pick the bones out of that. Hauling herself into the carved seat, she reflected gloomily that he'd probably think she was angling for the sympathy vote. And it wouldn't make any difference. His pride had been dented and he was raring for a fight, looking for a chance to lash out at her in revenge.

No. Wild horses wouldn't drag it out of her that she'd been self-conscious about her damaged breast. Let him think what he liked. She wasn't going to discuss something so personal and life-shattering with anyone, let alone Leon.

But he'd scared her with what he'd said. If Lexi was happy, if... Oh, yes, she thought in dismay, she could see that any child would prefer to live here and not London...

Hot, stinging tears burned like scalding water in her eyes and ran down her cheeks unchecked. Miserably she sopped them up with her tongue, little sobs breaking through her parted lips.

She was horribly afraid that what she had to offer Lexi was not enough. And yet John had been so sure that Leon resented looking after Lexi.

In a gesture of despair, her arms flopped over the arms of

the chair and her left hand hit something hard. She blinked.
A telephone.

Perhaps if she could talk this over with someone—a second opinion... She sat up, struggling to compose herself.
And after a while she picked up the receiver and dialled with
shaky fingers.

'John! It's me, Emma,' she mumbled when a curt voice
answered. 'I—I'd like to talk to you... I was wondering...could you come round? *Please?*'

Leon sat on the gnarled and twisted bole of an olive tree
which had been the felled victim of an ancient storm, its
branches still miraculously thick with leaf and flower. Olives
were tough. They took everything the climate could throw at
them and still bore fruit. He wished he could be so certain
of his own strength.

He didn't dare get in the car again. For the first hundred
yards he'd driven on adrenaline and then had realised he'd
swerved off the road twice, his tyres biting into the irrigated
soil which had played merry hell with the gleaming bodywork.

He'd kill himself if he drove home. And she wasn't worth
that...whatever her delights, and they were many.

So he'd abandoned the car and had set about calming himself down, refusing to think about the passion that had swallowed him whole and had turned the tables so disastrously
on him.

It had never been his intention to let Emma see Lexi if he
could possibly avoid it. He had meant to be seduced. To
declare then to the courts that this woman had not only committed fraud but that she'd slept with her brother-in-law the
first night she'd arrived on the island. And he would have
asked for an injunction to stop her seeing Lexi.

It had been a brutal and morally suspect ploy on his part
perhaps, but it would have given Lexi the ultimate protection.
And it had rebounded on him—big-time.

He ground his teeth together. Because he'd lost his head, he would now have to spend hours in Emma's company and watch her yearning to hold her daughter. Far from giving him a malicious pleasure, the prospect filled him with dread.

He took a deep breath and his nostrils were immediately assailed by wild honeysuckle and orange blossom. When his foot stirred the rich, red earth he felt suddenly overwhelmed by the love of his land and it swelled to fill his aching heart.

This had been Kyriakis land for generations. And, after him, it would belong to Lexi. He stilled. Sefton had let slip that Emma was determined to take Lexi back to England one way or another. Leon's jaw tightened. That was his worst fear. But his Lexi had her roots here and she must never live anywhere else.

Emma must be persuaded to go home. There was no other way. The ends would justify the means.

Determined on his course, he set off on foot for home. It was then that he heard a car coming up the lane to the villa. Suspecting who it might be, he hurried grimly through the trees and watched with growing anger as the car came to a jerking halt.

Emma emerged from the villa, her face white in the glare of the porch light. She spoke to John Sefton in a low voice and he replied.

Leon heard her utter a low cry. And then Sefton pulled her boldly into his arms.

CHAPTER SIX

IF SHE'D been in a different mood, she would have loved the walk to the house through the olive grove the next morning. John had been wonderful, comforting her into the small hours of the morning and advising her to persevere. His confidence had given her strength and after sleeping late she felt more optimistic and better able to cope.

But she was unbelievably nervous. In a sleeveless blue top and white shorts, with a cheerful pink rucksack on her back, she set off along the path to find Leon's house. She felt as if she were about to take an exam, her stomach churning uncomfortably. And when her footfalls stirred up the scent of mint and basil she gave only a passing thought to them instead of revelling in their combining scents.

Lexi was uppermost in her mind. It terrified her that her daughter wouldn't like her, or would pick up Leon's hatred and be suspicious—perhaps scared.

She'd spent long hours in prison learning Greek but repeating phrases to a tape recorder was a lot different to interpreting a child's chatter, especially with Leon possibly muttering vile things about her under his breath.

She winced. He wanted to make her suffer. All because his sexual pride had been wounded. Men! she thought darkly.

'I will get the better of him,' she muttered, scowling at the herby path.

But the way ahead had changed. The path had widened. She looked up and saw the ground rising gradually. And on a hill, perhaps half a mile away, sat a beautiful, old stone mansion, perfectly proportioned and graceful.

She stared at it wide-eyed. Doubts chased through her

mind. To live here, in this paradise, in a beautiful period house, would be any child's dream.

She frowned, thinking positively. If that child wasn't loved, then a cosy cottage somewhere in England and an adoring mother would be better. She'd buy a little house with the remainder of her stash of money. In the country. With chickens.

With that decided, she walked towards the house. Close to, it was very impressive, with Grecian pediments and huge shutters flanking the tall windows. And on the ground floor, French doors lay open to the cooling breeze.

Sick with nerves, she rang the bell and was admitted by a long-legged beauty in jeans and T-shirt. Emma gaped. This wasn't Marina! Some other female, a temporary 'auntie' for her child? she thought, choking with fury.

'Hello. Are you Emma?' asked Long Legs solemnly in an enchanting accent.

'I am,' Emma replied grumpily, sounding anything but enchanting.

'Come.'

The tall, willowy young woman swayed across a high and airy marbled hall, her easy manner in the expensive surroundings crushing Emma's self-confidence still further. It was a long walk. Eventually they reached the back of the house where Long Legs pointed through the open double doors.

'He's in the garden,' she said succinctly to Emma. And swept off, every step disapproving.

Emma's heart sank as she stepped onto the terrace. If everyone around Leon behaved like that towards her, then it would be impossible to convince Lexi that she was harmless.

Pale and trembling, she scanned the fabulous garden and quickly identified Leon, sitting beneath the shade of a rubber tree.

Her hand flew to her mouth to stifle her sharp intake of breath. *There was Lexi.*

A rush of tears clouded her view and she brushed them

away impatiently. 'Oh, sweetheart,' she whispered softly, a catch in her anguished voice. 'Oh, my darling, darling baby.'

With hunger in her heart she watched the sturdy little figure, dressed in a sweet little flowery top and matching shorts which came down to her dimpled knees. Love spilled from Emma's entire being. Someone had put Lexi's hair up in a pony-tail and had fastened it with a bright pink scrunchie but rebellious curls danced all around Lexi's small face.

Emma's heart melted. Her daughter was quite exceptionally beautiful. She let out a soft breath and felt a little better about the meeting. Love would bind them and break down all barriers.

With glazed eyes she watched her daughter happily arranging rose petals in a wooden truck: small piles of pink, white, red, and yellow. Emma felt a pang of pride that little Lexi should be so deeply absorbed in her sorting game, playing with an admirable concentration.

The need to run forwards and crush her sweet baby in her arms was unbearable. So she pressed her lips together and stayed silent behind a column, giving herself a chance to watch unobserved and to yearn openly for her child. Because soon she'd have to appear friendly but detached. Towards her own daughter! Emma's lip trembled at the injustice of that.

Her loving gaze saw the breeze ruffle the rose petals and ruin the neat piles and she smiled in motherly sympathy at Lexi's look of dismay.

'Daddeee!' Lexi wailed in English.

She gasped in horror, ice freezing her spine. Both Leon and Lexi whirled around and Emma hastily hid her face, gripping the pillar with rigid fingers, her head pressed hard against the cold unmoving stone.

'Oh, God!' she moaned, when she heard Leon's quick stride coming up the steps towards her.

'How long have you been there?' he growled, keeping his voice low so it didn't carry to Lexi's ears.

She flung him a furious glance. 'Long enough. She…she calls you *Daddy*! How dare you? In how many ways do you want to take my child from me?' she hurled back in a barely controlled undertone.

'I correct her,' he said quietly, his eyes cold and distant. 'But she persists. She has a mind of her own—as you'll find out.'

'What do you mean? Have you said something detrimental about me?' she demanded, her face hot with anger.

'I've said nothing. I wouldn't waste my breath talking about you. Well, are you ready? I suggest you find a more charming expression.'

With an effort she checked her temper. This was it. The moment she'd been waiting for. Her heartbeat thundered in her ears and the sick sensation coiled hotly in her stomach.

'I—I'm ready. Just one thing, Leon,' she said, her blue eyes wide with apprehension. She moistened her parched lips. 'You must give me a fair crack of the whip. If I suspect even for a moment that you're trying to influence Lexi's opinion of me, then I'm off to see John. I'll get the lawyers involved. Lexi must be given the opportunity to know and love her own mother. Do I make myself clear?'

'Crystal.' His eyes glittered. 'I imagine this is what you and Sefton talked about last night?'

She was taken aback. 'Umm…yes.'

'And this morning?' he enquired sarcastically. 'Or was he helping you with some other, more personal, service?'

She flushed, well aware of what he was implying. 'Do you do your own snooping, or do you get minions to do it for you?' she asked scathingly.

He smiled but it wasn't anywhere near humorous. 'Your evasion has answered my question. Just consider this, Emma. It's a mistake for a woman in your position to put herself about. Me, Sefton, who next, I wonder? Your life needs to be close to sainthood. Anything less and the odds shorten against you.'

Emma met his glittering eyes coolly even though she was registering the truth of what he was saying. She would have to be very careful. John had insisted on staying till she fell asleep. It had been a wonderful gesture but he knew she was under surveillance and he should have realised that Leon would misinterpret the situation.

'I have nothing on my conscience,' she said, her chin high. 'And now I want to meet my daughter.'

He frowned. 'You remember what we agreed?'

He was barring her way. He'd turn her away if necessary, even now. 'Yes, yes, I'm to say I knew her daddy,' she said in a choking voice. 'I'll keep to my side of the bargain—but no tricks on your part,' she warned.

He smiled again, his eyes bright and hard. 'I won't need any.'

Emma shivered. He seemed so confident. He raised his hand to attract someone's attention in the house and Long Legs glided silently to his side.

'Would you bring some coffee, Natasa?' he asked pleasantly.

Natasa dimpled. 'Of course. And freshly squeezed orange for Lexi? I have some biscuits I made this morning if you're interested…' She paused and raised a shapely eyebrow in query, sharing some private joke with Leon.

His eyes crinkled with laughter as he ruefully patted his flat stomach and Emma found herself gritting her teeth, uncharitably wishing that Natasa would vanish off the face of the earth. Emma couldn't translate his reply and that infuriated her even further, but it was evidently funny because they both fell into fits of giggles.

'Obliging girl,' Emma found herself saying sarcastically, like some jealous wife. She went pink with fury at herself. What did she care *how* obliging Natasa was?

'She's hell-bent on single-handedly altering my waistline by cooking like an angel.' Leon's face sobered as he gazed after the pendulum swing of Natasa's rear. Emma clenched her fists hard. 'She is a gem. A diamond among women.'

'Pearl,' she corrected shortly. 'It's pearl.'

'Not in this case. Diamonds are for ever.'

She felt her heart bump unevenly. 'Are you trying to tell me something?' she asked as coolly as humanly possible. 'Is Natasa likely to be a permanent fixture in my daughter's life?'

'Anastasia—Natasa—is welcome to stay here as long as she wishes,' Leon answered quietly.

What was he doing, she wondered in amazement, operating a harem? Against her better wishes, she imagined him coming home last night, angry and sexually frustrated—and hated to think of what might have happened next between him and the nubile Natasa.

'I hope she's nice to Lexi,' she muttered.

'Brilliant. Come and discover how happy your daughter is,' he goaded. She hurled a glare at him as they walked down the steps into the landscaped garden. 'Lexi,' he called gently. She looked up, glanced at Emma and continued to rearrange the rose petals with a frown of concentration on her small forehead. 'This is someone your real daddy knew in England.'

Emma held her breath, a smile frozen on her nervous face. 'Hello,' she said, speaking in Greek like Leon. She was pleased at his look of surprise.

Lexi gave her an old-fashioned stare and returned to her game. Emma gulped in disappointment. But what had she expected? Some kind of psychic recognition, and her daughter beaming at her in joy and running up for a hug? She sucked in a shaky breath. The answer, stupidly, was yes.

Leon was smiling smugly and easing himself into the comfortable cane chair. Emma marshalled her wits and went to kneel on the lawn beside Lexi, her hands gripped tightly together so she wouldn't do anything silly like grab hold of her daughter and frighten her witless by clutching her to her heart.

'I have a present for you,' she said lovingly in her carefully rehearsed Greek.

Lexi looked up from beneath dark Kyriakis lashes. And went back to sorting the petals. Emma's heart beat hard but she bided her time. This was a child not to be bought. It didn't matter—on the contrary, it showed great strength of character, she rationalised.

Patiently Emma waited and watched. She noted that Lexi's fingers were surprisingly dextrous. She didn't get that from Taki. He'd been clumsy. Her eyes shifted to Leon's hands which were long and slender and capable of great delicacy of touch and she was glad that her daughter had inherited that particular Kyriakis trait.

Emma ached with longing and it was taking all her bitterly learnt self-control to remain physically neutral. Lexi was so deeply engrossed, so utterly sweet. Any mother would have caught her up and hugged her breathless by now—but she wasn't any mother. She was on trial and this trial would have far-reaching consequences.

Casually she slid off her rucksack and began to undo the clasps, knowing Lexi was watching surreptitiously. Emma's fingers fumbled because they were shaking so much and she gave Leon an imploring look.

'You're on your own,' he drawled.

Then she felt a small, soft hand on hers and froze. Lexi was helping! Emma felt a huge rush of emotion to be so close to her child, to see the fair hairs gleaming on the smooth brow, the stubby little nose wrinkled in concentration... She couldn't *bear* it, she thought with an inner groan. This was torture...

Lexi moved back, the clasps undone and Emma frantically eased her tense muscles and gave her daughter a radiant smile.

'Thank you,' she said warmly, and searched her limited

vocabulary. 'You are clever!' she exclaimed. 'Look, this is what I have for you.'

She drew out the smaller pink rucksack and placed it in front of Lexi who looked at it uncertainly then checked with Leon—but his attention was fixed on something he'd seen to his right.

'Thank you very much,' Lexi said politely.

But Emma could see she was pleased. Already the contents were being investigated. Lexi lifted out the soft fabric doll and immediately took off the sun hat and peeled off the Velcro that held the dress fast. Underneath was a shocking pink bikini. Lexi beamed in pleasure.

Emma leaned forwards, hardly daring to breathe, and pointed out that the rucksack on the doll's back contained toy sun cream, a hairbrush, towel, sunglasses and flowery mules for the doll.

'Oh!' Lexi squealed excitedly and it was as if Emma had won a million pounds.

But then Lexi ran to Leon to show him and Emma bit her lip, forcing herself to remember that she was a stranger and a hug would have been most unlikely.

The doll was being investigated and the bikini was already half-off. Leon solemnly received the hairbrush and followed orders to tidy the yellow wool plaits, while Lexi persevered with the difficult task of fixing the sunglasses securely.

'You like it?' Emma ventured brightly.

But Lexi didn't look at her, she was too taken up with dabbing the sun cream bottle all over the doll's body.

Leon met Emma's tormented eyes. 'Go and say thank you nicely,' he prompted Lexi in a growly voice.

Her daughter put her arms around Leon's neck and cuddled him. That hurt Emma more than she could have believed possible. Her daughter loved someone else more than she loved *her*.

'Go on,' he urged.

'Thank you,' Lexi said solemnly to Emma, having scrambled down from Leon's lap.

'You're welcome,' she replied jerkily.

'Emma, come and have coffee.' Leon's dark eyes were upon her, their expression unreadable when she was expecting mocking triumph.

Feeling dispirited, she jumped up and sat in the chair he'd indicated as Natasa brought a tray to them.

'Thanks, 'Tasa. Aren't you stopping with us?' he asked in surprise, seeing that she'd laid the tray for just two people.

Natasa smiled fondly. 'Not today, Leon. I am making *tiropitta*.'

Amiably she stroked Lexi's bent head and the little girl looked up with a beaming smile that made Emma wince. There was another exchange between Natasa and Leon that was teasing and familiar, which ended with Natasa pretending to threaten Leon with the coffee pot.

Emma watched, isolated by their friendship, bewildered that she should be upset when Leon sat back and gazed after Natasa with a tiger-got-the-cream smile on his face.

'Right,' he said, grabbing the coffee pot. 'Lexi, up to the table, please.'

'Can't she stay there, playing?' Emma asked, seeing her daughter's reluctance.

'No,' he replied firmly. 'She must sit at a table if she wants to eat.'

'But—'

'There are no buts,' he said. 'That is the rule in this house.'

And to her surprise, Lexi meekly gave the doll a kiss, laid it down and clambered up to the chair that Leon was holding out for her.

'Good girl,' Leon said approvingly and was rewarded with a seraphic smile.

'Please-may-I-have-a-biscuit?' Lexi asked all in one breath.

'Certainly—uh...*one*!' he instructed in a shocked tone.

Lexi's hand hovered and Emma hid a smile as her daughter locked frowning stares with Leon, searching for any sign of weakness. He didn't waver. Unfazed, the little girl placed the one biscuit on her plate and broke it in half.

'Two,' she said perkily.

Leon pressed his lips together to stop himself laughing. 'I never really win,' he muttered to himself.

'I'm so glad,' Emma said drily. 'Lexi,' she went on with a fond smile, 'what will you call your dolly?'

The startling blue eyes regarded her steadily. 'Mama,' she said.

Emma choked on her biscuit. Leon slapped her on the back and put a glass of iced water in her hand.

'It's a temporary obsession,' he explained curtly in English. 'She wants to be like Soula.'

Lexi began to chat to Leon. Her conversation was so quick and occasionally garbled that Emma couldn't understand what she was saying. But her daughter was laughing and she could tell that the two of them were fond of one another and were at ease in each other's company.

Leon was ever watchful, she noticed, seeing problems before they arose. Without making a song and a dance about it, he moved Lexi's colourful plastic cup away from her exuberantly gesturing hands. Her daughter was impetuous and enthusiastic, she mused. Just like her.

And a moment later he heaved his wriggling niece back to the centre of her chair when it seemed she might fall off in her excitement.

He also gently asked her to slow down her frantic gobbling of her biscuit. Just like her, Emma thought again—she always ate fast. Her father had said she seemed eager to grab life by the throat—or teeth—and never did anything slowly.

'Did you like your biscuit?' Leon enquired of Lexi.

'Mmm-*mmm*!' she said. 'Did you?'

He grinned. 'I think we'd all like another one. Yes?'

Lexi clapped her hands. 'Yes, please!'

Emma was interested to see that he was a stickler for good manners, making sure that Lexi never spoke with her mouth full nor interrupted a conversation. She wasn't sure she would have been so strict with such a young child but her daughter seemed to be coping very well with the rules.

Perhaps, Emma thought gloomily, that was because he doted on Lexi and she on him. His body language told her that. And the expression on his face when he looked at the little girl was tenderness itself.

Emma felt utterly excluded by their mutual affection. This was no act for her benefit, nor to punish her. It was obvious that he had become both father and mother to her daughter. Hence his opposition to anyone who might take one of those roles away from him.

John had made a terrible mistake. She shrank into her seat, hardly noticing that the coffee was almost scalding her mouth. Leon adored her child. And that was why he'd felt confident in inviting her here.

She couldn't have spoken if she'd wanted to. She knew she'd gone pale, that tremors were capturing her body and draining it of strength. Her lips seemed glued together; dry and bloodless, arcing down in misery.

Lexi's sturdy little legs were swinging beneath the table. Leon caught one in his hand while he replied to something she'd said and his hand affectionately stroked the soft, baby skin.

Emma closed her eyes at witnessing such casual intimacy, the kind usually shown only between fond parent and daughter. He has claimed her for his own, she thought miserably, her heart bumping hard in her chest. *My child!*

'Emma. Are you all right?' Leon asked quietly in English.

'No,' she whispered.

'Do you want to go back to the villa, or do you want to come to the beach with us?' he asked gruffly.

'I—I'll come to the beach,' she mumbled.

'Sure? Haven't you had enough?' Leon queried. 'I think

I'd better rescue that.' He took the coffee cup from her shaking hands and she stared at it with blank eyes. 'Emma, this won't get any easier for you... Lex, if you've finished,' he said, breaking off, 'you can go and play. Let me wipe your mouth.'

Emma's heart lurched as he took out a handkerchief and delicately wiped the little mouth which had been pursed up in preparation for the ritual.

'Kiss!' Lexi demanded merrily.

'Sweetheart,' he murmured, gently kissing each rosy cheek.

Emma writhed and caught a fragment of something that Lexi was saying about love.

'Yes,' Leon answered huskily, his forefinger tucking a golden curl behind Lexi's small ear. 'I love you, poppet.'

Emma looked away, unable to bear any more.

'Listen to me,' Leon said softly in her ear. His low tone made her skin tingle. 'Don't do this to yourself. You've had long enough to see that your daughter is fit and well and very happy—'

'And she is loved,' Emma whispered miserably.

'Very much.' He sounded very gentle, almost as if he knew how badly she was hurting. But that couldn't be so. His only concern was for Lexi. 'Why did you put yourself through this?' he asked. 'You must have known that after two years with me her life would be established. I am her legal guardian. I have pledged to devote myself to her.'

She turned glistening eyes to him. 'I didn't think it would be like this. You—you gave John the impression that she was a nuisance,' she mumbled, choking over the words.

'That's not true.' He hesitated, glanced down at Lexi who was politely tapping his knee for attention, and he tied the ribbon which had come unknotted around the doll's improbably yellow hair. 'Either he's a terrible judge of character, or he was determined to think ill of me, or...or he wanted you to come here and be disappointed.'

'Why would he do that?' she said indignantly.

Leon shrugged. 'Perhaps,' he said, his eyes dark and watchful, 'he likes to be needed and he hoped you'd run to him for comfort.'

'I wouldn't...' Her voice tailed away. She had done just that. And John had seemed delighted, smiling as he'd soothed her, had stroked her back, and had held her tightly... She bit her lip, determined not to be thrown off course. 'Lexi must get to know me,' she said obstinately.

'Why? Don't you think she can live happily without you?'

Emma glared. 'Maybe now she can, but soon she'll want to know who her mother is,' she declared. 'She's already muddled, calling you daddy and naming her doll "Mama". That's not normal, Leon. She wants to be like Soula, who knows very well who she is and who her parents are.'

Leon winced. Soula was also muddled—Marina had seen to that. But Emma had a point. Lexi's searching for a parent was beginning to present a problem. The last thing he wanted was for her to end up an emotional mess like Soula. And keeping Emma out of the equation was surely the best solution. He could then deal with the problem quietly and lovingly, without Emma's emotional input.

He shuddered. He certainly didn't want anyone else having hysterics in the house. He'd had enough to last a lifetime.

'I understand what you're saying,' he said, 'but this is clearly painful for you—'

'I've been through pain before. And fear, and humiliation,' she cried passionately.

Her words reached deep inside him, wounding him as though she'd wielded a knife. Looking deeply into her eyes, he could see the scars of her life there, raw and naked and slashing across the clear blueness like a laser. Her lashes had become spiked with tears and her mouth had parted softly, the swelling curve of her lips trembling gently with misery.

Reluctant to let her into their lives, he suppressed his overwhelming sense of compassion and raked in a strangled breath.

'Then, why suffer any more?' he argued. 'Be glad she's safe. And go home.'

Emma moaned. It was tempting. To shut him out, this house, Lexi's happy face... To start her life again... There would be certain torment if she stayed. And her planned abduction was looking less and less likely with every second that passed.

But the moment she considered the idea of leaving, she knew she couldn't do it. There would be something unfinished about her life. At least if she tried to befriend Lexi and failed, she would know where she was, once and for all.

'I can't go without being acknowledged as Lexi's mother,' she said croakily. 'I know it'll be hard for me. But it's her right to know me. It's not much to ask, Leon, access to my own daughter.'

His eyes narrowed. 'But is that *all* you want?'

Caught off guard, her eyes flashed to his and revealed the truth. His sympathetic expression vanished. 'I—I'd expect to have her for holidays when she's old enough—' she began honestly, hoping to cover up her secret intentions.

'While she is still under age, she will never leave Zakynthos without me,' Leon said meaningfully.

'Then, I will claim my rights in court,' she said defiantly.

He looked over at Lexi, who was happily stuffing rose petals into the doll's rucksack. 'You'll be wasting your money—and Sefton ought to know that. Go to an independent lawyer here and learn the truth,' he said in a hard tone. 'The situation is this, Emma. She is under my care. You will be able to visit a couple of times a year—'

'I want more than that!' she cried.

'Then, you will have to live on this island. That was the ruling in the case of a friend of mine who was having similar problems with his German ex-wife. She had to give up her home and her job in Germany and come to live on Zakynthos. Or never see her children again.'

CHAPTER SEVEN

EMMA sat quietly, watching Leon reading a bed-time story to Lexi, her mind in turmoil. It could have been an idyllic day if the shadow of her daughter's future hadn't hung over everything they did.

They had taken a picnic to the beach below the house, walking through the glorious gardens which were alive with birdsong and thick with the scent of plant oils vaporising in the heat.

Dancing ahead of them, her daughter had looked the picture of happiness. Occasionally Leon had called out and the little girl had come running eagerly, to be shown delights: a gecko with its padded feet, tadpoles in a meandering stream, a snake's skull, and—most exciting—a huge eel lurking in a pond beneath a huge eucalyptus.

Each time Emma had bitten back her urge to be the one who expanded Lexi's knowledge of the world around her. But Leon had been able to explain in fluent Greek, of course, and she'd had to ask him to translate nearly everything he'd said.

Language had proved to be just one more barrier. Until Lexi unexpectedly had spoken in English.

'Marina was born and brought up in England,' Leon had said a little uncomfortably. 'She and Soula speak mainly English. Lexi will probably grow up bilingual—she has as many English words as Greek.'

It had been easier after that. She'd said nothing but had given Leon a hard, angry glare and had spent the rest of the afternoon concentrating solely on Lexi, building sandcastles, digging a pit for the sea to fill, and running squealing in and

101

out of the waves with her. Their shared laughter had been worth a thousand tears.

And once, she'd even lifted her daughter in her arms when a huge wave from the wash of a boat had rolled towards them. For a brief, glorious moment she had held the firm little body close, Lexi's excited giggle tickling her ear.

Then had come the demand to be put down and she'd had to comply, her arms suddenly horribly empty of her wriggling, much wanted burden.

As Leon finished the story and kissed Lexi's sleepy face, hot tears prickled in Emma's eyes, but she refused to cry again. The day had been full of bitter-sweetness and yet the joy had exceeded the sadness.

And now it was late, very late. Lexi had been determined to keep going till she was ready to drop and, because Emma was there, Leon had let her. However, she knew this was part of his plan for her to be convinced of Lexi's happiness.

Her daughter had certainly co-operated in that plan. That afternoon Lexi had refused to take a nap on the beach, but had consented to curl up on Leon's naked chest for a few minutes.

Sighing with envy, Emma had stared at them both: her daughter's small body squirreled into a ball, Leon's tanned and muscular length stretched out on a lounger beneath a huge sunshade.

Emma's throat had gone dry. It had been the most tender and heart-wrenching picture and she had found herself wishing fruitlessly that he was Lexi's father, not Taki.

Because his eyes had been closed, she had been free to feast her gaze on his tousled dark hair, which was breaking the line of his broad forehead. She had admired the beautiful jut of his strong nose, the carved arch of his mouth, and the power of his perfectly toned body.

And then Lexi: sweet-faced, pouting-lipped and infinitely adorable, lying so trustingly in Leon's adoring embrace. Her daughter would be safe with him. He would bring her up well.

Emma had turned away, fighting the sharp pain which had knifed through her chest. *She* adored Lexi. *She* would bring her up safe and well! And Lexi was flesh of her flesh, blood of her blood.

A grunt had interrupted her thoughts. Lexi had scrambled up and was bouncing on Leon's hard stomach till he'd lifted her off. Emma and Leon had exchanged amused glances at Lexi's desire not to miss a second of the day.

Emma sighed. She remembered the catch in her throat at the sight of her daughter at the water's edge, as she'd picked up handfuls of sand and had happily thrown them into the glittering waves. Funny little mite! she'd thought affectionately.

'Night, Lex,' Leon murmured, bringing Emma back to the present.

The little hand opened and closed in a heart-wrenchingly sweet attempt at a wave. 'Night.'

'Say goodnight to Emma,' he prompted.

'Goodnight to Emma,' Lexi obediently, wickedly, replied and they all chuckled.

'Goodnight, Lexi,' Emma said huskily, her voice shaking with emotion as her daughter pushed the new doll under the bedclothes. And she turned to leave.

'Night Mama.'

Emma froze, every nerve in her body electrified. Leon too, was visibly shaken. Slowly she swivelled back again, a smile lighting her face, her heart soaring with delight. It had happened!

And then, through her glistening tears of happiness, she saw that Lexi was hugging and kissing the doll. *Mama.*

Leon couldn't move for shock. Seeing Emma's joy and disappointment had shaken him more than he could have believed possible. And now, with a cold certainty, he realised that Lexi was showing the first outward signs of deprivation.

Appalled, he registered Emma's white face, heard her broken sob and felt his body turn to ice when she ran from the room as if the hounds of hell were after her.

He passed a hand over his forehead, rooted to the spot. Lexi's need for her own mother and father had only become apparent in the last ten days. But for a child of that age, ten days was a long time. He muttered a low curse. Events had escalated faster than he'd dreamed. He needed to take action—fast.

Emma ran out of steam halfway down the stairs. Incapable of continuing, she slumped in a miserable heap on one of the wide steps. Leon came to sit beside her. His whole body was tense for some reason and she gritted her teeth, so exhausted—both emotionally and physically—that she couldn't bear to do battle with him.

All she wanted was to be spirited back to the villa by some magic hand, to be presented with a cup of tea and then carried to bed. She felt she could sleep for England.

'Go away!' she grated fiercely.

'Emma! I'm sorry that happened,' he said shakily. Astonished by the sincerity in his tone, she searched his face. He seemed very upset. 'I'm sorry,' he repeated helplessly.

Bewildered, she mastered her trembling lip. 'I'd f-forgotten,' she mumbled, thrown completely into confusion by his hand, which was sympathetically stroking her cheek. 'The doll… I should have realised…but…' She couldn't go on. The joy had been too intense, the disappointment too wounding.

He put a comforting hand on hers. 'It was a bad moment for you.' He removed his hand and cupped her chin and she felt more muddled than ever. 'Poor Lexi. I've been blind.'

'Blind?' she repeated, her brain and her voice in a fog.

'To her needs.'

Emma's heart skipped a beat. She looked at him with huge, wondering eyes, her lips parted with breathless hope. Of course Leon didn't care particularly that she'd been hurt. But he did care about Lexi. And maybe he'd see that her daughter truly needed her. It was possible that he'd stop trying to get her on the next flight back to England and would allow the relationship to develop. She had a slim, but welcome chance.

'Leon,' she cried fervently, grabbing his arms in her desperation. 'You want me to give up and go home. But you can't keep us apart. It would be wrong. You can see that, can't you? She wants her mother.'

'Sure. A mother, perhaps. But…*you*?' he said gratingly.

She winced. 'You think I'm a criminal but I'm not. And even if I were,' she added hotly, 'does that make any difference to the fact that Lexi wants a real mother of her own? Not Marina, or Natasa, or any other woman you bring into your life, but *me*! I've only known her for a few hours today but already I can see that she has sensed that something's missing in her life. Let me be part of her world, Leon. She needs me.'

'You're asking too much,' he muttered.

'Not if you really do care about her,' she cried passionately. 'You'd put your own revenge and anger aside and do what's best for her.'

For a long time he contemplated her and she held her breath waiting for his verdict. 'I need time to work out the best way of dealing with this.'

'How long?' she whispered.

'I don't know,' he snapped irritably. 'As long as it takes. I wasn't going to let you near her originally. Part of me wishes I'd stuck to my guns—'

'And the other part?' she asked anxiously, scanning his frowning face.

'Is worrying what damage you'll do to both of us,' he growled.

'Why would I want to hurt my own child? That little mite…' Her words became caught up in her tightened throat. 'Leon, I'll be careful. Sensitive,' she promised desperately.

'You can set the agenda. I'll be her daddy's friend until you say it's time to tell her the truth—'

'It could be a long while.'

'I have the rest of my life,' she replied with heartfelt passion. 'What could be more important?'

'I do believe you mean that,' he muttered. 'I've never known anyone so determined.' He hesitated, his eyes brooding. 'I'll give it some thought. I will do what I consider to be best for Lexi. *Your* wishes don't come into it. And now stop restricting my blood supply.'

She looked down and snatched away her hands from his arms. There were marks where her fingers had been where her nails had dug into his flesh. 'Sorry about that. I got carried away—'

'You always do,' he said, his expression brooding.

Her victory was beginning to sink in. 'I feel very passionately about my daughter. I know you do too.' She slumped, feeling quite drained suddenly.

'It's been an exhausting day for you,' he observed softly.

'I've loved it,' she protested.

'Hmm. Love-hate, I think.'

That was true. But she wouldn't have missed it for the world. She fell silent, summoning up the will to stand and begin the long walk back. Groggily she got to her feet and she gripped the banister as if her life depended on it. Step by step she fumbled her way down the stairs.

There only remained the huge hall to tackle. She eyed it doubtfully but set off, her eyes fixed grimly on the massive wooden door. Behind her she could hear Leon talking to Natasa. And then he'd stridden past and was opening the door for her, an unreadable look on his face.

'See you tomorrow,' she said weakly, before he could suggest an appointment sometime in the future. And she stumbled helter-skelter down the steps outside.

'Wait. I'm going to walk you back.' A torch was flashing along the path ahead, picking out the way for her.

'I can manage,' she snapped, and spoiled her proud independence by tripping over her own feet.

Leon's arms caught her waist and she felt his warm body against her spine and buttocks before she could wrench herself free. He was aroused again. He'd do himself a favour if he hurried back to Natasa, she thought crossly.

'Stubborn woman! You're too tired to see straight,' he rebuked.

'Yes. And not in the mood for company,' she snapped.

Half tearful in her impatience with her irritating tendency to be feeble whenever she needed her strength most, she stumbled again. And this time his arm crooked around her waist and wouldn't be shifted.

'Stop fighting me,' Leon said in an unfairly low and husky tone. 'I can't let you go back on your own in this condition—'

'More than your reputation's worth,' she muttered sourly.

'It would look bad,' he agreed drily, 'if you were found in a state of collapse on my land.'

'I'd rather crawl back on my hands and knees than put you through such shame!' she flung, hot from the pressure of his hip against hers.

'You're unbelievably obstinate,' he said with a sigh. 'One of Lexi's endearing traits. If she wants to finish a task she's set herself, she'll do it come hell or high water.'

Emma raised a weak and fond smile. 'Good on her!'

She considered the trembling muscles in her legs and then the path stretching ahead. It looked daunting.

'Long way, isn't it?' Leon murmured, interpreting her frown correctly.

Her mind might be obstinate but her legs were begging for assistance. She heaved a resigned sigh. 'OK, Leon. You're right. I am shattered and in the absence of a minibus or a Zimmer frame, I suppose you'll have to do.'

'Was it…very difficult for you today?' he asked as they continued.

She sighed. 'Very. You were right. It hurt.'

'But you want to repeat the torture.'

She smiled ruefully, remembering it all. 'Of course. It was wonderful, too. She is adorable. I love her dearly.'

'You found it exhausting being with her.'

And how! Her limbs felt as heavy as lead and she couldn't prevent her body from drooping. 'I'll be fine once I'm fully fit,' she said in a tired voice.

'Toddlers are very demanding—'

'Are you suggesting I'm not up to being with her?' she said flaring.

He squeezed her waist. 'Relax. I'm not trying to score points. I'm saying that I understand. I suggest you have a rest tomorrow. Swim, laze around—'

'You're stalling me. I want to see Lexi,' she cried helplessly.

'I know,' he said soothingly. 'But I need time to think.'

'Can't you do that while I'm around?' she pleaded.

'No. I can't,' he muttered.

'I won't get in the way. I'll play with—'

'Emma,' he interrupted tightly, 'I can't think, I can't concentrate with you there. Accept that and do yourself a favour too, take a break. It was a struggle today, wasn't it? You pushed yourself to keep going but I saw how much of an effort it was towards the end. Do you want to burn yourself out before you've got very far? Does that make sense?'

He was right and she hated him for that. It upset her that she wasn't really well enough to see Lexi every day. A deafening silence fell between them. They trudged on, bruising mint and basil and thyme underfoot. She tried to find her breath but it had run away and her mouth was doing its stupid wobble again.

Leon stopped and gently held her. She stared bleakly at his shirt front. It was a strange blue-white in the darkness and she gazed in mesmerised fascination at the powerful rise and fall of his chest.

'I know you, Emma,' he said softly. 'You are normally full of boundless energy and enthusiasm, just like Lexi. But you're not yourself at the moment and it's obvious that you need to conserve your strength. Rest tomorrow. Sleep all day if you want, what does it matter?'

A sudden breeze played with her hair, whisking it about her face and he gently lifted golden strands away, his warm fingertips brushing her cool skin. She looked up and fell prey to his compelling eyes.

Petrified that she'd make the same mistake twice and inch forwards for a kiss, she tore her glance away and gazed stoically into the velvet night beyond his broad shoulder.

'You...you won't hold it against me?' she said jerkily. 'You won't point out to the courts that I couldn't be bothered to see Lexi, but preferred to laze around—?'

The tightening of his grip stopped her. 'No, Emma.' He seemed to struggle with his thoughts. 'If you must know...I don't want you bursting into tears or breaking up in front of Lexi. That won't do her any good at all. If you carry on driving yourself too hard, you might well lose control. I know your composure is being sorely tested because I have some idea of how you're feeling, being shut out of her life—'

'Yes, I know you do,' she said, remembering his problems with Soula.

His lashes lowered to hide his dark, impassioned eyes and she felt suddenly dizzy with weariness.

'You're swaying,' he said thickly. 'I should have got the car out. Let's get you back.'

They walked hip to hip like lovers, Leon's head bent over hers solicitously, though she knew it was because he was merely worried that she might keel over and have to be carried.

Her arm had found its way around his waist and she allowed it to stay there. For added support, she told herself, but knew that was a lie. She just wanted to sink into his arms and sleep, to wake with him beside her and to gaze at the beautiful angles of his face.

But he was her implacable enemy and would fight tooth and nail to keep her daughter, whatever concessions he granted her now.

The villa was ahead. After today's family fun, it would be silent and lonely in there. Depressed, Emma pushed Leon away.

'Thank you,' she said unhappily. 'Goodnight.'

He continued to walk beside her as she stumbled drunkenly along. 'I must see you to your door—'

'Checking up on me?' she blurted out, too miserable to think what she was saying. She wanted Leon: his sympathy, his body, his respect. And he was off limits. So she'd turn herself against him. 'Do you want to make sure I haven't got an orgy organised?'

'If you have, I hardly think,' he said, sounding gently amused, 'that you'd be up to it.'

'No. I'm sorry I said that,' she muttered, immediately ashamed of herself. She really wasn't cut out to be a bitch. 'You've been kind…gone out of your way to see me home—'

'Here, let me. I don't think you can cope with locks either,' he said, and she realised she'd been trying to put the key in upside down. 'I hadn't realised you were that shattered.'

She leaned against the door jamb, her whole body shaking. 'Lexi doesn't give her heart easily, does she?' she said with a doleful face.

'She takes her time. Weighs people up. Gives them that basilisk stare and waits to see if they run screaming,' he agreed.

'It pained me more than you could ever know,' she said dispiritedly. 'You said you'd put me through hell. Well…' she choked, tears blinding her '…you've succeeded.'

'Emma…'

He'd followed her in. But she'd had enough. She stood in the middle of the room shaking with tension.

'Go!' she said jerkily. 'Just *go!*'

'I...can't,' he said huskily.

'Why?' Emma wailed, wanting him, hating him, muddled, beyond coherent thought.

'I don't know. Or...perhaps I know too well. I—I feel some responsibility for you—'

'Too late!' She hurled the words hysterically, lurching towards the bedroom. 'I needed you years ago,' she said stormily. 'I needed you to believe me when I was accused of fraud. I needed you to tell me we were finished and you were getting engaged...'

It was too much to bear. She choked on her tears and gave up, slamming the bedroom door behind her and jamming a chair against the handle.

Somehow she dragged off her clothes, had a perfunctory wash and crawled into bed. It was only when she turned out the light that she heard the front door close. Leon had left. She burst into tears again.

Leon found it hard to concentrate. He'd slept badly, Emma's forlorn face had firmly stuck on the back of his eyelids, burning into his brain with the force of an indestructible laser image. Even now, at ten in the morning, she was in his eyes, his mind, and his body...

And he didn't even have Lexi to occupy him. Natasa had taken her to town to do 'women's things', 'Tasa had said, and the two of them had run to 'Tasa's car giggling with glee.

Emma's doll had gone too. Leon wasn't sure if he was glad or worried that it accompanied Lexi everywhere, into the bathroom that morning, for breakfast on the terrace, and then—duly coated in 'sun cream' and complete with rucksack just like Lexi—into the car.

His mind darted about like a butterfly. Thinking of golden

hair sweeping briefly, seductively over a softly curved cheek. Of a face tight with desperate longing, arms fidgeting because they couldn't do what they'd been made to do: cuddle a child. And the body...the body! He groaned.

After losing his second e-mail of the day and failing to make sense of a perfectly simple company balance sheet, he leapt irritably from his desk and grabbed some gear for the beach.

He needed an emotional break too. He'd swim till he dropped. And think of nothing, not even tip-tilted lips that needed kissing.

Twenty minutes later he knew it had been a good decision. Lulled by the droning of bees as he strolled through the garden, he let his tense body relax.

A griffon vulture soared overhead. Delicate mauve thistles carpeted the olive grove beyond. A faint breeze stirred the fronds of the date-palms, sending them clacking and as he approached the beach, swallowtail butterflies decorated the garrigue—the low herb undergrowth—like darting jewels.

He stood at the top of the sandy bay to admire its voluptuous sweep. And his pulses quickened to see another voluptuous shape. Emma.

He groaned, knowing he had to go back. And found his legs carrying him inexorably forward. She needed to be alone. To rest and recuperate. So did he—and he wouldn't get any rest with her around. His muscles always knotted up.

Right, that was agreed. They shouldn't be together. The fire was too easily lit in his blood...

But she was there. Alone. And something tugged him inexorably on, ignoring sense and caution.

'I'm surprised to find you down here,' he discovered himself saying quietly.

She sat up on the lounger, visibly flustered. He wasn't too composed either. Unlike yesterday, when she'd worn a one-piece, she was in a small and wonderfully revealing bikini which made the most of her slim body and spectacular curves. Her hands had come to protect her chest, an odd reaction, which had made his gaze linger there longer than wise.

His nails dug into his palms, which helped. He tried to look nonchalant and thought it would help if he sat down on the sunbed beside her.

'Sorry to intrude,' he said with unreal cheerfulness. 'I just fancied a swim in the sea.'

She smiled hesitantly, clearly weighing up his mood and to his surprise he found himself beaming in pleasure. Her smile broadened in response to his inane grin and he realised she was nervous. She was wondering if his verdict was for or against her.

Behind her sunglasses, her eyes were unreadable. He hoped the same applied to his because he was already lusting unmercifully.

'So did I.' Encouraged by his friendly nod, she went on. 'I—I had a long, long sleep and feel a lot better. And I'd…liked it here so much yesterday that…I wanted to spend the day here,' she said haltingly.

'Me too. Do you mind if I stay?'

He frowned. Why had he said that? She might object, in which case—

'How could I? It is your beach, after all.' She eyed him uncertainly. 'But I'll go if you're going to growl at me. I need a restful day for a change.'

'I won't growl,' he promised, managing to hold back a sigh of relief. 'I'm looking for an uncomplicated few hours, schlepping out. Deal?'

She grinned back at him and seemed delighted. 'Deal.'

Her head tipped back to enjoy the sun, the action raising the contours of her breasts. Leon tried not to notice his racing pulses, and studiously averted his gaze and fixed it sternly on the dazzling sea.

'I'm glad you feel better,' he ventured to say. And wondered why he felt that way and how banal his conversation was going to get.

'I really needed a break. I've been under a great strain for a long time,' she said quietly.

'I can imagine.'

Again, a pang of pity—and his low, caring voice must have conveyed that pity to her. But she'd brought her troubles on herself. He had to remember that.

And yet he knew he couldn't help feeling great sympathy for her. Lexi was her baby. And a stranger. He frowned, washed by pain on her behalf.

She sighed, the pleasure of that outrush of breath attracting his attention. Her eyes were closed in contentment, the sun gleaming on her pale gold skin. He felt his throat go dry.

'Where's Lexi?' she murmured.

He gave a joking groan. 'Buying up every pink dress in Zakynthos with Natasa.'

He checked himself. She'd winced and he realised he'd put his foot in it. It must hurt her to have some other woman doing things with her daughter.

'She…she's fond of Lexi,' Emma observed, turning her head to study him closely. 'Does…does Lexi ever call her Mama?'

It was his turn to wince. More and more he was beginning to realise that he couldn't exclude Emma from Lexi's life. But the implications of changing tack were alarming.

'Only once.'

'Once is enough, Leon!'

He looked deep into her startlingly blue eyes. 'I know. It upset Natasa. She made sure that Lexi knew that she wasn't in the running for that position.' From the anxious look on Emma's face, the relationship needed clarifying. And perhaps a little more than that. 'My sister-in-law,' he explained, 'adores children.'

'Sister-in-law!' It seemed the light had dawned. 'She's Marina's sister?'

He nodded and could see her brain turning over the information. 'Her husband died six months ago from cancer. For some reason she's convinced she'll never marry again and have babies of her own. Which is ridiculous, of course, but it gives her great happiness to spend time with Lexi. And I want 'Tasa to be happy. She nursed her husband devotedly and I admire her, and wish her well.'

'A diamond among women. Poor Natasa! It must have been terrible for her to lose her husband at such a young age. All her dreams, her plans for the future…' Her voice petered out.

Natasa's story seemed to have touched a chord with Emma. He saw that she was struggling with a profound sympathy, a kind of horror that went far beyond any normal reaction.

'Emma?' He touched her arm and she jumped.

'I—I was thinking. Was it quick?' she asked, her face pale.

'Her husband's death? Yes, mercifully so.' It seemed that she waited to hear more. 'They both came to stay with me. It helped her to cope. It meant she could forget normal household activities and concentrate on being with her husband. We knew it was terminal.'

'Difficult for you all,' she observed, her expression full of concern.

There was something about her that invited his confidences. He'd never spoken about Natasa to anyone outside the immediate family. And even to them he'd never revealed his own feelings. But suddenly he felt a need to open up.

'I think the worst part for me was when I heard her crying all alone at night,' he said quietly. 'I could do so much to help her, but there were some things she had to face on her own. That was hard for me to accept. I wanted to take away her anguish completely.'

'You can't,' Emma said. 'People have to go through that grieving process. She was mourning for her husband and herself. It's a mistake to think you can leap-frog misery. It has to be faced, and then it's been dealt with—and you're the stronger for it. You did all the right things, Leon.'

'Did I?' He wasn't sure.

'You gave her support when she needed it. She cares very deeply for you—'

'And I for her.' Without her, he didn't know what he would have done. She had been—and would be—his lifeline.

Emma's white teeth snagged at her lower lip. 'So…you're helping her to adjust. You're making her feel useful and she's fussing over you and Lexi like…like…a mother hen,' she finished jerkily.

He wasn't sure why she was on edge. Perhaps because she believed Natasa was taking over her role. Anxious to put Emma straight, he took her hand in his to capture her attention.

'Natasa will never be Lexi's surrogate mother,' he said gently. Her enormous eyes remained fixed on his hopefully and he knew he'd hit on the answer to her fears. 'And the reason she's here is that when her husband died she asked if she could help run the house. She needed to be with family for a while and needed an excuse to stay without feeling she was a parasite. My housekeeper was ready to retire, so it seemed a good arrangement.'

Emma frowned at their interlocked fingers. 'Wasn't there gossip, with you both living in the same house?'

'Not with Marina there too, and Soula. Natasa is devoted to her sister and everyone knows we are just an extended family. It's not an uncommon arrangement.'

'Poor Natasa,' she said again. 'I hope she finds happiness one day.'

Happiness. There were several levels of it. He was content enough. But once he had known a happiness that had filled every cell in his body with the joy of living. Would that rapture ever be part of him again?

'I think I'll go for a swim,' she muttered.

He watched her walking thoughtfully to the water's edge.

In the old days she would have turned a cartwheel or two in sheer exuberance, but she was different now. Sometimes the old impetuosity surfaced, but mostly she was sad and subdued. He wanted to change that, to see her laugh more frequently.

After a decent interval, he hauled off his T-shirt and ran into the sea, plunging his hot and tense body into the cool turquoise water. It was a while before he paused in his ferocious crawl and began to swim for pleasure. Eventually he turned on his back and floated, staring up at the bright blue sky. When he struck out for shore, he saw her towelling herself dry on the beach.

Decision time. He sat on the edge of the water, thinking of the emotional mess that Soula was in and how his calm, gentle influence had been worse than useless and soon he'd have to accept that and leave Marina and Soula to their own devices.

It hurt to admit it, but Emma was right. Lexi would probably be more balanced if she knew her biological mother. He watched the sea lapping over his feet. There were some things you couldn't stop. Tides and love being two of those.

But the danger for Lexi if he agreed—for his peace of mind! Perhaps, he thought, as the water swirled in a rush around his entire body, he could cope with the prospect of Emma's access visits. All he had to do was to make sure that she was never alone with Lex—not now, or any time in the future.

Aware that he was making a momentous about-turn, he jumped up and walked quickly to where Emma was sitting, her honey-gold body bolt upright in the lounger.

'You've decided! You'll let me stay and befriend Lexi!' she cried eagerly, when he was still a yard or so away.

His eyes widened in stark surprise. 'How the devil did you know?'

'I read you,' she cried happily.

'*Read* me?'

'The way you sat there, thinking—and your body language… Besides, I felt sure you'd do the right thing.'

He grunted and sat on the edge of his lounger facing her. 'Don't make me regret it, Emma,' he warned. 'If you harm that child—'

'I wouldn't!' she cried with elation, swinging her legs around to mirror his pose. 'Lexi's welfare comes first, I promise you that,' she said softly. 'Thank you for giving me this chance.'

'It's for Lexi, not you.'

Or was it? He didn't know any more, only that he felt as if a burden had been lifted from his shoulders. He'd see her often. Feed his eyes on her. Get to know her. Spirals of pleasure rippled through him, shortening his breath. Madness.

'That's why I felt sure you must agree,' she said happily.

'You hit a raw nerve.'

'Did I? Good!' she exulted.

'I don't want Lexi confused,' he continued, trying to quieten his own leaping nerves. But he couldn't get enough of her ecstatic face and her joy was lifting his soul. She seemed to glow with life. And he wanted to kiss her till she couldn't draw breath. 'We do this gradually. Be guided by me.'

'Yes, Leon,' she agreed with a laugh. 'Oh, I'm so happy!'

She jumped up, her face rapturous. And, impulsive as ever, she bent forward and kissed both his cheeks. Fatally, he had imprisoned her face between his hands before he knew what he was doing. And their mouths met, first clumsily, then fiercely as Emma's euphoria carried her beyond the realms of caution.

Then she pushed at his shoulders. Reluctantly he let a gap form between their lips and his hot eyes met her troubled blue ones.

'I can't believe I just did that!' she exclaimed, her hand in front of her soft mouth.

Ditto. He managed a casual grin. 'You always did need to let off steam.'

Scarlet with embarrassment, she nodded, seizing on his excuse with alacrity. 'That's it! And I will!' she cried, leaping up.

And to his delight, she ran along the firm sand by the lapping waves, turning a series of perfect cartwheels.

CHAPTER EIGHT

'I THOUGHT we'd feed the animals,' Leon said casually the next morning, when he and Lexi arrived at her villa, as they'd arranged.

'Animals?' Emma asked, smiling broadly to see Lexi jumping up and down excitedly.

'Chittens,' Lexi explained loftily, holding out a soggy and distorted lump of bread. It had clearly been squeezed fiercely in her little hand for some while and Emma's eyes softened with amused affection.

'Chickens and turkeys, goats, sheep and geese,' Leon said indulgently. 'Come on. I'll show you. Lexi saved that from breakfast, didn't you, sweetheart?' He repeated that in Greek and she nodded so vigorously that her scrunchie fell out of her silky hair.

'Here. I can do it,' Emma offered eagerly.

But Lexi pulled away, glaring at Emma from under her lowered brows with an expression so like Leon's that it caught at her throat. And she tried not to mind the rejection. It was early days yet. But, despite her reasoning, it still hurt.

'Hold the scrunchie for me, will you Emma?' Leon asked casually. He put down his own bag of stale bread, scooped up Lexi's curls into his hand and gave them an admirably fashionable twist.

She was grateful to him for involving her. The smile she bestowed on him was pure gold and Leon responded with a conspiratorial wink as he fixed the hair problem with a deftness born of long practice.

'The animals belong to the caretaker,' Leon explained, when they were eventually on their way—a tickle, a cuddle

and a ride on his shoulders later. 'He rang to say that the
turkeys had chicks so I thought Lex might like to see them.'

The smallholding lay beyond a field of low currant vines
which marched across the red, rich soil in military ranks.
With Lexi's legs wrapped suffocatingly around his neck, his
head reluctantly doubling as a drum for her small hands,
Leon led the way beneath a bower of wild honeysuckle to a
lemon grove, seemingly alive with cheeping grey chicks.

'There they are,' he cried, lowering Lexi to the ground.

'Chittens!' Lexi cried with joy, and hurtled after them.

'She's got my finesse,' Emma said ruefully, seeing the
turkey chicks scatter in alarm as the blonde bombshell approached. 'Delicate as a stampeding bull.'

'Enthusiasm, and it's wonderful,' Leon corrected with a
grin. He scraped a hand through his mussed hair.

'So long as you're not a chitten.' She giggled.

Leon laughed and ran to catch Lexi's hand and to show
her how to win the confidence of the chicks. With great patience he taught her to throw her bread as far as possible at
first and then increasingly closer and closer.

However, Lexi's aim wasn't too good and Emma and Leon
kept chuckling as one or two of the tiny chicks narrowly
missed concussion from the heavy lumps.

'Hello, chittens!' Lexi whispered, awed, as they cheeped
with enthusiastic recklessness around her feet.

'Chicks.'

'Chits.'

'Stand very still, sweetheart,' he said lovingly, and Lexi
turned into a rigid statue, only her fingers daring to move.
Which made her aim even worse.

Leon gave Emma some bread and, with it, a sideways grin.
He's wonderful, she thought, admiring his patience with her
over-eager daughter. And she tried hard to understand his
slow and careful Greek when they went to dispense grain for
the chickens and to feed the other animals in the enclosure.

Then, by a clump of cornflowers, something caught her eye and she bent down to see what it was.

'Look!' she cried, her voice hushed in pleasure. 'I've found an egg.' It was freshly laid. She crouched down and smiled at Lexi. 'Hold out your hand,' she said in English, showing her what she meant.

A small and sticky palm was hesitantly extended and Emma gently slid the egg into it. The look on her daughter's face made her heart turn over.

'It's warm!' Lexi squeaked.

'Gently,' Leon warned, his voice low and soft. 'It will break easily.'

'Oh, oh, oh!' Lexi whispered, magnificently reining in her obvious desire to leap about in glee.

'For your breakfast,' Emma suggested, wishing she could be there.

Her daughter beamed at her, the blue eyes searingly bright. 'Yes. Thank-you-very-much.'

'My pleasure,' Emma whispered happily and her moist eyes met Leon's.

A searing flash of longing went through her and she turned away hastily. For a split second she had yearned for the impossible. That she and Leon and Lexi would be feeding chittens and finding eggs and loving one another for the rest of their lives.

But he despised her and believed she had not only defrauded innocent people, but had been the indirect cause of his brother's death. And, though he might not be averse to kissing her, he certainly wouldn't welcome her freely into his highly protected home.

The dream had been too welcome, the reality harsh. Unless she altered her plans radically, she would be taking her daughter away from all this. Her eyes widened. How could she do that to her child? This paradise…

She swallowed. It was her own fault. Leon had warned her that she'd realise Lexi's future lay here—and that the knowledge would be painful to accept. And she'd recklessly brushed aside his caution, seeing it as a threat. But perhaps he'd been right. Doubts gnawed at her, spoiling the happy moment and her stomach felt suddenly hollow.

'We're going back to Emma's villa now. The animals are all breaded-out.' Leon's voice was warm and gentle, close to her ear.

She shivered and tried to perk up. 'For a swim?' she suggested unsteadily.

Lexi let out a whoop and charged off. Leon threw Emma a grin and ran after her. She heard her daughter wailing—presumably she'd fallen over—and Leon's soothing murmur, a childish giggle, and his deep laugh. How easily a child's distress could be smoothed over.

I want him, she thought. And not just physically. Someone to soothe her hurt, to be there when she needed him. A shoulder to lean on and a friend to share her day, her moments of joy.

Emma stifled those thoughts at birth. Life wasn't that forgiving and Leon certainly wouldn't be.

Later that afternoon, after exhausting games in the pool, Lexi fell fast asleep. Tenderly Leon placed her daughter's limp form on a lounger beneath a walnut tree and joined Emma by the poolside where she sat dangling her legs in the warm water.

'She liked the egg,' he said, easing himself down to the tiled edge.

She smiled. 'Almost as good as the crown jewels.'

'Better. She's fascinated by nature. I'm up all hours of the night trying to keep a few steps ahead of her. I'm OK identifying beetles, but not too hot on finches,' he said ruefully.

'What about bees that look like Zeppelins?' she squealed, as she ducked away from the attentions of a huge insect with iridescent wings. 'Crikey. It's got a buzz that sounds like a chain-saw!'

'Keep still. It won't harm you,' Leon advised, laughing.

The giant bee proved him a liar by doing a circuit of her head, clearly preparing to dive-bomb her and then line up for an emergency landing.

'Help!' She grabbed frantically at Leon.

'I...ooooohaargh! What—?'

He overbalanced and they both toppled into the water, coming up spluttering and laughing. The mock menace on his face made her squeal and she struck out for the steps at the far end of the pool.

Of course he caught her. Emma shrieked when he grabbed her and then became aware of someone else shouting. Still clasped in his firm grip, she jerked her head around to discover a tight-lipped Marina standing on the edge of the pool, clad in a black leather basque and a pelmet skirt, and with her hands on her hips in an attitude of frosty disapproval.

Surprisingly, Leon kept his hands on her waist. 'Hello, Marina. This is Emma—' he began courteously.

'Instead of fooling around with the criminal classes,' Marina snapped nastily, 'how about paying attention to your niece?'

From the increased pressure on her waist, and the clenching of Leon's teeth, Emma expected him to put Marina in her place with a few well-chosen epithets. Instead, he merely said, 'Lexi's asleep.'

There was a splash. Emma jerked her head around and realised that a child of five or six years of age in a pink party dress and with ribbons everywhere conceivable—Soula, without question—was calmly and maliciously throwing objects into the pool. A chair. Her sunglasses. Emma gasped. A towel—

Leon launched himself across the pool in a whoosh of water and hauled himself out.

'Soula, for heaven's sake!' he rebuked.

The little girl screamed and ran away from him, pushing

whatever she could find into the pool as she went. Two mugs, a plate, an orange and Lexi's jelly shoes.

'Now look what you've done!' screeched Marina.

'Soula,' Leon said quietly, restraining his temper with difficulty as a small teak table hit the water, 'please don't do that—'

'Don't come near me!' Soula shouted, stamping her feet. 'Mummee! *Mummee!*'

Emma was horrified by the extraordinary vehemence of Soula's appeal to her mother. The little girl flung herself at her mother's knees and was immediately soothed.

Marina and Leon stared at one another: she spitting fire and hatred, he—oh, thought Emma, her heart going out to him—he was hurt and frustrated with a tortured expression on his face. Sadly she clambered out of the pool, wondering what to do and afraid that Lexi would wake even though Leon had said she slept the sleep of the dead. She headed for her daughter just as Leon hissed, 'Take Lexi in!'

Hastily Emma scooped up the floppy little body, holding it close to her. My child, she thought shakily. In my arms at last but for the most awful reason.

Unsteady on her feet and nervous of her bundle, she climbed the steps with great care up to the villa, then sat in the nearest chair with her, cradling her close.

My baby, my baby, her heart was saying as she gazed down on the sleep-soft face. Oh, my darling baby! She kissed Lexi's head, feeling guilty. It was as if she was violating her daughter's rights. She gulped and restrained her urge to squeeze Lexi tight and kiss every inch of the sweet face.

When she looked up to the scene outside, she saw that Leon was standing over Soula, his hands on his hips.

'Soula, you can't go around doing that!' he said in a rasping voice.

'She's upset because you forgot Lexi was going to Maria's party,' Marina yelled. 'We had to waste time coming here and she'll have missed the clown—'

'I said Lex wouldn't be going,' he replied. 'She didn't seem bothered. Her mother is here—'

Emma looked down sharply. Lexi had given a small sigh. Stealthily, trying not to disturb the sleeping child, she rose from the chair, intending to move back out of earshot. She held her breath and froze. Lexi's eyes opened—and then closed again.

'But you promised,' shouted Marina as Emma cautiously moved further into the open-plan room. 'You can't break that promise.'

Faintly she heard Leon's groan and she paused, straining her ears to listen to his reply. 'That was a week ago, before Emma came—'

'You said you were going to fling the little cow out on her ear!'

Lexi's eyes snapped open. She registered Emma's face, and burst into tears.

'Hush, sweetheart,' Emma murmured, but there was no response from the stiff little body. 'It's OK. It's me.'

She longed desperately to say, It's Mummy. Despite all her attempts she couldn't comfort Lexi. Almost in tears herself, she tried everything she could to soothe the struggling, wriggling and weeping child, but to no avail. And that upset her desperately.

And then Leon was there, taking Lexi from her and holding her sobbing daughter tight, wrapping his big arms around her.

'She didn't hear anything, honestly,' Emma wailed in agitation. 'She just opened her eyes and cried—'

'It's OK, Emma. She was startled.'

Gradually Lexi's sobs lessened as his reassuring voice murmured softly in her small ear.

Startled. By the sight of her own mother. She let out a moan.

Leon was kissing the small, damp face, making a game of capturing the tears with his mouth and smacking his lips noisily. When he pretended to eat her nose and ears and declared them tasty too, she dissolved into giggles, her tears forgotten.

So easy, thought Emma sadly. If only she could comfort her own child. But she wasn't loved. She was a stranger.

Oh, God! she thought, wrapping her arms tightly around her pain-slashed body. I've lost my child. Will I ever get her back?

'The party—' Marina had appeared at the back door.

He let Lexi down to the floor. 'I'll ask her,' he said with apparent calm. But his hands were clenched into fists.

Emma's eyes flashed. She wasn't letting her daughter go off with a mad clothes-horse and her destructive child.

'Leon,' she said grimly, 'a word.'

He took one look at her and seemed to know what was in her mind.

'Natasa is driving,' he said quietly. 'She'll be responsible for Lexi.'

'But—'

'Trust me. Would I put her in an unsuitable situation?'

'N-no—'

'It's none of her business!' Marina snapped.

'She's Lexi's m-o-t-h-e-r,' he said, spelling the word carefully. 'She has every right to be concerned for her daughter's welfare.'

His amiable tone was carefully monitored for Lexi's benefit and Emma detected steel in his eyes when he looked at his ex-wife.

Marina's mouth looked dangerous, ready to spit venom. Emma braced herself, fearful for what Lexi might hear.

'Do you think so? That woman killed your brother!' Marina flung the words, fast and furious. 'Have you *forgotten*—?'

As Emma gasped, Leon crossed the floor in a flash. 'Don't say another word,' he murmured pleasantly. 'Or I'll be tempted to violence. Let me have Lex's party dress. Go and wait in the car. She'll be out in a few moments if she's coming. You've gone too far this time, Marina. We'll talk when you get back.'

Aghast, Emma sank into a chair and stared blankly into space. She'd been so wrapped up in her own problems that she hadn't thought of things from his point of view—however wrong that view might be.

How could a man *like* a woman he thought had been responsible for his brother's death, let alone feel fond of her? And his approval and respect was what she longed for—like Natasa. But there was no evidence to prove her innocent. So he'd always blame her. She groaned.

'I don't want her to go!' Emma whispered in panic when she and Leon were alone again. Fortunately Lexi had become engrossed in playing with her doll.

'I do,' he said firmly. 'There are things I have to say to you immediately—and I need time to do so.'

'But you said I could be with Lex—'

'I did. That was before the scene out there really developed—'

'Scene? It was more like Armageddon!'

'You're exaggerating, Emma,' he said gently.

'Not where Lexi is concerned.'

'It needs explaining. The party is a sleepover. Natasa will watch over her. She keeps a tight rein on her sister and Soula. And Marina doesn't shout at Lexi. Only me.'

'And Soula?' Emma's hands had tightened into fists, ready to defend her child.

'Soula isn't interested in anyone other than herself,' he said bleakly.

'Leon—' she cried, aghast that a father should feel so badly about his child.

'Give me time. I'll explain.'

And he talked gently to Lexi, dangling the pretty baby-blue dress—far more attractive than Soula's—as a lure and soon he had persuaded Lexi into its soft folds, his tone eager and excited as he spoke of the delights ahead.

But when they'd waved goodbye, his cheerful expression was wiped from his face as if a giant hand had erased it. With a hard expulsion of air from his lungs, he sat down heavily on the sofa and, through the open door at the far end of the room, he gloomily surveyed the debris floating in the pool.

Emma ignored it. He needed her more. 'Leon, don't worry,' she said gently, sitting beside him and tentatively stroking his shoulder. 'Lexi didn't hear anything she shouldn't, I'm positive. It...it was just me who made her cry.'

'But she *could* have heard. So far she hasn't, but...' He sucked in a long breath. 'And now you're thinking that this isn't paradise after all,' he muttered bitterly. 'And you'd be right.'

He looked at her, his eyes bleak and infinitely pained and in an instinctive action she took his head in her hands and laid it on her breast, enfolding him in her arms and rocking him.

The scene she'd witnessed had been appalling. Not the kind of thing to risk exposing a child to. She had ammunition, she thought sadly, to put before the courts. And it gave her no pleasure.

'I don't understand,' she said, stroking his dark, shining hair. A lump came into her throat. 'Why, if you and Marina hate the sight of each other, do you let her stay with you? You're divorced. You don't have to make each other's lives hell.'

He drew away a little and heaved such a despairing sigh that she felt like cuddling him and kissing him better.

'Leon,' she whispered, afraid that she cared too much. 'Tell me,' she begged. 'I want to help if I can.'

His arm came to rest around her shoulders and he pulled her close. 'Hold me,' he said simply. 'That helps.'

With concern in every fibre of her being, she did as he

asked. And soon, when his breathing had settled to a more normal rate, she ventured again.

'Marina. Soula.'

She bit her lip, worrying that the child would be a terrible influence on little Lexi. And the rows must be distressing, if that was a sample. Her eyes widened as she remembered something.

'When you were visiting me in prison, Marina was looking after Lexi!' she said in horror.

'Not exactly,' he replied. 'It was Natasa who took charge. But if I'd said Marina's sister-in-law was caring for your daughter, you would have gone ballistic. Look, let's clear the pool then get dressed and make a cup of tea,' he said shakily. 'And I'll tell you everything.'

In silence he walked out and dived into the pool, lifting the objects out. Emma and he then sluiced them under the pool shower and dried some, leaving the sun to dry the others.

Then they went back inside. Alarmed by his brooding lethargy, she watched him walk slowly up the stairs to the bedroom where he'd left his clothes. His steps slowed overhead and she found herself listening out for him anxiously as she hurried to her own bedroom, showered and scrambled into a simple scoop-neck T-shirt and denim button-through skirt, dragging a quick brush through her hair.

Rushing out, she put just a little water in the kettle and grabbed a couple of mugs and two teabags, opting for speed over elegance. The tea was made by the time he came down, steam coiling up from the mugs which she'd placed on the low marble table in front of the sofa.

She watched his slow progress down the stairs and her heart missed a beat. Edible as ever in the mint green shirt and stone chinos, he had a vague, distracted air which wasn't like him at all.

'Sit down,' she said taking charge. She occupied one end of the sofa and intended him to feel he could reach out for whatever comfort he needed so she patted the space beside her. 'I want to know it all.'

When he came over it seemed natural that he should pull her against him again so they were curled up together, her head on his chest, her arm flung loosely around his waist.

'It goes way back,' he began softly. 'You accused me of abandoning you when I got engaged. It wasn't that simple.'

'No?'

To her surprise he kissed the top of her head and she stopped breathing for a moment. He turned her till they were gazing into one another's eyes. He smiled, and said huskily and with infinite sadness, 'I did love you.'

Her breath knifed in sharply, in small shuddering gasps. Then she gulped.

'Then…why did you break my heart?' she asked, quite bewildered.

His finger traced her hairline. Her eyes flickered shut, long lashes veiling the pained blue beneath.

'Duty,' he replied harshly.

'Leon—'

His mouth found hers, softened in a gentle kiss that made her moan—and then was gone.

'We'd been out to that students' charity run, remember? We made love in my digs and arranged to meet the next day. You were wearing a bright blue shirt and jeans and you had your hair up, as you did just now when you were swimming.'

She couldn't believe he'd remembered. 'Then…we said goodnight,' she said jerkily.

Leon tensed. 'And later that same night, I had a call from my father. He was, to my surprise, in England. He'd come over with members of the Christofides family. We had been linked in business partnership with them for several generations,' he explained. 'Father sounded upset. We arranged a breakfast meeting for seven o'clock in his hotel.'

Emma listened to the low, tortured tones with apprehension. She had never known Leon so subdued.

'It was an arranged marriage, wasn't it? A dynastic affair—'

'Not exactly,' he replied slowly. 'The problem was that Marina, who's the only daughter and heiress of Anton Christofides—my father's dearest friend—was in trouble.'

Emma's head shifted imperceptibly so that she was looking up at him. She knew what trouble meant.

'Pregnant?' she asked sharply. 'By *you*?'

'No, no, Emma.' He squeezed her reassuringly and she subsided, her heart pounding. 'By a tourist.' Bitterness invaded his tone.

'What? Are you saying...Soula isn't your child?' she squeaked.

'Exactly,' he muttered. 'Marina was only just seventeen and quite a handful. Very wilful and spoiled rotten. Her father was out of his mind. The shame...'

'They...' She tensed and so did he, warily watching the look of sheer horror that was spreading across her face. 'They made you marry Marina to cover up what had happened?' she cried in outrage. 'And you agreed? How could you, Leon? How could you?' She battered her fists against his chest in frustration and he caught her wrists in self-defence, wrestling with her. 'It's gross,' she complained. 'You loved me. I loved you.' Wriggling, she tried to escape him but he wrapped his legs around her body and held her fast. 'Let me go!' she sobbed. 'I can't believe you could do such a thing. *Let—me—go!*'

He was silent. Hot-faced and furious, she squirmed till her T-shirt was rucked up and in danger of revealing her naked breasts beneath.

'You're a rat! You ruined my life for the sake of a—a spoiled female who'd—'

Leon's mouth enclosed hers. For a few moments she fought its pressure, her head whirling at the wonderful sense of liquidity in her bones. And then she began to allow the pleasure to flow through her, helpless to resist its insistent beat.

'Emma.' He grated her name urgently against her lips, dropping kisses there which were so delicate and tantalising that she stupidly flung her arm around his neck and snaked her body against his. 'You must let me explain.'

'Wait a minute! You're lying!' She raged, coming to her senses. She'd remembered something. 'It wasn't a sudden surprise to you at all. I was there. I saw the banner, the menu—'

'They'd been done here, on the island, as an urgent order before everyone left. They were so sure I'd agree.'

Emma saw that Leon's eyes were still drugged with desire and she battled with her hunger and her love. Feeling like that was madness. He'd all but destroyed her with his sense of duty. Had sent her hurtling into Taki's arms. And Taki's ruthless domination. Two years in jail. *The loss of her child.*

What had she been thinking of?

Cold, her eyes shimmering with anger, she said jerkily through clenched teeth, 'OK. Make your excuses. But make them good, Leon—because I'm close enough to ruin your chances of fatherhood for ever.'

CHAPTER NINE

JUDGING by her glittering rage, Leon thought tautly, she could well carry out her threat. He took the precaution of removing his hands from the sweet firmness of her back and waist and, in an effort to protect himself, he hauled her up a little. In doing so, she ended up straddling his pelvis.

It was a mistake. She shuddered throughout her body and as he felt her deep heat seep into him he momentarily lost the plot. She was throbbing. And so was he.

They stared, appalled, at one another. A tornado seemed to be filling his head, ripping out whatever brains and conscious thought he'd had in there, to leave just sense and sensation.

He muttered a curse and found his place in the story by sheer dogged effort of will. She would understand even if he had to force every word down her throat. No one was going to call him a rat. He'd acted as honourably as he could. A tiny little voice told him that, from Emma's point of view, that could never be so.

'Dammit, Emma!' he snapped, savage in his frustration for sex and for her understanding. 'You weren't there. You didn't know what it was like.'

'Enlighten me,' she said flaring, her chest heaving.

The movement of her untrammelled breasts, hard-tipped and hovering far too close to his hands, combined with the pooling heat between them, almost sabotaged his mind again.

Where the hell was he? He shut his eyes tightly and it came to him and when he opened them again he was only briefly diverted by the puffy little breaths she was taking through her parted lips.

She thought the worst of him. And that was infinitely unjust.

'Do you think I didn't argue?' he demanded roughly. 'That I didn't tell them I was in love? I was reminded of my *duty*.' He spat the word out, hating it and what it had done to his life. 'Both my family and hers put pressure on me. They were depending on me—I was the only person who could help. There *was* no one else, I realised that immediately. Understand my dilemma!' he demanded urgently. 'These were people I was close to. They were turning to me to solve a desperate situation. I've always admired and respected Anton Christofides. He's my godfather—and in my country that role creates a special bond between the child and godparent. He's been like a second father to me. I care about him deeply. And there he was—this confident, assured and highly respected man—looking utterly distraught, despairing even, and begging me to save his daughter from dishonour.'

He raked his hand through his hair, bleakly remembering the chilling sense of inevitability as he'd tried to come up with any other solution than the one that had been proposed.

'It was a nightmare,' he muttered. 'All the time I could hear Marina sobbing her heart out in the other room. She was virtually a child, however wilful, Emma! And then they brought her out to persuade me. She flung herself at me and pleaded with me to agree. I've never known anyone so hysterical. She had a razor in her hand and I wasn't sure if she was going to slit her own wrists or mine! Do you know what that's like? To have someone's life depend on you? Should I have turned my back?' he cried passionately. 'At the very least I would have lost my father's respect—the father I loved and honoured above all men. I would have lost my extended family, Emma, and destroyed people I loved. But, far worse than that, Marina might have carried out her threat to kill herself...'

He broke off, choking as the past heaved back in graphic clarity: the despair, anger, pity... 'And the baby, Emma,' he said, choking on the words. 'She swore she'd have an abortion if I didn't marry her.' His mouth twisted at the horror of it. 'I couldn't bear that. I couldn't be responsible for the death of her child.'

Emma was quiet now, her eyes full of sympathy. She curled up against him again, reaching up to stroke his forehead. He realised it had been creased in a worried frown. But this meant so much to him. For years he'd wanted to clear the air.

'You could have told me all this at the time,' she said grumpily.

'No, that wouldn't have worked. If I had seen you, I would never have gone through with it. When I knew I had to agree, for Marina and her unborn baby's sake, I had to block you out of my life. It was better that you should hate me. It meant I wouldn't be tempted to change my mind. I had to believe that I could come to love her and her child,' he said passionately.

'Did you?' she asked in a small voice.

'No—though I tried. Oh, I loved Soula at first but Marina was always difficult. And my wife in name only.'

His eyes grew bleak. The days had been a nightmare, tiptoeing about the hysterical Marina, ducking flying objects and listening to her screeching over some trifle. A lost lipstick, a mislaid flight ticket… God! He'd never known such people existed.

'Leon…?' Emma touched his face, her eyes full of questions.

He blanked out the hell of those years and tried to sound dispassionate.

'I'm the head of the family. That's what I must do.'

'Your duty.' There was a pause as they both considered that. 'But,' she said breathily, sending shivers of air across his jaw, 'you're not exactly thrilled with the situation.'

'No,' he admitted. 'It's hell. So far Lexi hasn't been affected—Marina and Soula keep to themselves most of the time and I'm merely a wallet on legs. But…God, I don't know what to do for the best sometimes,' he finished moodily. 'I've made a mess of things. I should have left them to their own devices and not confused Soula with my house rules—but it's hard, seeing a child being brought up with widely differing values to yours.'

'What do you think Marina wants in life?' she asked.

'Money,' he answered without hesitation.

'Love, Leon,' she corrected. 'We all need love.'

He was silent, his heart in total agreement. And then said quietly, 'I couldn't give that to her. A roof over her head and financial security, yes, courtesy, sympathy, time…but not love.'

Emma saw the link. She'd had none to give to Taki, because she'd squandered it on Leon. And the marriage had foundered.

'I think you should let go,' she mused. 'All the time you're around, it's not giving Marina a chance to strike out and find her soul mate. It isn't any of your business how she brings up her child, and you seem to be the catalyst for their anger. As far as prospective boyfriends for Marina are concerned, you'd put anyone off,' she said bluntly, omitting to explain that men would feel intimidated because he was so charismatic.

'That's exactly what I've decided. I'm talking to Marina in the morning. I'm going to suggest she talks to her father about living with him again. She's visited him a couple of times and I think he and his new wife are happier to have her around, especially if Natasa lives there too. Marina's calmer when Natasa is around. I'll see what they all think. Trouble is, I'd lose a housekeeper.' He rubbed his chin reflectively. 'The caretaker's wife might help out there. Donika's working on the land at the moment. She's always asking me to find her an indoor job. I'll ask her. I'm sure she'd jump at the chance.'

It seemed settled. 'You'll miss Natasa.'

He smiled and her jealousy unfurled its claws. 'I'll miss her biscuits but my waistline will be reprieved,' he said, smiling wanly at his little joke. 'But, yes, I'd miss her.'

'She'll be able to visit,' Emma said, finding her generosity hard to believe.

He said nothing but stroked her hair absently, as if his thoughts were far away. Emma reflected that Marina's fling had not only ruined her own life, but many lives. Leon had tried to do what was right—and in doing so had destroyed his own happiness. She felt very sad. They might have been married now with children of their own.

'Oh, Leon,' she whispered jerkily.

She felt the air between them quiver and lifted her head to judge his expression. His lips had parted, his teeth shining white in the darkness of his face. The drowsy, sultry expression in his eyes served as a warning but she couldn't—wouldn't—heed it.

This was the man she'd loved and lost, the man she'd respected and had adored with every last breath in her body. And he was still that same man. He'd surrendered his own happiness for the sake of a frightened teenager and her unborn child. And now he was hurting and she wanted to ease his pain, to wipe it out as if it had never been and to make his heart whole again.

She smiled at him hazily. Everything had changed. He wasn't heartless—far from it—and she still loved him. Terribly, recklessly, profoundly.

For a brief, wonderful moment, her own heart opened like a flower. And then it closed up again when she realised that she had to protect herself. Her eyes became dull. He might have loved her once—and still lusted after her—but he had a devastatingly low opinion of her.

'Emma,' he murmured seductively.

'Tea,' she said jerkily. 'Getting cold.'

'To hell with the tea.'

'This doesn't change anything,' she said frantically.

'Doesn't it?' His eyes glittered.

'No.' She bit her lip, steeling herself to ignore the mesmeric stroking of his hands as they moved up and down her arms, and the hot message in his liquid eyes. Needing to escape, she wriggled in his grip and found herself being pushed back.

He was kissing her, ignoring her moans of protest, driving his mouth into hers till it throbbed, one hand supporting her spine and crushing her against him, the other running up and down her bare leg which had somehow wound itself wantonly across his thigh.

How had it done that? she wondered. It was almost as if it wanted to encourage him. Appalled, she wrenched her mouth from his and said the first thing that came into her mind.

'I need to ring John.'

He scowled. 'Later.'

'No, please, Leon—'

'Why the desperation?' He bit the words out. 'Won't I do?'

'It's not that—'

'What then?' he challenged. 'If you're so free with your favours—'

'You brute!' she said choking with incredulity, managing to pull herself back a little. Her chest heaved in anger, and her temper was made worse by the miserable sense of disappointment and sexual loss rushing through her shaking body. 'You never believe me. In your eyes I'm a criminal with no morals at all—'

'Right.'

'And I leap into bed with anyone I fancy—'

'Yes!' he hissed.

'Well, you're wrong on all counts!' she said fuming. 'John's nothing other than my lawyer and my friend—'

'And stays the night with you.'

'Once. Because I was upset,' she yelled. 'And he left at three. He comforted me—'

'All innocent? Never made love to you?' Leon queried in frank disbelief.

'No!'

'Never *touched* you?'

'Umm…'

Her eyes flickered. And she found herself being lifted, Leon's fury carrying her halfway across the room before she could gather any kind of protest together.

'He kisses you. He touches you. So can I!' he hissed, pausing in mid-stride.

Then his head descended and the fires ignited more fiercely than ever. She did her best to grit her teeth and stop herself from coiling her hands around his neck in compliance. And somehow she summoned up the strength—and the voice—to protest.

'Don't treat me like this! You have no right!'

His eyes silvered. His reply was a burning kiss which softened and sweetened, becoming so tender that she thought her heart would break with sorrow. Still holding that kiss, transfixing her with dreams of what might have been, he began to move towards the bedroom again.

He felt drunk. Unable to believe he was acting so badly. But he couldn't stomach the thought of Sefton…

He felt her gasp and gentled the pressure of his mouth which had become fierce and bruising again. Gently he swept his lips over her jaw, hating his weakness for her, unable to understand why she aroused such explosive emotions in him when he'd always been rational and considerate to a fault.

But emotions there were. Pity. Anger. Compassion, jealousy—oh, God, the jealousy! And such fevered desire… His mouth caressed her high cheekbone, the sight of her half-closed eyes making his pulses race. Reverently he kissed each quivering lid and exulted in her throaty moan.

His shins suddenly hit the bed, jarring his body and he fell with her onto the soft quilt, his senses befogged by the heady perfume of roses somewhere in the room.

'Tell me no,' he said huskily, covering her body with his.

'Nnnnoooo,' she whispered languorously.

'Not totally convincing.'

Lazily he let his fingers trail across the soft warm skin just above the waistband of her skirt. She jerked and writhed and he caught her arms to imprison her, letting his mouth swoop and mimic the caress of his fingers while she gasped in pleasure, her legs wrapping around his body while she pleaded implausibly for him to stop.

So he did. And she blinked several times, her mouth sulky with disappointment. He waited, his breath locked in his lungs, his eyes fierce with desire.

Feebly she tried to hit him, forgetting her legs were keeping his body close to hers, and then she muttered something angrily and wrenched free, tumbling with him on the bed, over and over, kissing and moaning, tangled with him in a hungry desperation as hands and mouths and teeth and limbs strained to ease the explosion of longing.

Beneath him she moved in her old, wanton way, her eyes luring, her body firing him to unbelievable abandon. She was everywhere, her hair teasing his cheek, her yielding body urgently thrashing with his, her mouth wandering at his throat and her heart beating violently against his chest.

He wanted to devour her whole, to take her in and make her his. To wipe away all other men she'd known and to leave just the memory of his body, his mouth, the pleasure he could give her.

Her tongue slicked along his collar-bone and he shuddered.

'I want you so badly,' he croaked.

Her mouth opened and no sound emerged. So he kissed it, the sweet pressure bringing an ache to his heart. He looked at her with dark hunger in his eyes and knew he had smashed her resistance. His mouth enclosed hers, his tongue tasting her as he slid his hand to the top of her thigh and met warm, wet silk.

Emma cried out, a needy cry that brought an answering

spear of need in him. Rhythms pounded mercilessly in every part of his body: the thud of her heart and his, the movement of her hands over his back and the leaping, dangerous pulse of heat beneath his fingers which called to a deep answering pulse within his very manhood.

Her throat arched, his mouth urgently moved there, branding it with searing kisses. And then he lifted her, crazed with her, intoxicated and utterly incapable of anything other than actions of raw instinct. In a fierce movement he'd pulled off her T-shirt and had shrugged away his shirt, pulling her to him.

Skin on skin. Thunder roared in his ears. It was unbelievable. The feel of her. The softness…

She moved in a deliberately provocative way, an insistent gesture which she repeated, the hard peaks of her breasts describing a circle against his chest and its shuddering muscles.

'Kiss,' she moaned, taking one breast between her hands and offering it to him.

Every cell in his body reacted. With a deep, visceral groan, he lowered his mouth and took the dark, pulsing nipple in his mouth. Emma jerked as his tongue flickered and tasted and she grabbed at his hair when he closed his eyes in bliss and suckled greedily.

'Other one.'

Without gentleness, she dragged his head from her breast to satisfy its twin, his nose and chin deep in the lushly cushioned mound.

'Touch me again,' she whispered.

Instead, he brought her hand to ease his own agony. And she understood, always had, knowing what she did to him and that something between them blazed so fiercely that no man, not even Leon, could keep under control.

At her touch, he bucked and drew back, his eyes glazed with passion. Gently he unbuttoned her skirt and eased down the frivolous blue briefs inch by inch over her glorious thighs.

For a brief moment he buried his face in the golden triangle of hair, promising himself greater delights later. She uttered little moans of pleasure as his mouth enclosed her sweetness and then she was kicking off her briefs with frantic legs.

And then, when he fumbled with his own belt, she reached up. She seemed to be in a mist, as if a veil had drifted over his eyes, and her body simmered before him, beautiful and golden in its nakedness but annoyingly out of focus.

Then he felt her remove the rest of his clothes, gasping his name when he was kneeling above her, naked too. Gently she took him between her hands, but he couldn't bear the waiting.

'No. I want *you*,' he urged breathily.

'Leon…'

'Now!'

'Oh, yes,' she cried and pulled him down, arching up to him, demanding his mouth, her arms guiding, helping him to slip into that paradise…

'Emma!'

He didn't know if he'd spoken aloud or not. Didn't care. Silky liquid enclosed him, warm, tight, exquisite, each gentle movement a sweet torment. But Emma didn't want gentleness. Her hands grasped his muscled buttocks and urged him on.

His body took over. In the back of his mind he knew he'd meant to pleasure her slowly, to drive her wild with desire. But this was too much. His mouth lunged at hers and his rhythm increased, primitive, long and deep thrusts which seemed to strip his mind of everything but the sensation that they were joined as one person and would never be parted.

Tears wet his face. Emma. Emma, Emma, called his aching heart and she was calling him, crying his name over and over again, gasping into his mouth, licking his salty tears—or were they hers?—and all the time the volcanic emotions in his body were rising, higher, higher, the heat and sweat and total sense of freedom and release making him yell with her as they rolled around the bed. And his movements became shorter, harder, faster. Their voices deeper, huskier. Kisses fiercer. Hands more frantic.

It was happening. Shooting up through his body like a torrent, flames of heat burning his skin, each pore electrified, faster, faster…

'Emma, *Emma*!' he yelled.

But she was silent, shuddering, jerking, a seraphic smile on her face. He realised he'd come down to earth again though they were still united and he wanted to keep it that way, warm, tingling, the sweetest feeling in the world. The sweetest woman.

He smiled back. She sighed deeply and her eyes closed, her entire body limp. Carefully he eased himself over her so that he bore most of his own weight, and snuggled up, his face close to hers. Still linked, he thought muzzily. If only that could be true for ever.

His brain wasn't working too well. It was a moment before a slow frown found the energy to work a line between his brows. What had he wished? Confused, he gave himself up to gazing at her. It was sex talking. Nothing else.

He eased away.

'Don't go,' she mumbled incoherently, her arm flapping in vague protest.

But he felt ice clutch at his heart. And swung around so he was sitting on the edge of the chaotic bed, his hand clearing his eyes of…someone's tears. Hence his blurred vision. And he was gritting his teeth. Finding his brain. It was in there somewhere. His pulses still galloped mercilessly but they'd soon calm down.

Eyeing the distance involved, he made a good stab at lurching towards the bathroom.

'Wharr-you-doin'?' Emma slurred.

'Shower.'

Her mutter showed she didn't think much of that but he

grimly staggered to it and turned it to cold. Taking a deep breath, he stepped in, suffering his penance.

Better if he'd done this before, not after. How could he have been such a prat? The freezing needles of water seemed to wake him up out of his stupor. So what kind of man makes love to a woman he despises?

Marina was right. This was the woman who'd single-handedly destroyed his family business without regard for the consequences, sparing no thought for the hundreds of people she'd left without the security they'd planned for.

Recompensing those people had broken his father and had hastened his death and, Leon reflected grimly, it had given *him* sixteen-hour days and no social life while he'd built up the family fortunes again, scheming, planning, networking, and begging for investment. He slapped his fist into his palm. This was also the woman who drove his brother to a terrible and violent death.

And he'd just made love to her.

'You'll get pneumonia!'

He looked up. Through the curtain of water he could see her, a sheet wrapped around her incomparable body. Her fingers were testing the temperature of the water and she was looking at him in sheer amazement.

He discovered that he was shivering violently and stepped out, his eyes blazing so black and hard that she took a step back.

Grabbing a towel, he snarled, 'I don't care.'

She cringed against the tiled wall. 'Leon..!' she whispered in shock.

From under ferocious brows he scowled. 'It's done. A mistake. Can't be undone,' he said shortly, grabbing towels to warm him.

And he wanted to wound her as he was wounded, ripped apart by desire for her, his self-respect torn to shreds and left bleeding on that rumpled bed. His head came up. Rivulets of water poured down his face from his saturated hair and he mopped at them with the end of the towel. He wanted her to see his eyes and the loathing there.

'It got a bit out of hand, didn't it?' he said, mimicking her pitiful excuse earlier.

She gasped. 'Get dressed and get out,' she whispered.

'My *pleasure*,' he growled, towelling vigorously.

She left. He heard her collapse on the bed. Wondered if she was all right. And checked himself. She was a big girl. She could look after herself, only too well.

Then he remembered he had to get his clothes from the bedroom. As he gathered them up, finding they'd been hurled into odd places with surprising force and distance, he glanced at her surreptitiously.

She lay curled up in a ball just like Lexi and for a moment his heart lurched before he could steady it again. She was very still, her face almost hidden in her shielding arms.

'My shirt's underneath you,' he said coldly.

She didn't move and he was forced to lift her hips. He looked at her sharply. Tremors were rippling through her entire body.

'Emma?'

'Go away!'

He hesitated. 'Do you need medicine or something?'

She sat up with a sudden violence, her eyes spitting fire. 'Yes. I need love. I need a man who doesn't use me. Do you know what you've done, Leon? Do you?'

'Yes,' he said bleakly. 'Do you? Or do you think you had no part in what happened, no input, no desire?'

'Don't,' she muttered, covering her face with her hands.

He pulled them away. 'Look at me.'

When she did, he wished he hadn't asked. Her eyes reproached him, making him feel ashamed of himself. He made a helpless gesture with his hands. He didn't understand what was happening to him, only that they couldn't be near one another.

'The truth is, Emma,' he said tightly, 'we're destroying

each other. This can't go on. We have to separate or…' He paused, fighting for breath.

'Or what?' she whispered.

'Get each other out of our systems. There'll never be a middle way for us, Emma. You know that, I know that. So it's in my bed, or out of the country—and the choice is yours.'

'I—I'm not ready to leave! Lexi doesn't know—'

'You've seen your child. You know she'll be fine with me. I'll find some way of solving Lexi's need for parents.'

'What?' she cried.

'I don't know. But…' He couldn't believe he was saying this, that he was urging her to leave. He wanted her so much that every bone in his body was aching. 'Do the decent thing and get on the next plane,' he said in a strangled tone. And the jealousy surfaced, searing and bitter in his gut. 'Ring Sefton and take him with you. He's desperate to give you what you want. If he hasn't done so already.'

'What is it with you about John?' she cried hotly. 'Are you jealous or something?'

'Yes,' he yelled, grabbing her shoulders. 'I don't want anyone else to touch you but me. It sickens me to think of other men making love to you. And it crucifies me to want you. It degrades me—'

'And if I was innocent?' she said bitterly.

'But you're not.'

'If.'

His mouth tightened but he couldn't prevent the wishing from showing in his eyes. 'It's not worth discussing,' he said gratingly. 'I want you out of here in the morning. Make your arrangements.'

It was hard, leaving. His feet were unwilling—his whole body, too. But he got out eventually, her words still ringing in his head. *'If I was innocent.'* He sucked in a shuddering breath, every muscle in his body screaming as he tried to get that idea out of his mind. Because the implications were too alarming to contemplate.

CHAPTER TEN

EMMA rested. She would need all her strength if she was to fight for what she wanted: to clear her name and to be accepted as Lexi's mother. And then…she shut her mind to that. But Leon's jealousy had given her hope.

Later, she rang John and he came over. They went out to a taverna in the nearby beach resort of Alikes and she thought how much Lexi would enjoy being here, with a different pony and trap clip-clopping and rumbling past every few minutes.

John seemed pleased that she was leaving the villa and arranged to pick up her things in the morning. He wasn't so pleased when she said she was going to lay siege to Leon's house till he let her see her daughter.

'Abduct her and let's get home,' he advised.

Emma stared at him in shock. 'I couldn't possibly,' she protested, putting down a forkful of red mullet. 'She doesn't know me. She'd be terrified—'

'Oh, she'll soon get used to you,' he said airily.

'No, John. I'm not doing that to my daughter. How can you suggest that?'

He took her hand and looked into her eyes. 'To save you distress,' he said gently. 'Poor Emma. This must be awful for you. You must be at your wits' end—'

'Don't make me a victim, John,' she said with a frown, suddenly sensing that he'd always done that. 'I'm determined to see this through properly.'

'But why?' he argued. 'When we can be up and off in

twenty-four hours? You with your kid, just as you wanted it? She'll be OK. Kids can get used to anything—'

'No.'

She removed her hand, suddenly disliking his sweaty touch. How could he be so insensitive to Lexi's needs?

'So you're going to camp outside Kyriakis's place, hoping to catch a glimpse of her as they drive out—and you think that's going to bring you and her closer together?' he said sarcastically.

'It won't come to that,' she said firmly. 'Leon won't be able to cope with the scandal of his sister-in-law parked on his doorstep like a lost parcel.'

'I thought I was here to give you advice?' John said sulkily.

'You are.' She patted his arm consolingly, feeling bad that she'd dragged him over and had taken no notice of him since. He had devoted an extraordinary amount of time to her. 'I'm terribly grateful for what you've done. But John, I did make it clear that I'd never take Lexi until she was happy in my company.'

He caught her hand and kissed it, holding it fast when she tried to retrieve it. 'Emma, I wish you'd listen to me. Let's do it. If you won't take your daughter now, then you must see she'll never be yours. From what you tell me, Kyriakis has established himself in Lexi's heart. Isn't that true?'

'Ye-e-es,' she said slowly.

'He's going to make this as difficult as possible. And my enquiries here suggest that you won't make much headway legally. You'd be condemned to flying over here once, perhaps twice, a year and being faced with a child who doesn't want to be with you. I know this is painful, but I think you should give up. Come back to England and start a new life. Emma,' he declared, his eyes shining, 'let me take care of you. I can heal your pain. I'd do anything for you.'

Her eyes widened. Leon had been right! Appalled that she'd given out the wrong messages to John, she searched for a gentle let-down. And in searching she let her gaze swing absently to the taverna opposite.

Where Leon sat, glaring. She gulped. Of course. She was constantly being watched—in case she did something to ruin the wretched Kyriakis name. Like steal a child's ice cream or something, she thought waspishly.

John's eyes narrowed. Following her glance, he saw Leon and let her hand drop. 'Now, that's an opportunity I can't miss. I'll go and have a word,' he said casually.

Emma blinked. He'd always been edgy about meeting Leon before. 'About what?'

'Oh, tell him you're leaving the villa, where you'll be, that kind of thing.'

He seemed to take a long time about it. She'd worked her way through a rolled filo pastry pudding and a chocolate ice cream before he came back. Leon had listened to John without moving a muscle, his dark eyes menacing.

'That's done,' her lawyer said with satisfaction. 'Ready to go back?'

She would have liked a walk along the beach perhaps, but presumed he must have things to do. 'Sure. I'll have an early night.'

'Me too.'

It wasn't until she was fighting off John's attentions on the doorstep of the villa that she realised he'd expected her early night to include him.

'No, John,' she cried in panic, grappling with him. 'Don't spoil everything—'

'Come on. We're great together. When you were in my arms the other night—'

'You were comforting me,' she protested, leaning back till she felt her spine would crack. This was like Taki all over again. She felt herself weaken as terror struck through her, fuelled by the terrible memories of her husband's abuse. '*Please*, John,' she whimpered desperately.

'Leave her alone, Sefton,' came Leon's quiet and ominously calm voice.

Emma breathed a sigh of utter relief as John's vice-like grip eased. She would be all right. Surveillance had its advantages after all.

'Keep out of this,' snarled John, his face distorted with rage.

Leon came right up to them. 'Let her go, or you'll find yourself on the next plane to England. With your own personal resuscitation team,' he said pleasantly.

Emma was immediately released. She moved away, rubbing her arms.

'Goodnight, Sefton,' murmured Leon. Muttering, John stalked to his car and Leon turned his hooded eyes on her. 'All right?' She nodded dumbly. He held out his hand. 'Key.'

Trembling, she fumbled uselessly in her bag. And dropped it, and its contents onto the path. They both bent to gather everything up. Leon, inches away, looked into her eyes.

'Are you really all right, Emma?' he asked huskily.

'Shaken up. Disappointed,' she admitted. 'I know. You told me so.' She stood up. 'But thank you. It saved an ugly scene.' She shuddered.

Leon put an arm around her shoulder. 'And Sefton's manhood is intact,' he observed with a wry smile, unlocking the door and switching on the lights for her.

She allowed herself a faint smile too. 'I would definitely have kneed him,' she agreed jerkily.

'Can you manage or do you want me to stay?' he asked neutrally.

'I'll be fine once I've got my breath back. It—it happened to me once before, that's why I panicked. I wasn't so lucky that time.'

Leon's jaw clenched. He hesitated for so long that her heart began to beat erratically, and then he turned away and began to walk down the path, giving a brief wave of his hand as he did so.

*   *   *

Awake early, she tidied and cleaned the villa and left her stuff in an empty shed which she'd seen when they'd been feeding the animals. She stuck a note on the door to her lawyer that was brief and to the point. 'Will be in touch. Have found accommodation. Emma.'

She hadn't, of course, but she'd do that later, once she'd wrung concessions from Leon.

It wasn't till she'd almost reached his house that she remembered he was having a heart-to-heart with Marina that morning, and wouldn't thank her if she turned up in the middle of it.

So she sat down in the orchard amongst the wild fennel and oats and daisies, and idly watched clouded yellow butterflies flitting about. After a while she felt a little restless and set off for a walk.

Ahead, half veiled in a mist, sprawled the mountains, grey-green from the thousands of olives which clad their sides. Small hills rose from the flat valley floor in front, their tops crowned with pencil cypress and low white buildings.

This was all of Leon's land. Each plant irrigated, tended lovingly, the cherry, fig, apricot and almond trees making little islands in the sea of currant vines and small hay fields. She came across a field of melons and, beside it, a field of scarlet poppies. Lizards basked on a stone well-head and chickens—chittens, she thought with a lump in her throat—ran about the undergrowth.

She leaned against the trunk of an olive tree whose girth suggested it must be several centuries old and felt a love for the island steal over her, catching her unawares. She tried not to love it, tried to find flaws. Wrong language. Strange letters unlike any alphabet she'd ever known and hadn't yet mastered. Miles from home, the culture she knew.

That was all she could come up with. Not a lot. Could she live here? Her heart and her head told her that Lexi would be happier on the island. And she… She inhaled slowly and let the breath out again. She wanted to be Lexi's mother properly, not just for weekends.

There was something more. She wanted Leon too. But she'd already realised that, since he held her responsible for destroying his family, their relationship could only be based on sexual attraction. Though that was a start. And it was the only thing she had going for her.

Her pulses raced at the very thought. He hadn't been shocked by her damaged breast—hadn't even mentioned it. He must want her very much to have ignored the scar.

Maybe, as her lover, he'd listen to her when she tried to explain about Taki and her role as financial director. Her brow furrowed. Problem was, there wasn't any evidence for that. It would be her word against that of a Kyriakis. Not much hope there, she thought gloomily. Her eyes glinted. But she had to try.

When she checked her watch and found it was lunch-time she decided to head back. She'd walked a long way and by the time she arrived at the front of Leon's house—it had to be the front, for maximum embarrassment to him—she was not only very tired but the sky had clouded over and drops of rain were beginning to fall.

She took a deep breath and knocked on the door. It was opened not by Natasa but by Leon.

'Yes?'

'I've come to see Lexi,' she said humbly.

'Not today, thank you.'

'OK.' She sat down as the door was closing and prepared for a long wait. But the door opened almost immediately.

'What are you doing?'

'Waiting,' she said over her shoulder.

'For?'

'You to change your mind.'

'It's raining.'

'I've noticed,' she said gravely.

The door closed. Emma muttered something to the Fates

who'd chosen to make today of all days the time they let the heavens open, and she put her bag on her head in a vain attempt to keep the rain off. It didn't help. The water ran over it and onto her knees.

Thunder cracked, making her jump. And almost immediately there was a lightning flash. The Fates then decided to make a good job of washing the island and instead of rain they produced a wall of water which hit her with such force that she was reduced to crouching in a miserable heap while the torrent beat the ground ferociously and thus flung red soil up at her.

She was soaked through in minutes. And then suddenly the rain ceased. She looked up cautiously and saw a giant coloured umbrella above her.

'Get inside,' yelled Leon above the pyrotechnics of the storm which was still raging beyond the umbrella.

Oh, hurray, she thought gleefully. And scuttled in.

'You look appalling.'

'Thanks,' she said ruefully, her face glistening with water.

He glared. 'Every time I decide something, you sabotage it.'

'I'm very sorry,' she said, doing her humble bit again.

'Upstairs with you,' he growled. 'Have a bath and get warm.'

'Thank-you-very-much,' she murmured.

'Not funny.'

It was, she thought. Her first goal had been achieved. Shivering, she meekly followed him up the stairs though she was so weary that he reached the top long before she did and he waited impatiently, his fingers drumming on the banister.

'Look at you,' he scolded.

She did. Drenched, her body shedding cinnamon-coloured mud and water, her hair plastered to her head, she knew she must look a sight. The carpet must be in a similar condition too. Guiltily she turned to check and saw the wet red earth trail leading back to the front door.

'Oh, crikey.'

'Wait there.'

He clamped his lips together and turned on his heel while she slumped and dripped. Returning, he held out an enormous bath sheet and wrapped it around her like a cocoon. And then he picked her up, carrying her mummified body through a vast and breathtakingly beautiful bedroom and into a bathroom beyond where he deposited her on the sea-blue tiles.

'I'll find some clothes for you. They'll be in the bedroom. Come down when you're done.'

She nodded, not daring to say anything in case it offended him. She felt shattered but peculiarly perky and her mouth was liable to run away with her for sheer elation. Wriggling out of the bath sheet she locked the door, ran the bath and peeled off her wet things.

After selecting some expensive-looking herbal bath oil, she emptied a prodigious amount of it into the deepening water, turned off the taps and slid in with a sigh. Her head nestled back against a padded headrest. The bath was wide enough for two people side by side, she thought muzzily.

Her eyes closed as her brain considered that fact. Perhaps this was the moment when she'd fall asleep and Leon would break the door down and come crashing in, afraid she'd drowned.

She stayed soaking for ages, half hoping he might do just that but eventually common sense told her that he hadn't had that grumpy face for nothing and he wouldn't break that lovely panelled door anyway.

So she got out, dried herself slowly, wishing someone else could do that for her, and padded into the bedroom to see what delectable item he'd pinched from Marina's wardrobe. It was a man's shirt and jeans.

Ignoring them, she prowled around looking for a hairdryer but didn't find one and had to content herself with wrapping a small towel around her wet hair like a turban.

There was a rap on the door. It was sharp and imperious and she knew it must be him.

'Are you dressed?'

She hoicked the bath sheet around her more securely. 'Near enough,' she replied, and sat down heavily on the bed, her limbs far too tired to help her to stand.

He came in and sat in an easy chair. 'I thought you ought to know. Marina's left with Soula and Natasa. She spoke to her father and he was happy to have his daughters and grand-daughter back in the family home.'

'And his wife?'

'She says she can cope if Natasa is there, exercising her calming influence. Anton Christofides is turning a wing of his house into a large, self-contained apartment so they won't move in immediately.'

Emma blinked, not knowing what she should say. 'Was there a scene?'

'Not when I told her I'd settle a large sum on her,' he said cynically.

'Generous.'

'She's irritating and difficult but I feel great sympathy for her,' he muttered. 'She had a child when she was just a frightened kid herself, and a husband who didn't love her.'

'Where's she gone in the meantime?' Emma asked, touched by his compassion.

'To the villa—temporarily. It was her design. I told her she ought to take that up professionally. She's talented. Natasa thinks so too. Marina was quite excited at the prospect.'

'Good,' Emma said warmly.

'Where are *you* staying?' he barked.

Emma shifted, longing to curl up properly on the bed but she was worried that he might think she was issuing an invitation.

'Nowhere. Yet.'

He looked out of the window where the storm was still

raging. 'You can't go out in this.' She remained mute. There wasn't much she could say and the warmth of the bath was making her sleepy. 'What are your intentions, Emma?' he snapped.

'Go to sleep,' she mumbled and let herself fall back to the pillow.

Somewhere in the dim recesses of her mind she heard him muttering under his breath and the cool whisper of linen being draped over her tired body. And then she fell into a dark and deep well of sleep.

It seemed a few moments later when she woke. The rain was still falling in torrents outside and it seemed to be night. She yawned and stretched, then froze. A pair of eyes were looking at her.

A light snapped on and the eyes turned into Leon. 'Hungry?' he muttered, looking wonderfully tousled and grumpy.

She wondered if he'd been there all the time and gave a little shiver. 'Umm...yes, I am, Leon.'

'I found a hairdryer for you. Come down when you've used it,' he said curtly. 'And stop being Miss Meek and Mild. I prefer you to shout and laugh.'

She grinned and sat up, prepared to do either of those if necessary, but he'd gone.

It took ages to sort her hair because it had dried in coiled lumps inside the towel. But eventually it looked good enough. She couldn't say that for the rest of her.

Leon's shirt needed the sleeves turned up till there was a huge roll of material at her elbows. If she fastened the top button then the collar dug into her neck every time she looked down and if she left it open the shirt gaped a bit. She opted for gaping.

Beneath the knee-length shirt, the jeans collected in sad folds above her bare feet and it had taken all her efforts to make the belt hold up the weight of all that unsupported denim.

'Hallo? Here I am,' she called, standing uncertainly in the empty hall.

Leon appeared after a moment, looked her up and down, did his famous scowl and turned back, indicating she should follow him with a curt flip of his hand.

'Feta cheese salad,' he said abruptly, when they'd fetched up in a large kitchen.

'Lovely.'

She beamed, and tucked in, looking around. Expensive floor tiles, coffered ceiling and royal-blue wooden cupboards. A marble table, comfortable chairs and three wrought-iron candelabra. Murano glass downlighter adorned with angels. Stylish objects—a piece of driftwood, a large shell, a wooden bowl of realistic artificial cherries—casually placed as if by accident, but looking absolutely right. Gorgeous. If this was another sample of Marina's taste, then she'd make a great interior designer.

Leon cleared his throat and she looked up expectantly.

'You'll have to stay here tonight and don't say, Yes, Leon.'

She stopped herself from giggling at his monotone delivery. She was in for the night. Goal number two!

'Thank you,' she murmured and decided to go for gold. 'Have you worked out how to help Lexi with her parent problem?' she asked innocently.

He scowled beautifully. 'No.'

She tried not to look pleased and set about rubbing salt in his wounds. 'Poor kiddie. She's such a sweetie and it'll be awful seeing her become more and more paranoid—'

'Emma,' he roared, banging his fist on the table and making her—and the crockery—jump. 'I'm worried stiff. You're not helping—'

'I am, I can,' she said earnestly. 'You know why I'm here, don't you?'

'Because you're an obstinate, difficult, stroppy, mule of a

woman who doesn't know when the odds are stacked against you,' he growled.

'Well, yes, there's that,' she conceded smugly.

He glared. 'And?'

Now the moment had come, she was losing courage. It was such an outrageous suggestion in the cold light of a kitchen.

'This is…so difficult,' she said, twiddling her fork in the salad aimlessly.

'That's never stopped you before,' Leon said caustically.

Her mouth twitched. No. It hadn't. She leapt where angels feared to tread.

'OK,' she said, but keeping her eyes lowered on her frantic fork. 'I have a proposition.' There was a silence and in that silence she suddenly noticed her desperately unsexy clothes. They wouldn't help at all. Putting her fork down, she clasped her hands in front of her and managed to undo another button. 'Well,' she began, letting her hands fall to her lap.

'Yes?'

It was only a small, barely spoken word, but it had carried heat and lust and passion. And when her eyes flickered up, she rocked back, knocked breathless by the sizzling impact of his sensual expression.

He would agree, she thought, tense with excitement. Her hands shook.

'You offered me a choice,' she said huskily.

Something quivered in the muscles of his face, as if each one had tightened in sequence. She had to lick her lips or she wouldn't have been able to continue. And it was so important. Her tongue slicked over them again, and the simmering darkness of his eyes dried her throat. Pools of heat were making her focus on her hungering body and she had to redouble her efforts to speak.

'I—' She swallowed, wanting to hurl herself across the table and ravish him, to tear off his shirt and ease the tempestuous turmoil claiming her entire system. 'I said once I'd do anything for Lexi. I imagine you would, too.' He nodded slowly. 'She needs to know me, we've already agreed that. And I understand why you want me to leave…' Agitated because he sat there without saying anything, other than the hot message he was projecting from every inch of his body, she staggered to her feet and began to pace up and down the kitchen. Her physical urges had to go somewhere. Her brows drew together. 'I've forgotten where I was.'

He seemed to have trouble finding his place in her outburst too. 'You understand why I want you to leave,' he provided eventually.

'Oh, yes. Right. However,' she said, prowling furiously, 'I've decided *not* to leave the island.'

'Ah-h-h.'

It was a whisper. Husky, deep and laced with such feeling that she found her steps getting even faster and infinitely more erratic.

She sucked in a huge breath and launched her suggestion, rattling it off at high speed without giving him a chance to interrupt.

'And, to start with, I want to stay in this house because that'll suit us both. When you think about it, you'll see it makes sense. I will get to know Lexi quicker that way because I can pop up and take a rest whenever I need and yet I'll be around a lot of the time gradually becoming part of Lexi's life, so you'd have to put up with me for a shorter time than if I was commuting. And after a while she'll accept me as her mother and—and she'll be happy and then…then I can leave and find somewhere to live on the island and Lexi will know she has a mother and I can see her often and write to her and telephone…' She ran out of breath and dreams and stopped abruptly.

'You…want to…live in this house?' The silence was deafening, the pause unbearable. 'You know what that means,' he growled. It was her turn to nod, her eyes enormous in her pale face. 'Let me get this straight,' he said, his voice oddly strangled. 'You're saying that, for Lexi's sake, you'd risk being used for sex?'

It wasn't like that, she told herself. It wasn't just sex. Maybe that was *his* attitude towards her at the moment, but she'd convince him of her innocence somehow and then his feelings would change.

It was a huge gamble. But worth going for. She stared at the floor, willing her nerve to hold.

And realised in dismay how stupid she looked. With all the striding about, the jeans had unfolded and hung around her ankles, the belt having given up entirely and having allowed the waistband to slide precariously to her hips so that the crotch appeared somewhere around her calves.

It dawned on her that it hadn't been sexual tension that had put a strain on his muscles. He'd been trying hard not to laugh.

'You…said you'd do anything to get Lexi,' he said in a rasping.

'I did,' she squeaked.

'Even making yourself available in exchange for access?'

She knew that Leon must be trying to discover how far she'd go to be with her daughter. It was the, Will you sleep with me or any other man I might name and, if you will, then you're a slut? kind of question.

She might as well answer. Her hopes of finding the love they'd once shared could now take a running jump. She'd become a figure of ridicule.

'If that's the price,' she mumbled crossly, glaring at the clumsy jeans and hauling them up.

She knew he was looking at her, his stare rooting her to the spot even though her gaze was fixed with unlikely intensity on the floor. The atmosphere burned around Emma as, presumably, Leon battled to stop himself from laughing out loud.

'Agreed,' he said, when she had abandoned all hope of an answer.

'Thank you,' she said in a small voice.

'There's a condition.' He waited but she was too miserable to comment. 'You cut all contact with Sefton. No calls, no visits, no letters, no e-mails—nothing.'

Dubiously she chewed her lip. 'He knows where he stands now, Leon. I still need him as my lawyer here.'

'Lawyer or fellow abductor?' he asked flatly. 'I have details now of the route you've planned. He told me in Alikes yesterday evening. If I were you, I'd forget Sefton and his little games. They could result in you never seeing your daughter again.'

Her eyes rounded in dismay. 'Why would he tell you?' she asked, pink-faced with horrified embarrassment.

'He's been warning me of the possibility ever since my first meeting with him, Emma. He doesn't want you to succeed.'

'Why?' she cried, baffled.

'He doesn't want you saddled with someone else's child, don't you see? And Sefton's the type who needs women to be dependent on them. You filled that bill very well all the time you were in prison and desperate. He played the hero. I'm not denigrating what he did for you, only his motives. The moment you looked like showing strength, he backtracked and did everything he could to make sure you ended up miserable and needy. You're not totally convinced, I can see. But will you believe me if I say that I even know he's brought over clothes and toys for Lexi, to keep her amused during the journey?'

Betrayed, she thought. Her plan would never have worked—John would have seen to that, and Leon would have had her stopped before they even set sail from the island.

She was horrified. 'We made plans...'

'I know.' His eyes were grave.

'I would have lost her for ever.'

'Without doubt.'

'How could he do this to me?'

'He had his own agenda. You were supposed to fit into it.'

She trembled. Choking with dismay, she took a step towards him and tripped over the jeans, grabbing the table in frustrated fury at her own clumsiness.

'You think I meant to whisk her away from everything she loved,' she cried, desperate that he should understand. 'But I wouldn't do anything so cruel. John and I argued about that but I insisted that Lexi and I had a stable and loving relationship before we—we—'

'Snatched her. How could you even think of doing that, Emma?' he asked quietly.

She gulped. 'I told you before,' she wailed. 'John had reported that she was a millstone around your neck. I couldn't bear that, Leon. I thought of my baby, being suffered by you because it was your duty, your wife and daughter treating her badly, and—and it made me *mad*.'

Her vigorous movements had dislodged the jeans again and she muttered curses under her breath as she tried to leash the belt tighter around her middle.

'And now you know different?' he asked throatily.

She flicked a glance at him, ready to complain—if he was laughing—that it wasn't her fault he couldn't find her any female clothes. But his expression was implacable and only his eyes gleamed as if in amusement.

'Now I know different,' she agreed, tossing back her hair and hanging onto the gaping shirt for grim death, 'I have no intention of ever taking her away. She's settled here happily and she loves you. I hope she'll come to love me too. As I said, if all goes well, I'll live on Zakynthos and find a job. I've only ever wanted the best for Lexi. Honest,' she said earnestly. 'I thought I was best. Now I think she needs us both. You can trust me. I swear I won't abduct her.'

He was frowning and she held her breath, then she realised she was dragging the shirt hard over her breasts and he was probably worried that she'd rip the seams or something. Her fingers eased up and so did his frown.

'Believe me,' she pleaded when he just sat there.

He blinked as if he'd been thinking of something entirely different. 'I believe you,' he said slowly. 'But I will take precautions nevertheless. I don't want you to go anywhere without me. I need to watch over you, Emma. This house will be your prison. That's reasonable under the circumstances, isn't it?'

'I've known worse prisons,' she muttered, wriggling uncomfortably in the jeans. 'This one's got a swimming pool.'

His mouth tightened, definitely, she realised, to hide a smile. She sighed. Her appearance was wearing down his resistance. He'd roll about on the floor in hysterics soon.

'Then, you agree.'

'Of course.'

Absently she pushed up the sleeves of the baggy shirt which had flopped down over her hands and had been dangling unappealingly. What did she look like? He'd never want her after this. Bang went goal number three.

'Emma…where are your clothes?' he asked tautly. 'The villa was empty when I dropped Marina there.'

She hitched up the jeans again, longing for a sexy dress with a slit skirt. Or even a dull Auntie Maud dress that fitted her vaguely. Then Leon could stop busting a gut trying not to fall about laughing.

'In a shed near the goats and sheep and things,' she replied meekly.

He grunted. 'They'll have to wait till tomorrow then. I'm not going out in this weather. Are you finishing that?' he asked belligerently, pointing to her mangled salad.

'Not hungry any more,' she replied, subdued.

He scowled. 'Then I'll take you up. You can have Taki's old room. It's not been used and all his stuff's there but I'm sure that won't bother you.'

She glared back at him from under her brows. Was that a

dig, to remind her of what she was supposed to have done? Taki's possessions had been taken from the house the day after she'd asked for a divorce and had been shipped to Zakynthos. Taki had obviously intended to skip the country.

'Why should it?' she said with a shrug. The shirt slipped off her shoulders and she sulkily tugged it back again.

Leon's intake of breath alarmed her in its ferocity. 'Don't do that,' he roared, leaping to his feet.

Her eyes widened in bewilderment. 'Do what?'

'Look sexy in whatever you wear,' he yelled savagely.

Emma's eyes widened even more. 'What, these old things?' she cried, wondering if he was being sarcastic. One glance at his mouth and she knew he wasn't. 'Leon,' she croaked, putting up a defensive hand.

'Oh, no,' he said menacingly, 'you don't get out of your agreement like that.'

And suddenly her back was against the wall, Leon was kissing her, the shirt was slipping and she didn't care and firecrackers were going off in her head.

'Bonfire night,' she mumbled crazily.

'I'm consumed,' he said, breathing hotly in her ear.

She shivered. 'Me too. Take me to bed, Leon.' Looking dazed, he drew back, and then grabbed her hand to pull her to the door. But she resisted. 'Wait a minute.' She wasn't spending a moment longer in the jeans. Couldn't have walked in them anyway. With trembling fingers she unleashed the belt and let them drop to the floor, stepping out suddenly untrammelled.

They began to run. Into the hall, up the stairs, into the bedroom where she had first bathed, slept and changed. There he tore off his clothes and hers, driving her against the door and then, in a tumble of arms and legs, to the thickly carpeted floor.

I love you, she said in her head. And she knew then that she wouldn't settle for an occasional relationship with Lexi, and some lusty sex with Leon whenever she visited. She wanted to live with them both for ever and no one was going to stop her.

Her heart swelled as she kissed him, adoring the feel of his toned skin beneath her mouth. Licking him, tasting, eating... Her hands touched his leaping heat and she gazed lovingly into his eyes.

I love you, they said. His teeth drove into his lower lip as if she'd injured him. Shaking, he caressed her breasts. And then his hands paused. She could feel his palm curving around the deep dent where her scar was and she realised that she'd forgotten about it—and that he couldn't have noticed it at all the last time they'd made love.

He was still, looking at her with shocked eyes. Oh, God! she thought. He finds me ugly. It would be the end. He'd never want her. Never fall in love with her. He'd avoid her like the plague and they'd be strangers, meeting on the doorstep every time she came for Lexi.

She felt tears swim into her eyes. One day she'd be faced with Leon's mistress or his wife...a stepmother for Lex. She couldn't bear it.

She pushed his hands away. 'I disgust you, don't I?' she mumbled unhappily. 'I know it's hideous. But it's still me in here,' she said in a blaze, choking on her tears. 'And if you don't like the way I am then all our problems are solved. You won't be tempted to make love to a woman you despise and I won't be tempted to encourage you.'

CHAPTER ELEVEN

UPSET, she tried to scramble to her feet. He pulled her down again and they struggled for a moment till the tears were overwhelming her and she just lay in a miserable heap, weeping. And she was horribly aware that he was tense and tellingly silent beside her, just staring, not touching, not even comforting her.

'You don't have to say anything,' she mumbled. He was appalled. She could see the horror in his eyes. Blind with tears, she sat up, her hands crossing over her breasts. And she realised that she'd instinctively covered her breasts when they'd made love in the villa. Hence his disgust now. 'Where's Taki's room?' she asked croakily. 'P-point me in the right direction and I'll g-get out of your hair,' she said jerkily through her sobs.

'What…?' He sat up too and cleared his throat. 'What happened?'

'Cancer,' she muttered sulkily.

His intake of breath rasped harshly. 'Emma,' he whispered. 'Was that your illness? Why you get so tired?'

'Yes. Taki's room. Where is it?' she snapped.

Leon was in shock. He'd loved her breasts. They'd been perfect. Softly rounded globes, sweet to his lips, with wonderfully responsive nipples that leapt eagerly into his mouth.

And she'd faced the most terrible disease… He felt a gut-wrenching fear empty his gut and cause his stomach to contract fiercely. What was her future? She might *die*! The shock rocketed through him bewilderingly, thundering through his body and leaving it weak. Aghast, he met her wet-lashed eyes and fought his desperate urge to say mad things.

Like, *Don't ever leave me, you can't die, why you, of all people?*

'I'm so sorry,' he growled inadequately instead.

She looked at him with pitiful eyes as if her world had come to an end, the tears pouring down her unhappy face.

And whether it was unwise or not, he couldn't let her go. Gently he stroked her arm, trying to ignore his own fear, his own needs, and to concentrate on hers. She thought she was ugly. That he didn't find her sexy any more. He smiled ruefully to himself. If only!

'Take your hands away from your breasts,' he said quietly.

'No.' She shook her head violently. 'You've seen me. Isn't that enough? Do you want to humiliate me more?'

'Seeing isn't enough for either of us.'

Ruthlessly he unpeeled her fingers, wet with salty tears, and kissed every inch of each breast. She winced and jerked back when his mouth brushed the scar but he was too strong for her and after a juddering moment of tension she gave in.

'Is that good?' he murmured.

Emma couldn't believe what was happening. It was good. She let out a low moan, revelling in the glorious feel of his firm lips touching where no one—even she—had touched with such gentle worship.

It made her cry to see him loving her there, devoting delicate, sweet kisses to that cruel slash into her femininity.

'Don't cry,' he murmured, raising his head. 'It's all over now. Isn't it? It is, tell me it's over,' he demanded urgently.

Bewildered, trying to stop her sobs, she found herself being crushed in his arms. He was trembling. She couldn't understand why. And then he'd pushed her back a little, his eyes intent on hers.

'Is it over?' he repeated fiercely.

She felt her heart beat faster. Had she got it wrong *again*? 'Why does it matter so much to you?' she asked breathlessly.

Leon stared. 'I—I'm just asking. It affects Lexi, doesn't it?' he said, sounding irritated.

She hoped it was for another reason too. But she didn't dare to totally trust her intuition. It had been wrong so many times before. Her imagination had leapt to conclusions that were way off the mark.

'I'm in the clear,' she assured him and couldn't mistake the way he sagged in relief. He was stroking her breast again as if his caress could heal it. And perhaps he was right. She did feel whole again. Her delighted smile lit up her face. 'I'm expected to live to one hundred and three providing I don't break my neck doing cartwheels.'

Leon felt his heart buck at her joke. All he wanted to do was to hold her close and block out the moment when he'd thought she, so passionate, such a lover of life, might die before her time. His eyes closed in a fervent prayer of thanks.

When he opened them he saw that she was smiling, but wilting. 'Come to bed,' he said in a gravelly voice. 'And tell me about it.'

Tenderly he pulled back the sheet and helped her in, then joined her, drawing her into his arms and holding her as if she were fragile china.

'When did it happen?' he asked quietly. 'You looked pretty rough when I visited you in prison. Was it then?'

'Well, the shock of being charged with fraud can't have helped, and I'd felt too sick with worry to eat, but it had started before then. Though I didn't discover the lump till I *was* in prison. The oncologist talked to me and said it could have been due to the stress of my marriage…'

She clamped her lips together but he put a questing finger beneath her chin and lifted it so that she was forced to meet his eyes.

'What stress?' he asked grimly.

'You won't want to know. Leave it. Best unsaid.'

'No. I don't want there to be any secrets, Emma. The time for that is past.'

She lowered her lashes but his finger was insistent and made her look at him again.

'I have to know,' he said gently, his eyes soft with compassion.

'I made an awful mistake,' she said sadly. 'Taki was very sweet and attentive when I was getting over you. I suppose I fell for him because he seemed to have some of your characteristics. But once we were married I realised that he was obsessively jealous of you, and had married me just to hurt you. I told him that was crazy, you'd dumped me.'

'He was right. It did hurt me,' he said, living that pain again. He'd hated his brother then, and had been ashamed of himself for feeling that way. It had seemed as if Emma had betrayed him, but logic told him that she had a right to fall in love with anyone she fancied. 'You say he was jealous?' It was news to him.

'He talked about you all the time,' she admitted. 'It didn't help our relationship. I kept comparing you two.'

Something leapt within him. 'Oh?' he enquired casually.

'Leon…I think you should know that he didn't like you much. He thought his father favoured you. Teachers, friends…everyone.'

He was stunned. 'I never knew. Go on.'

She bit her lip. 'Oh. Well…our relationship went downhill.'

It seemed she'd come to a halt in her story. 'That was the stress?' he asked with a frown. 'I can see it was tough being married to someone you didn't love, but not that bad, surely?' His eyes narrowed as he read the expression in her eyes. 'There's something else, isn't there?'

'He was…rough.'

Leon's throat dried. 'How rough?' he growled.

'He got drunk. Because he felt such a failure compared with you,' she explained. 'And he'd come home and shout and fling things and sometimes he'd hit me and—'

Again the compression of her lips. God. Taki had struck her! He thought of her body being bruised, the fear on her face, the misery she must have suffered and could hardly contain his anger. 'And?' he prompted ominously.

She jerked her head away, her eyes lowered. 'He—he made me sleep with him when I didn't want to.'

His chest expanded with a huge, indrawn breath that rasped at his lungs like a saw. 'You mean he raped you?' he asked, clenching his fists in fury.

'Only the once,' she said, ridiculously down-playing what had been a sickening moment.

'Oh, Emma!' He groaned.

'No. I'm not a victim, I refuse to be. I'm not making light of what he did, but he's not going to ruin my life because of his jealous, drunken assault,' she said quietly. 'I've blocked it out of my mind. I don't like to think about it. The past had some nightmare moments and I can only move on and keep fit if I put it aside and look to the future.'

'You're amazing,' he found himself saying in wonder.

She sighed and snuggled up, nuzzling her face into his neck. He couldn't believe what she'd gone through. A rush of feeling filled his head, demanding that he protect her from harm in the future. She wouldn't suffer any more. She'd had enough, he vowed.

'How did you feel when you were told you had cancer?' he asked quietly.

'Terrified. It was like walking into a brick wall. I have no recollection of the rest of that day at all. I was terribly emotional and went into a state of total depression, with days of crying.'

'You were scared of dying,' he said sympathetically.

'No. Of not seeing Lexi,' she cried. 'The only thing I feared was that I'd die without ever seeing her again. That's when I decided that come hell or high water I'd see her and form a relationship with her. So I set about making myself well. And here I am and now you know why I'm so determined that she should know I am her mother.'

'She will. I'll make sure of that,' he said, terribly moved

by her fortitude. Lesser women would have crumpled. Not Emma. His mind whirled with admiration. She deserved success. 'One day, very soon, she will call you Mummy.'

'Leon.' She flung her arms around his neck, her eyes alight with joy. 'You really mean that?'

'Only,' he protested, pretending to choke, 'if I'm not throttled first.'

Hastily she withdrew her arms. 'I went too far again, didn't I?'

'You did.' Laughing, he kissed her slowly and sweetly. 'And now, let's see if you can go too far in another direction.'

'Oh, Mr Kyriakis,' she whispered, hugely demure and fluttering her eyelashes frantically. 'I thought you'd never ask.'

He laughed again. 'Wait there.'

'Where are you going?' she protested, as he clambered out of bed and grabbed his dressing gown for decency.

'We're going to celebrate.'

'Celebrate what?' she asked.

He looked at her, golden and glowing, her skin so flawless, hair gleaming, eyes bright, and he could hardly breathe. Swallowing the extraordinary lump of emotion, he said softly, 'Your life.'

She beamed. 'That's lovely, Leon. I'll drink to that.'

He was out of the room before she could say anything else. As he ran down the stairs he felt his spirits soar. Amazing, he mused, hauling a bottle of champagne from the cold store, how the probing finger of death could put life into perspective.

He knew now that he wanted Emma. Wanted her to stay and live with him, to be in his bed.

Eagerly he raced up the stairs again, two flutes and the champagne in his hand.

'I've gone off the boil,' she said haughtily.

'No problem,' he said with a grin.

The bottle would have been nicely shaken up from all that

running. Aiming it warily at the bathroom door, he eased the cork out. It exploded very satisfactorily and, as Emma squealed with excitement, he let it foam all over her, dragging back the covers to do a thorough job.

'Brute. Look at the bed. And it's all over me.' She gasped.

'So it is,' he said in satisfaction, his voice suddenly husky as he leaned over her, and began to lick it off. He shrugged out of his robe and let his body slide over hers, enjoying her look of mute, shocked delight. 'Perhaps,' he said, almost losing his voice entirely as he began to work over her glistening skin, 'you could do the same for me.'

It took a long time. And he never finished. Before he'd even reached her knees she'd captured a crucial part of his anatomy in her hands and was stroking with such maddeningly strong rhythms that he couldn't bear waiting any longer.

He felt a great tenderness as he made love to her. Almost as if his heart was filled to overflowing with something intangible. The physical sensations were just as intense, his passion for her as volcanic, but an undefinable quality had entered their loving. Something profound and bewildering, a feeling of warmth and contentment. A feeling of coming home.

He kissed her deep scar with great gentleness, wanting to take away all the pain it had ever contained. She shuddered with pleasure and the gaze she turned on him all but tore his heart asunder.

'I love you,' she whispered.

Her mouth met his. For a moment he didn't—couldn't—respond. And then, swept away in an emotion he couldn't explain, he kissed her back with a fierce poignancy that powered its way through his body until only physical energy could scatter its bitter-sweet pain.

Their bodies were one. Every breath they took, every beat of their hearts, every sigh. Gently, with agonising slowness, he moved within her, showering her face with kisses as he did so, his hands caressing each swollen breast.

He began to lose his mind, crazy thoughts darting through his brain. That they would be like this for ever. That he would do anything to make her stay, whatever her past. That this was love for him too. He wanted it to be. So badly. And he let himself pretend it was, because the mere thinking of it intensified his feelings and both fired and delighted his shuttered heart.

Lying beside her afterwards, hearing her breathe, made him happier than he could ever remember. He watched as she fell asleep, kissing her nose on impulse and getting a grunt for his pains.

If he loved her, he thought soberly, his conscience was in for a bumpy ride. He had to talk to her, see if there was anything in her claim that she was innocent. Find evidence. But how?

Three weeks was a long time in politics. It was also a long time in a child's life, Emma thought happily as she and Leon walked along the flower-decked street in pretty Alikes, with Lexi grasping their hands and being given swings in the air.

'One, two, three…wheee!' she and Leon went.

'Again,' demanded Lexi.

'We're at the taverna now, sweetheart,' Emma said, gazing at her daughter fondly. Lexi looked adorable. She wore a baby-blue T-shirt with 'I'm Gorgeous' printed on it and matching pedal pushers dotted with ladybirds.

'Ah,' cried the meeter and greeter. 'Good evening, beautiful lady.' And he bowed to Lexi, taking her hand and leading her to a prime position.

Emma beamed. Everywhere they went with Lexi she was met with smiles and admiration. And if there were tears, a dozen macho men would come running up to divert her, beating the women by a short head.

This was their favourite restaurant. Lexi could watch the

ponies go by and wave at them while she waited to eat, nearly falling off the balcony in the process.

Not that entertainment was lacking. Almost immediately the waiter brought the menus, plus a paper turkey for Lexi, whose fantail could be opened and closed repeatedly. Till it broke, and the vigilant waiter brought her another. And later, Lexi's ice-cream pudding managed somehow to support not only a paper parasol and flag, but a sparkler as well.

Such simple things give pleasure, Emma thought, gazing at her daughter's ecstatic face. For her, a sparkler. For me, seeing my child is happy.

After their meal they strolled along the beach arm in arm by the calm indigo sea, with Lexi perched atop Leon's shoulders. Emma was deeply content. Every night in Leon's arms she saw a greater fondness in his eyes. It was almost like the old days.

But not quite. He hadn't given himself fully to her—and wouldn't, till she was cleared of all her imagined crimes. Soon she must talk to him about the innocent part she played. And she could only hope that he'd believe her.

'Haven't seen that before.'

She followed Leon's gaze to an unlit children's playground, lurking in the dark with just the moonlight illuminating it.

'Whoopee!' she cried, breaking away with Lexi and running to the slide.

'Kids,' called Leon scornfully after them.

'That's us,' she said, unabashed.

The two of them came down the slide squealing and Leon put aside his superior male act and joined in. It was all very childish and silly but Emma found herself laughing more than she had for a very long time.

In the half-dark—which somehow made it all funnier— they sampled the swings, the roundabout and a rocker then the see-saw, laughing hysterically when Leon's weight stranded Emma and Lexi high in mid-air.

Gasping for breath and clutching aching stomachs, they walked back to the car, with Lexi chatting nineteen to the dozen.

'Lovely day, lovely evening,' Emma said dreamily as they drove back.

Alerted by the sudden silence from Lexi, Leon looked in the driving mirror and smiled. 'She's asleep,' he murmured fondly. 'How about just you and me having a meal out tomorrow night?'

'You only want to play on the slide without Lexi squealing in your ear,' she teased.

'I thought we'd go upmarket,' he said with a chuckle. 'Somewhere elegant where we can be grown up and you can wear that green dress that makes my knees tremble.'

She was secretly thrilled to know that. 'Don't choose anything on the menu that requires a steady hand then,' she advised.

'I think I can control myself.' He gave her a hot glance. 'Till we get in the car.'

'I'm too old for back seats.' She sniffed.

'It reclines.'

'It would.'

'Here we are, my darling,' he said softly. 'Home.'

'Home,' she repeated, awash with love.

The next day was spent on a nearby beach, searching for crabs under rocks and fishing off a small jetty. Lexi loved the sea urchins that lurked like dark black blobs in the sea, and she never seemed to tire of watching the mullet and bream and wrasse swimming lazily by beneath their dangling feet.

Donika, the caretaker's wife, was now a firm favourite with Lexi and she had agreed to babysit for the evening. When Emma and Leon were ready they went to Lexi's room to read the bed-time story and say goodnight.

'Oh.' Lexi gasped, looking at Emma in awe. *'Poli oraya!'*

'*Efharisto*,' Emma said, thanking her. And surveyed Leon, a feast for the eyes in his perfectly tailored oatmeal jacket, white open-neck shirt and biscuit trousers. 'Leon's beautiful too, isn't he?'

He went pink and said something about choosing a story. But she noticed that when she and Leon sat on either side of Lexi, her daughter kept glancing up at them both and stroking their arms contentedly.

'You're quiet,' Leon observed, when they were on their way to the restaurant.

Emma turned shining eyes to him. 'I was thinking how happy I am,' she said softly. 'You can't imagine how much pleasure it gives me, to be with you and Lexi.'

Yes, he could, Leon thought. And yet their growing intimacy as a family carried with it a bitter-sweetness. More than anything he wanted to help Emma to prove her innocence. Only then would his friends and relations accept her, and only when her reputation was clear could she be truly happy.

He reached out a hand and held hers briefly. 'I'm glad. I'd give you the world if I could,' he said huskily.

'I'll settle for a *souvlaki*,' she said, but her eyes were warm and she leaned her head on his shoulder in a gesture of affection.

It was his favourite restaurant, high on a hill above Zante town, overlooking the sweep of the bay. From the vine-covered terrace where they sat they could see the whole town laid out before them, its lights gleaming in the sultry night.

In the background a man was singing *Kantathes*, the love songs of the island. Emma looked more beautiful than he'd ever seen her. He could hardly take his eyes off her and all the time emotion was swirling inside him, depleting his appetite. They held hands across the table and he marvelled at the love in her sparkling eyes.

He kissed Emma's hand. 'Would you like a brandy, or port, or a coffee?'

Her face glowed in the candlelight and his breath caught at her vulnerability. He didn't want her to be hurt, to be unhappy.

'Let's go home,' she whispered.

As they drove off, he felt his heart fill up. He had to help her. It was obvious to him that she was innocent of fraud—she was far too honest for that. He looked at her, singing softly beside him, and wanted desperately to make her life perfect.

'Emma, tell me again,' he said urgently, 'how your job as financial director was arranged.' The happiness in her face was erased in a flash. Her hands twisted in her lap. 'Help me to understand,' he said. 'Start at the beginning so it's clear in my mind.'

Her mouth pursed and then she began. 'After marrying Taki, I was very busy, working all hours as a financial assistant in an insurance company. I didn't have much spare time. Taki said he wanted me to be the financial director for the Kyriakis bank and I told him it was impossible. He explained I could get a huge salary for doing nothing and he could easily do the work for me. It was a very common arrangement between a husband and wife. He got me to sign a document which I read—and it all seemed above-board. I had no reason not to trust him. He brought other papers for me to sign later, which he said were virtually the same as the first document so I just put my name at the bottom as he suggested. I know it was stupid and I should have read them, but he was so tetchy, so I did what he asked, even when I'd given up work to look after Lexi when she was born. I had to trust him. It was a family business, and all the profits were going to him anyway.'

He frowned. 'But there's no evidence of any kind to back up your side of the story?'

'None that my defence could come up with,' she said dolefully.

'There must have been files, accounts—'

'Apparently when the Inland Revenue swooped, the office had been stripped clean.' She hesitated. 'Leon, I know you won't like hearing this, but it looks to me that Taki knew he was in trouble and had taken steps to hide the evidence. He was certainly in an awful mood the fortnight before. Violent, drunk... That's when I said I wanted a divorce. And he was out all hours of the night.' She sighed. 'He could have burned the books or thrown them in the river. And then a week before the Revenue descended, he was killed, as you know.'

'He rang me a few days before his death,' Leon said in a low tone. 'He told me about the divorce and said he was resigning his post at the bank. He was coming home, and asked me to—'

God. He was a fool. Sharp and clear, an image came into his head. The container of Taki's effects, shipped out *before* the Revenue's investigation. He swore loudly and put his foot on the accelerator.

'Leon!' she protested. 'What are you doing?'

'Sorry.' He eased off a little but stared fixedly ahead, desperate to get back. 'Taki's things are in the house.'

Her gasp told him that she knew what he was thinking. They were both silent and tense. He took a short cut and thistles slapped against the sides of the car as he negotiated the narrow lane. Never had the journey seemed so far.

Gripping the wheel, he tried to concentrate on the road but it was difficult. Bubbling up came wild hopes that tempted him to put his foot down and scream around the roads as if the hounds of hell were on his tail.

'Deal with Donika,' he called, slewing to a halt outside the house and leaping from the car.

His heart was in his mouth as his quick stride swallowed the ground, the steps, hall, stairs...

'Please let something be here,' he muttered, reaching the door to Taki's bedroom. It was a chance. Thin and wild, but nothing more. A friend of his had unpacked the container and he'd never stepped foot in the large suite of rooms. He flung open the door and stood stock-still in amazement.

Inside, it was like Aladdin's cave. Antique furniture was crammed into the room together with silk rugs, Lalique *objets d'art*, art deco clocks and figurines and oil paintings. Impatiently he scanned the expensive clothes, electronic equipment and luxury items. His brother had lived well. A shiver went down his spine. Perhaps too well.

He could have kicked himself. If he'd only come in, and seen all this, maybe he might have wondered how Taki had acquired all these goods. And he might have done a little detective work of his own.

His gaze alighted on a stack of boxes and files piled against the wall. For a moment he stared, unable to believe his brother's deviousness. And then he clambered over a heap of designer jackets and with shaking hands he began to open the boxes, hurling papers aside when they proved to be useless.

'Oh, my God!' he heard Emma say.

'Donika? Lexi?' he enquired curtly, scanning a document.

'All fine. Let me help, Leon,' she cried, scrambling to join him.

'It's got to be here, got to be!' he exclaimed, ripping open another box. She was looking at him oddly and he paused. 'What?'

'You care,' she said gently. 'You want me to be innocent.'

'Of course I do,' he yelled, frantically scything through the contents.

'Why?'

'Because I love you, of course, you…' Had he said that? He blinked, suddenly still. He grinned at her. 'I love you,' he crowed and swept her into his arms.

'Oh, Leon.' She sighed, when they came up for air.

'I love you,' he said in delight, unable to stop himself. 'Love you,' he yelled. 'I do. I really do.'

Emma giggled. 'No need to sound so surprised. And now

let's seal that subtle declaration by proving I'm innocent,' she suggested excitedly.

They fell on the boxes with renewed enthusiasm. And then he found the account books which had been missing. Two sets. All in Taki's hand. Letters from Taki, rearranging pensions and selling off shares and then details of a Swiss bank account containing more money than Taki could ever have earned.

Leon was appalled. There was enough evidence here to have damned his brother. When they'd finished checking the last document, they had found nothing, not one thing that showed Emma had ever been a part of her husband's fraudulent scam.

Dusty and dishevelled, Leon sank to the floor, shaken by the shame and the awful realisation that his brother had caused unbelievable suffering to the woman he loved.

'My brother,' he whispered, white with shock. 'My own brother!'

CHAPTER TWELVE

EMMA took him by the hand and led him to his bathroom where she gently removed his clothes and hers, and showered the dust and memories from both their bodies.

'How can you ever forgive me?' he asked passionately.

'It was Taki, not you,' she said soothingly.

'But I didn't believe you—'

'I was fooled by him at first, too,' she reminded him. 'He was miles away from you—how could you know how his hatred of you had turned his mind? He always said he wanted to be richer than you are. He found a way of achieving that. Besides, I was the one under investigation. There was nothing to point the finger at him. That's why I was so frustrated. I couldn't prove my innocence. He'd been too clever.'

Leon seemed to be in a total state of shock, just apologising and blaming himself for the misery she'd suffered. So she dried him and led him to bed where he lay on his back, his muscles tensed alarmingly while he stared hazily at the ceiling.

'You lost your reputation, your job, your freedom and your child,' he said hoarsely.

All that seemed so long ago. Water under the bridge. And the future was looking just wonderful. She smiled.

'But I won a lot more. And I'll get the rest back, won't I?' Lovingly she kissed his shoulder.

'I can't forgive myself,' he muttered.

'If I can, so can you,' she said with a laugh. 'Leon, I'm happy. Ecstatic. You love me. There's only one more thing I want.'

He rolled over, his eyes glistening with unshed tears. 'Cup of tea?' he said jerkily, attempting a joke.

Emma smiled. 'Lexi, you nut case. And,' she murmured, sliding her hand over his chest, 'something else, for the time being.'

He kissed her, his mouth desperate on hers. For a while he was like a tiger unleashed, his passion white-hot, each kiss more torrid than the one before. And gradually, soothed by her languorous movements and slow, seductive caresses, he grew less frantic and more tender.

'I love you,' he whispered, his voice cracking with emotion.

'I love you back,' she said in a purring voice, stretching her feline body luxuriously.

His mouth descended and she gave herself to him, utterly content.

They had been building up to the big moment all day when Leon would tell Lexi that Emma was her mother. And now they all settled themselves on the sofa and Leon put on the video for them all to watch.

'That is Emma,' he said, as the picture came up. 'I knew her a long time ago. She was my best friend. I loved her a lot.'

Sitting between them both, Lexi watched with enjoyment, laughing when Emma fell into the pond. 'Again, please,' she cried. So it was rewound and played once more.

Leon turned the television off. 'Emma knew your daddy, remember?' he murmured, cuddling Lexi close. Emma held her breath. 'Sweetheart,' Leon said gently, taking Lexi's small hands in his, 'do you like Emma?'

Emma quivered as her daughter flung her a big smile.

'Lots,' Lexi said, clapping her hands.

Emma felt a huge lump of emotion clogging her throat. This was the moment she'd been waiting for. Leon was clearly nervous. He swallowed.

'Lexi, you are a big girl now,' he said flatteringly. 'Big enough for me to tell you something special.'

Lexi's eyes grew enormous as Leon took a deep breath. Emma held hers, every nerve in her body screwed up in apprehension as Leon continued.

'Sweetheart, you are a very lucky girl.' He stroked Lexi's soft cheek and kissed it while Emma felt her stomach knot up unbearably. 'Emma,' he said gently, 'is your mummy.'

Lexi blinked at Leon and then up at Emma who sat with tears in her eyes.

'Yes. I am your mummy, sweetheart,' she said huskily.

At Lexi's wriggle, Leon released his arms and the little girl slid off his lap. Emma smiled shakily and opened her arms to her beloved child.

But Lexi stood frowning. And then she ran out into the garden.

There was an appalled silence. Emma couldn't speak, couldn't think and had become frozen like a statue in her seat. She felt Leon get up and move to the open door, his feet sounding heavy and slow on the tiled floor.

Desolation swept through her. She stared blankly into space, unable to believe what had happened.

'She's talking to the doll you gave her,' Leon said, from somewhere far away.

'Calling it Mama?' she choked.

'Darling,' he whispered and she knew she'd been right. 'Come here,' he begged. 'I can't let Lexi out of my sight. Come and sit with me.'

She couldn't. There was no life, no energy in her body. 'I feel sick,' she mumbled, and rushed off to the bathroom.

Wiping her face later, she looked at her reflection in the mirror and wondered where the pale, tragic-eyed woman had come from. It seemed that the happiness of the past few days counted as nothing. She knew that was ridiculous, that she and Leon were made for one another and would be lovers for the rest of their lives, but…

'Oh, Lexi!' she moaned.

Suddenly she wanted Leon. With a sob, she ran out to him,

absorbed his groan of utter relief and the frantic worry on his face, and hurled herself into the welcoming circle of his arms.

He rocked her like a child. 'She'll get the hang of it,' he assured her. 'Give her time.'

'And if not?' She snuffled into his shoulder.

'She will. She cares for you. Hey, darling, sometimes I'm jealous of you two girls giggling together.'

She wouldn't be cheered up. She felt even too numb to cry now. The ravages of the past few minutes had gone deeper than tears. She feared that she might never claim her daughter.

Leon eased her to the top step. They sat with their arms around each other watching Lexi whispering to her doll. Leon got out his handkerchief and blew his nose loudly. Miserably Emma looked at him and saw that tears were trickling from his eyes and he was blinking, trying to stop them before she noticed.

'Oh, my darling,' she whispered, laying her head on his shoulder.

He kissed her forehead. 'I love you so much,' he said brokenly. 'I want Lexi to love you too—'

He muttered irritably as the phone set up its insistent ringing. 'Cursed thing! I'll put it onto the answer-machine—'

'No. You answer it,' she whispered.

Dropping a quick kiss on her head, he left her. She didn't dare go into the garden. Lexi might be upset if she did. Emma bit her lip hard. She never imagined she'd ever be jealous of a doll in a bikini, she thought, trying to raise her own spirits. It didn't work. The coil of nausea lurked like bitter gall in her stomach.

My child, she thought, tormenting herself. My baby! She had come so far, fought so hard and yet a tiny little girl had shattered all her dearest hopes.

'Lexi,' she mumbled, consumed with misery. She pressed

a hand to her aching heart and tried to believe that it would
be all right, one day.

And suddenly she saw that Lexi was scrambling up onto
a low drystone wall—something she'd been told never to do.
Before she could call out, Lexi was on top of it and had
slipped.

Emma ran like the wind, her spine freezing at the blood-
curdling scream. Lexi got to her feet and began to run to her,
wailing at the top of her voice.

'Mummy. Mummy!'

'Oh-h-h!' Emma shuddered as her arms enfolded her
daughter, their tears mingling. 'What is it, darling? Where
does it hurt?' she asked with a sob.

'I f-f-fell.' Lexi wept, pointing to her knee.

'It's all right,' she said shakily. 'Mummy will kiss it better.' Emma bent and kissed the grubby little knee, tasting a
tiny smidgen of blood. My daughter, she thought, her heart
singing as she hugged the snuffling child. My darling daughter.

'What's wrong?' came Leon's anxious voice.

And Emma didn't mind when Lexi slithered from her
grasp and ran to him. Blurry-eyed she rose, feeling she could
weep for joy.

'And Mummy kissed it better!' Lexi was saying with all
the pride of a hero discussing his war wound.

'Uh-huh.' Leon's voice cracked completely. He glanced
up at Emma and cleared his throat. 'That's what mummies
do,' he said softly.

'I said to dolly,' Lexi said, 'my mummy has come.'

'I see. That was kind,' Emma said.

'Can you be my daddy?' Lexi asked earnestly, as Leon
dabbed at her knee with a handkerchief.

He smiled. 'I would like that,' he said fervently. 'Emma?'

'Need you ask?' she whispered, feeling far too weak to
stand unaided.

Shaking with emotion, Leon swept them both into his embrace: the two people he loved most on earth. He felt quite delirious.

'This is an odd place and an even odder moment for a proposal, but I can do the bended knee and flowers and wine later. Just now,' he whispered to Emma, 'I have to know if you'll marry me. I love you with all my heart. I want to be with you for ever. Please say yes,' he urged fervently.

'Oh, Leon, as if I'd ever refuse you. Yes, yes,' she said breathily and, overjoyed, he kissed her.

'Do mummy and daddies,' said Lexi horribly loud in his ear, 'do kisses too?'

He dropped a quick peck on the baby cheek. 'Oh, yes,' he said, feeling like shouting with happiness. 'Lots.'

Emma laughed. 'I love you both so much,' she said breathlessly.

It was dreadfully late by the time the excited Lexi had gone to sleep. Emma sat on the terrace with Leon, curled up in the big cane chair with him, and listening to the frogs pulsing in the background while the bats laid on an aerial display. Somewhere in the distance she could hear the electronic call of the scops owl, and the occasional bark of a dog echoed across the peaceful valley.

'Got any champagne on ice?' she asked casually.

He gave a wicked chuckle. 'Two bottles. One for each of us.' His mouth met hers in a long, thorough kiss.

Emma felt drunk already. 'Seems a waste to pour it down our throats,' she murmured and, encouraged by his passionate growl, led the way indoors.

Helen Brooks lives in Northamptonshire and is married with three children. As she is a committed Christian, busy housewife and mother, her spare time is at a premium but her hobbies include reading, swimming, gardening and walking her two energetic, inquisitive and very endearing young dogs. Her long-cherished aspiration to write became a reality when she put pen to paper on reaching the age of forty, and sent the result off to Mills & Boon®.

Don't miss the next story by Helen Brooks, THE MILLIONAIRE'S PROSPECTIVE WIFE, coming in September 2005, in Modern Romance™!

THE GREEK
TYCOON'S BRIDE

by
Helen Brooks

CHAPTER ONE

'YOU'RE not seriously telling me you're actually considering going to Greece, Jill? You can't, you just can't.' Sophy tried very hard not to glare as she looked at the small, slim girl sitting opposite her but it was hard. 'You don't owe Theodore's family a thing and you know it. Michael is seven years old now and they have never so much as acknowledged his existence.'

'Well, they didn't know about it for the first couple of years,' Jill said reasonably.

'And when they found out? You'd have expected some sort of contact—a letter, a phone call, *something*.'

'According to Christos, the family did try to write but they never received an answer to any of their letters.'

'And you believe that?' Sophy's voice was scornful, her violet-blue eyes expressing her opinion of Jill's in-laws as forcefully as her voice.

'It *is* possible, Sophy.' Jill gazed miserably at her twin, her own violet-blue eyes dark and tragic and her face very white. 'Theodore was a very proud man, excessively so— you know that. He said he would never forgive them and he meant it. He…he could be implacable when he made up his mind about anything.'

'But he would have talked to you about it,' Sophy pressed urgently. 'At least to tell you he'd received some correspondence?'

'No.' Jill turned away, busying herself folding some washing she had just brought indoors. 'Not necessarily, not if he'd already made up his mind. When we got married he told me I was his family from that point on and that he

5

had no other, and he meant it. I wasn't allowed to even discuss them, if you want to know the truth.'

Sophy stared at her sister's bent head and not for the first time wondered how happy Jill's marriage had really been. But that was irrelevant now anyway. Six weeks ago Theodore had been killed in a freak accident when the car he had been driving had been crushed by a falling tree at the height of a bad storm.

With that in mind, Sophy now said gently, 'But the funeral, Jill? They never even came to Theodore's funeral.'

'Christos told them it had been Theodore's wishes.' And at Sophy's loud snort of disbelief, Jill raised her blonde head and looked straight at her sister. 'It was true, Sophy. There were letters which Theodore had placed in Christos's safe-keeping some years ago. I didn't even know anything about them until Theodore died and then Christos felt he ought to tell me before he sent them to Greece. I think he suspected what they contained.'

'Letters?' Sophy took a quick gulp of coffee as she watched Jill continue to fold the washing in the big wicker laundry basket on the kitchen table. 'Letters to whom, exactly?'

'To his family. In…in the event of his illness or death. Of course he didn't expect it would happen so soon or suddenly—' Jill stopped abruptly, taking a deep breath before she continued, 'Anyway, Christos and I made the decision to open the letters and read them before we sent them, the day after the accident, and then…then we destroyed them. But Christos felt he had to phone the family and just say Theodore had left instructions he didn't want them there.'

Jill now stopped speaking, laying her head on the edge of the laundry basket in front of her and bursting into tears. Sophy jumped to her feet, rushing to her twin's side and putting her arm round Jill's shaking shoulders as she said urgently, 'Oh, love, what is it? Come on, everything will be all right.'

'They were awful, Sophy.' As Jill raised streaming eyes, she was choking on the sobs she was trying to stifle. 'Really awful. So bitter and hard and cold. I…I couldn't send them. Not to his mother and everyone. Think how they'd feel after what has happened to Theodore. So—' she reached into the laundry basket and extracted a newly dried handkerchief from the pile of sweet-smelling washing '—so I burnt them. I burnt them all. Do you think that was wrong of me?'

She raised haunted eyes to her sister's face and Sophy stared at her, her blue eyes reflecting her concern for her beloved twin. 'Of course not,' she said softly, smoothing back a lock of fine, ash-blonde hair from Jill's brow. 'What good would it do to just perpetuate all the misery? Heartache breeds heartache.'

'That's what I thought.' Jill dabbed at her eyes as she said, 'Christos said the decision had to be mine and mine alone, and once I'd made it he said he agreed with me, but it's been like a lead weight round my heart ever since. Theodore gave those letters to Christos, believing Christos would do what he wanted, and I…I burnt them. He would never forgive me if he knew.'

It seemed to her that Jill's husband had majored in unforgiveness, Sophy thought grimly. She had always had reservations about Theodore and the two of them had never hit it off, something Sophy knew Jill had sensed from the first time she had introduced them. Consequently Jill had been guarded in anything she said about Theodore and for the first time the two girls had had an area in their lives in which they were less than totally frank with each other, although neither of them had acknowledged it.

It had been less of a problem than it might have been, owing to the fact that within three months of Jill meeting

Theodore—just after the two girls had finished university— Sophy had been offered a wonderful opportunity on the strength of her degree in Maths and Business Studies to work in London as a trainee buyer for one of the top fashion companies.

She had left Cambridge—her home town—within the month, just days before Jill had discovered she was pregnant with Michael, necessitating a hasty register office wedding which Sophy had attended before shooting off back to the capital. From that point the twins' lives had gone in very different directions—Jill looking after her family and helping her husband in his very successful restaurant business, of which Christos was a partner, and Sophy following her own star in her dream career and rising to her present position of fashion buyer.

Sophy had always held the private opinion that Theodore had got her sister pregnant purposely, knowing Jill was unable to take the Pill due to being the one woman in several hundred thousand it made ill—but she had been wise enough to keep her suspicions to herself. However, over the years she had seen her sister change from the bright, sparkling, happy creature of former days to a mere shadow of the old Jill: quiet, withdrawn and totally under her dominant husband's control. But Jill had never complained and had always changed the subject when Sophy had tried to ascertain if all was well, and so she had had to leave the matter of Jill's marriage alone and respect her twin's privacy.

'So…' Sophy brought their attention back to the letter lying at the side of the laundry basket which had started their discussion in the first place. 'You feel you ought to go and meet Theodore's family, then.' She could understand her sister's decision a little better in view of what had transpired, although it still felt like allowing a lamb to walk into the wolf's den.

'Just for a short holiday, like they've suggested. They can meet Michael and, more importantly, Michael can meet them and get to know the only grandparents he has.' The twins' father had walked out just after they were born and their mother had died some years ago.

'And then?' Sophy asked gently.

'Then we'll come back and carry on like before,' Jill said quietly. 'I can help Christos in the business; we've already talked about that, and Michael can carry on at his present school with all his friends. I wouldn't even think about staying out there, Sophy, if that's what you're worried about.'

She didn't know what she was worried about exactly, except that if the family were anything at all like Theodore they would persuade her easy-going sister that black was white. Jill had always been the malleable, docile one, acquiescent to a fault and utterly unable to stand up for herself.

'Look, if you're uneasy about me going alone with Michael, why don't you come too?' Jill said matter-of-factly. 'Theodore's father has already offered to pay for me and Michael and a friend—his suggestion, Sophy. He wrote I might feel more comfortable if I brought a friend along too. I'd much prefer you to come with me but I thought you'd probably be too busy. I know you've been backwards and forwards to Paris like a boomerang the last few weeks and I didn't want to add to your stress levels!'

'That's all finished now the collections are reviewed,' Sophy said thoughtfully. 'The next few weeks will be more low-key, besides which I've still got some holiday left from last year, let alone this! When are you thinking of going?'

'Any time. I'll fit in with you,' Jill said quickly. 'Do you think you could come, then? Oh, Sophy, it'd make all the difference!' And she burst into tears again which immediately settled the issue as far as Sophy was concerned, without another word being said.

Jill needed her. The job, work commitments and anything else came a very poor second to that.

The Greek airport was typical of all airports, crowded and noisy and confusing, but the journey had been relatively comfortable and Michael's excited chatter had kept both women occupied and taken their minds off the forthcoming meeting with Theodore's estranged family. Sophy had been busy with making sure their luggage was intact and that Michael didn't disappear for the last few minutes—Jill being in something of a daze—and so she only became aware of the tall dark man waiting for them when Jill gripped her arm and breathed, 'Sophy, that's Andreas, Theodore's brother—it has to be. Look how he's watching us.'

She turned to look in the direction in which her sister was staring, keeping one hand on Michael who was jumping about like a small jack-in-the-box, and then became transfixed herself as her eyes met the hard, black, narrowed gaze riveted on the women.

There was no time to make any comment because in the next instant the man was making his way towards them, his tall, lean powerful body cutting through the crowd as though it didn't exist.

'Mrs Karydis? Jill Karydis?' His voice was deep and gravelly and strongly accented, and dark eyes flashed from one twin to the other, eyes that were set in a face that was cold and handsome.

Jill seemed to have gone into some sort of frozen limbo, and after waiting a second Sophy was forced to say, 'This is Jill,' as she indicated the pale silent figure at her side, 'and Michael too of course,' as she brought her small nephew in front of her. 'How do you do, Mr...?'

'Please call me Andreas.'

As soon as she had spoken, he had transferred his attention to Jill, who was gripping Sophy's arm as though her life depended on it, and still didn't seem able to speak. And then, as he held out his hand, Jill seemed to come to life—much to Sophy's relief—saying, 'Hello, Andreas,' as she let go of her sister's arm. 'Thank you so much for coming to meet us.'

'It is a pleasure,' Theodore's brother said coolly.

Sophy could well understand Jill's present state of shock because she was feeling a bit that way herself. The man in front of them was nothing like Theodore—which was a relief in one way. Theodore had been just a little taller than Jill, his light brown hair and brown eyes pleasant but unremarkable, and his body stocky if anything.

His brother was aggressively handsome, at least six foot tall, with a powerful top-heavy masculinity that didn't detract from the lean muscled body's impact on the senses. His eyes were not dark brown, as she had thought, but a deep compelling grey, and his hair was black—jet-black.

But there was one area in which Andreas's resemblance to his brother was evident: there was no sign of softness about him at all. He could have been fashioned from a slab of granite.

And then Sophy had to recant the last thought as the grey eyes fastened on Michael's inquiring young face, and, letting go of his sister-in-law's hand, Andreas knelt down in front of his young nephew and said softly, 'Manchester United, eh?' He nodded gently at Michael's tee-shirt—his favourite, which Sophy had bought her nephew for his last birthday—as he said, 'I, too, am a fan of the football. We will have to have a kick around together, yes? You would like this, Michael?

'*Yes.*' It was said with great fervency. And then Michael added, his voice quieter, 'You're my daddy's brother, aren't you?'

Andreas didn't move and his face didn't change as he said softly, 'Yes, Michael, I am your daddy's brother, which makes me your uncle. This is good, eh? This means that already we are friends?'

Brown eyes, very like Theodore's, stared into grey, and for a long moment Michael surveyed his new uncle. And then, coming to a decision which was self-evident, he smiled sunnily and nodded.

Andreas ruffled the boy's hair before standing again, and Sophy was glad of the extra moment or two. This big, virile male was a little daunting, to say the least. Before he had spoken to Michael, she would have said he didn't seem quite human, but then the complete metamorphosis had thrown her even more.

And then Andreas was looking directly at her, his grey eyes smoky dark and almost black, and his voice was smooth and expressionless as he said, 'And this must be Sophy, yes? Jill's letter did not prepare us for the event of there being two of her; she said merely that her sister would be accompanying her.'

Sophy stiffened immediately. She and Jill had been devoted to each other from tiny children, but both girls had always fought for their individuality from those around them, recognising that the fact that they were identical was a mixed blessing.

Some people automatically assumed that because they looked so uncannily alike they functioned with one brain and one voice. The truth of the matter was that they were dissimilar in temperament and behaviour. In fact, they were almost direct opposites.

'How do you do, Andreas?' Sophy said politely, but with a certain edge to her voice which was not lost on the dark man watching her so intently. 'I'm Jill's twin, as I'm sure you've guessed.' She forced a cool smile and hoped he'd take the hint.

Andreas nodded, his gaze going over her steadily as though he was endeavouring to read what she was thinking. 'I am pleased to meet you, Sophy,' he said evenly, before turning again to Jill with an abruptness which made Sophy feel she had been cursorily dismissed. She blinked, staring at the cold male profile with a feeling of dislike as she heard Andreas say, 'The car is waiting outside, if you are ready, and I know my parents are anxious to welcome you into their home. Shall we go?'

'Yes, of course. Thank you,' Jill said quickly.

Andreas had summoned a porter with an inclination of his head as he had been speaking and Jill's quiet voice fell into an empty void as he spoke to the young man in rapid Greek.

Jill looked, and had sounded, utterly bemused, and as Sophy watched her sister smooth her straight silky fringe with nervous fingers, she frowned to herself. Jill was supposed to be coming here to relax and meet Theodore's family in a spirit of reconciliation, and in Sophy's opinion the Karydises were darn lucky her sister had bothered to make the effort, considering past history. This brother certainly needn't act as though it was the family doing Jill a favour, she thought aggressively.

She watched her sister's face, framed by its curtain of wispy ash-blonde hair which hung to her shoulders, and noted the tension written all over it with a further deepening of dislike for Andreas Karydis. She flicked back her hair, which was shorter than Jill's and cut to frame her face in a gleaming chin-length bob, as her soft full mouth tightened. Who did this family think they were, anyway? Royalty, by the look of it.

And then she cautioned the quick temper which her mother had always insisted came from her father's side of the family, and of which Jill had no trace. She didn't know what Andreas was thinking; she could have read all this wrong. Maybe the distant, aloof manner he had displayed with her and Jill was habitual with the man. Jill had told her that Theodore's argument with his family had begun long before he'd met her, but that when Theodore had chosen an English wife it had been the final straw.

That had been in the early days of her sister's marriage, and when she had asked Jill why Theodore had quarrelled so bitterly with his kith and kin and come to England, Jill had been vague and changed the subject.

It had been two or three years later before her sister had admitted Theodore had refused to discuss his past life with his wife, and that she had no idea what had caused the rift. Even Christos, whose name Theodore had been given by a friend of a friend back in Greece before he'd left his native land, and with whom Theodore had struck up an immediate rapport on seeking him out on arriving in England, did not know, according to Jill.

A mystery. And Sophy had never liked mysteries. Everything had to be clear and straightforward, as far as she was concerned; she couldn't have married Theodore for all the tea in China! Not that he would have asked her in the first place. A rueful smile touched her mouth. Jill's husband had always made it plain in a hundred little unspoken ways that he'd had as little time for her as she had had for him. She had just never been drawn to the strong, silent, macho type of male; Heathcliff might be great in the book but a dark, brooding, moody type of man would be sheer murder to live with, as far as she was concerned.

And then she came out of her reverie as, the luggage being in place on the trolley, Andreas turned and took Jill's arm, saying politely, 'Shall we?', his glance taking in Sophy and Michael before he strode off with Jill pattering along at his side.

Sophy smiled stiffly and hoped she hadn't betrayed the jolt her senses had given as the piercing eyes had met hers.

Strength and authority seemed to radiate from the man and it was too much, too overwhelming to be comfortable. Even the clothes he wore were a representation of the dark power that was in every glance, every gesture. All around them were colourful dresses and bright shirts, Bermuda shorts and cheeky tee-shirts vying with more elegantly flamboyant clothes worn by both sexes, but still undeniably cheerful and showy.

Andreas was wearing a brilliant white shirt, open at the neck, and plain charcoal trousers, and he was a monochrome of severity in all the brightness.

As they exited the building the full force of the June sun hit, the heat wrapping them round like a hot blanket, and Michael's awe-struck voice as he said, 'Wow! It's really, *really* hot,' brought his uncle turning round with a smile on his face.

'England is not so warm, eh?' he said indulgently, his tone of voice and the look on his face completely different with his small nephew than it was with the two women. 'It is normally in the eighties here in June, but even hotter in July and August. You will find yourself spending much time in your grandparents's swimming pool, I think. Like a little fish, eh?'

'A swimming pool?' Michael was elated, his big brown eyes shining. 'They have one of their own?' he asked in wonderment. He had recently learnt to swim at the local swimming baths and, although barely proficient, adored the water.

Andreas nodded. 'But one end is very deep,' he warned quietly, his eyes smiling into the little round face topped by a mass of curly light brown hair. 'You must never venture into the water unless you are with a grown-up, Michael. This is a rule for all the children who visit my parents's home, yes?'

'Who are the other children?' Michael asked immediately.

'Relations and friends of the family. Do not worry, little one. You will meet them all in good time,' his uncle said easily.

Andreas had been leading them across the vast car park as he had talked to Michael, and now, as he approached a long sleek limousine complete with driver, Michael's eyes nearly popped out of his head. 'Is this your car?' he asked breathlessly. Cars were his passion. 'Your very own?'

'Yes, do you like it?' Andreas asked, smiling at the enthusiasm.

Sophy had been viewing the light exchange between the two with something akin to amazement, and as she glanced at Jill she saw the same emotion in her twin's eyes. The youngest member of their little party was clearly not in the least intimidated by his formidable relation!

'It's beautiful,' Michael breathed reverently, stroking the silver metal with a respectful hand. 'And this is my favourite colour.' He walked round the car slowly, goggle-eyed.

'Mine too.' Andreas grinned at the small boy, and the two women exchanged a cryptic glance, reading each other's minds as they so often did. It looked as if Andreas and Michael were friends already.

The chauffeur had been busy piling the luggage into the cavernous boot of the vehicle, and now Andreas called him over, his voice composed as he said, 'This is Paul, my driver and also my friend.' As the small lean man smiled a smile which showed blackened teeth, Andreas continued, 'Mrs Karydis, Paul, and my nephew, Michael. And this is Miss…?' as he included Sophy in the sweep of his hand.

'Sophy Fearn. *Mrs* Sophy Fearn,' Sophy said, smiling sweetly into the gnomelike face of the driver. The 'Mrs' was a small victory, nothing at all really, but it felt wonderful to be able to trip Theodore's brother up on even a tiny detail.

There was a startled pause for just a second or two and then Andreas recovered immediately, his hard, handsome face hiding his thoughts as he said quietly, 'I do apologise, Sophy. I was not aware you were married but of course I should not have assumed.'

No, you shouldn't. Sophy held his eyes for just a moment, allowing her gaze to say the words she couldn't voice, and then she smiled coolly, her voice polite and unconcerned as she said, 'Not at all, Andreas, it's perfectly all right. And I'm a widow actually,' she threw in for good measure.

The grey eyes widened for a split second and again she knew she had surprised him. 'I'm sorry.'

Sophy was aware of Michael fidgeting at the side of them and knew her nephew was longing to ride in the car, and so she kept the explanation brief, merely shrugging as she said, 'My husband died three years ago and time helps.' She hoped, she did so hope he wasn't as crass as one or two of their friends had been with their sympathetic remarks after Theodore's death along the lines of, 'Such bad luck, the pair of you having such tragedies,' and 'I can't believe you've both lost your husbands,' as though she and Jill had been unforgivably careless.

But Andreas merely nodded, the compelling eyes holding hers for a moment longer before he opened the door of the limousine and helped them in, his manner formal in the extreme.

It was the first time he had touched Sophy, and the feel of his warm, firm flesh through the thin cotton sleeve of her light top was unnerving, although she wasn't quite sure why.

Once inside the overtly luxurious car, Michael's oohs and ahhs filled the air space and provided a bridge over any difficult moments, and then Paul was negotiating the big car out of the car park and they were on their way.

'Have you been to northern Greece before?' Andreas asked politely after a few minutes, his glance taking in both women.

'I haven't been anywhere,' Jill answered quickly, 'apart from a holiday in France with a load of other students when we were at university, but Sophy's always dashing off somewhere or other abroad with her job. She's used to travelling.'

'Really?' The dark gaze focused on Sophy's face.

'A slight exaggeration,' Sophy said quietly. 'I'm a fashion buyer so I have to pop over the channel now and again, and there's been the odd visit to Milan and New York, but most of the time I'm sitting at my desk with piles of paperwork in front of me.'

'A fashion buyer.' It could have been her imagination but Sophy thought she detected a note of something not quite nice in the deep voice. 'So you are a career woman, Sophy? An ambitious one?'

It was a perfectly reasonable question and if anyone else had asked it she wouldn't have minded in the least, but somehow, coming from Andreas Karydis, it caught her on the raw. 'I'm a woman in an extremely interesting job which I've worked very hard to attain and enjoy very much,' Sophy said coolly, 'but I don't care for labels.' It was dismissive but she kept it polite. Just.

She felt Jill shift uncomfortably at the side of her but Theodore's brother appeared quite unmoved, his eyes holding hers for a moment longer before he nodded unconcernedly, turning to Jill again as he said, 'I might be prejudiced, of course, but I consider this part of Greece one of the most beautiful. Halkidiki is mainly an agricultural area with pine woods and olive groves, and you'll find it's picturesque but with a timeless feel about it. In many places the people's way of life is still little affected by the twenty-first century, and the land is lush and green with wide open spaces and plenty of golden beaches. It is a pity you did not come in the spring; the fields are hidden under a blanket of flowers then, although they are still pretty in summer.'

'Have you lived here all your life?' Jill asked nervously after a few seconds had ticked by in silence.

Andreas nodded, and then the piercing gaze swept over Sophy's face for an instant as he said, his mouth twisting sardonically, 'But, like your sister, I travel a little. My father has olive, lemon and orange groves on his estate, but his main interest has always centred in shipping. Now he is older he prefers to take things easy and leave the main bulk of the Karydis business interests to me to handle. This suits us both.'

Jill nodded and said no more, but Sophy's mind was racing with a hundred and one questions she knew she couldn't ask. Was Theodore's family as wealthy as this car and the way Andreas had been speaking was making her think they were? Had Theodore been the younger or the elder son, and were there any more brothers and sisters? What had caused Theodore to leave this wonderful part of the world and make a new life in England? Question after question was presenting itself to her, but she forced herself to turn and look out of the car window as though she wasn't aware of the big dark man sitting opposite her, Michael at the side of him chattering away nineteen to the dozen.

They had been travelling along a wide dusty road with rows of cypress trees flexing spearlike in the faint hot breeze on either side, but now they approached a small village dozing gently in the noonday sun. The glare of whitewashed walls was broken only by purple and scarlet hibiscus and bougainvillaea, and chickens were pecking desultorily here and there at the side of the road, their scrawny legs only moving with any purpose when the limousine nosed its way past.

'Oh, there, Jill, look.' Sophy nudged her sister as she pointed to a spring some way from the road, where a collection of women had brought amphora-shaped earthen jars to collect the pure sparkling water, the overspill from the spring filling a trough from which a small brown donkey was drinking. 'Isn't that just lovely?' The two women were quite entranced.

'The water is quite untainted,' Andreas said quietly. 'Most of the villages have their own water supply plumbed in these days, but still the women prefer to come to the meeting place and chat and gather the water for their families in the time-old tradition. I think maybe very few people have the need to see the doctor for this epidemic called stress which is so prevalent in the cities, eh?' he added a touch cynically.

'Will I be able to drink from a stream like that?' Michael asked hopefully, 'at my grandparents's home?'

All attention drawn back inside the car, Sophy saw Andreas was smiling indulgently, his voice faintly rueful as he said, 'I'm afraid not, Michael. Your grandparents have all the conveniences of the twenty-first century, which includes water coming out of taps. However, if that were not so you would not be able to enjoy your own pool during your stay, so maybe it is not so bad?'

The village passed, the car took a winding road where the occasional stone house set among lemon, fig and olive groves broke the vastness of green fields baking under a clear blue sky.

'Why are those ladies wearing big boots?' Michael asked his uncle a few minutes later, pointing to where sturdy women were busy working in the fields, their legs encased in enormous neutral-coloured leather knee boots and big straw hats on their heads. 'Aren't they too hot?'

'It is for protection against the bite of snakes,' Andreas said soberly. 'It is not wise to work in the fields without them. This is Greece, little one. It is very different from England.'

He was very different too. Andreas was giving his attention to his small nephew, and it gave Sophy the chance to watch him surreptitiously. And she dared bet he was just as dangerous as any snake. How old would he be? She looked at the uncompromisingly hard handsome face, at the firm carved lips and chiselled cheekbones, the straight thin nose and black eyebrows. He could be any age from his late twenties right up to forty; it was that sort of face. A face that would hardly change with the years.

Theodore, at thirty-six years of age, had been eight years older than she and Jill, and in the last couple of years before his death had put on a considerable amount of weight and lost some of his hair. His brother was as different from him as chalk to cheese. But that happened in some families.

And then Sophy came to sharply as she realised he had finished talking to Michael and that he was looking straight at her, his eyes like polished stone and his eyebrows raised in mocking enquiry.

She flushed hotly, turning away and staring out of the window as her heart thumped fit to burst. He might *look* different, she qualified testily, but inside he was certainly a one hundred per cent Karydis, all right. Arrogant, cold, self-opinionated and dominating.

She had never understood what had drawn her sister to Theodore and how she could have remained married to him all these years, although once Michael had been on the way perhaps there had been little choice about the matter. Whatever, she couldn't have lasted a week, a day—an *hour* with him! And, although she was sure Jill was unaware of it, her sister was already beginning to lighten up a bit and show more evidence of the old Jill who had become buried under the authoritative weight of her husband.

This might be exactly what it was purported to be—a pleasant holiday for Jill and Michael to meet their in-laws and establish a long distance relationship for the future, but for herself she wasn't so sure about the purity of the Karydises's motives. And there was no way, *no way* she would stand by and see her sister come under the oppression of another dictator, be it Theodore's parents or his brother or the whole jam pack lot of them.

She straightened her shoulders and lifted her chin as though she was already doing battle. She would keep her eyes and ears open whilst she was here. She had always been far better than Jill at picking up any undercurrents, and she was doubly glad she had made the effort and accompanied Jill out here.

The Karydises might find Jill accommodating to a fault and somewhat naive, but they would discover her sister was a different kettle of fish if they tried to pull any fast ones!

CHAPTER TWO

IT WAS another half an hour before Andreas announced they were close to his parents's home, but the journey through the Greek countryside where the vivid blue backdrop of the sky had provided a perfect setting for small square white-washed houses with red tiled roofs, pretty villages and countless olive groves, and the odd dome-shaped spire dazzling in the sunshine, could have continued for much longer as far as Sophy was concerned. Apart from one factor, that was—the proximity of Andreas in the close confines of the car.

Since the moment he had caught her watching him she had been very careful to avoid any eye contact, but she knew without looking at him every time the grey gaze was levelled in her direction and it was unnerving. *He* was unnerving.

She hadn't met a man who exuded such a stark, virile masculinity before, and the open-necked shirt he was wearing had enabled her to catch a glimpse of the bronzed, hair-roughened flesh beneath which had caused her stomach muscles to tighten. And she liked that reaction even less than her earlier irritation and dislike because it suggested a kind of weakness.

It wasn't as though she *liked* the caveman type, she told herself crossly. Matthew had had the sort of looks she was drawn to: thick fair hair and blue eyes, a slim, almost boyish frame and classical fine features in an academic sort of face. Matthew had been gentle and mild, non-threatening, and that was her ideal man. Matthew. Poor, dear Matthew.

As the car turned off the main road into what was vir-

23

tually a narrow lane, Sophy's thoughts were far away. She and Matthew had met at university and she had liked him right away. He had been funny and warm and easy to be with and, although at uni they had just been friends, once she had moved up to London—Matthew's home territory— their relationship had moved up a gear, and they had slowly begun to get to know each other better.

They had been married for just eight months before Matthew had fallen ill, and it had been a happy time. He had been her first lover and their sex life had been tender and comfortable, which had summed up their life together really, Sophy silently reflected, as the car came to a halt outside a pair of eight-foot-high wrought-iron gates set in a gleaming white wall.

And then, within two months of the liver cancer being diagnosed, Matthew had died, leaving her alone and utterly devastated.

Friends had rallied round and her job had helped, but it had been a full twelve months before she had felt she was beginning to enjoy life once again. And she hadn't dated since, in spite of several offers; shallow affairs weren't her style, and whether she had just been unlucky or men as a whole assumed a young widow was fair game she didn't know, but certainly the ones of her acquaintance seemed to assume a dinner and a bottle of wine meant a bed partner. And the married ones were the worst of the lot. It had been quite a disillusioning time, if she thought about it. She frowned to herself, oblivious of her surroundings.

'...Aunty Sophy?'

She came out of her reminiscences to the realisation that Michael's chatter had been directed at her for the last few moments and she hadn't heard a word. 'I'm sorry, darling,' she said quickly. 'I was day-dreaming. What did you say?'

But Michael was talking to his mother now, and it was left to Andreas to say quietly, 'He was merely pointing out the gates opened by themselves, courtesy of Paul's remote control of course.'

Sophy nodded, forcing herself to meet the level gaze without blinking. She noticed his grey eyes had turned almost silvery in the blinding white sunlight, throwing the darkness of his thick black lashes into startling prominence and yet earlier, at the airport, the grey had been nearly black. A human chameleon, she thought drily, and no doubt his nature was as enigmatic as his appearance. Some men liked to project an air of mystery.

More in an effort to show she was not intimidated than anything else, she said politely—the car having passed through the gates and into the spectacular gardens beyond—'It must be wonderful to live in such beautiful surroundings. Have your parents always lived here?'

'For the last thirty-two years,' Andreas said softly. 'I was actually born here twelve months after they first moved in.'

So he was only thirty-one; he seemed older somehow. And then her attention was taken by Jill who touched her arm, her voice awe-struck as she said, 'Look, Sophy, banana trees.'

They were travelling very slowly down a long winding gravel drive, the tyres scrunching on the tiny pebbles, and either side of the car was a cascade of vibrant colour. Masses of exotic, brilliantly coloured flowers and small shrubs were set strategically among silver spindrift olive trees, and the feathered leaves of jacarandas and the broad polished leaves of banana trees were also etched against the blue sky. The effect was riveting.

And then the car turned a corner and a long and very beautiful house was in front of them, its white walls and deep red roof perfectly complemented by the riot of colour at its many balconies, the same lacy ironwork reflected in the veranda which ran the full length of the house and which again had bougainvillaea, anemones, lobelia and a host of other trailing flowers winding over it.

'Oh, *wow*!' Michael, with the innocent ingenuousness of a child, verbalised what both women were thinking as he turned to his uncle, his brown eyes wide, and said, 'Are my grandparents *very* rich, Uncle Andreas?'

'Michael!' Jill turned as red as the scarlet roof. 'You mustn't ask things like that, darling,' she said reprovingly.

'Why?' Michael stared at his mother in surprise.

'Because it isn't polite.'

Polite or not, it was a pretty valid point, Sophy thought bemusedly. She could see tennis courts to the left of the house and Andreas had already mentioned the swimming pool; these people were *loaded*. She had always thought Theodore was nicely set up—what with his restaurant business and the lovely house he and Jill had lived in—but this, this was something else. Why hadn't Theodore ever said he came from such a wealthy family?

Jill must have had the same thought because her voice was small when she turned to Andreas and said, 'Theodore never talked about his family, Andreas, as I suppose you've guessed. You'll have to excuse our surprise.'

There was a moment's hesitation on Andreas's part, and then he surprised both women as he leant forward slightly, saying quickly under his breath, 'I understand this, Jill, but I would implore you not to reveal it to my mother. My father and I would expect nothing else, but she…she is desolate and it would serve no useful purpose to know he has not mentioned her to his wife and child. You understand?' he added urgently.

'Yes, yes of course.' Jill stared at Andreas as he settled back into his seat and then glanced once at Sophy.

Understand? She didn't understand anything about this family, Sophy thought militantly, but she was *so* glad she had come here with Jill. If the parents were anything like their offspring, they might soon be on the next plane home rather than enjoying a couple of weeks in the sun! Overwhelming wasn't the word for it.

However, she had no time to reflect further as the car had drawn to a halt at the bottom of the wide, semi-circular stone steps leading up to the house, and Andreas had already exited, turning to extend his hand as he helped both women out on to the immaculate drive.

The heat struck again with renewed vigour after the cool air-conditioning inside the limousine, but it wasn't that which caused the colour to flare in Sophy's cheeks. For a brief moment as she had slid out of the car and risen to stand beside her sister, she had been just a little too close to Andreas. Close enough to sense the muscled power in the big frame next to her and smell the faint, intoxicatingly delicious scent of his aftershave, and she couldn't believe how her body had reacted.

Fortunately the front door to the house was already opening and all attention was diverted to the couple standing framed in the aperture. 'There are your grandparents, Michael,' Andreas said very softly as he touched his small nephew on the shoulder. 'Would you like to take your mother and say hello?'

'Sophy?' Jill had turned to her, her hand reaching out, and Sophy said quickly, 'Take Michael and introduce him, Jill. I'm right here, don't worry.' She smiled encouragingly, her eyes warm, and after a split-second of hesitation Jill turned and did as Sophy had suggested leaving Sophy and Andreas standing together at the bottom of the steps.

That the women's swift exchange had not gone unnoticed by Andreas became clear in the next moment when, Jill and Michael now out of earshot, he said softly out of the corner of his mouth and without glancing down at her, 'So, it is true what I have read. I have always wondered if the text books are right.'

'I'm sorry?' Her voice was as quiet as his and Sophy didn't take her eyes off her sister and nephew either. Immediately Jill and Michael had reached the couple standing at the door to the house they had been enfolded in Theodore's parents's arms; Michael's grandfather lifting him up and hugging him to his chest, and Jill's mother-in-law embracing the younger woman with an embrace which looked to be welcoming. Sophy relaxed slightly.

'Dominant twin and submissive twin?' Andreas drawled coolly.

It was less an observation and more an implied criticism, and directed specifically at her. Sophy recognised it at once and, true to her nature, rose instantly to the challenge. 'It is both dangerous and naive to believe everything you read, Mr Karydis,' she said icily, her eyes leaving the party framed in the doorway and sweeping with cold dislike over the dark profile next to her. 'I would have thought you knew that?'

'So it is not true, then?' he returned evenly, the phantom of a smile playing round the hard mouth suggesting he found her attitude amusing rather than anything else.

She opened her mouth to fire back another put-down but Jill was already turning back down the steps, calling her name as she urged her sister to come and meet Theodore's parents. All Sophy could do was to stitch a bright smile on her face and keep it there during all the enthusing of how *very* alike they were, and how *amazing* it must be to have a mirror image, and so on and so on. But there was no edge to Theodore's parents's greeting—unlike their younger son's—and Sophy found herself relaxing still more. After a little while the five adults and Michael entered the huge, marble-floored hall behind them which was vast by any standards.

Evangelos, Theodore's father, was an older version of Andreas, but try as she might Sophy could see nothing of

Jill's husband in the tall, handsome man in front of her. And Dimitra, Theodore's mother, was not at all what she had expected. The doe-eyed and still quite exquisitely beautiful woman was clearly overjoyed to see her grandson and daughter-in-law and couldn't take her eyes off Michael. 'He is so like my Theodore at that age,' she said brokenly more than once, clutching hold of her husband's arm as though for support. 'You remember, Evangelos? You remember his curls and what a pretty child he was?'

Sophy saw Andreas and his father exchange a glance over the top of Dimitra's light-brown hair which was liberally streaked with strands of silver, and it was Andreas who gently walked his mother through to the beautiful drawing room off the hall, the others following with Evangelos.

'I am sorry.' Dimitra's glance included Sophy as well as Jill once they were all seated and she had composed herself. 'I just wasn't expecting Michael to be so like his father. It…it is wonderful, of course, but…'

As the older woman's voice trailed away and an awkward silence ensued, Sophy said quietly, 'Just at the moment a mixed blessing? But that will pass and it's perfectly understandable in the circumstances. Jill was only saying on the plane coming over that, having had Michael, she could understand a little of what you must be feeling.'

Jill flashed her sister a grateful glance and took her cue, moving off the sofa on which she and Sophy and Michael were seated and kneeling down in front of Dimitra before taking her mother-in-law's hands and saying softly, 'I would like us to be friends and for you all to get to know Michael, Dimitra. I know it won't take away the pain of your loss, but perhaps in time you could feel a little part of Theodore is still with you in the form of your grandson?'

'Oh, my dear…' Now the tears were pouring down

Dimitra's face as she held out her arms to Jill and Jill, still kneeling, hugged her mother-in-law.

Andreas cleared his throat before saying to a now silent and subdued Michael, 'How about if I show you the pool? You would like this? And also your grandfather has something in the garages that might take your fancy. Have you ever sat in a Lamborghini, Michael?'

'A Lamborghini? A real one?' Michael was over the moon.

'And there is a Mercedes too in your favourite colour,' Andreas told the small boy in a stage whisper, 'but don't tell your grandfather I've told you. Perhaps you and your aunt would like to come and see now and we can have a cold drink by the pool, yes?' The question was spoken in a tone which made it rhetorical.

Sophy stiffened slightly. It was one thing to remove Michael from the overwhelming emotions throbbing about the room, but from the way Jill turned and looked at her as Andreas spoke she knew her sister wasn't at all sure about being left alone with Theodore's parents, even if things did seem to be going well. And Jill was still the only person she was concerned about.

She squared her shoulders. 'I don't think—'

And then, to Sophy's surprise and anger, she found herself lifted up from the sofa by a determined, strong hand at her elbow. 'Come along, Sophy.' Andreas was smiling and his voice was soft and pleasant, but the granite-hard eyes were another matter. 'Ainka is going to serve refreshments in a few moments, so it is better I tell her now we will have ours by the pool in the sunshine. It is lovely there this time of the day.'

She glared her protest at his cavalier treatment. 'Now look—'

And then she found herself literally whisked across the room and out of the door, Michael padding along behind them, and it wasn't until Andreas had shut the drawing room door and had pointed down the wide expanse to his nephew saying, 'That door down there, Michael. That is the way,' that she came to her senses. And she found she was mad. Spitting mad.

'Let go of me, this instant!'

It was a soft hiss—Sophy was well aware of Michael's ever-flapping ears—but none the less vehement for its quietness, and Andreas immediately complied, his voice as low as hers as he said, as they both watched the small boy dance off down the hall, 'Your sister and my parents need time to themselves, Sophy. Surely you see that? This is an important time for them all.'

'What I *see* is me being man-handled and Jill left alone at a difficult time,' she snapped hotly. 'That's what I see! And who do you think you are, anyway, telling everyone what to do?'

'My parents's son,' he bit out with soft emphasis.

'And I'm Jill's sister,' she snarled with equal ferocity.

'What on earth do you think they are going to do to her in there?' Andreas asked testily, lifting a hand to Michael who had now reached the end of the hall and was waiting for them.

'I've no idea, have I?' Sophy returned cuttingly. 'Jill and I don't know you or your family from Adam! All we do know is that, for some reason, you all fell out with Theodore years ago and there's been no meeting point until now.'

'You cannot lay that at my parents's feet. My mother was inconsolable when he left Greece and would have done anything to bring about a reconciliation.' He glared at her, only moderating his expression when Michael called to them impatiently. 'And there was no "falling out" in the way you have suggested. My brother left Greece because *he* wanted to and in the same way it was Theodore who cut his family out of his life.'

'He had a family, Jill and Michael,' Sophy snapped back quickly. 'And, from what I can gather, the fact that he married my sister was the final nail in his coffin. Well, let me tell you that he was lucky to get her! Darn lucky, in my opinion. Jill is worth ten of any high society girl he might have had paraded in front of him by your parents.'

'Now, look here—'

'I don't have to look anywhere, Mr Karydis. Jill might be inclined to give you all the benefit of the doubt, but I tell you here and now that my sister and Michael are my only concern. I don't have to like you, any of you, and I intend to make sure that Jill's good nature is not taken advantage of. Now, you promised Michael a look at the pool and the cars, so I think we should get on with it.' She glowered at him, her eyes shooting blue flames, before she turned to face Michael fully and arranged her features into a more harmonious whole.

As she went to walk away, she felt his hand catch her wrist again and she shot round to face him, grinding out through clenched teeth, 'You touch me once more, just once, and so help me I'll forget Michael is standing there watching us and give you the sort of come-uppance you should have had years ago.'

The stunned outrage on his face almost made her smile— almost—but she was too angry to fully appreciate that it was probably the first time Andreas Karydis had ever been well and truly castigated. And by a mere slip of an English girl at that.

As his hand dropped from her arm she swung round and made her way to Michael—who was hopping about with fretful eagerness—sensing Andreas was just behind her, and then they were all entering a long corridor leading off the hall. The kitchens were on one side and—according to

Andreas's terse voice—the resident housekeeper and the maid's private quarters on the other.

Andreas stopped to poke his head round the kitchen door and ask that their refreshments be served in the pool area, and then they continued to the end of the corridor and passed out of that door into the grounds of the estate and into hot bright sunshine.

Sophy let Andreas and Michael walk in front of her once they were outside for two reasons. One, she wanted to let Andreas establish a nice easy rapport with Michael for the little boy's sake and for the atmosphere to lighten generally, and two, she found she needed to dissect all that had been said and determine if she had been hasty at all. The truth of the matter was that she was feeling slightly guilty about some of what she'd said, and the more she went over their conversation in her mind the more she acknowledged she had gone too far.

She bit her lip as she glanced at the tall powerful man and small boy in front of her, the blistering afternoon sun beating down on one jet-black head and a smaller golden-brown one. Oh, darn it—what a way to set the ball rolling!

She had only been in Greece two minutes and she'd already dug a big deep hole for herself as far as Andreas Karydis was concerned! Not that it bothered her personally, if she was being truthful—he was a hateful, arrogant pig of a man and she thoroughly loathed him—but she was here as Jill's sister and Michael's aunt, and Andreas was Jill's brother-in-law and Michael's uncle. Unfortunately, the family connection was close.

They had almost reached the Olympic-sized swimming pool which glittered a clear blue invitation in the sultry heat but, although the magnificent surroundings and acres of landscaped grounds were breathtaking, their beauty was curtailed by her thoughts. Which had become clearer in the fresh air.

It was a less than auspicious start to their two weeks in Greece! Sophy groaned inwardly. But maybe Andreas wouldn't be around much anyway? They'd established earlier in the car that he had his own property some miles away, so apart from an odd call or two to be polite he probably wouldn't waste his time calling on his brother's widow and her sister.

But then there was Michael. And the two of them seemed to be getting on very well. Which was good—great, in fact. Of course it was. Or it would have been, if Michael's uncle had been anyone rather than Andreas! Oh, she didn't know what to think any more and she had a headache coming on. And it was all Andreas's fault.

'Why don't you sit down in the shade?' Andreas suggested as they reached the pool area and he turned round to look at her, his voice expressionless as he pointed to the far corner of the tiled surround where the dark shade produced by an overhanging and thickly blossomed tree was broken into patches by dappled sunlight. 'The sun can be fierce to the uninitiated.'

'Thank you.' It was stiff but the best she could do. The whole area was scattered with plump sun loungers and several tables and chairs, and she could see a vast brick-built barbecue in one corner and a pretty wooden sunhouse in another. Sophy glanced about her and then forced herself to say, 'This is very pleasant, idyllic in fact.'

He nodded, leading the way to a table and four chairs, and they had no sooner seated themselves than Christina, the plump little housekeeper, appeared, pushing a trolley containing an iced jug of lemonade and three glasses, along with a plate of sweet pastries and another of small rich cakes. A large bowl of fruit and several smaller bowls of different kinds of nuts and dried fruits was also placed before them, Christina smiling and nodding at them all before she ruffled Michael's curls and waddled back off to the house. It was some snack, Sophy commented silently.

'I like her.' Michael was blissfully unaware of the tense atmosphere as he helped himself to a nut-filled and honey-flavoured pastry. 'I like *everything* here.' He took a big bite of the sugared pastry before adding, 'Don't you, Aunty Sophy?'

Sophy sipped her lemonade and her voice was carefully neutral when she said, 'Yes, it's lovely, Michael.'

Andreas was looking at her, one eyebrow raised provocatively and she couldn't believe anyone could say so much without uttering a word. 'This is good,' he said gravely, 'as you have two whole weeks to enjoy everything.'

If there was one thing she loathed it was sarcasm, Sophy thought militantly, glaring again before she could stop herself.

As soon as Michael had finished his pastry he made his way to the pool edge, sitting down and removing his socks and shoes and dangling his feet in the water as he hummed a little tune to himself, completely happy for the moment as only children can be.

Sophy had had to restrain herself from stopping the child's move, but Michael's departure had somehow heightened the tense atmosphere to breaking point. She was almost relieved when Andreas said quietly, 'He seems remarkably well adjusted already to the loss of his father,' as he turned to look at her.

Sophy made the mistake of meeting the dark eyes trained on her face, and the way they all but pinned her to the spot brought a thudding in her chest which made her hand tremble slightly. 'They…they weren't close,' she said stiffly, wrenching her gaze away with some effort. 'Theodore spent most of his time working.'

In actual fact she had always felt Theodore was a severe father and that Michael feared rather than loved him, but she wasn't about to tell Andreas that. Besides, she could be wrong. She had only seen the two of them together a few times.

'You didn't like my brother.' It was a cool observation.

Surprised into looking at him again, she saw the intense eyes were narrowed and thoughtful but not hostile. Nevertheless she wasn't about to trust him an inch, and she stared at him for a moment before responding, 'What makes you say that?'

'Am I wrong?' he asked smoothly.

'He was Jill's husband and she loved him.'

'That's no answer,' he said softly.

'It is to me.' She raised her chin, her soft mouth tightening as he continued to study her with what Sophy considered to be intrusive intensity. 'The only answer you're getting.'

'You're very defensive about your sister's marriage,' he said at last, his body inclining slightly towards her as he spoke.

Was she? She didn't think she was, but certainly there was something about Andreas which made her uptight and on edge. 'No, I'm not,' she said sharply, moving her body irritably. 'But I happen to think their relationship was their own business.'

'I agree absolutely,' he said with silky composure, 'but if I remember rightly it was *your* attitude towards Theodore I was remarking on.' He smiled what Sophy considered a supercilious smile.

'And as you've only met me today and haven't seen your long-lost brother for years, I would suggest any remarks of that nature are extremely presumptuous,' she shot back quickly. Game, set and match.

He settled back in his seat, shifting his large frame more comfortably, and her senses registered the movement with acute sensitivity even as she steeled herself not to reveal a thing to the lethal grey eyes. He was very foreign, very alien somehow—far more than Theodore had been—but she didn't think it was altogether his Greek blood that made her feel that way. It was the intimidating nature of his masculinity, his bigness, the muscled strength which padded his shoulders and chest and the severe quality to his good looks. There was no softness anywhere, and in spite of herself she recognised such overwhelming maleness fascinated even as it threatened.

He looked cynical and hard and ruthless, but sexy too, very sexy. She bet he would be dynamite in bed.

The thought was such a shock that it literally brought her upright in her seat. She couldn't believe she'd thought it about him.

'What is it?' The grey gaze hadn't missed a thing.

'Nothing.' She forced her voice to sound cool and remote. 'But I would prefer to get back to the house now, if you don't mind.' She eyed him firmly, sensing what his answer would be.

'I do.' His voice was very smooth. 'There are still the cars to see, if you remember?'

'It's Michael who's interested in cars, not me,' Sophy said sharply, 'as you very well know. I don't want to see them.'

He stared at her with an enigmatic smile which didn't reach the cold intent eyes. 'That is a pity,' he drawled easily, 'because you are going to see them.'

'I see.' She was glaring again, she thought angrily, but she just couldn't match his irritating composure. 'Hospitality and putting a guest at ease aren't your strong points, are they, Mr Karydis?' Each word was coated in sheer ice.

He stiffened at her words and then laughed quietly, his face hard. 'Would you be offended if I said it depended on the guest?' he said with insulting politeness. 'Or that women like you make me think my countrymen were right to wait until 1952 before they gave the female sex the right to vote?'

'Oh, how very chauvinistic of you, Mr Karydis,' she said cuttingly. 'I gather you are one of those rather pathetic males who feel threatened by any woman who has a mind of her own and isn't afraid to use it? What's your view of the female sex? But no, let me guess. Our destiny is to be kept pregnant and barefoot, is that it? We're all supposed to fall into your strong male arms and beg you to make love to us?'

'If that is a subtle invitation, Sophy, you should wait to be asked,' he said reprovingly.

She knew it was a calculated jibe to get under her skin but in spite of that she couldn't disguise the furious anger his cool baiting had produced. It turned her cheeks scarlet and her eyes fiery as she spluttered, 'You, you—'

'Male chauvinist pig normally fits the description but you have already used that one,' he said calmly. 'However, being such a woman of the world I am sure you can find a more original definition if you try.'

He was laughing at her! It was there in the barely concealed curve of his lips and the glitter of amusement in the dark eyes, and Sophy would have given the world to be able to slap the smirk off his handsome face. But there was Michael just a few yards away, and it wouldn't do the little boy any good at all if his aunt suddenly attacked his new uncle, Sophy cautioned herself desperately. Although it would certainly relieve her stress levels.

And as though he had read her mind, Andreas added softly, 'Now, please, Sophy Fearn, do not force me to carry you kicking and screaming to the garages. It might upset the family.'

'And of course the family is everything,' she snapped hotly.

'Just so.' The grey eyes narrowed ominously. 'I care very

much for my parents and I am sure you care about your sister, so let us at least put on a facade of being civil, yes? It is only for two weeks, after all.'

Sophy drew on every little bit of will power she possessed and took a deep hidden breath. She had never met anyone she had disliked more—or so instantly. He was a brute, an arrogant brute, and she loathed and detested him, but this visit was not about her or her feelings. She had come to Greece to look after Jill and Michael and make things as easy as she could for them, and a feud with Theodore's brother simply wasn't an option in the circumstances.

She raised her chin a little higher, forced her voice into neutral and said flatly, 'I can manage two weeks if you can.'

'Excellent.' He rose to his feet and held out his hand to her. 'So, we will take Michael to see the cars and then return to the bosom of the family, yes? Smiling and calm.'

Sophy gritted her teeth as she ignored his hand and stood up. Thank goodness, thank *goodness* Andreas didn't live with his parents. With all the best intentions in the world, she didn't think she could have stood two weeks of seeing this man every day.

She looked at him as he walked across to Michael after a mocking smile, her senses noting the comfortable, almost animal-like prowl with which he moved. She felt shaky inside and that made her angry with herself. He had wound her up to screaming point and it was the first time she had allowed anyone to do that.

Unbidden, her mother's wedding photograph suddenly flashed onto the screen of her mind. She had found it one day when she was about eleven or twelve, hidden in the attic where she and Jill had been rummaging about when their mother had been at work. Their mother had spent nearly every waking hour working in an endeavour to keep a roof over their heads and food on the table, and although they had never wanted for anything on a material level the two girls had virtually brought themselves up.

From the time they had first asked questions about their father their mother had refused to discuss the man who had let her down so badly, but her bitter silence had spoken for itself. The twins had never dared to press the matter and they had assumed their mother had destroyed any photographs that might have been taken, so when they had discovered the picture of the handsome smiling man and his radiant happy bride they had pored over it for hours.

Their mother's fragile fairness had seemed even more delicate beside the tall dark man at her side, and she had been looking up at her handsome husband so adoringly, so reverently, it was clear to anyone how much she had loved him.

Their father had not been looking at his new wife but straight into the camera, his stance confident and self-assured and his handsome face wearing an expression of cool self-satisfaction which had bordered on the arrogant.

It had somehow fitted exactly the bare facts they knew—that their father had run off with a local beauty queen just a couple of months after they had been born, and had never bothered with them from that day on or even spoken to his wife again.

Jill had seemed to take the photograph in her stride but somehow, and Sophy couldn't have explained why, it had eaten into her soul like a canker. Their father had been aggressively handsome, very masculine and dark with a magnetism which had leapt off the paper. And she had hated him. Hated his swaggering bumptiousness, his insolent good looks and the dark charisma that had trapped her mother into a life of lonely, back-breaking hard work and embittered memories. He had ruined her life and he hadn't given a damn.

'Aunt Sophy? Come *on*.'

Michael's impatient, childish treble brought Sophy out of the dark void and into the bright June sunlight again, but for a moment she stared almost vacantly at the small boy standing in front of her. And then she forced herself out of the blackness.

'Uncle Andreas is going to take us to see the *Lamborghini*.' Michael clearly couldn't understand how anyone could fail to recognise the importance of this momentous event, and as Sophy looked down into the little eager face she found herself smiling and her voice was soft when she said, 'Lead on.'

As before, Sophy hung back and let the other two walk a few paces in front of her, and as she followed the large figure of Andreas and the small dancing boy at his side through an arched trellis wound with richly scented white roses, she found herself looking across a velvety smooth lawn which stretched beyond the pool area and curved back round the house in the distance.

The air was rich with the heavy, warm perfume of the scented bushes and landscaped flowerbeds surrounding the green area, and she noticed several flowered arbours complete with low wooden benches as they passed. It was like a stately home in England!

The Karydis family must have an army of gardeners to keep the grounds in such perfect condition, she thought idly as she walked on. Everything was immaculate.

Pristine tennis courts stretched behind the row of pretty red-roofed garages at the rear of the house, and Sophy stood looking into the distance as Michael oohed and ahhed behind her, climbing quickly into the Lamborghini and sitting agog as Andreas went through the controls with his small nephew.

Jill had unwittingly married into fabulous wealth, that much was for sure, but what on earth had made Theodore cut himself off from his family the way he had? Although Andreas seemed to have his brother's cold, authoritative nature, Evangelos Karydis had appeared quite warm and friendly and Dimitra even more so. Still, it was none of her business, not really, Sophy told herself silently. Only in as much as it affected Jill, that was. But one thing was for sure…

She turned and glanced back at the occupants of the Lamborghini, her face flushing in spite of herself as Andreas's eyes met hers for an instant, a disturbing gleam at the back of the grey. She was going to make very sure Jill made no commitment to this family, either in terms of herself or Michael.

She didn't trust these people, she didn't trust them at all, and the big dark man so deftly charming his small nephew at the moment she trusted least of all.

CHAPTER THREE

JILL was chatting quite happily when they re-entered the drawing room a little while later, and although Sophy was pleased to see her sister apparently relaxed and at her ease she felt a moment's disquiet too. Jill had always been the one to take everyone at face value and blithely assume people were as nice and straightforward as they appeared to be, and Sophy had picked up the pieces of her sister's trusting heart more than once when things had gone wrong when they were young girls. But this wasn't a case of schoolfriends being two-faced or a boyfriend letting her sister down. This was the Karydis family—Jill's in-laws and Michael's grandparents—and that was something very different. And it could be very dangerous.

Michael ran to his mother immediately, full of the swimming pool and the cars, and as Sophy stood in the doorway for a moment Andreas turned and looked straight at her. His voice was low as he murmured, 'Smile, Sophy. My parents will think you do not like them if you look at them like that, and that would never do,' but in spite of the silky sarcasm coating the words the threat underlying them was very plain.

She started slightly before she could control the action and then responded immediately to the challenge, her eyes fiery and her gaze fearless as she said, 'No one tells me what to do, Mr Karydis. Least of all you,' her voice as quiet as his but with a quality that made his mouth tighten. 'Remember that, will you?'

She had annoyed him. Good. Sophy brushed past him and walked across to the others, the satisfaction she felt at

43

puncturing his massive male ego just the slightest putting
a smile on her face as she said politely, 'You have a beautiful home, and the grounds are quite magnificent,' as she
glanced at Dimitra and Evangelos.

'Thank you, my dear.' Dimitra smiled back at her. 'And
I understand you have been a tower of strength to Jill
since—' She faltered and then swallowed quickly, continuing almost immediately, 'Since Theodore died.'

Sophy opened her mouth to make some polite social reply, but then as she looked into Theodore's mother's eyes
she saw what Jill had seen. Pain, anguish, an almost tangible desperation that her son's wife and sister-in-law
would like her, and it swept away anything but the desire
to comfort the grieving woman in front of her. She sat
down and then leant towards Dimitra.

'I've helped a little,' Sophy said gently, 'but I know how
important it was to Jill to come here and meet you, and for
Michael to get to know his grandparents.'

Dimitra's gaze moved to Michael as she murmured, 'So
much lost time. So many wasted years and heartache.'

'But now Jill and Michael are here and this is a new
beginning,' Andreas's voice said just behind Sophy, the
warmth of his breath touching the slender column of her
neck and making her shiver inside. 'Yes? And you will
have many happy sunny days gossiping and putting the
world to rights, no doubt.'

His voice had been tender, indulgent, and as different to
the way he had spoken to her as it was possible to be,
Sophy thought. But she didn't understand any of this. According to Theodore, the break from his family had become
set in concrete when he had married an English girl, and
yet here was his family welcoming Jill with open arms.
Something didn't add up.

She continued to worry at the thought like a dog with a
bone once the little maid, Ainka, had shown her to her truly

sumptuous room next to Michael's, Jill's being on the other side of her son's. It had been suggested the two women rested before they freshened up and changed for dinner at eight. Andreas had offered to take Michael to the pool for a swim—an invitation his nephew had accepted with alacrity—before the child had his own tea and was put to bed by his mother, and now the house was quite silent.

Sophy lay down on the massive double bed the room boasted but after five minutes or so gave up all thought of a nap, and walked across to the wide glass doors leading on to her balcony.

The luxurious bedroom and marbled en-suite were decorated in cool pinks and pastel blues and lilacs, reminiscent of a bunch of sweet-peas, and the efficient air conditioning had made the temperature comfortable, but as Sophy drew back the gossamer-thin voile curtains and opened the doors the heat struck with renewed force, reminding her she was in a foreign country.

The balcony was furnished with a small table and two chairs, and was a riot of colour with masses of white and purple hibiscus and bougainvillaea winding over the wrought iron, and tubs of scarlet geraniums set on the biscuit-coloured tiled floor. The scent was heady and the tiles were so hot they burnt her feet before she flopped down on to one of the chairs with a little sigh of pleasure. This was more like it!

She was wearing a thin, sleeveless summer dress which she now hoisted up to her thighs as she stretched her long legs out to the rays of the sun, letting her head relax back over the edge of the chair as she shut her eyes and let the warmth toast every bit of her. Gorgeous. Gorgeous, gorgeous, gorgeous. It would do Jill the world of good to relax and soak up some sun for a couple of weeks, and it was clear Michael intended to make the most of his unexpected holiday. Perhaps things would work out?

And for herself? She continued to slump motionless in the chair as her thoughts moved on. She'd been in dire need of a break for months, if she was being honest. Although she and Matthew had decided a family wasn't for them for years, and that they would both put all their energies into their careers and then each other—in that order—it had been different after he had died. She had driven herself at a frantic pace then, and it had somehow become a habit. The rewards had been great, of course, and her job was certainly one in a million and she counted herself incredibly fortunate to be in such a position, but...nevertheless she was worn out. Exhausted. She hadn't realised just how much until this moment. She felt she could sleep for a week.

She must have fallen into a light doze because when she heard voices below the balcony it was as though she was emerging from thick layers of cotton wool. She opened her heavy lids slowly and moved just as cautiously as she silently straightened in the chair, wincing slightly as her neck muscles gave protest at the awkward position she'd adopted as she slept.

'Can we come to the pool again tomorrow, Uncle Andreas? Please? Can we?' Michael's voice, high with excitement, caused Sophy to peer through the screen of green leaves and flowers which hid her from sight as effectively as a small wall.

Michael was below, his curls wet and dripping and his small body gleaming like a baby eel's, but it wasn't her nephew who caused Sophy to become transfixed as her heart almost stopped beating and then raced in a most peculiar way.

Andreas was walking at the side of his small charge and he had clearly been more than a watchful bystander, as his brief—very brief—black trunks and the towel slung casually over one broad male shoulder indicated. His thickly muscled torso was tanned, and the black hair on his chest glistened with droplets of moisture before narrowing to a thin line bisecting his flat belly as it disappeared into the swimming trunks.

There wasn't a shred of fat anywhere on the hard, lean frame, nor on the powerful thighs or sinewy arms and legs. He was a magnificent male animal in the prime of life, and the easy way he was moving and the total lack of concern at the fact that he was as near naked as he could be showed how comfortable he was with his body.

Sophy was not comfortable. Anything but, in fact. She knew she was ogling him—there was really no other word for this shameful, clandestine spying—but once she had seen him she found she just couldn't draw her eyes away.

Growing up in an all-female household had caused her to be a little shy with the male sex in her youth, and Matthew's fair, almost hairless body had not prepared her for what she was seeing now. Nothing had prepared her for what she was seeing now! It was one thing to have the odd fantasy about idols of the silver screen, or indulge in a little imagining of how this icon or that would appear unclothed and in the flesh, but quite another to have that flesh—acres and acres of it, or so it seemed to her fevered gaze—hitting her between the eyes. Because that was what it felt like. And she couldn't ignore it.

She had been holding her breath in stunned fascination and then, as Andreas and Michael walked past on the ground below and disappeared into the house, she let it out in a long, low whoosh and sank back in the chair again, her heart pounding.

She held her hands up to her cheeks and discovered they were burning, which was ridiculous—*really* ridiculous— she told herself irritably. She wasn't some nervous little schoolgirl or a weak, trembling sort of female, for goodness' sake.

Her career brought her into close contact with strong, determined and often ruthless individuals of both sexes, and she was used to dealing with any eventuality on a day to day basis. And she had been *married*; the male form held no mystery for her. At least she'd thought it didn't.

She bit her lip as she gazed over the balcony into the blue sky above, the sun now pleasant rather than hot as evening began to temper its heat. She wasn't going to think about this any more, she told herself firmly. She was going to go back into the bedroom and take a shower, and once she had washed her hair and sluiced away the strain of the journey—and Andreas Karydis—she would use lashings of the new, expensive body lotion she'd treated herself to just before leaving England.

She had well over an hour to pamper and titivate herself and she needed every minute because—and here her eyes became midnight blue—she intended to look like a million dollars tonight. She needed to show Theodore's brother that she was a cool, composed and sophisticated woman of the world and that all his nasty taunts and obvious dislike of her didn't mean a thing. She couldn't care less, in fact. He could be a cardboard cutout for all the effect he had on her!

She continued to tell herself the same sort of thing all the time she got ready for dinner, and by the time she popped in to Michael's room to say goodnight to the little boy the power of positive thinking had done its work. She felt like she could take on a hundred Andreases, especially when Jill's eyes widened and she breathed a 'Wow!' at the sight of her sister.

Michael was almost asleep and, after kissing him goodnight, both women tiptoed from the room. Once on the landing, Jill looked at her twin admiringly. 'You look absolutely sensational, Sophy. Is that one of the dresses from that collection in Paris you told me about?' she asked approvingly.

'Uh-huh.' Sophy grinned at her sister as she gave a little twirl, the coral gown of Fortuny-style pleats accentuated by Swarovski crystal hugging her slender figure. 'One of the perks of the job, although it still cost me an absolute fortune. I allow myself one extravagant purchase once in a blue moon, but this was the most expensive yet.' She rolled her eyes expressively.

Jill was still in her towelling robe, and now Sophy said, 'What are you going to wear tonight?'

'I'm not sure.' Unlike Sophy, Jill had never been the slightest bit interested in clothes, and it was fair to say that anything of any worth Jill possessed had been given her by her twin. 'Come and help me decide?' she entreated quickly.

Once in Jill's quarters, which were furnished exactly the same as her own but with a colour scheme of warm hyacinth blues and purples and sharp bright white, Sophy gazed at the clothes she herself had packed for her sister, Jill being unable to decide what to bring. Only something special would do.

'This.' Sophy extracted a pale lavender gown, the bodice of which was complemented by geometric paillette detailing in raw silk. 'We're going to knock 'em dead tonight, sis, or die in the attempt. Okay?' she said encouragingly.

'I haven't worn this since you gave me it,' Jill admitted with a feeble attempt at a smile. 'Oh, Sophy, I'm so nervous. Now I've had time to think, this is all out of our league, isn't it? I never dreamt Theodore came from such a background.'

'You got on fine with his parents,' Sophy reassured her firmly, 'and they seem to just be grateful you and Michael are here. Just be yourself, sis, and that will be enough, and take it from me—in these dresses we certainly won't look like the poor relations. The Right Honourable Jill and Sophy, more like!'

'Oh, Sophy.' But Jill was smiling now, and once she was dressed sat chatting quite naturally while Sophy put her sister's hair up in an elegant knot.

Ainka was waiting in the hall when the two women came downstairs, and she led them to the huge ornate dining room where the others were sitting just outside its patio doors enjoying a cocktail in the dying sunlight.

'How charming you both look.' Dimitra's voice was genuinely warm and her husband offered his own compliments, but Sophy was too busy coping with what her first sight of Andreas in evening dress had done to her senses. The scattered ones that remained, that was.

He's magnificent, she told herself silently. Magnificent and threatening and dangerous. The formal clothes brought a ruthless quality to the brilliant dark good looks that made her shiver deep inside, and wish the evening was over rather than just beginning. She'd been right, so right to be wary of this man.

She heard him murmur something flattering to Jill before Dimitra and Evangelos drew her sister to one side, asking if Michael had settled down for sleep, which left her standing rather awkwardly at Andreas's side.

Ainka had handed her a large fluted glass of champagne cocktail before leaving, and now Sophy concentrated on the delicious effervescent drink as Andreas turned his piercingly dark and keen gaze on her, saying softly, 'You are a credit to your profession and quite beautiful.'

'Thank you.' She smiled politely and took a sip from the glass.

The words themselves were innocuous enough but there was an edge to his manner Sophy didn't like, an edge of criticism, although she wasn't going to give him the satisfaction of knowing she'd recognised it. She'd rather die.

'Do I take it you dressed Jill too?' he asked mildly.

'What?' She had turned her gaze away from him but now her eyes flashed to his dark face. She had been right. He was definitely put out about something.

'Your sister,' Andreas said smoothly. 'Clothed by Sophy Fearn? Or am I wrong?'

His accent was slight and his English was perfect, but the faint inflection it lent to the deep husky voice made her stomach muscles curl as she said tightly, 'No, you are not wrong, Mr Karydis. Do I take it you disapprove of what Jill is wearing?'

'Not what she's wearing, no,' he returned softly, 'just the motive behind it. *Your* motive, Sophy. And if you address me as Mr Karydis one more time I shall not be responsible for my actions. The name is Andreas, as you very well know.'

She ignored the latter comment, her chin well up and her voice icy as she said, 'So you credit yourself with mind-reading ability as well as everything else, is that it? Do explain, Mr Kar—' She stopped abruptly as the lethal grey gaze turned to shining ebony. 'Do explain,' she continued after a slight pause, 'my obviously base and wicked motives for giving Jill a super dress she could never afford otherwise—a dress, I might add, which was a birthday present six months ago,' she finished triumphantly.

'I'm not questioning your initial motivation,' he returned silkily. 'I'm sure you only wanted to bless your sister with a delightful gift and give her much pleasure.'

'Oh, thank you so much,' she cut in sarcastically. 'How kind.'

'But you encouraged her to wear the dress tonight because you look on my family as the enemy, an enemy which needs to be guarded against at all times. The dress was your way of pointing out that Jill has done very nicely without us in her life—as is your attire, I might add.' He eyed her imperturbably.

'What a load of nonsense,' Sophy lied vehemently, her voice low enough for the others not to hear but carrying forced outrage.

'Do you really think my parents wish to harm Jill or Theodore's son?' Andreas asked quietly. 'Are you really so poor a judge of human nature? They are generous, warm-hearted people who have never knowingly hurt anyone.'

'Something which I'm sure can't be said of you,' Sophy shot back before she had time to consider her words.

She stared at him, inwardly horrified but outwardly icy calm as she waited for his reaction, and when it came it wasn't the explosion she expected. 'So,' he drawled thoughtfully, his hard mouth twisting slightly, 'it is me you feel you have to armour Jill and yourself against. Yes?'

There was nothing she could say and so she merely glared at him, her violet-blue eyes sparking. Hateful, *hateful* man!

'Have you always been such a fierce protector?' he asked, his voice so soft now she could barely hear it. 'And, if so, why did you let your sister marry my brother? He could not have made her happy and certainly Michael has no idea of what a father is.'

She was too amazed to hide her shock, but it was at that moment Dimitra turned, calling them to join the others to which Sophy responded with a promptness she knew was not lost on Andreas. But she couldn't help it. Jill had been right—they *were* out of their league here and she still wasn't sure what was going on. This family was like a proverbial minefield.

Sophy had downed two champagne cocktails before Ainka called them into dinner, but she felt she needed a little Dutch courage. She knew every time Andreas's dark eyes flashed over her and it was often, often enough for her to feel constantly shaky inside. That in turn made her angry with herself and churned her stomach still more. Which was ridiculous, darn it. He was just Theodore's brother.

Jill, on the other hand, was chatting away to Dimitra as though the two of them had known each other all their lives; Evangelos looking on indulgently and joining in the women's conversation now and again. In fact, everyone seemed at ease and relaxed apart from her, Sophy thought irritably.

But it would be better once Andreas left. She supposed she should have expected Theodore's brother would be around for the first few hours, but having his own home meant he would just call by now and again. Didn't it? She prayed it did, Sophy reiterated as she finished the first course—a delicious soup made with yoghurt and garlic and fresh vegetables—and looked at the dishes Ainka was piling on to the table.

She was sitting next to Dimitra with Jill opposite her and Andreas at the side of Evangelos, who was heading the table, so she had found it easy to avoid the granite-grey eyes. Nevertheless Andreas's dark, brooding presence had the effect of making her all fingers and thumbs, and when she knocked over her wine glass—white wine, fortunately, and not red—she wasn't really surprised. The whole evening was an accident waiting to happen!

'Oh, your beautiful dress.' Dimitra looked aghast at the puddle in Sophy's lap, which Sophy was hastily mopping with her table napkin. 'You must sponge it down with water or it will stain.'

'It's all right, really.' She knew her face was fiery but she was so furious with herself she could scream. So much for the calm, cool, cosmopolitan woman of the world, she thought bitterly as she felt the wine soak through to her panties. Talk about pride going before a fall! What on earth was Andreas thinking?

What he was thinking became evident in the next moment when he rose to his feet, pushing back his chair with the backs of his legs before walking round the table and drawing her up with an authoritative hand at her elbow.

'Come and repair the damage in the downstairs cloak-room,' he said in a tone which left her no choice but to obey when married to his grip on her arm. 'It won't take a moment and it would be a shame to spoil such a delightful dress.'

Was she the only one who could hear the sarcasm in his voice? Sophy asked herself as she submitted to being led from the room with as much grace as she could muster. Apparently so, from the smiles and nods from the others. They clearly thought Andreas was playing the perfect gentleman. The manipulative swine!

She waited until they were in the hall and the dining room door was closed before shaking off his hand with enough venom to make the dark eyebrows rise. 'Thank you, I can manage perfectly well now,' she said stiffly. 'I've dealt with worse than this before.'

'Oh, I have no doubt you can look after yourself, Sophy,' he said from his vantage point of six foot plus, staring down at her delicate fairness with hooded eyes. 'You might look as though a breath of wind would blow you away, but there is a backbone of steel in that fragile frame, is there not?'

'Don't tell me, you disapprove of that too!' she returned frostily. No doubt he was one of those men who preferred his women to be for ever batting their eyelashes and playing dumb. She knew his type all right.

'Did I say that?' he asked in a tone which suggested suppressed amusement. 'Now, be fair, did I?'

Nothing could have got under her skin more than to think he was laughing at her, and her voice sharpened as she said,

'You didn't have to. You can say talk more effectively without saying a word than anyone I've ever met.'

'Another snap decision.' He stood back a pace, folding his muscled arms and staring down at her for a second or two as she glared back at him. 'What a little harridan you're going to be in a few years,' he observed nonchalantly, before taking her arm again and whisking her over to a door to the right of the dining room which he opened with his free hand. 'The cloakroom,' he stated unnecessarily as Sophy surveyed a room large enough to swallow at least half of her little London flat. 'Now, let's see about getting you cleaned up.'

In spite of his comment about the backbone of steel he was making her sound as though she hadn't got a grain of sense, Sophy thought furiously, her anger blinding her to the fact that Andreas had entered the cloakroom with her until it was too late to protest. She stared at him as he casually began to fill one of the bowls—of which there were three—with cold water. 'What are you doing?' she managed at last.

'Cold water is best for white wine.' He raised innocent eyebrows.

'I'm not referring to the wine stain,' she said tightly. As he very well knew. 'I'm perfectly capable of sponging down my own dress.'

'What kind of host would I be to let you struggle alone?' he countered with a charming smile which didn't fool Sophy in the slightest, especially when she looked into those glittering eyes.

'I'd prefer to struggle, actually.'

'Sophy, you are a guest in my parents' home.'

The eyebrows were raised again, she noted irritably, and they made her feel like an errant child who was having a tantrum. 'So?' she snarled tightly. What had that to do with anything?

'So I am not about to…abuse that position,' he murmured gently, the soothing tone positively insulting.

'I didn't think for a moment you were!' It had the added advantage of being absolutely truthful, something Andreas couldn't fail to recognise. 'Of course I didn't.'

He stared at her for a long moment and by the end of it Sophy had to grit her teeth in order not to look away. He had been leaning against the wall whilst they talked, and now he levered himself upright, his eyes taking on a distinctly pewter quality as he ground out, 'You really are the most—' before stopping abruptly, and visibly controlling himself.

'The most what?' she countered swiftly, her defiance strengthened by the fact that she couldn't see he had anything to complain about. She had agreed with him, for goodness' sake! That was a first if nothing else. And she hadn't accused him of trying to take advantage of her— just the opposite, in fact. What was the matter with the man? He disliked her as much as she disliked him, she knew that, so why was he all bristling male ego?

'Forget it.' It was cold and abrupt. 'Just forget it.'

'No, hang on a minute.' As he turned to go, she caught at his sleeve, a tiny part of her amazed at her temerity. 'You obviously have something to say, so say it.'

'It doesn't matter,' he bit out grimly. 'You are Jill's sister and I am Theodore's brother. That is all. We are bound through family ties to get on with each other as well as we can over the next little while. If you would like to deal with the matter of the dress, I will then escort you back to the dining room,' he added with stiff formality. 'I will wait outside.'

She could feel bunched muscles under her fingers and, unbidden, a picture of how he had looked earlier, tanned and dark and uncompromisingly virile, made her breathless and took any tart rejoinder she might have made straight out of her consciousness.

She remained staring at the door to the cloakroom a good ten seconds after Andreas had left, and then roused herself to get to work on the dress. The material was wafer-thin, as was the lining, and after sluicing handfuls of cold water over the stained area she patted it carefully with one of the cloakroom's fluffy towels which dried it almost immediately.

The recovery mission accomplished, Sophy stared at her reflection in the full-length mirror for a few moments. She was too flushed, she decided critically. Too bright-eyed. It was the champagne, of course, that was *definitely* all it was, but she had better dab her hot cheeks with cold water before she went back to the others.

By the time she opened the cloakroom door she was feeling a little more like herself, and when Andreas levered himself off the opposite wall where he had been waiting for her she managed a fairly cool smile as she said, 'I'm sorry to have kept you waiting but there was no need for you to stay.'

'It is no problem.' His gaze was remote, implacable, and it made her want to gabble. Instead she kept her mouth tightly shut as they walked back to the dining room, and it was only when she sat down in her chair and felt taut muscles relax that she realised just how tense she had been.

The meal was wonderful, and as course followed course Sophy realised Christina's cooking was first class. The housekeeper made an appearance at the end of the dessert stage when she bustled into the dining room with the coffee, Ainka following with a tray containing a carafe of ouzo—a spirit distilled from grapes—and another of iced water.

Sophy had been hoping she could escape to her room; the slow leisurely style of the last meal of the day in Greece meant they had been at table for over two hours. And two hours of Andreas Karydis was enough for anyone!

But as Christina poured a cup of the heavy sweet coffee for everyone and Ainka filled the women's glasses with iced water and those of Evangelos and Andreas with ouzo—the women having declined the spirit—she realised she had at least another half an hour or so of social chit chat to get through, just to be polite. And, the thing was, she wouldn't have minded if it was just Theodore's parents and herself and Jill present, but Andreas's dark presence on the perimeter of her vision was keeping her as jumpy as a cat on a hot tin roof. And he knew it too.

At half-past ten, when her nerves were stretched to breaking point, she rose jerkily to her feet. 'I hope you'll excuse me, but I have a slight headache,' she said politely to the room in general, allowing her glance to brush each face briefly before it concentrated on that of Dimitra's. 'I think I'll turn in, if that's all right. Thank you for a lovely dinner and for making me so welcome,' she added with a warmth which was quite sincere. 'It was really very kind of you to include a third party in Jill's invitation, and I do appreciate it.'

Through the ensuing effusive reassurances from Evangelos and Dimitra that *of course* she was very welcome in their home, and that as Jill's dear sister she *must* count herself just as much a part of their family as Jill and Michael, Sophy was very aware of the cool scrutiny of the tall dark man standing watching her across the other side of the table, although she ignored him.

Andreas had risen when she had stood up—he had the social etiquette down to a fine art, if nothing else, Sophy reflected a trifle nastily—but he hadn't added his voice to those of his parents. Not that she had expected him to do so.

He simply stood there, silent and enigmatic, his glittering

gaze trained on her flushed face and his big body relaxed and still, looking at her as though he was a scientist studying some rather repellant bacteria under a microscope.

Sophy smiled again, wished them all goodnight in as bright and carefree a voice as she could manage and left the room quickly, forcing herself to restrain the urge to break into a trot once she was in the hall and making her way towards the stairs.

'Awful man. Awful, awful, *awful* man.' She found she was muttering to herself once she had reached the sanctuary of her room and stopped abruptly, kicking off her high heels as she walked over to the bed and flung herself down on the soft covers with a little sigh of exasperation.

She couldn't let Andreas get to her like this. She had only been in Greece for a matter of hours and here she was all knotted up and at loggerhead with Jill's brother-in-law. And she was supposed to be here to *help* Jill and Michael, to smooth their path as it were—not enter into war with a member of the family.

They had got off on the wrong foot, but hopefully, now he had made the polite overtures of welcome his parents had obviously required of him, his presence at the house would be minimal. And if Dimitra and Evangelos were really as pleasant as they appeared to be, the next two weeks might roll by quite happily.

But it was strange… Sophy's clear, unlined brow wrinkled as she rolled over on to her back and gazed up at the pale blue ceiling which had rather impressive little fat cherubim fashioned in each of its corners. As far as she could recall, apart from those first few minutes when they had arrived at the house, Dimitra and Evangelos had mentioned their eldest son hardly at all. Now that wasn't normal in the circumstances, was it?

She had left the balcony windows open whilst she went down to dinner and now, as the thin, flimsy drapes moved with the warm evening breeze, she heard the sound of voices from somewhere outside. Andreas must be leaving, but as the drive was at the front of the house and her room was situated at the back overlooking the landscaped grounds, beyond which stretched the swimming pool, she could distinguish little of the conversation beyond Evangelos's voice calling something in Greek, probably goodbye.

It was quite dark outside, but once on the balcony Sophy breathed in the rich scented air and looked up at the moon brushed free of clouds. She felt restless tonight, and although she hadn't lied about the headache she didn't feel like going to sleep. She massaged her aching temples slowly.

The night was soft and warm, a night for lovers, for passion. A night for endless caresses and whispered promises, for reaching the heights.

And then she caught hold of her errant thoughts sharply, utterly amazed with herself. What had got into her tonight? she asked herself bewilderedly. She must have had too much wine. Why was she feeling so disturbed and edgy, fretful even? This wasn't like her. She was always perfectly in control of herself.

She heard the sound of a car's engine and the scrunching of tyres on the drive which signalled Andreas's departure, either by taxi or maybe he had called out his driver to pick him up. Whatever, he was leaving and that was the main thing.

But with Andreas's name came the clear picture of how he had looked that afternoon after leaving the pool— tanned, dark, virile, dangerous.

And suddenly Sophy knew why she was feeling the way she did.

CHAPTER FOUR

As WITH every other unpleasant thing which had come her way in her twenty-eight years of life, Sophy faced the fact that she was sexually attracted to a man she thoroughly disliked head-on.

It was galling in the circumstances, and she could just imagine the satisfaction Andreas would feel if he knew—which meant he must never find out. What made the situation all the more unpalatable was that she had never felt this way before and she couldn't understand why it had happened now, so fiercely and without warning. And with Theodore's brother, of all people.

She paced the bedroom, her eyes stormy and her mouth tight with self-deprecation. The truth of the matter was she had never met a man with such lethal magnetism before, she admitted after a good ten minutes of self-analysis, not in a day-to-day setting of close contact anyway. Oh, there had been the odd male on the Tube or at a function or something, whose good looks had had that extra dimension which had made her heart beat faster, but not like this. Not like Andreas Karydis.

But it didn't matter. It didn't, not really. She was panicking because she felt things were out of control—but they weren't, *they weren't*, she reassured herself grimly. Everything was fine. All her life, from when she had been a little girl of three or four and had realised she and Jill hadn't got a daddy like everyone else—and moreover that there was something shameful and secret about the fact, judging from her mother's reaction when they asked questions, she had imposed an almost obsessional self-control on herself.

61

And when she had found out the truth about her father and had seen what loving and trusting a man to distraction could do to a woman, she had consciously vowed she would never let herself be manoeuvred into such a humiliating position. Life—her life—was built on constraint and determination and absolute autonomy, and within those restraints she was happy. She had met and married Matthew, hadn't she? And they had been united in agreeing each of them would follow their own separate career and destiny within their relationship. It had worked. It would still be working if he hadn't died.

She stopped her pacing and walked into the bathroom, turning on the shower before slipping out of her clothes and allowing the cool silky water to bathe her hot skin.

She was just overtired, that was all. Theodore's death, the awful funeral and trying to support Jill and Michael at the same time as giving her job the hours it needed had taken it out of her. She worried about Jill, she couldn't help it.

She had always felt more like Jill's mother than her sister, she reflected ruefully as she lifted her face to the refreshing spray. And although she had always tried to hide her concern about Jill's choice of husband, her initial misgivings had grown with the years rather than decreased.

What had Andreas meant with that crack about Theodore? She frowned as she tried to remember his exact words. Oh, yes, he had said Theodore couldn't have made Jill happy and that Michael had no idea of what a father was. She would ask him what he meant by that, the next time she saw him. He couldn't make remarks like that without explaining himself fully, and there was a sight too much cloak-and-dagger stuff concerning Theodore, in her opinion!

Once back in the bedroom and with sleep a million miles away, Sophy picked up one of the novels she had brought with her from England, climbed into bed and adjusted herself comfortably against the heaped pillows. She would read for a few minutes before settling down to sleep, she decided, and put all thoughts of a certain tall, dark Greek out of her mind.

An hour later she was more wide awake than ever and couldn't remember a line she had read. The book could have been written in double Dutch for all the sense it had made to her whirling mind. She threw it down irritably, annoyed with herself.

She had heard Jill come upstairs just after Andreas had left, and some time after that all the lights had been extinguished downstairs and now there was only shadowed blackness beneath the balcony windows. The whole house was asleep. The whole *world* was asleep, she told herself restlessly, wondering why it was always so much worse to be awake when you knew everyone else was sleeping peacefully.

She settled herself down, resolutely switching off the lamp at the side of the bed. She *was* tired and her body was calling out for rest; it was only her mind that seemed determined to solve all the problems of the universe!

After half an hour of tossing and turning, the light went on again and Sophy swung her legs out of bed, her face frowning. Okay, so she couldn't sleep, but she'd go stark staring mad if she had to remain in this room another minute. She would go for a walk in the gardens. In fact, she could take her swimming costume with her and if there was enough light she could perhaps have a swim in the pool. It was as warm as a summer's day in England.

The decision made, she dressed quickly in light cotton combat trousers and a thin but warm cashmere jumper she'd brought with her, just in case the night was a little chilly after the intense heat of the day. After grabbing a towel and her costume, and slipping on a pair of flat pumps, she opened the door to her room cautiously and peered out on to the landing. Everywhere was silent and dark. She felt a moment's trepidation which she ignored.

She made her way carefully downstairs by the light of the moon shining through the windows, and then paused in the massive hall, suddenly uncertain. What if the place was alarmed and she roused the whole house?

Well, she'd just explain she was hot and bothered and had decided to take a midnight swim, she told herself firmly. And with the huge wall surrounding the property and the fact that Evangelos's estate was miles from the nearest village, there probably wasn't an alarm anyway.

There wasn't. In fact, the door at the end of the corridor leading off the hall wasn't even locked, and Sophy passed quietly through into the cool scented darkness of the night with no trouble at all, breathing a little easier now that hurdle was over.

Once outside, she found the moonlight was lighting up the grounds almost as bright as day and her way was quite clear. She breathed in the perfume of the sleeping vegetation in great gulps as she walked down towards the pool, suddenly finding herself grinning. This was great, quite an adventure, and it had been years since she had acted on impulse.

Her footsteps quickened as she lightly skimmed the lawn and ran down through the arch of roses into the pool area, and after kicking off her pumps she had stripped off the trousers and jumper and donned the swimming costume in seconds. The pool appeared even more enormous in the moonlight, and the far end under the trees was in deep shadow which caused her a moment's disquiet before she told herself not to be so silly. She walked to the shallow end of the pool as the cool breeze drifted over her skin and ruffled the silk of her hair.

She dipped her toe in the water and then squeaked as the cold water hit her nerve-endings. It felt *freezing*!

She was just about to jump in, knowing it would take ages if she tried to do it gradually, when something—a movement, a ripple or maybe just her sixth sense—caused her to pause, her heart beginning to thump madly as she peered into the blackness.

'Is…is anyone there?' She felt slightly ridiculous speaking to thin air, but something wasn't right.

Nothing happened for what seemed like an hour but in reality was no more than a second or two, and then an unmistakable voice said quietly, 'It's me, Sophy. Andreas.'

Andreas? *Andreas?* She heard the swish water made when a body was cutting through it and then after a moment saw a dark shape come out of the shadows and into the tiny glittering waves lit by moonlight. And in the same instant she glanced over at the chair where she'd thrown her clothes and awful realisation hit. She'd thought she was alone and she had been completely naked for a few moments. Had he seen? What was she thinking? *Of course* he had seen. A blind man would have seen!

'You rotten, low, conniving—'

'Hey, hey.' He paused to tread water in the middle of the pool, his face shadowed planes and angles in which only the glitter of his eyes was truly discernible. 'What have I done now?' he asked with every appearance of hurt surprise.

'What—?' Words failed her and she had to take a hard pull of air before she could continue. 'What have you done? You know *exactly* what you have done, so don't come the old soldier with me,' she bit out furiously. 'You let me change into my costume without a word to warn me you were here. You're absolutely disgusting!' she finished scathingly.

'I didn't even see you until it was too late,' he said

mildly. 'You flitted in here like a breath of moonlight and proceeded to whisk off your clothes in two seconds flat. When I realised I was no longer alone, you were already…'

'Naked!' she spat angrily.

'In a word, yes.' He swam closer, hard muscled arms slicing through the dark depths to emerge briefly in the moonlight, silver and gleaming. 'Is it my fault you are one uninhibited lady?' he drawled softly when he was closer.

'I am *not* uninhibited,' Sophy hissed furiously, bitterly resenting the innuendo that she was quite happy to take off all her clothes in front of a virtual stranger.

'So you're inhibited?' he asked in tones of hateful sympathy.

'No, of course I'm not.' She glared at him and then stamped her foot. 'And don't try any of your mind games on me, Andreas Karydis,' she warned furiously. 'I know your little tricks.'

'That's an improvement.'

'What?' She glared at him, resenting the easy tone.

'You actually called me by my first name. Of course, the Karydis came after, but I still count that a step forwards.'

She just didn't believe this man. She stared at him before drawing herself up and saying icily, 'You can count it any way you want, but I still think you're disgusting. To spy on people like that! It's totally beyond the pale.'

'I wasn't spying on you, Sophy,' he said silkily. 'Any more than you were on me earlier.'

'Me?' He couldn't, he *couldn't* know about that?

'On your balcony?' he reminded her gently. 'You happened to be there and I happened to be underneath; I understand that perfectly. And tonight I happened to be in the pool and you…' He let his voice die away and smiled up at her instead.

Sophy had always considered herself a very non-violent person but right at this moment she wanted to commit murder. 'That is utterly different and you know it,' she managed through gritted teeth. 'There was no time for me to make myself known.'

'My point exactly,' he said appeasingly.

His hair was wet and black and he raked it back with one hand as he stood up, the water now reaching to just above his waist. His eyes hadn't left hers but he made no attempt to get out of the water, perhaps sensing she would run if he did.

'I...I'm going back to the house,' she said tightly. 'I didn't come down here to bandy words with you.'

'Of course you didn't,' he agreed smoothly. 'You came here to swim, so swim. No one is stopping you.'

Oh, yes, they were. The swimming costume she had brought with her was a modest one-piece affair in black lined silk. It was perfectly decent but she almost felt as naked as she had been a few minutes earlier with those lethal grey eyes fixed on her.

His maleness was even more flagrant in the dark shadows of the pool and, far from being chilly as she had been a few minutes before, she now felt feverishly hot. She wanted to moisten her dry lips but, knowing he would read the gesture for what it was—nerves—she restrained the impulse, and said instead, 'I came here to be alone, actually.'

'Don't be childish.' He turned in the water as he spoke, taking off for the deep end with a ruthlessly powerful drive. 'There's plenty of room for both of us in here, and I promise I won't talk to you or interfere with your swim in any way. Okay? Does that satisfy you?'

No, it didn't satisfy her at all, but Sophy felt as though she were between the devil and the deep blue sea, or perhaps the devil and the deep blue swimming pool was more correct.

She was still in the same position when Andreas swam back, his voice decidedly mocking now as he said, 'Fright-

ened of the big bad wolf, Sophy? Is that it? Believe it or
not, I have actually seen a woman naked before and the
sight of your body—although undeniably a nice bonus on
a night like this—will not turn me into a sex-crazed monster. You'll be quite safe.'

Impossible man! But the overt derision settled the matter
and when he again turned and swam away Sophy wasted
no time in entering the water. Once the first shock of the
cold had abated she found it was pleasant, and after three
or four lengths of the pool when she steadfastly ignored
the dark figure cutting backwards and forwards in the opposite direction to her she found she was quite warm.

However, after some ten minutes or so in the pool, when
Andreas had said not a word, the silence had become so
loud Sophy felt like screaming to break it. Instead, at the
point where their bodies passed each other, she said a trifle
breathlessly, 'I thought you had gone home. There was a
car earlier?'

'That was my driver, Paul, arriving, not me leaving.'

'He's here too?' For a moment she almost expected the
little gnome like man to pop out from behind a bush.

'There were some papers I wanted my father to look at
tonight before he went to bed, and it was easier for Paul to
bring them and a change of clothes for me so we could go
straight to the office from here in the morning,' Andreas
explained briefly, before swimming in the opposite direction.

His eyes had been black in the shadows and the bulk
and breadth of him somewhat alarming so close to, his teeth
gleaming white and the drops of liquid on his face and hair
catching the moonlight as he had talked. Sophy felt a stirring in the pit of her stomach, a flood of sexual awareness
that was impossible to deny. She continued on her route,
splashing a little more than was necessary as her arms and
legs seemed unable to follow the commands of her brain.

Andreas spoke the next time they passed. 'You couldn't sleep?'

'No. There's been so much happening today and, I suppose, a strange bed and all that...' Her voice tailed off breathlessly.

'I never have a problem sleeping in a strange bed,' Andreas said huskily, the gentle teasing in his deep voice causing her further problems with her coordination.

She just bet he didn't, Sophy thought hotly as they went their separate ways again. A woman in every port, if she knew anything about it. *Several* women in every port, in fact.

'Don't overdo it on your first session.'

'What?' This time she did actually swallow a mouthful of water and spluttered a bit before she could say, 'I was just thinking about getting out, actually.' Away from his disturbing presence.

'So was I,' Andreas said immediately.

'Oh, right.' Brilliant. She had been hoping to exit fairly gracefully and hurry back to the house whilst he was still in the pool. She had noticed this swimming costume, which was quite proper and respectable when dry, seemed to have taken on the effect of a second skin when wet, clinging to every curve and contour with a determination that was positively wanton. And she knew exactly what would happen when her breasts met the cool night air; her nipples were already hardening and stretching the silk still more.

She scrambled out of the pool with more haste than aplomb, conscious of Andreas in the water behind her, but once she had grabbed her towel and wrapped it round her sarong-fashion, she found the nerve to turn and face him. She was surprised to see he was still in the pool with something of a winsome expression on his hard handsome face. 'What's the matter?' she asked cautiously. Why wasn't he getting out?

'A slight problem.' He sounded quite cheerful as though it wasn't really a problem at all. 'I thought I would be alone down here, you see.' He smiled innocently.

'So?' She stared at him, puzzled. What was he saying?

'So…no trunks,' he said with magnificent matter of factness.

'No *trunks*?' She had been swimming with a naked man—and not just any old man, either, but Andreas Karydis! 'What do you mean, no trunks?' And then, as he went to get out of the pool she added hastily, 'No, stay where you are. I know what you mean. I just don't know why! Why you didn't tell me at first, that is.'

'Because you would not have come into the pool and you have enjoyed your swim, yes?' he answered silkily. 'Have you not ever…how do you English say, skinny-dipped?'

'No, I have not,' she answered a trifle indignantly. What did he take her for, anyway? 'It's not exactly encouraged in the local baths in London,' she added caustically.

'But when you have been abroad?' he persisted softly. 'Not then?'

'On a beach with hundreds of other people? I think not,' she said hotly.

'Ah, yes, I see your point,' he agreed thoughtfully. 'Then you must indulge whilst you are here, Sophy. It will be quite safe late at night down here. No one comes.'

'You came tonight,' she reminded him tightly.

'Ah, yes.'

'Where's your towel?' she asked feverishly, glancing round as though it was going to come hopping towards her of its own accord. What a ridiculous situation to be in!

'I didn't bring one.' And, at her slight groan, 'Do not worry, I was wearing a robe. It is somewhere down there.' He pointed to the shadowy tables and chairs at the far end of the pool. 'I can look for it, if you like?'

'I'll get it.' She leant over the pool and handed him her towel as she added, 'Dry yourself off with this while I get the robe and wrap it round yourself.' Please. *Please.*

She didn't stop to see if he obeyed her or not, she simply scuttled off into the shadows, her eyes searching for the robe. She found it almost immediately lying on a chair but waited for a good couple of minutes before she turned round and retraced her steps. A football team could have dried themselves in the time.

Andreas was sitting on a chair by the pool, the towel wrapped low around his lean hips and his long muscled legs stretched out in front of him. He was the epitome of the relaxed male, his face open and innocent as she approached. 'Great, you've found it,' he said approvingly, and then, as she shivered, added, 'You're cold, Sophy. Put it on; I don't need it.'

Put it on? His robe? The robe that had his very definite male smell all about it and seemed an extension of the man himself? Was he mad? And her shiver hadn't been due to cold—far from it. She caught his eyes wandering over her breasts, their tips hard and pointed as they thrust against the wet black silk, and she folded her arms as casually as she could as she said, 'I'm fine, thanks. Keep the towel and leave it outside my door in the morning. I'm just going back to the—'

'Sit down, Sophy. We need to talk,' he interrupted her easily.

'Andreas, it's the middle of the night.'

'All the better for what I need to say,' he returned coolly.

'I don't think—'

'For crying out loud, woman!' He rose in one swift movement that made her fear for the towel, taking the robe from her suddenly numb fingers and wrapping it round her before she could protest. 'Now sit down and listen, will you?' he said a trifle irritably. 'I need to talk to you about

Theodore. That is one of the reasons—the main reason—I stayed on tonight. My father feels it is only fair to acquaint Jill with the full facts but he and my mother find it difficult to talk about this, for reasons which will become clear to you. He has therefore asked me to explain. I was going to ask to see you both tomorrow morning before I left for the office, but perhaps it is better to tell you informally like this and then you can explain in your own words to Jill.'

She stared at him as she sank down on to the seat he indicated, aware that this must be something very serious from his tense expression but finding it difficult to concentrate on anything at all with the lemony masculine fragrance of him all about her. But the robe *was* warm and the night air distinctly nippy, she told herself silently, ignoring the tingling heat that was spreading through her and which had nothing to do with the texture of the material and all to do with Andreas Karydis.

Andreas sat down again, pulling the towel tighter round his thighs—for which small mercy Sophy was very grateful—and then remained looking at her for a moment or two without speaking.

The shadowed darkness was quite silent, apart from the odd call from the numerous insects and night-life in the vegetation surrounding the pool, and the scent of magnolia was heavy on the air when at last Andreas began to speak.

'You have to understand what I am going to tell you from a background of the Greek way of life,' Andreas said quietly. 'And especially how it was some forty or fifty years ago. It was a man's world, then; maybe it still is, especially in the smaller villages where the family is very patriarchal and a woman's role is very clearly defined. My mother was born in just such a village, a fishing village far away from here in the south.'

He paused, looking away from her and across the pool, and Sophy realised he was finding this very hard. 'Andreas, you really don't have to explain anything,' she said quickly, negating everything she had thought earlier in the house.

'Unfortunately, that is not so,' he contradicted quietly. 'My father has asked me to tell you it all. Jill is Theodore's wife and there can be no secrets within the family, although it is up to her exactly what she tells her son.'

He paused again, and then said, 'My mother is a very beautiful woman even now; when she was younger she was quite exceptionally lovely. In the village where she lived there was a man. He wanted her but she did not want him, so in order to make sure she married him he waited his opportunity and, when she was separated from her friends one night, he raped her. She was fifteen years old.'

'Oh, Andreas.' Whatever she had expected it wasn't this and her shocked face spoke for itself.

'This man had two fishing boats and was considered good husband material by my mother's family. When he went to my mother's father and told him what he had done—my mother had been too ashamed to tell anyone— it was agreed he would marry her immediately. The shame, you see, was all on my mother's side, according to her family; this man was just acting as a man must.'

The bitterness was tangible and now Sophy didn't say a word, but she realised that in the telling of his mother's story she was seeing a side to this big, ruthless, hard individual she hadn't realised existed. A tender, softer side that could feel hurt.

'The day after the marriage had been agreed, a storm sprang up whilst the fishing boats were out. Two were lost. This man was on one of them. My mother was glad he had died—she hated him—but a few weeks later she realised he had not left her after all; his seed had taken root and was growing inside her.'

'Theodore?' Sophy whispered in horror, drawing the folds of the robe more closely around her.

'Yes, Theodore, my big brother,' Andreas said so harshly she winced. 'It was three years before my father's yacht made an unscheduled stop at the village harbour one evening, three years of hell for my mother at the hands of her so-called family and neighbours. She was made to suffer in a hundred different ways for the "sin" she had committed.'

He drew in a deep breath and when he spoke again he had control of his voice. 'My father's yacht had engine trouble and he noticed my mother helping pack fish from the night's catch. Without a man of her own, she was expected to do most things herself. For my father it was love at first sight and he did not rest until he had persuaded her to marry him and leave all the past behind her—except Theodore, of course. She loved her son in spite of the way he had been conceived. And so he brought her and the boy north—he was rich enough to buy her a new beginning in a place where she was respected as his wife—and brought up Theodore as his own son.'

'And he found out,' Sophy said half to herself, the heady sweet smell of the magnolia flowers suddenly a mockery in view of the painful story she was hearing. 'Theodore found out.'

'Yes, he found out,' Andreas said flatly, 'and, being his father's son, he vented his spleen on my mother. You think I am unfair?' he added tightly as she looked at him with wide eyes. 'I am not, Sophy. We never got on, I and Theodore, and when I was informed of the reason he had taken off for England I could see why. His father's blood ran hot and strong in his veins. He was an aggressive youth, given to fits of temper and with a streak of pure malice for those who crossed him. Maybe those first three years stayed somewhere in his subconscious, I don't know, but he was fiercely proud and possessive.'

'He blamed Dimitra?'

'Oh, yes, and one night he and my father rowed violently and came to blows. My mother tried to separate them and he said the most unforgivable things to her; she has never been the same since. In spite of everything she had gone through before she married my father she had never been crushed, not until that night. My father gave Theodore a sum of money, enough to start the restaurant business in England and so on, and Theodore left with my mother's pleas for him to forgive her ringing in his ears. *Forgive her!* Her! He was not worthy to lick her boots.'

'I'm sorry, Andreas. I don't know what to say.'

'You did not like him, did you, Sophy? You could not have liked him,' he said in response to her soft, shocked voice.

He was looking straight into her eyes now and for a moment the virile masculinity that was an essential part of him made her breathless. 'No, I didn't like him,' she agreed faintly.

'I have thanked God there is nothing of Theodore in his son,' Andreas said grimly. 'When I first saw the boy it was a shock; he is the physical image of his father, but that is all. Here inside, where it counts, Michael is free of the curse.'

He had placed his clenched fist on his chest as he spoke and as her eyes followed the gesture the maleness of him was again paramount. She shivered slightly, pulling the robe closer.

'You might think me hard towards my own brother,' Andreas said very quietly, 'but I learnt as a young child you do not extend the hand of love and comradeship to a rabid dog unless you want it bitten off. We never liked each other; long before Theodore discovered his parentage this was so. Part of his fury when he found out he was not my father's son was that he felt I had taken his place within the family.'

Sophy could find it within herself to feel sorry for Theodore but she was wise enough not to say so. Whatever Jill's husband had said and done before he had left his homeland had affected Dimitra badly, and it was clear Andreas would never forgive his half-sibling for the agony and grief he had caused their mother.

'Theodore said—' She stopped abruptly, not sure if she should go on—whether it was the right time to ask questions.

'Yes?' Andreas said a touch impatiently. 'What did he say?'

'He said the family cut him off for good when he married Jill,' Sophy said hesitantly. 'Obviously you'd all quarrelled before then, but he insinuated to Jill that his marriage was the final straw as far as his family in Greece was concerned.'

'That is not true.' Glittering grey eyes searched her face grimly. 'You have seen my mother, Sophy; do you really think she is capable of such bigotry? And my father worships the ground she walks on; he would have done anything to heal the breach between Theodore and my mother. For himself...' Andreas paused before continuing, 'I will not lie to you; he was bitterly angry with Theodore's attitude towards her, and his feelings are the same as mine, but neither of us have betrayed this to my mother. Theodore made her very ill—she had a nervous breakdown with the strain of it all after he had gone to England. My father could never have forgotten this if Theodore had lived, not even if the future had brought some kind of reconciliation.'

He had talked of Theodore being proud and unforgiving but Andreas and his father were just the same, Sophy thought. And then a little voice in her head said, But their attitude had been formed through love for Dimitra and what Theodore had done to her, whereas Theodore's stance had been taken through hate.

Was she making excuses for Andreas? The thought shocked her, intimating, as it did, that she wanted to think the best of him. Which was ridiculous considering the way they had been at each other's throats from the first moment they had laid eyes on one another. But he wasn't quite what she'd thought he was.

Sophy didn't like the way her thoughts were going and now said quickly, 'I believe you, of course I believe you. Dimitra is so sweet. She couldn't possibly have treated Theodore badly.'

'She is a wonderful woman,' he agreed quietly.

Andreas's voice unconsciously gentled when he spoke of his mother, Sophy noticed, and she had observed earlier the way he and Evangelos treated Dimitra like precious, rare porcelain. It must be nice to be adored by two such strong, powerful men; one a devoted husband and the other a loving son.

Again she drew her mind away from the path it was following, saying softly, 'Thank you for telling me all this, Andreas, and I'll make sure Jill understands how things are. I'm sure she won't find it necessary to tell Michael anything now or in the future; it's probably best he remembers his father the way he does now, which is as a remote figure on the perimeter of his life. Michael actually gets on better with Christos, Theodore's partner in the restaurant, than he ever did his father.'

Andreas nodded slowly. 'My father has been in communication with Christos and he has appreciated the man's tact and genuine consideration. It is good Jill has someone like him in the business.'

His face was closed and grim; he obviously had not liked having to reveal such intimate facts about his parents to a virtual stranger but it was hardly her fault, Sophy thought, before she warned herself not to be so touchy. She wasn't normally like this—but then, since she had met Andreas, she was beginning to realise there were things about herself of which she had had no idea. And she didn't like that.

She swallowed hard. 'I'd better get back,' she said awkwardly, rising to her feet with the robe still held tightly round her. She thought about offering it back but as it was quite on the cards for Andreas to pass her the towel if she did, she decided against it.

He had risen when she did and she found it incredibly difficult to concentrate on anything but the powerfully muscled body in front of her, hearing him say, 'I hope once these distressing matters are out of the way you and your sister and Michael will enjoy your stay in my beautiful country,' through hot prickles of rising sensation.

It seemed particularly ironic that the most civilised conversation they had had to date was being conducted with Andreas all but naked and she enveloped in his bath robe. She took a deep breath and managed a somewhat shaky, 'Thank you.'

His voice had been dark and smoky and his face wasn't grim any more; in fact, it was wearing an expression she hadn't seen before and it turned her limbs fluid. 'Do I frighten you, Sophy? Do you still see me as a threat?' he asked softly as her heartbeats accelerated to a hundred miles per hour.

'Of course not.' She tried for briskness but failed miserably. 'And I didn't see you as a threat exactly,' she lied firmly.

'Good.' He smiled, a slow, sexy smile and Sophy knew she ought to get the hell out of there but she was unable to move.

His eyes were as black as midnight and they held her wide blue ones with no effort at all, her lids falling half shut as his face came closer and his firm warm lips met hers in a light, almost teasing kiss. He drew her against his firm hard flesh, one arm round the small of her back as his other hand tilted her chin for greater access to her mouth.

He smelt of the cold, clean water and the night, and as her head began to spin the kiss deepened beyond the soft coaxing he'd employed at first. His lips and tongue were sensuous and experienced but he didn't rush her, his control enormous, as he pleasured them both.

Her hands were grasping the hard muscled flesh of his broad shoulders, although she had no recollection of how they got there and, although she was pressed so close to him now that she could feel the effect her body was having on his, she could no more have drawn away than flown to the moon.

He was kissing her deeply and slowly, building sensation upon sensation, and nothing in the world could have stopped Sophy from kissing him back. The hard pressure of his hair-roughened chest as he crushed her against him, the sensuous quality of his mouth, the overriding authority and power as he took the sweetness from her mouth with no consideration that she might refuse him was intoxicating. She couldn't believe how intoxicating.

She had never been kissed like this, never had such overwhelming sensations tearing through her flesh and making her moist and feverish in a man's arms. She felt as though she was on fire and he seemed to know just what to do to make the flames burn more fiercely.

There was a tight ache in her breasts, their peaks sharply tender, and it was bewildering because suddenly her body wasn't her own. She had always assumed she must have a low sex drive because Matthew's desire to only make love once every four or five weeks had never bothered her unduly. Their union had been comforting and reassuring rather than anything else, a relaxing and almost homely reinforcement of their friendship and high regard for each other. As had breakfast in bed on a Sunday and walks in the park.

But this, this took away her will and reason, shooting sensations to parts of her body she had never been aware of before. It made her want more, much more—made her dangerously out of control. The warning registered in her brain with enough force to cause Sophy to jerk back away from the warmth of him with a little cry of distress, the knowledge that she had been in danger of casting off every rule and principle she had lived by for the last twenty-eight years enough to bring her back to reality.

'Don't touch me!' Her voice was high and frantic, and through the rushing shame and humiliation that was pounding in her head a tiny part of her mind registered he obeyed instantly, even though his eyes were hungry and his muscled body taut and hard with passion. 'I don't want this! This is not why I stayed down here. You asked me to listen about Theodore, that's all.'

She was crying out against herself as much as him, against the insanity that had allowed her to lose all rhyme and reason the minute he had touched her. It was crazy, unthinkable—what she had nearly allowed. And with Andreas Karydis. *Andreas Karydis* of all people! She had only met him a few hours ago.

'Sophy, listen to me—'

'No, don't you dare come near me!' And then, in her panic and confusion, she said something unforgivable before she ran from him. 'You're just like them! Theodore and his father! Forcing yourself on women to get what you want.'

And then she was running from him, the robe slipping from her arms and falling on the ground as she sped across the cool tiles and then out on to the soft velvety grass beyond, careless of the clothes she had left behind as she ran as though the devil himself was at her heels. Which was exactly how she felt.

By the time she reached the sanctuary of her room, her breath was sobbing in her throat and the realisation was dawning that she had made a monumental fool of herself. She sank down on the bed, shaking uncontrollably as she relived the last few seconds with Andreas and what she had screamed at him. How could she? How *could* she have said he was like his brother and that madman who had sired Theodore? What a terrible thing to have thrown in his face.

She sat, shivering and shaking on the edge of the bed as she went over and over in her mind what had occurred, before she threw herself face down on the covers and cried her eyes out. A good ten minutes later, when her face was red and blotchy and her eyes so swollen she felt she was peering through two slits, she forced herself to emerge from the deep well of despair.

She would have to apologise to him for that last remark. The knowledge was like a hard lead ball in the pit of her stomach. It had been nasty and cruel, and most of all it hadn't been true. She had wanted what had happened just as much as he had, if not more. She groaned softly at her weakness, hating herself.

He was clearly the playboy type, or perhaps work hard and play hard was a more accurate description, but whatever—she had been nothing more than a brief dalliance as far as he was concerned. And she'd offered herself on a plate, after all.

Andreas was fabulously wealthy with the sort of personal charisma which would ensure the women were lining up in their droves. No doubt he only had to crook his little finger and a queue formed—and she'd fallen straight into line. No different to all the rest. Thank you very much for noticing me, Mr Karydis, and of course I'll keep your bed warm. *Idiot!* She gritted her teeth against the mental self-flagellation. Idiot, idiot, idiot! She had deserved exactly what she had got.

She should have listened quietly to his explanation for the split within his family; offered her condolences and reassurances that Jill wouldn't rock the Karydis boat; and exited gracefully. Instead— She bit her lip until she felt the salty taste of blood. Instead she had responded like a nymphomaniac to what he had probably intended as a brief goodnight kiss, and then accused him of intended rape. Virtually. Oh, what a mess.

She groaned softly, running her hand through her hair distractedly before sitting up and then sliding off the bed. A long, cool shower was a must and then she would lie down with a cold flannel across her swollen eyes. The family would think she had gone a few rounds with a boxer if she walked down to breakfast like this tomorrow.

She knew she had a reputation within the fashion fraternity of being icy cool and formidably in control of herself, and it was an image she had deliberately fostered during the last years. So what had happened in the last twenty-four hours?

Andreas Karydis had happened. It was stark and distinctly unsavoury, but it was the truth.

She chewed everything over whilst under the shower, and by the time she was tucked up in bed—the cold flannel in place and the light silky covers up to her chin—she had come to a decision. Tomorrow she would phone her secretary, Annie, and tell her to call the Karydis residence during the afternoon indicating Sophy's immediate presence was required back in London.

Okay, so it was sneaky, but she had seen enough of Dimitra and Evangelos to know that Jill and Michael were amongst friends here, and she could keep in contact by telephone with Jill and make sure everything went smoothly for her sister. She had never done anything like this before in her life but extreme circumstances called for extreme measures, and if ever a situation was extreme this one was. She needed to put as much space between herself and Andreas Karydis as possible, and if it felt like running away or ducking out of her responsibilities then that was tough—better that than staying. Oh, yes, indubitably.

Decision made, she was asleep in thirty seconds, utterly worn out by all the emotional turmoil.

CHAPTER FIVE

Sophy awoke the next morning to a gentle hand touching her forehead and Jill's concerned voice saying, 'Oh, Sophy, is your head no better? You should have said you felt so rotten. I didn't realise. Can I get you some aspirin or something?'

The flannel was still across her face, dried now but providing silent but eloquent justification for her swollen eyelids, and as Sophy sat up and put it to one side she knew she looked pretty bad from the way Jill stared at her. Guilt led her to say quickly, 'I'm fine now, Jill, really. It was just one of those headache things caused by the flight and the heat, no doubt. I'll have a shower and then come down with you to breakfast, shall I?'

'Breakfast's over; it's gone ten.' Jill pointed to the bright sunshine outside the window. 'I've brought you a tray Christina prepared for you, but there's no rush to get up. Have the morning in bed if you want. Evangelos and Andreas have gone into the office and Dimitra has taken Michael for a walk round the estate, so it's just the two of us for a while.'

'Right.' Andreas's name had brought a flood of colour into her face and Sophy quickly bent forwards, allowing the silky veil of her hair to hide her hot cheeks as she pretended to straighten the bedclothes. How she was going to face him again she didn't know.

'Isn't it just beautiful here?' Jill placed the tray containing warm, freshly baked croissants and preserves, fresh fruit and orange juice on her sister's lap, before strolling across the room and opening the glass doors leading on to the balcony so that the fresh, richly scented sunshine spilled into the room. 'I can't imagine what would drive Theodore to leave all this, can you? And Dimitra and Evangelos are so *nice*, Andreas too, although you'd hardly think he and Theodore were brothers.'

Sophy's silence must have spoken for itself, because Jill turned round and looked at her twin before saying tentatively, 'What? What is it?' as she saw the look on her sister's face.

'Come and sit down. I've got something to tell you,' Sophy said quietly. 'Or, better still, I'll join you on the balcony and we can sit in the sunshine while we talk.'

She related her conversation with Andreas almost word for word, and when she had finished speaking Jill remained staring out over the beautiful grounds bathed in brilliant sunshine for some moments before she said, 'It explains a lot.'

'I guess it does,' Sophy said quietly.

'Certainly why Theodore was so difficult to live with, even how we came to be married. He was obsessional about me from the first time he saw me, like his father seems to have been about Dimitra. I was flattered at first, I suppose, to have someone so crazy about me and I did love him then, in the early days.'

'And later?' Sophy asked very softly.

'He frightened me,' Jill admitted quietly as she turned to look straight into Sophy's blue eyes. 'He only wanted me to see him, think about him, talk to him. I…even think he was jealous of Michael because it took some of my attention away from him. He…he had these jealous rages if I even talked to someone on the telephone too long, and when he was like that there was no reasoning with him. Michael learnt to stay out of his way.'

'Was he violent?' Sophy sensed there was much more Jill wasn't saying. 'Physically violent, I mean?'

'Not at first, but after Michael was born…' Jill shrugged. 'I was careful to say and do nothing to upset him in the end.'

It was all Sophy's worst fears come true, and she stared at Jill's dear face before saying quietly, 'Why didn't you leave him, Jill? Or tell someone about it? Me, at least.'

'He would never have let me go,' Jill said flatly, 'and if I had attempted to leave him it would have ended in tragedy. You didn't know him, Sophy. As for why I didn't say anything…' She turned to look over the gardens again. 'Many reasons, I guess, but the main one was that I knew it wouldn't do any good and might do a lot of harm if he found out. You see, I'm not like you—I'm not a fighter. I never have been.'

'I wouldn't say I'm a fighter,' Sophy said in surprise.

'Well, you are.' Jill smiled sadly. 'Which is why Theodore didn't like you. He knew you would have rocked the boat and kept rocking it until he fell out!'

'Oh, Jill.' Sophy reached across and hugged her sister. 'I'm so sorry for the way your marriage turned out, but at least you've got Michael. He's a wonderful little boy.'

'And he makes every moment, good and bad, of the last seven years worthwhile,' Jill agreed warmly. 'A hundred times over.'

They talked some more before Jill wandered off to find Dimitra and Michael whilst Sophy got bathed and dressed, but long after Jill had left Sophy continued to sit in the sunshine. Her eyes were fixed on a mass of oleanders in the distance, the rich green clusters of foliage crowned with bursts of pink and white flowers quite beautiful, but Sophy wasn't really seeing them at all. Her vision was all within herself.

Would she ever have children? she asked herself silently, the conversation with Jill having sparked off a vague feeling of depression. She couldn't imagine going through life childless, and yet she had never really seen herself and Matthew in a family setting somehow. She had heard women remark that they were longing to have their partner's baby, but she'd never felt like that about Matthew. Was that wrong?

But Matthew had always been ill at ease with children, she reminded herself in the next moment, and the fragility of babies had frankly horrified him. When one of their close friends had asked him to be godfather to their first-born he had refused point blank, deeply offending the couple in question.

Now, in spite of Andreas's big, powerful build and aggressively masculine demeanour, she could picture him cradling an infant with the utmost tenderness, and his easy rapport with Michael had been immediate. He would be a natural as a father. Andreas Karydis as a father holding his newborn baby... Making babies with Andreas Karydis...

The harsh jarring call of what sounded like a peacock somewhere outside the confines of the grounds brought Sophy back to earth with a bump, and when she realised what she had been daydreaming about she went hot with mortification.

She was losing it, she really was! She'd be a candidate for the funny farm at this rate. She didn't know what had happened to her from the minute she had stepped foot in this country but she didn't like it one little bit!

She jumped up from the chair and stalked into the bedroom, her face set. But one thing had changed this morning; she was darned if she was going to high-tail it back to England like a little scared rabbit. Jill had called her a fighter and maybe she was at that, because now, in the cold clear light of day, the thought of running away was just not an option. She hadn't been herself last night—not in any way, shape or form—but that was last night and today was today and things were going to be different.

Andreas Karydis was just a man like any other; she had blown this whole thing up into something it wasn't. When she saw him again—*if* she saw him again—she would offer a cool apology for her last words to him the night before, at the same time as making it perfectly clear she had no intention of being so foolish as to repeat the exercise that prompted her outburst. Simple, she assured herself as she began to run a warm bath. No need for dramatics or rushing off home to England or anything else. She was a mature and competent woman who could deal with any hiccup life chose to inflict on her. Andreas might be rather a large hiccup, but a hiccup he was, nevertheless.

The three women and Michael spent a lazy afternoon by the pool after a light alfresco lunch. Jill and Dimitra insisted on it, declaring Sophy must take it easy after such a bad headache the night before. Their concern made her feel horribly guilty but Michael's transparent joy at being able to hop in and out of the pool all day eased her sore conscience a little. The small boy was clearly having a whale of a time and was already turning nut brown, although Jill and Sophy spent most of their time under the shade of the trees at the far end of the pool, mindful of the effect of the burning sun on their pale English skin.

After a couple of dips in the pool Sophy changed into a thin white cotton shirt top and long matching skirt, mid-afternoon. In spite of staying out of the sun her skin was turning rosy pink and she used that as an excuse to cover up. In actual fact, it was more the fact that Andreas might—just might—call by before returning to his own home, and if that happened she wanted—needed—to be as different from the girl he had met by the pool in the darkness of night as it was possible to be.

She lay on one of the loungers, the dark shade broken into patches by dappled sunlight, and idly watched Dimitra playing with Michael in the shallow end of the pool; Jill was fast asleep on another lounger at the side of her.

She wasn't aware of shutting her eyes, but the few hours of fragmented rest she had managed the night before must have caught up with her, because when she surfaced from a deep sleep it was to the realisation that the sun was no longer high in a blue sky but falling softly into the shadows of evening, and Andreas had taken Jill's place on the lounger beside her.

There was no smile on Andreas's face as he watched her eyes slowly focus and then widen as she sat up abruptly, and his handsome face was cold and still as she stuttered, 'I…I must have fallen asleep. What—where are Jill and Michael?'

'It is seven o'clock. Michael has had his tea and his mother is getting him ready for bed.'

There was a brooding quality to his presence and he looked devastatingly foreign, his formal shirt and loose tie, along with his suit trousers, indicating he was still in his office attire. The collar of his shirt was undone and revealed his bronzed muscled neck, and she noticed his eyes were so dark a grey as to be black, with a glittering fire in them that spoke of some emotion. Anger at her, no doubt, after last night.

She didn't stop to think, she just said, 'I want to apologise for what I said last night, Andreas. It was unfair and untrue. You aren't a bit like Theodore.'

He said nothing at all for a moment, and then moved in his seat, leaning back and stretching his long legs. 'Thank you. I won't argue with you.'

There was more than a touch of dryness in his voice but Sophy was relieved he hadn't been more difficult. 'Last night—' she waved what she hoped he perceived as a casual hand '—I was overtired and not thinking straight.'

'I see.' He let his dark gaze run over her soft blonde hair

and creamy, sunkissed skin, and she found herself flushing scarlet in spite of all her efforts to appear nonchalant and in control.

'I was not overtired and there was nothing wrong with my thinking,' he drawled with silky composure. 'I wanted to kiss you; I had been wondering what you tasted like from the first moment I saw you at the airport.'

She stared at him, immediately on the defensive. 'Look, Andreas, I'm here to keep Jill company, that's all,' she said quickly, relieved her voice sounded more firm than she expected.

He gave her a hard look. 'Do I take it you are informing me there will be no repeat of last night?' he asked expressionlessly.

'Exactly. I'm sorry.' She was relieved it had been so easy.

His frown changed to a quizzical ruffle which did the most peculiar things to her nerve endings. 'You're not at all sorry,' he said mildly. 'Right from the first you have been fighting me, have you not?'

First Jill, now him. Had she got 'fighter' tattooed on her forehead or something? 'Not at all,' she said carefully. 'I admit we haven't hit it off, though, but that's life.'

'The hell we haven't.' He straightened in the chair and she had to force her body not to react. 'Don't you recognise sexual chemistry when you feel it? The issue here is not that we haven't hit it off, Sophy, but that we've hit it off too fiercely for your mind to cope with. Your body, however, knows exactly what it wants.'

She couldn't believe he was sitting there saying these things to her with such a matter-of-fact tone of voice. She glared at him, her body stiff and tense and her face expressing her outrage. 'That's ridiculous,' she said icily. 'And you know it.'

He refused to accept her self-denial. 'No, it's the truth whether you like it or not.'

'I don't like it,' she shot back tightly. 'Neither do I appreciate the fact that you obviously think I'm the sort of woman who sleeps around.'

'You think because I kissed you I assume you sleep around?' Andreas said incredulously.

'No. Yes. I mean—' He was tying her up in knots! 'I don't wish to discuss this,' she said hotly, drawing the tattered remains of her dignity about her as she rose to her feet. 'I'm going to get ready for dinner. Goodbye, Andreas.'

'I've been invited to stay for dinner,' he said with suspicious meekness. 'Is that all right with you?'

'This is your parents's home,' she said primly. 'I wouldn't dream of suggesting you shouldn't stay. You must do as you please.'

'Thank you, Sophy.' He eyed her with barely concealed amusement.

He had risen with her, and now, as she felt his hand at her elbow, she drew in a deep breath and forced herself to show no reaction at all to his touch as they began walking back towards the house, even though she could feel the vitality and strength that was such an essential part of him flowing through his fingertips and making her flesh tingle. She wanted to shrug his hand away but it would be too crass, and so she concentrated on putting one foot in front of the other and ignored what the touch of his thigh against hers was doing to her equilibrium.

'Your clothes are in my car,' he said softly without looking at her as they walked. 'I didn't think it wise to leave them down by the pool as it might have prompted a question or two in view of your early departure after dinner, but I thought if I returned them to you last night it might have...disturbed you.'

Huh! She could hear the hidden laughter in his voice and her face was straight when she said tightly, 'Thank you.'

'My pleasure,' he returned smoothly. 'And I shall leave for my own home straight after dinner so if you feel inclined for another midnight dip, please do not hesitate on my account.'

'I won't,' she assured him with a tartness that made the dark eyebrows rise just a fraction in silent reproach.

For all the world as though he didn't know he had been deliberately goading her, she told herself savagely. But he had known all right. He was just loving this, all of it. But at least his quiet mockery sent hot pride flooding into every nerve and sinew and enabled her to march back to the house with her head held high and her back straight.

Sophy was applying the last light touch of make-up to her flawless skin before joining the others downstairs when the knock sounded at her door. Jill had already gone down some minutes earlier when Sophy had urged her to do so after her sister had knocked on her door, and Sophy had been pleased Jill had appeared quite happy to do so. Jill's confidence was definitely improving.

Thinking her sister had come to hurry her, she called out gaily, 'All right, all right, I'm ready, don't worry!' as she rose and walked to the door.

Andreas was leaning lazily against the opposite wall when she opened the door, and in spite of the fact that the previous night had prepared her for what the sight of the big, lean body encased in an immaculate dinner suit did to her senses, she found she had to take a breath or two before she could say, 'Oh I'm sorry, I thought you were Jill, come to tell me I'm taking too long,' as her cheeks began to burn with annoying colour.

'Take as long as you like.' He levered himself away and

reached for the small bag at his feet. 'Your clothes,' he offered imperturbably, his expression definitely sardonic.

His bronzed skin and black hair seemed ever darker against the light cream wall. He looked all male, the veneer of civilisation barely held in check. She caught the fanciful thought, angry with herself but shivering without knowing why.

'Thank you; I'm ready now.' She took the bag and walked across to place it on a chair, and when she turned back Andreas was framed in the doorway. His grey eyes lingered for a moment on the pure honey-tinted curve of her throat as she stood, slim and ethereal in the pale blue silk cocktail dress she had chosen to wear, and something in his gaze made her voice slightly breathless as she said, 'Won't it look a little strange if we go downstairs together? I'll wait a moment or two, if you like.'

'I don't like.' His voice was not hostile; rather, it had that thick smoky edge which had haunted her dreams the night before.

'But they might wonder—'

'Sophy, my parents and Jill have more important things to do than to wonder at the incredible sight of two people walking into the dining room together,' he said matter of factly, the sheer patience in his voice emphasising how silly she was being.

She nodded jerkily, wondering how it was that Andreas always made her feel like she was eighteen instead of twenty-eight, or perhaps a young gauche girl just entering her teens was more apt. Her normal cool common sense seemed to take one look at him and fly out of the window. Still, she was the only person who could change that so she'd better pull herself together. Right now.

She picked up the small silk purse in the exact shade of the dress and joined him on the landing, brushing past him as he stood aside for her to exit but with his hand still holding the door.

The contact, brief though it had been, brought a hectic pink flush to her cheeks as they walked along the corridor towards the stairs, but if Andreas noticed he didn't comment.

As they walked together down the wide staircase, Sophy slanted a surreptitious glance at him from the corner of her eye. The hard profile was giving nothing away. The strong forehead, black brows, straight thin nose and square chin could have been sculpted in granite for all the expression they held.

Sophy swallowed drily as her eyes rested a moment more on his firm, nicely moulded mouth before she dragged her gaze away. The memory of that kiss had been with her all day; even when it hadn't been in the forefront of her mind it had been lurking in her subconscious. She hated it but she didn't seem to be able to help it.

She could still feel how it had felt to be held so close to that big rugged body; even now her flesh was tingling at his closeness whereas he— She bit her lip hard as a mixture of self-disgust and irritation made her soft mouth tighten. He seemed quite oblivious to her supposed charms. And yet he had admitted down by the pool earlier that he felt the sexual chemistry between them every little bit as much as she did.

So what did that mean? That he could control himself better than she could? That thought wasn't to be borne, and it brought her sweeping ahead of him into the dining room with her backbone rigid and her eyes narrowed. She just had time to compose her face into a more socially acceptable expression before the others turned from where they were standing on the patio and called for Andreas and Sophy to join them.

The meal was as good as the night before and the conversation even better now Jill had gained enough confidence to do her part. Christina was a first-class cook and fiercely Greek, which meant most of the delicious dishes paraded in front of her Sophy hadn't tried before, but every one was excellent. Dolmades—meat and rice wrapped in vine leaves—and taramasalata—a compote of fish roes, garlic and lemon leavened by breadcrumbs—were two of Christina's staple dishes, but the table groaned with other succulent morsels.

Fried potatoes, slices of eggplant in batter, olives, cheeses, bowls of tomato, cucumber and peppers, seafood in various disguises, meatballs in thick sauce, plates of cold sliced veal, pork and lamb were all brought in at various stages of the long, leisurely meal. Sophy found souvlak—a pancake of brown meal garnished with tomatoes, peppers, onions and yoghurt and filled with thin slices of lean meat which had been pressed into a cone and cooked over a grill—to be especially to her liking, but it was all delicious. And Dimitra explained each dish in her soft gentle voice, giving a list of the ingredients and its Greek name along with the way they were cooked.

Evangelos's specialty was the wine, and at least three different varieties of both white and red had been brought out by the time the coffee and ouzo appeared.

It was an amazing lifestyle, Sophy thought, as she glanced round the beautifully decorated room beyond which the lights on the patio showed the gardens stretching away into the dusky night. Incredibly luxurious and opulent, and yet all the money in the world hadn't enabled Evangelos to do the one thing he had wanted with all his heart—to protect the woman he loved from further hurt in her life.

He had brought her out of the shame and misery which had been thrust upon her, provided the ivory palace of fairytale stories and more or less wrapped Dimitra up in cotton wool, but still the older woman had suffered to the point where her mental health had been broken when Theodore had rejected her so cruelly. And it had been cruel, wickedly cruel. She couldn't see Andreas treating his mother so badly, whatever the circumstances.

Immediately the thought materialised, the warning bells were clanging. What did she know about Andreas? Nothing at all beyond the fact that at times he could be just as hard and uncompromising as Theodore had been, so he might be quite capable of hurting Dimitra. Whatever, it was none of her business. This family was nothing to her beyond Jill's involvement with them. The old feud with its ongoing ramifications, along with the lives of Andreas and his parents, would soon be a distant memory once she was back in England; two weeks was just a brief flash of time in the overall span of things.

The air was heavier and more humid than it had been the night before, and when Dimitra suggested that they take their coffee on the patio to benefit from any slight breeze everyone agreed. Sophy especially was longing for a change of scene.

It was a little cooler outside and almost dark, the night sky of dark charcoal streaked with bands of silver grey and dull mauve. The scent of the climbing roses which twined all over the back of the house was rich and sweet in the warm air, and Sophy found her taut nerves were beginning to relax a little as she sat and sipped her coffee and listened to the others chat.

Christina had just bustled in and poured the women another coffee when Jill said, 'I think I'll just go and check on Michael before I drink mine,' turning to Dimitra as she finished and adding, 'Would you like to come with me?' Dimitra had apparently accompanied her daughter-in-law the night before when Jill had looked in on her son before retiring, and it had touched Jill how Dimitra had stood for ages just watching her grandson sleep.

As the two women stood up, Evangelos also rose, saying in an aside to Andreas, 'I'll make that telephone call to Athos to confirm the shipping dates now. I won't be long,' and before Sophy could blink she found herself alone with Andreas in the warm scented night.

She wasn't aware she had shifted uneasily until the smoky voice at her elbow said softly, 'Relax, Sophy. I'm not about to leap on you if that's what you are thinking.'

She made the mistake of turning to look him full in the face, and the dark sardonic gleam in the grey eyes informed her all too clearly he was loving her confusion.

'Don't be ridiculous,' she said stiffly, wishing she could think of a crushing retort to put him in his place.

'A kiss. I am to be hung, drawn and quartered for a kiss. Is that it?' he asked very quietly.

Put like that it sounded nothing, she admitted silently, but she knew—as well as Andreas did—that something vital and electric had leapt into being between them the moment his lips had touched hers. And if she hadn't called a halt, who knew what might have occurred in the perfumed darkness by the pool?

'You are determined not to mellow an inch, are you not? I am cast into the role of wicked philanderer and this will make it easier for you to ignore the truth,' he stated flatly.

'The truth?' she asked warily, wondering what was coming.

'The truth your body recognised from the first moment we met—that we are compatible sexually in a way that happens with few couples.' He looked at her, daring her to deny it.

'We're not a couple,' she pointed out swiftly, hot colour burning her cheeks, 'and you can't possibly say that, considering we've never even—' she paused for the briefest of moments before finishing '—slept together.'

'I am more than willing to put my theory to the test,' Andreas offered helpfully, leaning back in his chair as he crossed one knee over the other and surveyed her from laughing grey eyes, his face remaining completely serious.

Sophy gritted her teeth. 'How kind, but if you don't mind I'll decline your generous offer.'

He grinned openly then and she didn't like the rush of sensation that almost overwhelmed her as the hard, handsome face relaxed and softened.

He had slid into the seat Dimitra had vacated as the others had left, and now he stared at her for a moment before saying softly, the amusement dying from his face, 'You have the most beautiful eyes, do you know that? And they are a deeper violet than Jill's. Your hair is different too. Yours is a little paler than Jill's, silver almost, like moonlit water. You really are not so alike after all.'

He was close enough for her to be wrapped up in his male aura and it took a second for her to be able to say, her voice striving for lightness, 'There is no danger of mistaking us then?' as she tried to wrench her gaze from his.

'None at all.' He took one of her hands as though he had the right to do so, and when she instinctively tried to pull it away secured her fingers in one hand with her palm uppermost as his other hand casually stroked the soft full flesh. 'Soft and silky,' he murmured almost to himself, 'such fine transparent skin.' And then he had raised her palm to his lips, touching her flesh gently just for a moment.

A tingle shot straight up her arm and this time when she pulled away he let her go, settling back in Dimitra's chair more comfortably as his eyes narrowed on her flushed face. He folded his arms over his chest, and then said evenly, as though the rest of their conversation hadn't happened,

'Come out to dinner with me tomorrow night, just the two of us. I know a little place you would love down by the seafront.'

Was he mad? Sophy placed her hands in her lap and stared at him through the whirling in her head. 'No, thank you.'

'Why not?' he responded immediately.

He knew darn well why not! 'I don't want to,' she said ungraciously. 'Okay?' She eyed him defiantly.

'That's not an answer. Give me a reason. Is it because you are frightened to be alone with me, little English mouse? You think I will take advantage of you? Or perhaps it is yourself you are frightened of, eh? Maybe that is it?'

He was absolutely on the ball there but Sophy would rather have walked on red-hot coals in her bare feet than admit it. 'I am here to keep Jill company,' she said stiffly, 'as you well know. Not to go gadding off with every Tom, Dick or Harry.'

'Forgetting this Tom, Dick and Harry for a moment, you are saying you will not accompany me to dinner tomorrow night because of your responsibility towards Jill?' he said softly. 'That is it?' His expression told her all too clearly what he thought of that.

She glared at him but was saved the embarrassment of a reply by the other three emerging from the open doors of the dining room, Evangelos carrying another carafe of the milky white ouzo in one hand which he raised to Andreas, saying, 'It is a night for sitting and drinking while we put the world to rights, yes?'

'Sorry, but no.' Andreas rose lazily to his feet, his smiling face taking in the others as he said, 'I've some papers to look at tonight at home and Paul has been waiting outside for the last few minutes. I told him we were leaving at ten-thirty.'

'All work and no play?' Dimitra was smiling at her son

as she spoke and it was clear the bond between them was a strong one.

'That has never been one of my attributes—or failings, depending on which way you look at it,' Andreas returned drily. 'But it might apply more aptly to Sophy. Do you know she is insisting she cannot be my guest at the Pallini tomorrow because she is here only as Jill's companion?'

The dirty, rotten rat. Sophy was too taken aback by the effortless fait accompli to say anything as the others instantly voiced their insistence that of *course* she must go out for the night and enjoy herself. They wouldn't hear otherwise.

'You don't need to keep me company, Sophy, you know that,' Jill said earnestly.

Her voice had barely finished before Dimitra was saying, 'Please, Sophy, I hope we have not made you feel you are only here in some minor capacity. We love having you stay with us, my dear, but you are perfectly free to come and go as you wish, and I promise you we will take good care of Jill.'

Only Evangelos remained silent, his dark eyes on his son's face as Andreas smiled easily, saying, 'You see, Sophy? This is your holiday too, and you will be doing me a great honour in allowing me to show you a little of the real Greece while you are here, starting tomorrow night, yes?'

He had backed her into a corner and there was absolutely no way out without making it clear they were at logger-heads, and thereby upsetting everyone and causing tension. If ever there was a sly, underhand double-dealer, Andreas Karydis was one, Sophy thought furiously as she fought not to betray her thoughts.

And further proof of this came when Andreas turned to Jill, his voice pleasant as he said, 'Of course you are more than welcome to come too, Jill, although I thought you would prefer to remain close to the house in case Michael should wake up and want you.'

'Definitely,' Jill agreed at once.

As he had known she would. Sophy bent down and fiddled with the strap of her sandal, pretending it was undone, in an effort to hide the contortions her face had fallen into as she struggled not to scream abuse at him. Who did he think he was, manipulating everyone like this? Talk about a cheek! He thought he was so clever. It was a good thirty seconds before she could trust both her face and her voice, and even then her voice had a clipped edge to it when she said, 'What time would you like me to be ready?'

'Seven okay?' he returned easily, the charm fairly oozing out of him. 'And it's smart casual, not dinner dress, at the Pallini, unless you would like to go somewhere more formal?'

'The Pallini will be fine,' Sophy answered hollowly, wondering what the reaction would be if she threw the last of her cool coffee into his face.

'Until seven tomorrow, then.' He smiled at her, nodded at the others and kissed his mother lightly on the forehead before walking into the house, leaving Sophy sitting in a state of semi-shock as she listened to the others talking. She heard his voice once he was outside the house again—obviously conversing with Paul—and then the sound of a car's engine and the scrunch of tyres as it drew away.

Well, okay, Andreas Karydis, she thought furiously, I might be having dinner with you tomorrow night but that will be all. If you think for one second you can twist me round your little finger like you seem to do everyone else, you've got a big shock coming. She frowned to herself and then something made her glance up to see Evangelos watching her, his eyes—Andreas's eyes—narrowed and thoughtful.

She forced a smile and made a light, complimentary remark about the beautiful gardens, and Evangelos immediately switched into attentive host mode, the awkward moment passing.

But an hour or so later, when the four of them rose to retire, Evangelos caught her arm as they walked into the house letting Dimitra and Jill walk on ahead of them. 'He has annoyed you,' Evangelos said quietly, the words a statement and not a question. And he didn't need to mention Andreas's name.

Sophy thought about prevaricating but somehow, with Evangelos's kind eyes fixed on her face, it wasn't an honest option. 'Yes,' she said simply as they stood in the middle of the dining room looking at each other. 'He has.'

'You do not want to go to dinner with Andreas?' There was no condemnation in the question, merely mild and somewhat surprised enquiry. 'I think you will enjoy yourself at the Pallini.'

Did she want to be with him? The idea was thrilling on the one hand, but possessed of such danger she couldn't ignore the tension the thought produced. Also, the way he had manipulated her had caught her on the raw, to the point where she would have given anything to throw his dinner back in his face! And all these feelings, every one of them, was so alien to the calm, composed and matter-of-fact woman she normally was that she felt she didn't know herself anymore. So all in all, no—she didn't think she wanted to go to dinner with Evangelos's son!

Sophy was aware as she looked into the handsome face of Andreas's father that she was seeing Andreas as he would be in thirty years or so, and it took a moment for her to say quietly, 'I prefer to make my own mind up on such matters,' and this time she knew she *had* avoided a direct answer.

'I can understand this. Andreas can be…persistent when

his mind is set on something.' Evangelos's voice was apologetic.

Persistent? Persistent didn't even *begin* to describe it!

Sophy's face must have given her away because in the next instant Evangelos chuckled quietly, and his voice carried the amusement evident in his face when he said, 'It would be good for Andreas to find he cannot have things all his own way for once. He is used—' He stopped abruptly and then said, 'Pardon me, Sophy. May I speak frankly?' And at her nod, continued, 'My son is used to being the pursued rather than the pursuer, you know what I mean? He is wealthy and good-looking, and this has a magnetism all of its own for some women. Most women.'

Sophy stared at Evangelos, not at all sure if Andreas's father was warning her off his son or quite the reverse. 'This is not good for someone of Andreas's disposition,' Evangelos continued after a moment or two, 'because it produces a feeling of contempt in him for the women concerned. He is a highly intelligent man and tires easily of being told what he knows the woman concerned imagines he wishes to hear.'

Sophy nodded. Yes, she could understand that. Wealth and privilege brought its own problems. Her brow wrinkled. 'I don't quite see why you are telling me all this,' she said quietly. 'I have absolutely no intention of flattering Andreas's ego.' Not if he was the last man on earth!

'I know that, my dear.' Evangelos patted her arm in a fatherly fashion. 'I am merely explaining the reason for my son's lack of…sensitivity this evening.'

'Right.' She didn't quite understand where this was going.

'But one thing I would add, Sophy.' As she went to walk on Evangelos stopped her for a moment more. 'Andreas has had his fair share of hurt and disappointment, some of which—when combined with what I have already said—

has produced a cynicism which it has grieved me to see. He is a good man, a very good man but a complicated one.'

This whole family was complicated. Complicated enough to make her wish she had never suggested accompanying Jill out here. Sophy stitched a smile on her face with some effort and said quietly, 'I suppose we all are underneath the façade we put on for the rest of the world. My mother used to say—' She paused, not sure if she wanted to continue what she had started to say. This was Andreas's father, after all.

'Yes?' Evangelos asked mildly. 'What did your mother say?'

Sophy dismissed the feeling that she was letting Andreas's father persuade her to reveal too much. 'She used to say that men and women could only be their true selves with very young children and babies, or their pets. Never each other. With other adults there was always self-protection built in which formed its own natural barrier.'

'Do you believe that?' Evangelos asked quietly, his eyes intent on her heart shaped face.

Sophy shrugged uncomfortably. 'I'm not sure,' she said carefully. 'My father let my mother down very badly, so certainly after he had left us that was the case for her. Therefore it must be true for a percentage of people.'

'That is very sad.' Andreas's father shook his head slowly. 'For myself, I can say that I am totally myself with Dimitra, and, I believe, she with me. She knows everything there is to know about me—the good, the bad and the ugly.' He smiled at her, his last words aiming to lighten what had suddenly become a very heavy conversation, and Sophy smiled back.

'You're lucky,' she said simply.

'Sometimes we have to go out and secure our luck,' Evangelos murmured quietly. 'This is an age of instant gratification. Instant meals, instant money, instant relationships. But a relationship worth having doesn't happen without constant work and effort, not even the best of them.'

She stared at him, and then as he took her arm and walked her out into the hall where the others were waiting the moment passed.

But later, lying in the warm darkness of her bed, Sophy found she was more confused and disturbed than ever. Everything was wrong somehow and nothing was right, and yet she couldn't really put her finger on what was bothering her so acutely. She frowned irritably in the blackness, turned over with a little sigh and determinedly shut her eyes.

CHAPTER SIX

SOPHY didn't sleep at all well. She couldn't remember anything of the dark dreams that had troubled her during the night, but only that they had been of a nature to make her feel disturbed and distressed when she awoke early the next morning.

She showered and dressed, and acted as though she hadn't a care in the world during breakfast with Jill and Michael and Andreas's parents. After exploring the grounds with Michael and playing a couple of games of tennis with him, she and her small nephew spent the rest of the morning in the pool while Jill and Dimitra were taken shopping by Evangelos. Sophy and Michael were included in the invitation by Andreas's parents, but the look on Michael's face at the prospect of a morning spent in shops was enough to induce Sophy to offer to stay at the villa with him.

The others were staying out for lunch, so Christina organised a small simple barbecue by the pool for Sophy and Michael which was great fun, Michael's enthusiasm infecting Sophy.

Once they had eaten, Sophy insisted Michael wasn't allowed in the water for at least an hour and persuaded her nephew to curl up on one of the cushioned sun-loungers for a nap, a beach towel wrapped round him and the shade of a large tree making the temperature comfortable in spite of the baking heat.

Gradually through the morning, Sophy's face had become calm and relaxed in the young child's uncomplicated company, and as she sat sipping at a delicious glass of iced lemonade and watching him sleep, she felt peaceful for the first time since she had set foot in Greece.

She was purposely concentrating on nothing more controversial than the sleeping child, the bright sunshine and scented air, and the lone drone of tiny busy insects in the surrounding vegetation.

She must have drifted off to sleep herself because when the others returned they awoke both her and Michael, and they all spent a happy hour or two chatting over more iced drinks and watching Michael playing in the pool with the enormous plastic cheeky-faced whale Dimitra and Evangelos had bought their grandson.

It was a pleasant time, easy and unhurried, and when— at just gone half-past five—they all returned to the house, Michael to have his tea with Christina and the adults retiring to their rooms to rest before getting ready for dinner, Sophy found herself humming a little tune as she entered her sunlit bedroom. She'd just been overtired before, she told herself firmly.

She had just walked through to the bathroom to run herself a bath, fancying a long luxurious soak rather than a quick shower, when Ainka knocked at her door informing her there was a telephone call for Mrs Fearn and please could she come right away?

'For me?' Sophy asked in surprise, her mind immediately expecting Annie to be on the other end of the wire with some catastrophe necessitating her immediate return to England. She ignored the faint sense of panic and disappointment the thought conjured up and walked across to the bedroom extension, lifting the receiver and speaking her name clearly and crisply.

'Hallo, Sophy.'

The dark smoky voice could only belong to one man on earth, and for a moment the blood rushed in her ears like an express train. She licked suddenly dry lips and said steadily, 'Andreas?' as though she wasn't quite sure. No need to inflate the super ego any more than it was already.

'I am just calling to make sure that seven is still okay?' he said smoothly. 'I understand you have been taking care of Michael today, so if you would prefer to leave a little later after a siesta?'

'No, seven's fine.' She took a deep breath and hoped the gallop of her heart hadn't sounded in her voice. How come all the good the relaxing day had done her had vanished in a moment?

'Great. I'll see you a little later, then.'

She stood with the receiver in her hand for some seconds after the call had finished, until the sound of water reminded her about the bath and sent her hurrying into the en-suite. Suddenly the evening was there in front of her with all its capacity for potential disaster staring her in the face, and as she stripped off her swimming costume and shirt top her mind was buzzing. She should have said she was too tired, ill, anything.

She must not panic, she told herself silently. She would keep him at a distance with cool, reasonable politeness to-night; let him see he couldn't touch her emotions and that the physical chemistry between them was simply mind over matter. Which it was. Of course it was. Otherwise they were no better than animals.

By ten to seven she had changed three times. She'd felt the first dress was too revealing and come-hitherish, the second outfit of a cream linen summer suit too austere, and the third dress in bright bubblegum pink had wiped all the colour out of her skin. Now she surveyed herself in the mirror, her face tragic and her equilibrium completely blown.

The chocolate sequinned top with its spider-web thin straps dressed down beautifully with black jeans and strappy, high-heeled sandals, and she had fixed her hair into a loose casual knot, allowing a few tendrils to wisp about her cheeks and neck. She was wearing just a touch of shadow and mascara but that was all; the sun have given her skin a honey glow no cosmetics could improve and she only ever wore lip-gloss on her lips.

Would he think she had tried too hard? Or maybe that her outfit wasn't dressy enough, or even too dressy? These females who chased him—how would they dress? Designer labels to a woman, no doubt, with real 24-carat little rocks glittering on their necks and throats. She bit her lip hard at the way her thoughts were going and closed her eyes for a moment. Enough. Enough, Sophy Fearn. You don't have to compete with anyone—especially not where Andreas Karydis is concerned, for goodness' sake! Pull yourself together, girl.

She opened her eyes and decided on no jewellery at all except a pair of simple silver studs in her ears. Ready or not, here I come... The simple childish rhyme she and Jill had used so often in their games of hide-and-seek when they were young made her smile for a second. There was no doubt Andreas Karydis would be ready and perfectly in control, but she herself was quite a different matter.

She remembered again his compelling sexuality and the effortless ease with which he had kissed her and smashed through all her defences, and her heart began to pound madly. When Jill knocked the door the next moment and popped her head round to say Andreas had just arrived, it was almost a relief to know the moment was here and the waiting was over.

'You look gorgeous, Sophy, just right,' Jill said approvingly.

Evangelos had told the girls that the Pallini was a favourite with the younger generation, an excellent restaurant with its own dance floor and band but with an informal reputation that meant almost anything went in the clothes line.

'Are you sure?' Sophy asked anxiously. 'What's Andreas wearing? He hasn't dressed up, has he?'

'I don't think so.' Observant had never been a word which could be applied to Jill. 'Smart casual, like you.'

Smart casual could possibly have described the midnight blue silk shirt and beautifully cut black designer trousers that sat on Andreas's frame like an advertisement for sensuality, but sheer dynamite would have been more apt, Sophy thought weakly as she walked into the drawing room some moments later.

'Good evening, Sophy.' Andreas moved from his position at Evangelos's side to stand looking down at her, his grey eyes frankly appreciative. 'You look very lovely tonight.'

'Thank you.' She tried to match his smoothness but felt the warmth in her cheeks and knew she was blushing.

'All ready?' He turned as he spoke and raised a casual hand of farewell to the others who were all trying—unsuccessfully in the most part—to hide their interest in the proceedings.

Sophy was vitally aware of Andreas as they walked out to the car, and after smiling at the impassive Paul sitting in the front seat she climbed into the back of the sleek limousine, catching a whiff of expensive aftershave as Andreas climbed in beside her.

'Pallini's isn't far.' Andreas settled himself comfortably beside her, apparently unaware that he brushed her body once or twice in the process with a hard male thigh. She, on the other hand, felt the contact like electric shocks and had to apply rigid control not to let it show.

The whole point of the evening was to let this impossible man know she was quite oblivious to him, not behave like a cat on a hot tin roof, she told herself desperately.

She expected him to turn on the charm big time but, after the few brief words when they had entered the car, Andreas was quite silent as they left the estate and turned on to the narrow lane outside. They had reached the main road and been travelling for some minutes before he said quietly, 'Are you hungry?'

'So, so.' It was a beautiful evening, the sky still cornflower-blue and mellow sunlight slanting in the car window. 'Michael and I had a barbecue together at lunchtime and I made the mistake of eating the food he didn't want as well as my own,' she said a touch ruefully, 'so I'm not ravenous, if that's what you are asking.'

'Good.' He smiled at her, an easy smile that smoothed out the hard angles and planes of his face. 'I've reserved a table for nine; I thought it might be nice to take a stroll along the beach first. It is always beautiful in the evening, I think.'

'Fine,' she said with a wariness she couldn't quite hide, and then found herself stiffening as he leant across and took her hand in his. She stared into his eyes, her own wide.

'I am going to hold your hand, Sophy,' he said with the ghost of a smile twisting his lips. 'Okay? That gets that one out into the open. I shall probably hold it on the beach as well and put my arm round you, along with other little gestures that come naturally when a man is with a woman. I am not going to regress to the agony of adolescence with all its fumblings and awkwardness, so can you relax and accept you are out on a date?'

'A date?' She stared at him, horrified. And Andreas Karydis, even as an adolescent, would never, *ever* have fumbled, awkwardly or otherwise, her mind stated silently. 'This isn't a date. You're Theodore's brother,' she said a little stupidly.

'His half-brother,' he reminded her evenly, 'and as far as I know the one doesn't preclude the other. This *is* a date,

Sophy, whether you like it or not, and if you give yourself half a chance you might find you actually enjoy it.'

'Enjoy being with you, you mean,' she said before she actually thought what she was saying.

He smiled, apparently not in the least put out. 'Exactly,' he said drily, 'and don't expect me to apologise for suggesting such an outrageous notion, either. Woman is expected to be man's companion. It is the right and proper order of things.'

He was teasing her and she knew it, and she smiled weakly.

The long sandy beaches and clear turquoise water in the north of Greece were renowned for their charm, but the exquisite, gently shelving stretch on which the Pallini was situated was particularly lovely, being just off the normal tourist track.

They had just passed through a small town which had been a winding maze of narrow cobbled streets and tiny squares, with flower-bedecked tavernas and sugar white houses spilling out on to the pavements. Just outside the perimeters of the town, Paul had turned the car off the main road on to a well-used track, which had opened immediately to disclose a large sprawling one-storey building built of wood, with an enormous veranda stretching the length of it which was painted white.

Massive wooden barrels stood to one side of the building, and the front of it was decorated with fishermen's nets, huge shells, pieces of driftwood and other objects the sea had obviously brought to its door in its time. The effect was very attractive.

People were already sitting eating on the veranda as well as inside the massive restaurant, and other couples were idly enjoying a drink in the evening sunshine on the many scattered tables and chairs on the beach in front and to the sides of the building. Music drifted out on to the warm air along with the sound of conversation and laughter, and there was a definite buzz in the air.

In the distance across the white glistening sand, tiny waves lapped gently against the shoreline, the odd bird or two—along with two-legged creatures of the human variety—wandering along the beach in the warmth of the dying day. It was so foreign, so easy and relaxed and utterly Greek, that for a moment Sophy just stood and drank it all in once they were out of the car and Paul had disappeared. Sun, sea, sand…and Andreas at her side.

'What an unusual place,' she said at last, conscious of Andreas's eyes on her face in the moments before she turned and looked at him. 'And it seems to be very popular.'

He nodded, his dark eyes narrowed against the sunlight as he took her hand and began walking towards the building. 'A good friend of mine owns it,' he said quietly, and then, as Sophy bent and slipped her feet out of her sandals, he waited until she had straightened again before taking her hand and continuing, 'Nick's family is a wealthy one but he is the original bohemian. I think his father was despairing that he'd ever do anything with his life and then Nick met Iona, and within three months he had married her and bought this beach front, all of it. They built the restaurant and it was a success from day one. That was ten years ago.'

She couldn't resist saying, 'The love of a good woman obviously worked wonders then?' as she smiled mockingly.

'Obviously.' It was very dry.

'Is there living accommodation at the back?' she asked curiously as they approached the rambling building.

'Uh-huh. Just a kitchen and bathroom and one bedroom and sitting room. They live here eight months of the year and just retire to their house—a beauty of a place—for the winter.'

Sophy cast her eyes again over the wide sweep of sand

and sea lit by strong evening Greek sunlight. 'An idyllic lifestyle.'

'In many respects. The restaurant only opens in the evenings as they didn't want to lose sight of having time together, and they have an army of chefs and waiters now. However, money cannot buy everything.'

She raised her eyebrows questioningly at the statement, spoken as it was in an unusually sober tone for Andreas.

'Iona cannot have a child of her own,' he said quietly. They had reached the foot of the stairs leading up to the veranda now, and his voice changed as he said, 'Come and meet Nick and Iona and then we will walk a little of your lunch off, yes? Then you will have room for more.'

There was no time to reply before a little squeal from within the restaurant reached them, and in the next moment a small, slender woman with long brown hair reaching to her waist had flung herself down the steps and into Andreas's arms. 'Andreas! Oh, it's so good to see you! But you are very, very naughty. It has been months since you came to see us.'

'Don't exaggerate, Iona.' A long, loose-limbed and floppy-haired man had followed his wife and now he smiled at Sophy, holding out his hand as he said, 'You must be Sophy. I'm Nick and this limpet clinging to Andreas is my wife, Iona.'

During the next few minutes Sophy decided she liked Andreas's friends and that, if the circumstances had been different, they were the sort of people she would have liked to get to know better and spend time with.

Nick was the antithesis of Andreas, being so laid-back and mild-tempered that it was impossible to imagine him ever getting upset about anything, and Iona was just a sweetheart. Tiny, with huge expressive brown eyes and a gentleness about her that was very pleasant, she clearly adored her handsome husband, and he her. It was very nice to see, Sophy decided.

'Give me a bottle of wine and two glasses, Nick,' Andreas said after a while. 'We're going for a walk on the beach but we'll be back for nine. Has Iona made any of her famous tzatziki, by any chance? And it has to be Iona's, not one of your chefs, good as they are,' he added with a wink at his friend.

'Don't I always make some if I know you're coming?' Iona answered reproachfully.

'Always,' Andreas agreed easily, smiling as he bent and kissed Iona's smooth forehead. 'And it's always perfect.'

Sophy could hear Nick shouting orders in Greek to someone, and then he was back with a bottle of dark red wine and two enormous wine glasses which he passed to Andreas, saying as he did so, 'I've told Stephanos to save a couple of good portions of moussaka along with a bowl of extra prawns and shrimps. I presume you'll want your favourite main course after the tzatziki?'

'I've been tasting it all day.' Andreas grinned back.

Sophy was feeling acutely disturbed as they left the busy bustle of the restaurant and walked down the steps of the veranda on to the smooth white sand. She had left her sandals in Iona's care, and now, as she curled her toes into the warm powdery grains beneath her feet, she said quietly, 'They're lovely people. I presume they spoke English for my benefit?'

'They would want to make you feel welcome,' Andreas agreed softly. 'And, yes, they are two of the best.'

She didn't like what seeing him relaxed and off guard with his friends had done to her equilibrium. He had been different with Nick and Iona to how he had appeared before, even with his family. Younger, softer, more approachable. And infinitely more dangerous because this Andreas was more attractive than ever.

There were tiny shells here and there, shining and glistening as they made their way right up to the water's edge until the low hum of noise from the restaurant behind them was gone. Andreas had taken her hand in his as they had walked, the bottle of wine and the stems of the wine glasses hanging loosely in his other hand, and for some ten minutes or so he didn't break the silence which had fallen between them.

Sophy was breathing in the scent of the sea and sand and warm summer air, looking across the miles of calm tranquil turquoise water under the vivid, hard blue Greek sky as she concentrated on not thinking at all. If she started to think she was quite liable to panic, she'd admitted to herself at the beginning of their stroll, and so it was easier to blank her mind and let her senses soak up the beautiful evening. Ignoring the hard-muscled figure at the side of her was more difficult because her body seemed to have developed a life of its own since she had met Andreas.

'Over there.' Their area of beach was quite deserted now and Andreas was pointing to where a shelf of rock curved gently out of the sand, the water rippling daintily round its edges. 'The perfect place to sit and have a glass of wine and tell each other our life stories,' he drawled lazily.

She glanced at him quickly. 'I don't remember that that was part of the deal tonight.'

His grin flashed without apology. 'What would you like to talk about, then?' he asked very softly. 'The choice is yours.'

She decided to treat this lightly and gave him a noncommital smile she was rather proud of in the circumstances. 'Tell me about Greece,' she suggested evenly as they reached the smooth polished surface of the warm rock and perched comfortably, looking out over the glassy, still water.

Andreas gave her an amused glance from dark cynical

eyes as he poured two glasses of the rich blackcurrant wine and then handed her hers. 'You can get a guide book for that.'

The sun was sinking lower, flirting with the prospect of letting the moon have pre-eminence, and Sophy took several sips of the wine—which was perfectly wonderful—before she said, 'Okay, tell me about your work, then. Detail your average day. All men like to talk about their jobs, don't they?'

'When they are in the company of a beautiful woman?' Andreas said with a distaste that was not totally feigned. 'I think you have been associating with the wrong sort of man, Sophy.'

'You are being deliberately difficult.'

'Not at all.' He let his eyes sweep over her lovely face and something in his gaze brought the colour surging into her cheeks. 'Tell me about him, your husband,' Andreas said very quietly, all amusement gone from his dark face. 'Were you happy? Was he good to you?'

It was totally unexpected and for a moment all she could do was to stare at him, her eyes wide. And then she took a deep breath and said just as quietly, 'Yes, we were happy. Matthew was a good man and I loved him.'

The dark face didn't change by so much as the flicker of an eyelash. 'Is it painful to talk about him?'

'Painful?' She turned her profile to him, looking out to sea again. 'Not now,' she said slowly. The memories she had of Matthew were precious and warm, but they were in the past. She had moved on. 'But he didn't deserve to die so young.'

'Tell me what happened,' Andreas said quietly. 'I want to know.'

So she told him it all, from when she and Matthew had first met at university until the night he had died in her arms. 'I couldn't believe it at first,' she said quietly. 'He was my best friend and then suddenly he wasn't there any more.'

Andreas had said nothing whilst she had talked, but now he refilled her glass before saying softly, 'Did you mourn him as a friend or a husband, Sophy?'

'What?' She was too shocked to say anything more.

'I am sure you loved him, but fire can never be wholly content with water.'

'I don't know what you are talking about.' She glared at him angrily, not sure if he was criticising her or Matthew or whether any criticism was intended at all.

'Water is calm and tranquil, undisturbed by the more turbulent emotions that drive some men and women,' Andreas said softly. 'Some of the greatest statesmen in the world have had such attributes, but you…you were not meant to be the wife of such. Fire must be met with fire or else it slowly becomes quenched and reduced to the merest flicker. Fire is passion and wildness. It is fierce and frantic and life itself.'

Her chin was up, but something in the intensity of his voice caused her not to be as angry as she felt she should be. But he was all but telling her she shouldn't have married Matthew, wasn't he? Or at least that they would have proved to be unhappy in time—and all this when she'd only known him a couple of days. How dared he say whether they had been right for each other or not? But…somehow he wasn't being nasty.

'You didn't know Matthew,' she said coolly, 'and frankly you don't know me either, so I fail to see how you can say anything about our marriage.'

'I have heard and seen how you talked about him to-night.' His eyes had locked on hers and the rosy light that was now bathing the sky in the first signs of dusk made his bronzed skin and black hair even darker.

Sophy stared at him a moment longer and then slid off

the rock on to her feet. He couldn't be allowed to affect her so deeply. She took a gulp of the wine and then, as Andreas reached for the glass in her hand and took it from her, became still. He placed it beside his own glass on the smooth stone and then turned her into him, his hands about her waist.

'You are angry with me,' he murmured softly, but without any regret in his voice that she could hear.

'Why would I be angry?' she said icily, wishing she had the power to send him tumbling away from her if she pushed him, but knowing she wouldn't make any impression at all on the hard, muscled chest. 'You tell me I shouldn't have married my husband and that we were unsuited, when you never even met Matthew! How could I possibly object to that? Of course, some people might call it arrogant in the extreme, but no doubt that wouldn't bother you for a second. It wouldn't, would it?'

'Do you want a lie to smooth your ruffled feathers or the truth?' he asked mildly.

She opened her mouth to tell him exactly what he could do with his amateur psychology when his mouth closed over hers, hot and stunningly sweet as his hands moved her firmly into his body. It was a smooth and experienced move and allowed no opportunity for escape, not that Sophy was thinking of it anyway.

He explored her mouth leisurely but with an exquisite finesse that spoke volumes about his knowledge of women, and the scent of the sea and sand combined with the overwhelming enchantment that was taking her over.

Somehow her arms had wound round his neck, although she hadn't been aware of it, only that the smell and feel of him was all about her and she didn't want it to stop.

His hands were in the silk of her hair, turning her head to gain even greater access to her mouth before his lips began to cover her face and throat and ears in hot little burning kisses that made her moan low in her throat. And then the devastatingly knowing mouth was nibbling at her lips again, provoking a response that Sophy could no more have denied than she could have stopped breathing.

Andreas was breathing hard, his chest rising and falling under the thin silk of his shirt, but his control was absolute, and after a few last lingering kisses he moved her gently from him, looking down into her dazed eyes with an unfathomable expression. 'So, we know how we would settle any disputes between us, eh?' he said softly.

Sophy was trying to ignore the tingling in her spine and the slow languorous warmth that had weakened her limbs and sent her dizzy, but his words—with their underlying message of some sort of future involvement—sent a healthy shot of adrenalin into her blood. 'There is and will be no ''us'',' she said fairly steadily, 'so that's a purely rhetorical question, I take it?'

'You can take it any way you want to,' he answered pleasantly, but with just the faintest touch of steel underlying the smoothness. 'But for now we will return to the Pallini and eat well. We will smile and converse and speak of nothing more controversial than whether the moussaka is to your taste. You do like moussaka?' he added easily.

'Yes, Andreas, I like moussaka.'

If he noticed the cool flat note of control in her voice he didn't comment, merely gathering up the almost empty bottle of wine and the two glasses and following her as she began to walk back down the beach. And this time he did not take her hand. Ridiculously, Sophy felt bereft.

Sophy had not expected to enjoy the rest of the evening but—annoyingly—she found she couldn't help it.

The meal was wonderful but of gargantuan proportions, beginning with Iona's tzatziki, a dish made with yoghurt and garlic and served in two small bowls with warm chunks of fresh garlic bread to scoop it up with. The moussaka was heavenly but she was openly amazed at the amount Andreas put away, and he still found room for a healthy portion of a pastry dessert oozing with honey and cream and succulent red cherries.

They ate on the veranda overlooking the sea, the breeze off the water taking the edge of the humid heat and making it very pleasant. The sun went down in a riveting display of colour, rivers of red and gold and cinnamon flowing across the soft charcoal grey and midnight blue in a stunning extravaganza of nature at her best. It was hypnotic and spell-binding and the stuff dreams were made of.

And so was Andreas. Sophy knew he had set out to charm her, but in spite of herself she couldn't help responding. He was amusing and attentive, telling the odd funny story directed against himself with a wicked self-effacement that stated quite clearly he was deliberately being deprecative to win her round. The dark eyes flashed with humour and in the dim light his face had taken on something of the appearance of a handsome bronze statue, his features purely male and classical and his hair as black as the night.

She was enjoying herself, so much, and she didn't *want* to—but he made it impossible not to. And as though he had picked up on her thoughts, he leant closer to her as they sipped their coffee and brandy, his voice low and smoky as he said quietly, 'You should relax more often, but you find it hard to let go, don't you? If it wasn't your marriage that made you that way, then what? Because, deep, deep inside, I do not think you're like that.'

She stared back at him, suddenly finding the warm scrutiny unnerving. She opened her mouth to make some airy light comment but instead found herself saying, 'The way we were brought up, I suppose. My mother had to work all the time and Jill... Well, I guess I felt I had to look after her somehow. She always seemed younger than me, much younger, even though we're twins.'

Andreas nodded slowly. 'Your father?'

'Left the bosom of his family when Jill and I were a couple of months old,' she said, not as flatly as she would have liked. It was the wine, she told herself irritably. She had drunk just enough to make the mask slip a little. She had to be careful.

He had picked up the thread of bitterness. 'Your mother didn't marry again?' he asked softly.

''How could she? She worked all the hours under the sun; there was no time for socialising or meeting anyone. Besides, I think she still loved my father, although she would rather have died than admit it. She knew he was a weak, worthless rat but she couldn't quite let go.'

The faint air of bewilderment caused his mouth to tighten for a moment before he said, 'Do you ever see him?'

'I've never seen him.' Sophy straightened in her chair and the body language and the crispness of her voice told him the conversation was over. 'He might be dead, for all I know.' And then she smiled, a brittle smile, as she said, 'Could I have another brandy, please?'

A spirit of recklessness had taken her over and suddenly she didn't want to think any more. He had said she found it hard to relax and let go, and it was true when she thought about it. She had been on the treadmill of life for as long as she could remember, always being responsible and rational and in control. Even with Matthew it had seemed natural to them both that she would make the final decision on things. Not that she had minded, she told herself quickly, as though the thought was a betrayal; in fact, she had liked it being that way…hadn't she?

Suddenly she wasn't sure about anything—and it was a frightening feeling. The urge to chill out, to let her hair down without any thought of the consequences was as strong as it was dangerous, and she had to master it now, right this minute.

She felt obliged to drink the second glass of brandy when it came but washed it down with two cups of strong black coffee, the fleeting moments of devil-may-care foolhardiness vanishing almost as soon as they had arrived. But they were a warning, she told herself soberly, as she watched Andreas's face as he talked to Iona and Nick who had joined them at their table.

Andreas was a complex, enigmatic man and she didn't have a clue what made him tick. That kiss had told her he was as far out of her league, sexually and in every other way, as the man in the moon. And he was a man who liked women, and they liked him back.

Behind them in the distance where the beach road ran came the low whisper of cypress trees teased by the soft warm breeze, and the night sky was bright with stars, the moon sailing resplendent and proud surrounded by her lesser subjects. There were fewer people left now but the band was still playing, and the dance floor was not as crowded as it had been whilst they had eaten, just the odd couple dancing dreamily to a slow ballad.

'Come.' Andreas stood to his feet, extending his hand towards her. 'We will dance a little.'

'Oh, no,' she said immediately. 'I'm not a good dancer.'

She might as well have saved her breath because she found herself lifted to her feet with an authoritative hand and whisked through to the interior of the building, Iona and Nick following in their wake. She nerved herself for the moment when he took her into his arms and consequently was as stiff as a board, earning a little click of annoyance from Andreas. 'Relax, let the music lead you,' he murmured softly in her ear, his male warmth enclosing her in its own magic. 'It is not a sin to be young and carefree.'

Carefree, no. Careless, yes. And the two were dangerously entwined tonight.

'Is there anyone special in England?' he asked her quietly after they had danced for a minute or two.

'Not really,' she answered, trying to make it sound as though she had a whole regiment of boyfriends to choose from. 'Any relationships have to fit in with my work schedule, which can be hectic at times.' Or they would if she had any relationships!

'And your friends—your men friends—are content with this?' Andreas asked disapprovingly. 'Did Matthew fit in with your work schedule, too?'

'That's really none of your business.' It was hard to sound as vinegary as she would have liked when she was being held against his hard muscled frame, and his breath was ruffling her hair. But it was such a typical Andreas comment!

'Of course it isn't,' he agreed immediately. 'So, did he?'

Sophy's head shot up, her violet-blue eyes expressing her indignation. 'You really don't take no for an answer, do you?' she said tartly. 'I've never met anyone so confrontational.'

He smiled, tightening his arms. 'How clever of you to notice. So, the men in your life have always come to heel, yes?'

'I refuse to discuss this with you.' It was angry and hissed through gritted teeth, and suddenly—to Sophy's astonishment—Andreas threw back his head on a roar of laughter.

'Defiant to the last,' he murmured when he'd finished laughing. 'What is this myth about English women being so cucumber-cool, eh? You are more fiery than any Greek girl I know.'

Sophy gave him a dry look that made him grin again. 'Is that supposed to be some kind of compliment?' she said with a primness that made his smile widen. 'Greek style?'

'You don't like compliments?' he murmured silkily.

'Not when they can't be trusted.'

'What a suspicious little cat you are, my sweet.' He fitted her into him again and Sophy gave up trying to argue. She would never win in a war of words with Andreas; he was a man with all the answers. Which was another reason to keep him at arm's length.

Nevertheless she couldn't deny that she felt more alive than she'd felt for a long time, perhaps ever. But that wasn't just Andreas, she tried to reassure herself silently. It was the holiday magic of foreign parts; the warmth, the atmosphere, the sheer exoticness of it all. It got into your blood.

Sophy had expected they would leave shortly after they finished eating, but as the time continued to roll by she found the large group of people who were left were what Iona and Nick called their regulars—friends and patrons who regularly stayed until the early hours. And she didn't want to leave, not really. She was having too good a time.

The wine and ouzo was flowing freely and there was an earthier flavour to the mood inside the restaurant now. Iona and Nick sat with them at a table close to the dance floor when the four of them weren't dancing, and they were wonderful company. Nick was funny and Iona was droll and Sophy had never laughed so much in her life. She felt as if she'd known them for ever.

At one point all the men in the place linked arms and began a line of Greek dancing as the music got wilder and wilder, the women clapping and calling as the men stamped and whirled.

Sophy's eyes were fixed on Andreas. He was so different from how he appeared normally. Usually the aura of hard authority and command sat on him like cold armour, radiating ruthlessness along with the virile force that was at the essence of him. But like this, with his friends, he seemed open and relaxed, the cutting edges of his arrogance smoothed to silky softness.

But he was the same man, she reminded herself quickly, wrenching her gaze away from the dark, laughing figure and sipping somewhat frantically at the soft drink she had asked for earlier. He had a life force that was pure vital dangerous energy, an intensity of spirit that would always subdue and subjugate those around him.

Her fingers tightened on the glass and her heart began to thud. Why was she here? Why hadn't she made some excuse at the last minute? A headache or something along those lines?'

Because she had been curious. The answer was very clear in her head and suddenly there was no trace of the faint muzziness the wine had caused earlier. He fascinated her, like some dark alien being from another world, and she had wanted to be with him, wanted to learn more about him. It was almost a relief to acknowledge her weakness now she had let it out of her subconscious.

She had thought the more she learnt, the more she would be able to control this strange feeling she had for him; that in some way he would... What, exactly? Put her off him? Say or do something crass or gross? Maybe she had just *hoped* that would happen without really believing it.

The thoughts were terribly disturbing, and as a roar of laughter and shouting from the men finished the dance to the calls and claps from the women, she forced herself to come out of the deep void she'd sunk into. She would think of all this tomorrow, not now. For now she just had to be on her guard and sensible.

Sensible, level-headed Sophy. All her life these attributes had been tattooed across her forehead, put there by those who knew her best. 'Sophy will see to it.' How often had she heard her mother say that from when she was a tiny child? 'Sophy is my right-hand man.' And she hadn't minded, oh, she hadn't. Her poor mother had had enough to cope with; but now, when she thought about it, the pressure had always been there to take charge and supervise. To behave far older than her years.

'Bossy' had always been written on her school reports somewhere or other, along with 'Sophy has a mind of her own'. But those teachers hadn't known she had gone home to organise tea for herself and Jill from the age of five or six, often doing what housework she could and making it into a game for Jill who was disinclined to work unless she had to.

Oh, what was she doing, thinking all this now? She had never had thoughts like this before, so why now, in the most inappropriate of places? It must be the wine and the rich food.

'What's the matter?' She hadn't been aware Andreas had returned so quickly, but now he bent down and tilted her chin with his finger, his eyes serious. 'What's happened?'

'Nothing has happened.' She forced herself not to react badly.

'You've gone into Spartan mode again,' he said with quiet flatness. 'I can see it in your eyes. For a little while you forgot you mustn't enjoy yourself, didn't you?'

'Don't be ridiculous,' she said too emphatically. 'I often enjoy myself.'

'No, you don't, not really.' He bent closer and kissed her lightly on the lips. 'But you will if I have anything to do with it. Oh, yes, you will. And that is a promise, Sophy.'

And then he turned and spoke to Nick, leaving her sitting in stunned silence at the quiet intensity with which he had murmured the last words.

Why should she be keeping herself in a constant state of frayed nerves over this man? she asked herself silently. She hadn't known a moment's peace since she had first set eyes on him, not really. And she could hardly believe she hadn't known of his existence until a few days ago. She had to get this whole affair into perspective, and once she had done that... She bit down on her lip hard. Then she would know some peace again.

CHAPTER SEVEN

WHEN Sophy awoke to the sunlight streaming in to her room through the balcony windows she had left open the night before, she was surprised she had slept so well.

She and Andreas hadn't left the Pallini until gone three in the morning, and when they had walked along the beach to where Paul was waiting with the car, she had been convinced Andreas would try to make love to her on the way home. But he hadn't so much as kissed her, not until they had reached his parents' front door that was, and even then it had been the sort of social peck that didn't mean anything. Polite, brief and dismissive.

He had returned to the car immediately he had opened the door for her, sliding into the front with Paul this time and raising a laconic hand in farewell as the big car had executed an about turn and whisked off down the drive.

Perversely, his lack of ardour had thoroughly upset her, and she had marched up the stairs to her room, reiterating over and over again that she wanted *nothing* to do with Andreas Karydis and that she was glad—very, *very* glad— that he'd had the good sense at long last to realise that and admit defeat in the seduction stakes. Which that goodnight peck clearly said he had.

She had showered and washed her hair, swiftly blow-drying it before climbing into bed and pulling the thin cotton covers up to her chin as her mind had continued to dissect the evening frame by frame. After telling herself that she would be awake all night, she must have fallen immediately asleep!

She glanced at the little alarm clock she had brought with

her from England and was horrified to see it was eleven o'clock. *Eleven o'clock!* She flung back the covers and leapt out of bed. What must Dimitra and Evangelos be thinking? This was the second time she had missed breakfast and she'd only been here three days!

After a hasty wash in the en-suite bathroom, she threw on a light blue cotton top and matching shorts, and after brushing her hair into sleek obedience ran quickly downstairs without bothering with any make-up. She met Ainka leaving the drawing room with a duster in her hand, and the little maid informed her that the others had gone to visit friends of Dimitra after breakfast, who had a son the same age as Michael. 'Madam thought it would be good for the little one to have someone his own age to play with,' Ainka explained in her soft melodious voice, 'and you were sleeping so soundly, they did not wish to disturb you. Madam left instructions for your breakfast to be served in the sunshine on the patio, yes? I will bring it immediately.'

'Thank you, Ainka.'

So she ate in solitary splendour as she looked out over the beautiful grounds ablaze with sunshine, which was just what she'd needed in truth. It gave her a chance to compose herself and decide what she was going to say before she saw Jill, who, she knew, would want chapter and verse on the previous evening's happenings. She groaned inwardly and tried to marshal her thoughts.

She would be factual, she decided eventually as she finished the last slice of toast heavily covered with cherry preserve and licked sticky fingers appreciatively. Why did food always taste a million times better al fresco? Especially in the sunshine.

Yes, she'd be factual. She'd concentrate on the wonderful restaurant and Andreas's friends and the fact that she had had a lovely time. Their more intimate conversations, the kiss, his comment after the dancing—that she would keep to herself. Because it all meant nothing anyway and she didn't want Jill to get the wrong idea.

She shifted in her seat, suddenly restless. Why hadn't he tried to kiss her in the car, though? And all the way home she had been preparing herself with a mental list of excuses as to why she couldn't go out alone with him again, and then he hadn't even suggested repeating their date, anyway! She felt such a fool. And she couldn't remember ever feeling this way before. With every other man she'd known, either in business or on a personal level, she had always called the tune and had been in control.

She stood up abruptly, cross with herself and the whole wide world. She needed to take a brisk walk in the sunshine and get a grip on herself, she decided firmly. She had never been able to stand women—or men either, if it came to that—who blew hot one minute and cold the next, who were inconsistent and capricious, and here she was behaving like the worst of them. Wretched man! It was all his fault.

By the time the others returned for a late lunch, Sophy's face was calm again and her manner easy and relaxed—at least on the outside. But the outside was all that mattered, she told herself silently whilst patiently giving Jill a minute by minute account of the previous night's proceedings. She would deal with the inside when she was herself again, but privately. And each day that went by meant she was a day nearer to leaving this place—and Andreas. Strangely the thought was not as comforting as she would have liked it to be.

They all lazed the afternoon away by the pool watching Michael and his new little friend, Stevos—whom Dimitra had brought back to play with Michael for a little while— splashing about in the water. It should have been relaxing, Sophy thought wryly. Jill slept at one point, and she found herself watching her sister's lovely face with a mixture of bewilderment and self-annoyance. Why couldn't she be more like Jill? Jill never fought; she had even been able to live all those years with Theodore in a state of relative peace, whereas Sophy knew she would have committed murder in the first five minutes!

What would Andreas be like to live with? The thought was too dangerous to consider and she brushed it away like a troublesome insect, rising in one lithe graceful movement and shedding her shirt top to reveal her bathing costume beneath, which she had changed into after lunch.

She spent a riotous hour in the pool with Michael and Stevos, playing a noisy game of tag followed by an equally noisy game of piggy in the middle. The small boys had their tea together by the pool, and then when Evangelos and Dimitra rose and suggested driving Stevos home, Sophy came indoors to shower and change.

Now she was alone again she wouldn't admit to the flat feeling which had taken her over in the last couple of hours, nor of the secret expectation that Andreas might drop by on his way home from the office as he had done before. Instead she concentrated on her toilet, making as much effort with her appearance as she would have done for a huge dinner party rather than a meal with Jill and her sister's in-laws. Somehow looking good mattered today.

They had just started on the main course when the telephone rang, and the next moment Ainka appeared in the entrance to the dining room, stating Sophy was wanted on the phone. Somewhat mystified as to who would be calling her and assuming it *had* to be Annie with some kind of work problem, this time, she excused herself and walked out into the hall.

'Hello, this is Sophy Fearn,' she said carefully into the receiver, fully expecting Annie's apologetic voice in reply.

'Hello, Sophy Fearn.' The deep smoky voice made her name into a caress and in spite of herself she shivered. 'I was called to Athens today on business and I am stuck here tonight. I assume you're in the middle of dinner, knowing my mother's routine so I won't keep you. I'll pick you up about six tomorrow so be ready, okay? And don't eat too much lunch, this time.'

'What?' She stared into the receiver as her thought process hiccuped and stood still, and then managed to say, 'I don't think so, Andreas. I don't feel it's right to leave Jill like this, besides which it seems very rude as far as your parents are concerned.'

'We've been through that and the consensus of opinion is that it is rubbish.' There was no room for disagreement in the determined, cool voice. 'No one is thinking like that, Sophy.'

Bulldozer approach again. Sophy took a deep breath and said, 'Be that as it may, it's what *I* think.'

'I do not think that is the reason at all. You are frightened to be with me, that is the truth, is it not? Admit it.'

'Now it's you who's talking rubbish,' Sophy lied hotly.

'Prove it. Come out with me tomorrow night,' he said quickly.

'No.' It was a flat refusal and she didn't bother to dress it up with any more excuses. He'd just have to accept no meant no!

'That's settled, then. Six it is.' And the phone went dead.

She couldn't quite believe it. For a moment or two she was so taken aback, she just stared out into the immaculate quiet hall, hearing the low hum of conversation from behind the dining room door and then Jill's laughter and the rumble of Evangelos's distinctive chuckle through the buzzing in her ears. He had hung up on her. *Hung up on her.* And after railroading her into a date she didn't want and had said no to. An emphatic no. Well, he could take a running jump. She would not date Andreas again!

She waited until the burning in her cheeks had died down

and then walked back into the dining room, meeting Jill's inquiringly raised eyebrows with a careful smile. 'It was Andreas,' she said quietly, noticing the way Dimitra and Evangelos froze momentarily before they carried on eating.

'Oh, yes?' Jill had never been renowned for her tact, but Sophy had been hoping for once her sister might be a little diplomatic. It wasn't to be. 'Why was he calling you?'

'Just to say he had to go to Athens on business,' Sophy said a trifle limply, hoping it might encourage Jill to be subtle as she made her voice as dismissive as she could.

'Oh, yes, the Tripolos contract. You remember I told you about it, my dear?' Evangelos was talking to his wife but Sophy suspected it was more to save her further embarrassment than anything else, especially when he turned to include Jill and Sophy as he said, 'Andreas is a brilliant businessman. I would be lost without him, but sometimes I feel he works too hard.'

'That is because there is no one to encourage him home at night,' Dimitra said maternally. 'He needs a wife. I have told him this many times. It is high time he settled down.'

'Perhaps that is why he has not looked for one?' Evangelos returned with a wry smile and raised eyebrows.

'He thinks I am a fussy mother.' There was no rancour in Dimitra's voice and her eyes were full of love as she looked at her husband. 'But I know my Andreas. He will never be content with the beautiful, mindless creatures who throw themselves at him and have nothing in their heads but cotton wool. Nevertheless, he does need a wife, the right sort of girl.'

Dimitra's voice was light and her gaze was steady as she smiled at them all, but as they continued to eat Sophy felt Andreas's mother had been saying much more than the mere words indicated. Dimitra didn't think that she was making a play for Andreas, did she? Sophy asked herself in horror, nearly choking on a piece of green pepper as the thought hit and hastily taking a sip of wine.

Had Dimitra been trying to tactfully warn her off without saying anything direct? It might indeed look as though she had thrown herself at Andreas as far as his parents were concerned, considering he had taken her out to dinner last night and she hadn't got home to the early hours. What would they say if they knew he had asked her out tomorrow night?

She wriggled uncomfortably in her seat and found she had no appetite for the mouthwatering array of desserts Ainka brought in after the little maid had cleared away the other dishes.

Andreas clearly conducted his life independently of his parents, and that was fine—to be expected in a man of his age—but considering she was here as Evangelos and Dimitra's guest, she was in a totally different position.

She sipped her coffee thoughtfully, joining in the conversation with the others automatically but with her mind a million miles away as she considered how best to get a message to Andreas the next day to emphasise she definitely, *definitely* had no intention of seeing him on a one-to-one basis again.

Dimitra suggested they might like to have coffee on the patio again, the night being a humid one, and as they all rose to walk out into the scented night air Sophy felt a restraining hand on her elbow. 'Sophy?' Dimitra's voice was low as Jill and her husband disappeared out of the dining room doors, the long silky curtains billowing a little behind them.

'Yes?' Sophy forced a smile to her face as she waited for the polite cautionary word about Andreas she was sure would follow. She didn't blame Dimitra; one son had married an English girl and had been lost to her for ever, so it was only natural Dimitra would prefer Andreas to marry what she was sure his parents would describe as a 'good Greek girl', someone familiar with their culture and on their wavelength. Which meant any involvement, however transitory, with Jill's sister was not to their liking.

'Andreas wants to see you again, doesn't he?' It was a statement of fact, and followed by a little rush of words as Dimitra said, 'Oh, forgive me, my dear, for speaking to you in this way about a matter which is of no concern of mine, but I feel I just wanted to tell you...'

'Yes?' Sophy wasn't quite sure where Dimitra was coming from. There was none of the gentle aggression she had expected.

'He is not an island, although I know he gives that impression,' Dimitra said softly, embarrassment making her colour high. 'To the outside world he is Andreas Karydis, virtual head of a vast shipping empire which he controls by being hard, ruthless and clever. He has an intuitive knowledge of people which he uses to his advantage, but that has made him very cynical for one so young. He is not a fool, in other words.'

'I think I realised that in the first five minutes I met him,' Sophy said quietly. No one could think Andreas a fool.

'He likes you.' Dimitra's soft gaze was very steady, and Sophy suddenly realised Andreas's mother was made of sterner stuff than she had thought. 'And he doesn't like many people, I'm afraid. Oh, he will use them—the women too, if they are foolish enough to throw themselves at him—but he never allows anyone to touch the man inside. And the man inside is a good man. Of course, I am his mother and so I must confess to being biased. But I know he needs peace and happiness like everyone else.'

'Dimitra, I'm not looking for any sort of relationship at the moment,' Sophy said softly. Especially with Andreas. But she couldn't very well say that to his mother. And she wasn't quite sure about the liking part, either; she and

Andreas struck sparks off each other and there was no doubt the physical chemistry was there, but as for liking her... But she couldn't say that either—that it was good old-fashioned lust that attracted him.

Dimitra nodded slowly. 'I think I knew this. But...' She shrugged in a very continental way and didn't continue what she had been about to say. 'No matter.' She smiled at Sophy. 'You will not tell Andreas I have spoken to you in this way? He would be most annoyed with me.'

'Of course not.' Sophy still wasn't a hundred per cent sure exactly what way Andreas's mother had spoken! She rather suspected Dimitra had been trying to find out how her daughter-in-law's sister felt about becoming one of Andreas's 'women', and Sophy could well imagine there had been a velvet-coated warning in Dimitra's comment about women who were foolish enough to throw themselves at Andreas. And she didn't doubt there had been plenty.

Which made Sophy all the more surprised with herself when—she and Dimitra having started to walk across the room to join the other two outside, and Dimitra asking in a low undertone if she was going to see Andreas again—she answered in the affirmative. 'Tomorrow night,' she said quietly. 'He has asked me to have dinner with him. He's picking me up at six o'clock.'

Sophy determined she was not going to agonise over what to wear this time when, later the next afternoon, she emerged from the shower and stood in front of her wardrobe gazing at the clothes she had brought with her. She lifted a simple, pastel blue dress with an asymmetric hemline off one of the hangers and laid it on the bed, along with a cotton cardigan in the same colour. Decision made, she told herself firmly.

She dried her hair, applied her make-up and was ready

to go and sit with Jill and Michael at half-past five, Michael being in the process of munching his way through his tea on the patio.

'Very nice.' Jill smiled at her with her mouth but Sophy noticed her sister's eyes were troubled. 'You look lovely.'

'What's the matter?' Sophy asked directly.

'The matter? Nothing. Of course nothing's the matter,' Jill returned brightly, and then, as Sophy's wry expression didn't change, Jill said quietly, 'Don't get in too deep, Sophy. He is Theodore's brother, remember.'

It was said discreetly, in an expressionless voice, with Michael in mind, and Sophy's voice was equally flat when she replied, 'Half-brother, Jill. They only share the same mother, remember, and Dimitra is a love,' even as she asked herself why on earth she was defending Andreas. 'And Evangelos's a nice man.'

'Oh, I know, Evangelos and Dimitra are lovely but—'

Jill stopped abruptly, shaking her head as though she didn't know how to express her misgivings, and Sophy caught one of her sister's hands. 'Don't worry.' She squeezed Jill's hand very slightly. 'It's just dinner and he knows the score. I've made it abundantly clear I'm not looking for romance. He's not my type.'

'Andreas doesn't fit into a type,' Jill murmured ruefully.

The two women stared at each other for a moment, but there was no time for further confidences as the next instant a deep, dark voice from somewhere inside the house proclaimed the subject of their conversation had arrived early and Sophy's heart jumped.

She resisted the impulse to jump to her feet, rising slowly as she said goodbye and walking calmly through the open doors into the dining room, whereupon she made her way into the hall where Andreas was standing talking to Evangelos about a business matter, from what she could determine, before he looked up and saw her.

Her heart was thudding fit to burst but she looked cool and contained to the big dark man watching her so intently, his eyes narrowing slightly as he took in the gleaming silk of her hair and the classically casual simplicity of the sleeveless, fitted dress and matching peep-toe court shoes.

Evangelos made his goodbyes and exited via where Sophy had come from, presumably to see Jill and his grandson, leaving the two of them standing in a pool of sunlight in the hall.

'I missed you yesterday,' Andreas murmured softly, lifting a hand and tracing the outline of her small jaw with one finger.

He was wearing a beautifully tailored summer suit in pale grey, his white shirt and grey tie of the same expensive silk, and looked every bit the powerful wealthy tycoon.

Sophy blinked, the reality of him a hundred times more disturbing than all her thoughts over the last twenty-four hours. 'You barely know me,' she said as steadily as her racing heart would allow, 'so how could you possibly miss me?'

'Time's relative,' he replied, pinning her with his lethal dark gaze. 'How else can you explain the fact that you can know some people all your life and their impact on you barely touches the surface, whereas others...' He smiled slowly. 'Others become important within minutes.'

She didn't know how to answer that and so she said nothing, and after a moment or two he slanted a look at her under half-closed lids as he said, 'All ready? Goodbyes said?'

He made it sound as if she was leaving for good, and to bring things back into line with how she saw the evening progressing, Sophy said quietly but firmly, 'I can't be late again, Andreas. It isn't fair on the rest of the household.'

He looked hard at her and then glanced down at her feet. 'Where are they?' he asked in tones of great surprise.

'What?' She followed his gaze to her feet.

'The glass slippers. Isn't that what Cinderella wore?' he asked blandly, his eyes glinting his amusement. 'But don't worry, Cinders. You will go to the ball.'

'Very funny.' But she couldn't help laughing.

He took her hand, grinning at her as he said, 'Come on, woman, I haven't got time to bandy words with you. I'm hungry.'

Once out on the driveway Sophy was surprised to see a low, lean sports car crouching in front of them. 'Where's Paul?' she asked quickly. Three was safer than two by a long chalk.

'I don't use Paul all the time. I drove myself to the airport yesterday and I only got back an hour or two ago, so...' He waved his hand at the sleek silver beast in front of them. 'I'm quite a good driver,' he assured her modestly. 'Don't worry.'

She didn't doubt it, but the car was a sex machine with two low front seats and a powerful long bonnet and little else. It was not how she had envisaged the evening beginning.

Sophy gritted her teeth and allowed him to help her into the passenger seat, whereupon she had the uncomfortable feeling she was at eye level with the road. The inside was all leather, with a dashboard that looked like it had come out of a Bond film, and when Andreas slid in beside her she realised he was close. Very close. She swallowed hard and forced herself not to fidget.

The engine growled into life and the beast leapt down the driveway. 'Where...where are we going?' she managed as they exited through the gates, her stomach feeling as though it had been left behind on the drive. 'Is it far?' She hoped not.

'Surprise.' It was cool and laconic and she instantly bristled.

'I don't like surprises.'

'Force yourself,' he said pleasantly.

She gave up at that point. It was quite enough to try and keep body and soul together in this monster of a machine, especially with Andreas sitting so close she couldn't have put a pin between them, and his firm strong hands gripping the leather steering wheel on the perimeter of her vision as she stared goggle-eyed out of the massive windscreen.

Andreas drove like he lived, fast and ruthlessly, and more than once Sophy found herself praying that if—*if*—they reached their destination in one piece by some miracle, she would insist on a taxi home. Formula One was all very well but not her scene!

It was some ten minutes before she realised she had relaxed and was actually enjoying the ride, and as she cast a sidelong glance at Andreas she saw the hard firm mouth twitch slightly. 'Okay?' he murmured mockingly, his expression making it quite clear he had been aware of her nervousness and moreover had enjoyed it. 'The first time is not always the best.'

Barbarian. And he needn't think she was going to respond to the double meaning she knew full well he intended in that enigmatic sentence, either. 'I'm fine,' she said brightly. 'Are we nearly there?' Wherever there was.

'Another few minutes.'

It was another ten, but then the car was nosing its way quietly through automatic gates which closed soundlessly behind them and growling gently up a slight, tree-bordered incline to come to rest in front of a long, low, sprawling villa of mellow honey-coloured stone, its red tiled roof dappled by sunlight.

'This is your home,' Sophy accused uncertainly. 'Isn't it?'

Andreas cut the engine, settling back in his seat as he draped one arm round the back of hers. 'Do you mind?' he drawled easily. 'It's been a long forty-eight hours and I need to shower and change and relax. Paul's wife cooks better than any chef I know so you'll have a good dinner.'

'Paul and his wife live with you?' It reassured her fractionally. But only fractionally. This was the wolf's lair.

'They have their own separate annexe at the side of the house,' he assured her gently, having to go and spoil the moment by adding, his voice mocking, 'so you'll be quite safe, Cinders.'

'I never thought otherwise.' She glared at him, her angry irritation at his easy reading of her mind not helped by the wicked glitter in his dark eyes as he left the car.

'Little liar.'

She ignored that, trying to scramble out of the car, only to realise she needed the assistance of the hand he'd put out to help her, his eyes moving appreciatively over the length of golden tanned skin her skirt was revealing. By the time she was standing on the pebbled drive, her cheeks were as red as the full-blown, scarlet roses draping the arched porch.

The villa was completely concealed from the road by trees, but as Sophy turned to look fully at it she caught a glimpse of vivid blue beyond, the scent of roses, grass and sea combining to make her say, her eyes wide, 'Your house overlooks the sea?'

'Yes. The garden runs down to the beach,' he said lazily.

'How wonderful.' She had always adored the sea.

'Come and see for yourself.' He took her arm as the front door opened and a small, squat woman came waddling forward to meet them, the equally small figure of Paul just behind his wife, and after brief introductions Andreas led her into the house.

It was all wood floors and exquisite rugs, with an air of spaciousness and comfort that sat well with the big plump sofas and modern furnishings. There were five bedrooms complete with en-suites upstairs, Andreas informed her, and downstairs the space was divided into a large study, cloakroom, kitchen, breakfast and dining room, with a wonderful sitting room overlooking the beautiful three-tiered gardens which were enormous and, true to Andreas's word, ran right down to a beach of white sand.

Just outside the sitting room, which had one wall of glass inset with big glass doors to take in the magnificent view, shallow stone steps led down to the first tier of the garden which was pebbled and surrounded on three sides by feathered ferns and flowered bushes in great earthenware pots, in the middle of which sat several tables and chairs and upholstered loungers. More steps led down to the next two tiers of lawns embowered with vegetation, and then there was only an endless sweep of sand and blue sea beyond.

Cypresses flanked the sides of the garden and the scent of myriad blossoms was heavy and sweet, vying with the distinctive salt of the sea. The flowers and trees and green grass, the whiteness of the sand beyond and the dazzling blue of the sea in the clear, hard light was breathtaking, the sea appearing to be a flat shimmering sheet of blue watered silk.

'Beautiful, is it not?' Andreas spoke softly at the side of her, his eyes on her entranced gaze.

'Incredible,' she agreed faintly. Paradise on earth.

'There is only the occasional property dotted here and there along the coastline,' Andreas said quietly, 'and the beach is always empty. You can imagine you are the only person alive in all the world down there, and you never see another soul.'

'Hence the skinny-dipping?' It was out before she thought about it but she'd instantly imagined him cutting through the water.

He smiled, a slow, sexy smile. 'Hence the skinny-dipping,' he agreed softly. And then he bent and kissed her, a light, skimming kiss that nevertheless sent frissons of pleasure into every nerve and sinew. He smelt of the flowers and the sea and sunshine, and something else. Something very male and heady that curled her toes in her smart shoes and made her want to run her hands over his hard, broad shoulders and tangle her fingers in his hair, tugging his mouth closer and closer.

'Come and sit down and Alethea will bring you a drink,' Andreas said easily as he led her down the steps to a table and chairs shaded by the feathered leaves of a jacaranda. 'As well as being my driver, Paul makes the best cocktail you will ever taste, and at this time of the evening, after the sort of day I've had, nothing else will do. I won't be long.'

And so she sat in the captivating surroundings, her eyes roaming over the hypnotisingly lovely view as she soaked up the warmth and pungent, exotic perfume of the vegetation and sipped Paul's cocktail, which was as delicious as Andreas had promised.

Andreas joined her after a few minutes, his damp hair curling slightly on to his brow. It gave the hard, handsome face a touch of boyishness that was dynamite, and it took a moment or two for Sophy to be able to say, her tone airy, 'Enjoy your shower?' while she pulled herself together.

'Heaven.' He smiled at her, his tone easy.

He'd changed into a short-sleeved charcoal shirt and black jeans after the shower and he looked devastatingly attractive. Sophy's gaze jerked away from his to conceal the rush of sexual hunger that had taken her completely unawares, and she took a hasty sip of the cocktail, needing the Dutch courage.

Andreas stretched out long legs with a sigh of contentment, draining his glass in a couple of swallows and refilling it from the cocktail shaker he had brought out with him. After one long swallow he placed his glass on the table at the side of him and shut his eyes, his face raised to the sun. 'I want you to let me show you a little of my country while you are here,' he said quietly without moving. 'Some of ancient Greece.'

She glanced at the strong lean body and chiselled face, noticing how thick his eyelashes were as they rested on the tanned skin of his face, and her voice was a little throaty as she said, 'That's very kind, but it's not necessary.'

'Don't be so English.' It was mild but Sophy wasn't fooled by his relaxed manner. 'There are some wonderful sights not too far away, and it would only mean us staying overnight once or twice in the odd place. Thessaloniki has a superb museum holding the gold of King Philip, and at Pella there is the birthplace of Alexander the Great, and the earliest mosaics in Greece. You can't leave Greece without visiting the Acropolis and Mount Olympus, and there's the rock formations of Meteora and much more all within driving distance.'

Sophy hadn't heard anything more after the staying overnight bit. She drew a deep breath and said quietly, 'That's impossible and you know it. I couldn't possibly take off with you anywhere.'

'Why? You wanted me to tell you about Greece. I'm showing you instead, which is far better,' he said reasonably, 'now isn't it?'

'Not with Jill to consider, not to mention your work.'

He opened his eyes and sat up straighter. 'I'm the boss; I can take a few days holiday if I like,' he said mildly, 'and I know for a fact that Jill and Michael have been invited on a trip on Stevos's parents's yacht. If Jill knows that you will be otherwise occupied, she wouldn't feel so bad about leaving you.'

'Jill didn't say anything to me about a trip.' Sophy felt ridiculously hurt that Andreas knew more than she did.

'Perhaps because she doesn't know yet,' Andreas

drawled lazily, 'but Stevos's father works for me and he told me what he had in mind. I thought it was an excellent idea.'

Sophy stared at him. If it wasn't the height of presumption, she could almost imagine that Andreas had put Stevos's father up to this, but that was too ridiculous. He wouldn't do all that just to be with her. 'Whatever, I couldn't possibly just take off with you,' she repeated firmly. 'You know I couldn't.'

He sent her a mildly amused smile that didn't reach his eyes. 'You could do exactly that,' he argued gently.

'Whatever would your parents think?'

'That I was being the perfect host?' he suggested softly.

'Ha!' She glared at him, hardly able to believe he was serious.

Andreas considered her for another moment. 'Is that rather cryptic exclamation supposed to mean something?' he asked at last.

He was being purposely obtuse. 'You know exactly what it means,' Sophy fumed, swigging the last of her cocktail in her anger, and ignoring the warning the fuzziness in her head was trying to give her regarding the potency of Paul's cocktails. 'It would look as if—' She stopped abruptly, seeing that the amusement had now crept into his eyes and that his firm mouth was twitching slightly. He was laughing at her! She gritted her teeth and continued, 'As if we were more than just friends.'

'Separate rooms, I promise.' He surveyed her from under dark brows. 'And I'll make that clear to everyone, although why on earth two adults of our age have to answer to anyone but ourselves beats me,' he finished as though she was being unreasonable.

'Because I'm not like that and I don't want your parents to get the wrong idea,' she hissed tightly. 'I wouldn't dream of going to bed with someone I hardly know.'

'Exactly.' His smile was as sharp as a knife. 'And the best way to get to know someone is to spend time with them, right? We'll explore together, eat together, be together. No strings attached and strictly on your terms. You are Jill's sister, Michael is our shared nephew, so we owe it to them to be nice to each other, yes?'

'That's the worst line I've heard yet.' She scowled at him to prevent her lips twitching with amusement at his transparent hypocrisy. 'I can't believe you'd use an innocent little boy to get your own way.'

'Neither can I,' he said with a remarkable lack of remorse. 'It just shows me what lengths you've driven me to. You ought to be ashamed of yourself,' he added reprovingly.

'Me?' There was no way, no way on earth she would agree to such a crazy, dangerous suggestion. 'Me ashamed of myself?'

'Say you will come, Sophy.' He'd risen swiftly to his feet, pulling her up with him, and as always his accent gave her name a sensuousness an English voice couldn't hope to achieve. He kissed her, hard and long and very completely, and by the end of it her breath was shuddering and her legs were fluid. The heat of the sun was warm now rather than hot, the fierceness of the day mellowing to a delicious caress, and overhead a lone gull wheeled and circled in the air currents calling its melancholy cry to the wind. Nothing seemed real any more, only Andreas…

'Just a few days out of real life,' he whispered coaxingly against her mouth, teasing her with his tongue. 'A golden time to remember.' His hands came up to frame her face and they were gentle, incredibly gentle for such a big man. 'It will be good.'

He kissed her again, tasting and teasing until she kissed him back, and then his hands followed the smooth line of her throat, over the soft swell of her breasts where they lingered to caress the peaks into tortured life before continuing to the narrow span of her waist. 'Just a few days,' he murmured again.

He kept the pace slow, kissing her deeply one moment and then returning to cover her forehead, her temples, her eyelids, her cheekbones in hot little burning kisses that made her mouth search for his long before he assuaged its hunger once again.

The blood was surging through her veins now in a riot of sensation, the scent of him all about her as his lips and his hands continued to work their magic.

She could feel him trembling as he pulled her hard into the length of him, the kiss suddenly deepening into sheer hot and heady passion as she felt the power of his arousal against her softness. And then, almost as though he had recognised his control was slipping, he moved her away from him slightly, kissing her hard one last time before he said, 'Say yes, Sophy.'

She opened heavy lids, shattered and breathless by the flood of feelings he'd ignited and her head whirling. 'Andreas—'

'Say yes,' he commanded again, his dark eyes glittering as they looked down into her flushed face. 'Nothing will happen that you do not want, I promise you this.'

'You promise?' Her eyes were still dilated with desire. 'Separate rooms and nothing heavy?'

'If that is what you want.'

'It is.'

'Then so be it.'

And it was done.

CHAPTER EIGHT

'YOU'VE done *what*?'

Jill's voice was a screech and not at all like its normal soft self. Sophy stared at her sister, glad she'd waited to tell her about her trip with Andreas when they were alone. Dimitra and Evangelos had taken their grandson to visit some friends who ran riding stables, but Jill—who preferred her horses in fields at a safe distance and had no interest in equine pursuits—had opted to stay at the villa.

'I've said I'll go on a little sight-seeing trip with him for a couple of days,' Sophy repeated flatly. 'That's all. And I've made it clear it's not a Mr and Mrs Jones thing, if that's what's bothering you. He's booking separate rooms.'

'I can't believe I'm hearing this. Is it the sun, or what? Something's addled your brain.' Jill stared at her, her eyes wide.

Sophy had been thinking the same thing herself, right from the moment the limousine had dropped her home the night before and she had watched it draw away, Andreas's big figure next to Paul's suddenly becoming that of a near stranger again. But it hadn't felt like that when she had been with him at his home. The whole evening had been wonderful, magical, and the full enormity of what she had promised had only hit when she had stood by herself on the steps watching the car move away.

'I mean, you've always been the one who's tried to stop me doing daft things,' Jill continued plaintively. 'This just isn't like you, Sophy. And with Andreas, of all people.'

No, it wasn't like her. Sophy tried to quell the panic that had been churning her stomach at intervals ever since she had sat in her room last night. She had only managed a couple of hours' sleep. 'It's just a couple of days,' she repeated, as much for her benefit as Jill's. 'It doesn't mean anything.'

'I'm sure it doesn't, not to Andreas.' And then, as Sophy winced visibly, Jill said quickly, 'Oh, I'm sorry, sis, I am really, but I don't want you getting hurt. Andreas is… Well, he's just one of those men who's got everything, isn't he? And the women love him. He's more than able to look on this as a little flirtation and no doubt he's expecting you to do the same. A good time had by both and no regrets sort of approach. But you aren't like that. The trouble is…'

'What?' As Jill's voice trailed away, Sophy repeated, 'What were you going to say?'

'The trouble is, you look so different on the outside to how you are on the inside,' Jill said woefully, suddenly reaching out and clasping her sister's hands in her own. 'I didn't realise it when we were younger. I took you completely for granted, I suppose, but the way Mum was and us never knowing him, our father—' neither Jill or Sophy had ever been able to bring themselves to use the more familiar term of 'dad' '—affected you much more than it did me. You used to look after me, shield me from so much, but the consequences of all that mean you're—'

'What?' Sophy said again. 'Come on, Jill. Spit it out.'

'Damaged,' Jill said reluctantly, waiting for the blast.

'*Damaged?*' Now it was Sophy's turn to show outrage. 'Excuse me, but hold your horses here, Jill.' She wrenched her hands away, standing up and moving away from the patio where the two of them had been enjoying morning elevenses in the sunshine, before turning and facing her sister again, her face scarlet.

'I am most certainly not damaged,' she bit out firmly, 'and if anyone but you had had the cheek to say that they'd

have had a good slap. I can't believe you've been thinking
that about me.'

'Sophy, listen to me.' In her agitation Jill was wringing
her hands, and as though suddenly becoming aware of it
she placed them palm down on the top of the patio table.
'I'm not criticizing you, far from it, but you need to have
everything in order in your life; you always have done. You
have to be in control.'

'That's not a crime,' Sophy shot back quickly, 'or a personality defect. In fact, most people would look on it as an
asset, if anything. It's got me a great job, anyway, now
hasn't it?'

'And men?' Jill said very quietly. 'You've always gone
for the easy-going, academic type. Impractical in the main,
quiet, certainly unassuming. Nice, caring sort of men.'

'So?' Sophy glared at her. 'There's nothing wrong with
that, either?'

'So you can't put Andreas in that category, not remotely.'

They stared at each other for a full minute before Sophy
retraced her steps and sat down again, taking a long gulp
of coffee. 'I know that,' she said more quietly. 'I do *know*
that.'

'It's obvious there's something there between you; it has
been from day one,' Jill said softly at the side of her. 'Even
his parents recognised it. But whereas for Andreas this has
probably happened—' She stopped abruptly, colouring
slightly.

'Hundreds of times?' Sophy put in tightly. 'Is that it?'

'Well, yes. But you aren't like him. They don't know
you like I do, and I know that for you to be like you are
he's touched something deep inside. He'll hurt you, dev-
astate you, and he won't even know, Sophy. Don't you *see*?
He won't even realise.'

Sophy listened numbly to her own subconscious fears

being spoken out loud. She didn't try to argue with Jill any more because she knew her sister was only speaking the truth.

This fierce attraction she had for Andreas *was* something outside her understanding, and it frightened her as much as it thrilled. Even last night, when she had been wrapped in the magic he had created, she had been aware of the danger. Perhaps that was part of it—a sort of crazy rebellion against all the years of conforming? Most teenagers had their insurrectionary stage but she had never been able to indulge in such a luxury.

'If I say I know you are right and that I'll make very sure not to get involved, does that help?' she said after a few moments. 'If I promise to keep him at arm's length?'

'It does if I can be sure you really mean it and you aren't just saying it to make me feel better,' Jill said in true blunt sisterly fashion. 'But I've seen the way you look at each other.'

'I mean it.' Sophy raised her head and looked into the mirror image facing her with such concern. 'I promise. The thing is, I want to go, Jill. I've never felt so alive as I've felt the last few days and I want to have some fun, for once. I won't do anything silly, and Andreas knows I've got no intention of sleeping with him, but I just want to be with him for a while.'

'If that was supposed to make me feel better, it doesn't,' Jill said ruefully.

'Best you're going to get.' Sophy forced a quick grin. 'So, you'll be getting an invitation to go lording it on Stevos's father's yacht, and I'll be touring the country with one of its most eligible males. We never dreamt of that when we were sitting on the plane coming over, did we?'

'Oh, Sophy.' Jill's voice was troubled. 'Be careful.'

Two days later, when Sophy emerged into bright sunshine with her overnight case crammed to bursting, she glanced across the drive to where Andreas was sitting waiting for her in the sports car, the roof rolled back and his black hair shining in the white light. He looked every inch an icon of the silver screen.

She must be mad. The same thought had occurred at five-minute intervals all during the last forty-eight hours, but since talking to Jill a number of things had clarified in her mind.

Like Andreas himself had said, this would be a few days out of real life—a golden time to remember. She didn't intend to treat it anymore seriously than he did. She was physically attracted to him and she had to admit she liked his company—when he wasn't being confrontational and difficult, that was—but now she had acknowledged both those things she was in a position of control again. He knew the score, she hadn't tried to mislead him in any way—just the opposite—and he was quite prepared to accept this wasn't going to be a full-blown affair in the physical sense. She'd been totally up front and honest.

Anyway… She smiled at him as he raised a lazy hand in greeting. He probably secretly felt it was the best thing all round. With Jill being an in-law, it wasn't the most sensible thing in the world to have a fling with her sister. Too messy and potentially problematical, and she knew from little remarks Dimitra had let drop over the last few days that Andreas ran his life with a ruthless uncomplicatedness.

Yes, she could handle this. She could. But she was still probably mad! But a little summer madness was excusable, wasn't it?

The morning air was warm and moist, the sun blazing down out of a crystal blue sky, and as Sophy ran lightly over to the car Andreas slid out of the driver's seat and opened the small boot for her case.

'Good morning.' He kissed her full on the mouth before stepping back a pace, his eyes roaming over her clear creamy skin and blonde hair. She was wearing white cotton trousers and a white silk top and no make-up, and didn't look a day over twenty-one. 'You look like the essence of summer.'

'Do I?' She grinned back at him, determined to start as she meant to carry on and keep things light and amusing. She let her eyes run over the big muscled body clothed in black denim shirt and jeans, and wrinkled her smooth nose consideringly. 'You don't,' she pronounced at last, slanting a mocking glance out of blue eyes.

'Thank goodness for that. In the car, wench.'

That conversation set the tone for the most deliriously happy few days of Sophy's life. Andreas knew the surrounding country like the back of his hand and the first morning they went straight to Thessaloniki, Greece's second city, where they visited the Acropolis and Sophy stood spellbound by the panoramic view, before they paid a visit to the gold of King Philip.

They ate lunch mid afternoon in a tiny inn perched high on a flower-covered hillside, before continuing on to Pella where they browsed in the museum for a while along with seeing the superb ancient mosaics. It was fascinating and enthralling and slightly eerie.

Andreas took her to a small sweet little café with tiny carved wooden balconies and white-painted walls after they had emerged into languid evening sunshine, and they sat watching the world go by while drinking rich red wine and eating *keftedes* and warm garlic bread at a little table outside.

The evening sky was full of muted colours flowing into a lake of gold by the time they left, and they wandered through dusky streets where the odd intermittent barking of a dog or once, the unmistakable sound of a bonzouki could be heard. It was peaceful and timeless and possessed of a charm that couldn't be translated into words.

Their hotel was a modern one and, true to his word, Andreas left her at the door to her room, kissing her very thoroughly before he left. It took her a long time to get to sleep.

And so one golden day followed another. They talked and they laughed together, touched and tasted each other, but all within the constraints Sophy had set. She felt she had got to know Andreas better than she had ever known anyone in her life and, perversely, in the same breath, that the more she got to know him the less she seemed to understand.

When he suggested on the afternoon of the third day that they spend a couple of more days together she didn't object, dutifully phoning Jill to explain and to ask her sister how she and Michael had enjoyed the yacht, and then returning to the car and to Andreas with the others wiped clear from her mind the moment she put the telephone down.

They visited the spectacular Byzantine monasteries perched high on the cliffs at Meteora, the olive groves of Amphissa and much, much more, but on the night of the fourth day Sophy cried long and hard once she was alone in her hotel room.

Perhaps it was just that the idyll had ended and they had to go back to the real world the next day? she asked herself flatly, when—at two in the morning and utterly unable to sleep—she stepped on to the balcony of her small hotel room and sat looking out over quiet streets sleeping under a calm, deep midnight-blue sky pierced with stars. And soon she would be back in England, back in the frantic pace of life that she had thought she loved but which now seemed so far away.

Why hadn't Andreas tried to make love to her? The thought she had been ignoring for the last two or three days

wouldn't be denied any more. She hadn't expected he
would be so crass for the first twenty-four hours or so, and
she knew she had *told* him this trip had to be a platonic
one, but why hadn't he pushed things? He was that sort of
man, wasn't he? The sort that took what he wanted, regardless of anyone else? Wasn't he?

Of course, she would have fought him and made it clear
an affair wasn't on the cards, but she didn't understand
this…control. It could only mean he had mastered the feeling he had had for her. And yet the way he kissed her, the
way he held her *wasn't* platonic. She had expected him to
try and cajole her, to use his infinite experience to sweep
her off her feet—something! But he wasn't conforming to
the mental summing up she had made of him before the
trip.

She frowned to herself, her face feeling tight after the
tears she had shed earlier and her mind in turmoil. There
had been Jill warning her to be on her guard before she
had left, and Andreas hadn't put a foot out of place. It
would be funny if it wasn't so humiliating. And she did
feel humiliated…and hurt, which was utterly unreasonable,
of course. She ought to be glad he'd kept to their bargain.
It had saved any unpleasantness and meant they could part
as friends when she left for England.

Andreas was in the room next to her; what would he say
if she knocked on his door and asked to go in? She had
had the odd crazy thought like this one over the last few
days—impulses to reach up and tug his mouth down to hers
at the strangest moments, or suddenly throw herself into his
arms and ask him to make love to her. Impulses she'd denied, but which refused to lie down and die. It was high
time she was back at the villa with Jill and Michael. She
nodded silently at the thought. Andreas had exploded into
her life with all the dark force of a nuclear missile and
embedded himself deep in her psyche. No one had ever

affected her like this and she didn't recognise herself any more.

She shivered, although the night was warm and humid, and stepped back into the bedroom. She was just about to close the balcony windows when she heard the ones next door flung open.

A single thickness of white-painted brickwork on both sides of the balcony gave the rooms privacy, but she could distinctly hear Andreas sigh as he sat down on one of the wicker chairs the balconies contained, and then she heard the chink of a glass.

He couldn't sleep, either. She wouldn't have believed how comforting the thought was as a little tingle of something like excitement slid down her spine and her heart began to pound. Perhaps he was thinking of her? Maybe his body and mind were as restless as hers—knowing full well what was needed to assuage the craving that was part pain, part pleasure.

Should she call out softly to him? Suggest they share a nightcap together as they were both awake? And if by any chance one thing led to another—well, it wasn't a crime, was it? She wanted him, needed him, tonight. She ached for his touch.

The sudden realisation of where her mind had gone came like a physical jolt, and it was in that second Sophy realised that much more than her body was involved in her feelings for Andreas. She had fallen for him. Okay, so she wasn't sure if it was love or not—certainly this emotion was as different to the quiet, comfortable contentedness she'd felt with Matthew as it was possible to be—but something in her spirit had been drawn to him from their first meeting and she had started fighting it from that point, too.

'Oh, no…' It was just the faintest of whispers and he couldn't possibly have heard it, but she covered her mouth tightly with the palm of one hand none the less.

Not Andreas Karydis. She couldn't have been so stupid. He was everything she *didn't* like in a man, so how had it happened? He was arrogant and forceful and intensely physical, and in spite of the good time they had had over the last days she didn't doubt for a minute that he could be utterly ruthless and subjective when he had to be. Or when he wanted to be. And he had already made it abundantly clear that he wanted her physically and that was the point of his interest. Dress it up how you like, that was what it boiled down to.

She stepped quietly away from the windows which she left slightly ajar, fearing he would hear if she tried to shut them again, and fumbled among her things for the packet of painkillers she'd brought with her. The weeping she'd indulged in earlier, combined with lack of sleep, had created a nagging ache at the base of her skull, which had got distinctly worse in the last few minutes.

She wasn't going to think about anything any more. She took two of the painkillers with a drink of water and climbed back into bed, drawing the stiff hotel covers over her tense body and willing herself not to cry again. She would be more level-headed in the morning; everything always seemed at its blackest in the hours before dawn.

When Sophy came downstairs in the rather quaint, old-fashioned hotel they had booked into the night before, Andreas was already seated, reading the newspaper, at a table for two in the far corner of the small, flower-festooned dining room. He was sitting next to an open window which overlooked the hotel's pretty cobbled courtyard, which was complete with a sparkling fountain, and for a moment Sophy stood still in the doorway as she looked at him before he became aware of her presence.

The white sunlight picked up a sheen of blue in the jet-black hair and he was frowning slightly as he read, a little habit of his she had noticed over the last few days.

There was something so magnetic about his good looks, his whole persona, she thought weakly. And yet it wasn't really his looks, nor even his powerful body or dark sexiness. She couldn't find words, not even to herself, to explain the age-old call, but it was there, and it was virile and consuming and infinitely dangerous.

Being with him so closely over the last few days had confirmed what she had sensed the first time she'd met him—that women would want him, and badly. He would only have to lift his little finger and they'd come running. To get emotionally involved with a man like him would be a constant agony of wondering. Wondering if one female, more gorgeous or just plain predatory than the rest, had managed to get his attention. Wondering where he was if he was late any time and whether this was the day you would be replaced in his affections. Wondering how long you could hang on to him and to your sanity...

'Miss Fearn?' The young waitress who had served them dinner the night before was at her side, and as Sophy came out of the black thoughts she smiled at the pretty face but didn't correct the girl, letting the Miss ride because it was simpler. Perhaps if you got involved with a man like Andreas you had to let a lot of things ride to keep things simple, she thought bleakly. Other women's come-hither smiles and his responses, a phone call that was supposedly a wrong number, the faint odour of a different perfume to her own or a trace of lipstick...

She had listened to friends and colleagues list all those things during marital or long-term break-ups in her time, and on each occasion she had thought of her mother and the pain her father must have inflicted on a woman whose only mistake was to love her husband utterly. *And whatever her father had had to draw the opposite sex, Andreas had it tenfold.*

She followed the waitress across to the table automatically, forcing a smile as Andreas looked up at their approach. 'What is it? You look pale. Are you unwell?'

He was all concern, but she couldn't keep the thread of stiffness out of her voice as she said, 'No, no I'm all right. I just didn't sleep too well. The bed was lumpy.'

'I told you we should have gone to a more modern hotel, but you insisted you found this one picturesque.'

The tender indulgence with which he spoke was untenable, and her voice was sharp as she said, 'I'm not complaining, merely answering your question.'

Her tone straightened his face and narrowed his eyes, but after a long look at her white complexion he merely said quietly, 'I have waited for you before ordering. I intend to have croissants followed by a full English breakfast. What would you like?'

Sophy glanced up at the waitress. 'Just croissants and coffee for me please.' She had snapped at him and been unforgivably rude; if she hadn't realised it herself the touch of steel in the square jaw would have told her. But this…whatever it was—flirtation, tenuous dalliance, sexual game—had to stop. It had to finish where it mattered, in her head.

She was getting in too deep and Jill had been right after all. He was tying her up in knots and she wasn't even sure if he was aware of it. All she did know was that the more she was with him, the more she fell under his spell, and what would be the outcome? What *could* be the outcome? A brief affair and then a lifetime of regret. He had pursued her because he wanted her physically and she hadn't fallen into his arms like his other women. She appeared unattainable and that had intrigued him.

She remembered her mother saying once, with pathetic

pride, that she had worn her white dress on her wedding day with every right to do so. Whether it had been due to her principles or a strategic plan, her mother had netted her father because she hadn't given him what most other females had been only too ready to give, but it hadn't altered the basic character of the man. Nothing could do that. She'd be fooling herself to think otherwise.

'Okay, what has happened?' Andreas's voice was very quiet.

Sophy glanced at him and found the grey eyes were tight on her face, his own countenance expressionless. She took a deep breath before she could say, 'I don't know what you mean.'

'Don't give me that.' It was low and controlled but intense. 'You are a different woman to the one of the last few days,' he said grimly. 'This Sophy is the one who looked at me with such dislike at the airport, but I thought we had left that behind us.'

'Don't be silly.' Even to herself her voice sounded desperate. 'How could I have looked at you like that when I didn't even know you? And how could anything have happened since last night?'

'This I do not know but I intend to find out,' he said softly.

'There's nothing *to* find out.' This was awful, and it was all her fault. 'You'll just have to take my word on that.'

'So you are the same happy, sparkling-eyed girl of the last few days?' he bit out caustically. 'Is that what you are saying?'

She stared at him miserably. 'It's the end of the sightseeing,' she said flatly. 'Time to…to get back to normal.'

'Normal?' He flung the paper to one side and leant close to her, taking one of her wrists in his hand as he stopped her instinctive jerk backwards. 'And what is your definition of normal, Sophy? Nothing about this relationship is normal as far as I can see.'

'Please, Andreas.' His fingers were like steel and soon people would begin to notice. 'You're hurting me.'

'Whatever it is that holds you from the past is like a lead weight round your neck,' he grated softly, 'and, believe me, Sophy, it is not normal. You asked me for time and I have given you time, but you are acting as though I forced myself on you last night rather than taking umpteen cold showers and walking the floor until dawn. What the hell do you want from me, anyway?'

'Nothing,' she shot back quickly. 'I want nothing from you. I didn't ask to come on this trip; it was your idea. Remember?'

He let go of her then, settling back in his seat as his eyes continued to hold hers, their grey depths shining silver. 'Yes, I remember,' he said softly after a few seconds had ticked away in a screaming silence that was painful.

The waitress chose that moment to bustle up with coffee and croissants, managing—whether by chance or design—to brush Andreas's shoulder with one ripe breast as she placed their food in front of them. The fact that Andreas didn't appear to notice the manoeuvre was scant comfort to Sophy, and the other woman's actions seemed to confirm everything she was thinking.

'She likes you.' As the waitress disappeared in a flourish of black cotton and lacy white apron, Sophy's voice was very low. Part of her couldn't believe she'd actually said it out loud.

'What?' Andreas had been about to pour them coffee but now he froze, his eyes narrowing still further. 'Who likes me?'

'The waitress,' Sophy said woodenly. 'She likes you.'

'What the hell are you talking about?'

'She wanted you to notice her.'

'Well, I didn't.' He poured two cups of coffee, settled back in his seat again and then stood up, his voice a growl as he said, 'Damn it, I'm not sitting here like this when I want to talk to you, and I sure as hell can't do it in here.'

He pulled her up none too gently and then, despite her protests, all but frogmarched her out of the dining room and out of the hotel into the street outside. He didn't say a word as he whisked her along the pavement to a little dusty square at the end of the street, but after pushing her down on a gnarled wooden bench, sat down beside her. 'I've got the feeling I missed something back there,' he said grimly, 'and I do not like that. Now, explain.'

She stared at him, at the handsome face now set in dark angry lines, at the big broad shoulders and powerful chest, and suddenly wished she was back to yesterday morning when life had been golden.

There was a radio blaring somewhere and a baby crying in the old, gently decaying houses surrounding the square, but apart from a couple of pigeons pecking somewhat lethargically at a piece of stale bread, the place was deserted. 'I want to go back to the hotel,' she said stiffly. 'Right now.'

'Tough.' He eyed her implacably. 'If I'd got what I wanted we would have spent the last four days in bed instead of skirting the issue.' He was clearly determined not to let her off the hook.

'What issue?' She tried not to think about the bed bit.

'You know damn well what issue,' he growled softly. 'The issue of us, and don't say there isn't an us because we wouldn't be here now if there wasn't.'

'There isn't—'

He cut off her voice by the simple expedient of taking her mouth in a kiss that had no gentleness but was all fire and thunder. His lips were urgent and burning as his fingers tangled in her hair, and he crushed her against him almost angrily, forcing her lips apart and exploring her mouth with an arrogance that spoke of possession.

He hadn't kissed her like this before, and although she struggled for a few seconds the swift, hot and insistent flow of desire that immediately scorched her nerve endings was too strong to fight. She wanted him, wanted to be held by him like this.

She fell against him, there in the square in the bright hot sunlight as the kiss deepened still more, his mouth savaging hers, and as always when he so much as touched her the rest of the world faded away.

'*Diabolos.*' It was Andreas who pulled away. 'You say there is no us when I could take you here, now, in the open and you would not resist me?'

Sophy lifted her chin, her heartbeat threatening to choke her as she struggled to control the alien passions his lips and body invoked. 'It was just a kiss,' she said numbly.

He nodded, his eyes merciless. 'But if we had been in your room or mine and I had not stopped, what would it have been then? You want me every little bit as much as I want you, and I am done playing these games. I have been patient and still you fight me, even as your body betrays you every time I touch you. You have been married and so it is not sexual inexperience that holds you back.' He glared at her, his mouth grim.

There was sexual experience and then there was sexual experience, Sophy thought bitterly, and she didn't doubt for a moment she knew none of the tricks and sexual gymnastics a man like Andreas would expect of a woman.

'So, what is it?' he continued relentlessly. 'Why do you continue to fight me and yourself? Are you afraid of me?'

She had to make him see that there could never be anything between them and only the truth—or a limited version of it—would do that. She nerved herself and said quietly, 'Yes.'

His eyebrows rose at the unexpected honesty and he tensed for a moment, before visibly forcing himself to relax and gentling his voice as he said, 'I don't understand, Sophy. Why? What have I done to make you fear me?'

'It's not what you have done.' There was no easy way to say it. 'It's what—who—you are.'

For a moment she was frightened at the look which came over his face, but instead of the explosion she expected his voice was even more controlled when he said coldly, 'Let's take the first definition as the one you really meant, shall we? What, exactly, do you think I am?'

'You…you like women and they like you.' Put like that it sounded ridiculous, and Andreas wasn't slow to capitalise on the fact.

'In other words, I am a normal heterosexual male,' he stated with silky softness. 'Are you telling me this is my crime?'

'No.' She swallowed painfully. He wasn't going to make this easy, but then she hadn't expected him to. 'What I mean is, women will always chase a man like you. There's something about you…' This was going even more badly than she'd feared. 'It's not really your fault,' she finished weakly. 'But I…I don't want to be one of many. Some women can handle that but I can't.'

'Let's get this straight.' His face and body were rigid with rage, only his mouth moved in the carved structure of his countenance and his eyes were as cold and as hard as the rest of him. She didn't recognise the man in front of her as the Andreas she knew, this was a stranger. She could see now how he could effortlessly take over his father's empire and run it even more efficiently than Evangelos; he had only to display a fraction of the ruthlessness that was staring out of his face and any opposition would crumple. He was formidable and she felt scared to death.

'You are saying that I am a philanderer, a womaniser, yes? A Don Juan who keeps his brains in his trousers?'

She flinched a little at the crudity, her eyes opening wide with shock. 'No, no, I'm not saying that.' And she wasn't…was she? She suddenly realised she didn't know what she was saying. 'Just that it would be only natural for you to—'

'Spread myself round a little?' he cut in brutally. Dark colour flared across the hard cheekbones, his grey eyes narrowed and points of steel. 'And you have been thinking this all along, I take it?' he ground out slowly. 'Even the last few days? How charming.'

He was looking at her as though he had never seen her before and now hot panic was surging through her as she realised the enormity of what she had done. She should never have said anything, she told herself wretchedly, but even now a little voice deep within answered, But you had to, you had to. You couldn't have a relationship with a man like Andreas.

'So I am one of those weak and distasteful characters who sleep around and have a different woman for every day of the week?' He rose, staring down into her horrified face with hooded eyes. 'I think we had better get back to the hotel. The sight-seeing, as you pointed out earlier, is over,' he bit out rawly.

'Andreas, don't be like this. Please don't be like this.'

'Like what? Believe me, Sophy, if a man had said half of what you have I would have taken pleasure in rearranging his face. You have labelled me as a stud stallion from the first moment we met and yet you were the one who informed me you do not care for labels.'

The contemptuous statement was nothing less than the truth and his withering scorn brought her shoulders hunching as she too rose from the seat. She had no defence. None.

'Even the worst criminal knows of what he is accused

before he is condemned,' Andreas bit out disgustedly, 'but you sat safe in your little ivory tower and was judge and jury. How many times did I inadvertently say or do something to add weight to my sentence? Did you find it amusing that I was so obviously interested in you? Did you look forward to the moment when you would throw it all back in my face?'

'No!' This had all gone so terribly wrong. 'No, of course not,' she said desperately. 'It wasn't like that. I thought—' What had she thought? She didn't know now. 'I thought we could be friends,' she said helplessly.

'Friends?' He smiled a thin smile that was merely a bitter twisting of his lips. 'There was never any possibility of us being friends, Sophy, so do not lie to yourself. It was always going to be all or nothing.'

He turned from her, leaving her with no choice but to follow him as he walked out of the square and began striding towards the hotel, his body language stating all too clearly he was done with her. She had got what she wanted and she couldn't bear it.

The journey back to Halkidiki was one Sophy wouldn't have wished on her worst enemy. Andreas drove fast and furiously, his face grim and his hands gripping the steering wheel as though he wished it were her neck.

They stopped for lunch in a small town between Dion and Thessaloniki, and after Sophy had tried to apologise and Andreas had cut her off with a voice like ice, she had to force the food past the massive constriction in her throat. She managed it, just, but it sat in her stomach like a stone the rest of the way back to the villa. Which was only what she deserved, she thought.

As they passed through the gates of the estate, the afternoon sun was still high in the sky, and as Sophy saw the familiar building in front of them after they had turned a corner in the long drive she had to fight an absurd desire to cry. She had been so happy when she had left here a few days ago, and now things couldn't be worse. And it was her fault.

'Andreas?' As the car came to a halt she spoke quickly before she lost her nerve. 'I know you are angry with me but could we at least put on some kind of show so as not to upset the others? They won't understand.'

'*I* do not understand,' he shot back violently, before taking an audible breath and flexing his hands on the steering wheel. He breathed deeply once or twice and then said, 'Of course we can be civil, but I think it will be best if I do not trouble you again during the rest of your visit. There are many matters awaiting my attention at work, so this will be quite acceptable.'

He had exited the car before she could say anything more, striding round to the passenger door and helping her out with a formality that made her heart bleed.

Once in the house, Ainka met them in the sunlit hall with the news that the others were out for the day and wouldn't be home until late, and then disappeared upstairs with Sophy's case.

'Thank you for…for showing me around.'

Sophy's voice was small, and Andreas glanced down at her, his face hard. And then he became still when he noticed the tell tale sheen of the tears she was trying to hide. '*Diabolos.*' It was a low muttered oath, and when he took her arm, marshalling her roughly into the dining room and slamming the door behind them, she didn't try to resist.

'This is crazy—you know that, don't you?' His voice was not quiet or conciliatory and the room crackled with tension. 'You insult me and then you look at me the way you did just then. What the hell is the matter with you?'

'Nothing.' All the way home in the car she had been praying for him to give her another chance, to at least let her explain the unexplainable, but now the moment was here all the fears of twenty-eight years rose up in a flood again. She wanted him too much, that was the trouble. She loved him. She had been fighting it for days but now she had to admit it. She loved him in a way she had never loved Matthew, never imagined herself loving, and that made his power over her unthinkable.

'Nothing? You can say nothing?' He gave a harsh bark of a laugh but his voice had been agonised, desperate. 'I touch you and you melt for me—that is not nothing. I do not believe you have ever felt this way before because I know I have not.'

She didn't want to hear this, *couldn't* hear it. She had to believe she was doing the right thing, the only thing.

'Listen to me, Sophy.' He took her arms in his, holding her in front of him as he looked down into her face with burning eyes. 'There was a girl once, many years ago. We were going to be married and then I found out she was playing around. The same old story that happens a hundred times a day. I finished it but I told myself I would never meet anyone else I cared for like I did Larissa. And then I met you and I knew I had never loved her as I was meant to love.'

'No.' Her face was white. 'No, you don't love me.'

'Yes.' He shook her slightly, his body rigid. 'I've had relationships since Larissa but I have always known, and the women have too, that they couldn't go anywhere. But this is different.'

'You thought you loved Larissa but now you say you didn't,' she whispered through pale lips. 'You would say the same to me in time. Someone would come along, someone younger and prettier. And we hardly know each other, anyway,' she finished desperately.

'I have known you from the beginning of time,' he said softly. 'I recognised it that night by the pool, and so did you.'

'No.' She tried to struggle free but he wouldn't let her. 'I don't want this. I don't want you.'

'You want me.' His voice was as hard as steel.

'No.' Fear made her cruel. 'I despise the sort of man you are.'

'Despise me?' His voice was harsh again. 'You couldn't respond like this to a man you despise.'

The kiss was as savagely challenging as his words and continued to be so until she stopped struggling. By the time the force had gone the power of his mouth was holding her more effectively than anything else could have done, and she was accepting his hands and his mouth blindly.

Each one of his kisses was more urgent, deeper, hungrier, and she was answering the desperate need with a desire to match his, passion sending rivulets of sensation into every part of her. His hands had slid under the soft material of her top, sliding over the silky skin beneath as he explored her rounded curves until she moaned beneath his lips.

His tongue was probing, thrusting, sending electric currents coursing through her body as she melted against him, the relentless plundering of her mouth and the sure firm hands on her body creating a throbbing in the core of her that she'd never experienced before. Her body felt hot and molten, and she was no longer sure who was leading and who was following, she just knew she wanted more.

'You see, Sophy?' His voice was shaking, the tremours that pulsed the big male frame echoed in hers. 'You see how it is?'

She couldn't deny the messages her flesh was sending to his, but his voice was a subtle intrusion into the world of colour and light and sensation beneath her closed eyelids, and she opened heavy lids, her mind dizzy.

'This is real,' he said softly. 'I am real. Me, Andreas Karydis. I want you because I love you. Do you understand?'

She wanted to believe him. With all her heart she wanted to believe him but in the final analysis she dared not. She had seen what loving a man with all one's heart and mind and soul and body had done to her mother, and she couldn't cope with that sort of consuming emotion. It had been safe with Matthew; she had been in control and, although life had never been exciting or possessed of highs and lows, it *had* been her life. She had held the strings and kept her autonomy.

And suddenly she saw very clearly what she had to do. Struggling for calmness, she backed away from him, praying she would have the strength to say it all without breaking down.

'I understand,' she said quietly, 'and I love you, too.'

He waited, knowing from the look on her face and the tone of her voice that in spite of her confession something was still terribly, terribly wrong.

'And because I feel like I do, I can't be with you, Andreas.'

He did react then, taking a step towards her which was instantly checked when she said, her hands raised to ward him off, 'Please listen to me. I…I'll try to explain and then you'll see there can't be any sort of future for us.'

She told him it all, starting from the first time, as a small child of perhaps three or four, that she remembered asking about her father. The picture in the attic, her difficult childhood, the heartache and bitterness of spirit that eventually killed her mother, it all came pouring out. 'Jill said something recently that I vehemently objected to,' she finished sadly. 'She said I was damaged. I hated that—it suggests some sort of victim thing—but none the less she's right. I can't change the way I am and all I'd do was to make us both miserable and destroy anything we had, even if—' She stopped abruptly.

'Even if?'

She raised her chin at his soft voice. 'I was going to say even if you are not like my father,' she said jerkily. 'You see, you see how it is? I don't believe you, Andreas. I can't trust you. I care too much to be able to do that. All the time I'd be waiting. No one can live like that.'

She knew from the unmasked agony in the beautiful silver-grey eyes that he knew she meant it. 'So you run back to your insulated little bubble in England, is that it?' he grated. 'Where you consider yourself impregnable. To a life that is risk-free. A life that will eventually dry you up and shrivel everything that makes you you. Fear will turn you into a lonely young woman and then a lonely old one, and it is a poor bedfellow. You have met me now; I shall be there in your head even if you shut me out of your flesh. You can't go back to the way things were before you came here.'

'I can try.' She had to do this for both their sakes, but it was killing her. 'It will be me that suffers, after all.'

'You still don't get it, do you?' He stared at her, his face set and the note of pleading gone from his voice. 'You as an individual finished the day we met. When you suffer, I suffer now. We are in this together. Your pain is my pain, the same as your joy and happiness would be my joy and happiness. Don't you see what you have done, Sophy? You have become part of me and you won't alter that by going away.'

'You'll meet someone else one day.' Even as she said it she knew how trite and insulting it sounded after what he'd just said.

'Thank you.' It was cutting.

Sophy tried to think of something else to say but failed utterly. They remained staring at each other for a moment more before he said, 'Your mind is made up,' and it was a statement of fact, not a question. Nevertheless, she nodded her answer.

He nodded himself, the action curt. 'Goodbye, Sophy.'

'Goodbye.' She felt sick with pain and panic, but deep inside the alternative path—to reach out to him, to say she would love and trust him as he wanted—was as unthinkable as ever.

He gave her one last searching look and then walked across to the door, opening it and passing into the hall beyond without looking back. She heard the front door open and close, and then the roar of the powerful engine on the drive outside.

He had gone. He had left her as she had demanded she be left and he wouldn't try again. Not after all that had been said.

She had got what she wanted and the future couldn't have been more desolate.

CHAPTER NINE

THE rest of the week was torturous but eventually the morning dawned when they were flying home.

Sophy had related the true state of affairs to Jill once her sister had got back to the villa on the day she and Andreas had parted, and Jill had nobly forgone any 'I told you so's', but to Dimitra and Evangelos Sophy had just said she'd enjoyed the sight-seeing trip but Andreas had mentioned he had plenty of work to catch up on. She didn't know if they believed her and she didn't actually care; she was so consumed with misery that, selfishly, nothing else mattered but Andreas.

From a comment dropped at the dinner table the day after she and Andreas had returned from their trip, Sophy learnt from Evangelos that Andreas had flown to America that morning on urgent business and wasn't expected to return for a couple of weeks.

She had been amazed how the news had hit her. The fact that there was no likelihood of seeing him again should have relieved some of her tension and strain, but instead it had sent her falling into a deep well of despair that seemed bottomless.

She combated her wretchedness by forcing herself to appear normal—playing with Michael, chatting to Dimitra and steering the conversation away from Andreas any time she and Jill were alone and her sister tried to bring his name up. She knew Jill meant well and was worried she was bottling all her pain and anguish, but Sophy could no more have discussed the situation than she could have sprouted wings and flown.

Funnily enough, the morning of their departure was a rainy one—the first rain they had seen since landing in Greece. Sophy felt slightly guilty that she welcomed the drizzle but the overcast sky and grey clouds fitted her state of mind much better than the radiantly blue sky and bright sunshine of the previous weeks.

This time it was Evangelos who drove them to the airport, in the prestigious and beautiful Mercedes, much to Michael's delight. The little boy sat at the front with his grandfather and he chattered the whole way to the airport, taking the strain of having to join in any conversation from Sophy who was in the back with Jill. Dimitra had opted to say goodbye at the villa rather than in the cold neutrality of the airport terminal, and she had been weeping as the car had drawn away. However, the fact that Jill had promised to fly out for another visit at Christmas had made her tears not altogether unhappy ones.

Evangelos parked the car and loaded their suitcases on to a trolley, but as the little party made their way into the building he suddenly stopped dead, almost causing Sophy and Jill who had followed behind him and Michael to cannon into his back.

'What on earth…?' they heard him mutter, before he turned round and said, 'Over there, look. It is Andreas, isn't it?'

Sophy looked. It was. An instinctive and primitive fear made her want to run, but she wasn't sure if it was away from him or to him. Instead she just stood absolutely still as she watched him walk towards them. He looked cool and disturbingly calm.

'You're in America,' Evangelos said accusingly.

'Clever me.' Andreas answered his father but his eyes were on Sophy's white, tight face.

'When did you get back?' Evangelos asked bewilderedly. 'And surely the negotiations aren't completed yet?'

'I landed half an hour ago and I fly back in a couple of hours and no, the negotiations aren't complete,' Andreas said expressionlessly. 'However, I've some negotiations of my own which are a damn sight more important. Sophy and I are going for a walk, so you can get the coffees in and we'll see you later.'

'The plane leaves in a couple of hours. Sophy needs to book in,' Evangelos began, but he found he was speaking to thin air, Andreas having taken Sophy's arm and marched her away.

'What…what are you doing?' She found her voice at last but it emerged a shaky whisper.

'Changing schedules, cancelling meetings and flying halfway across the world,' Andreas answered drily without looking down at her. 'Pursuing a woman who has driven me mad from day one.'

He looked every inch the dynamic tycoon in a crisp grey business suit and white shirt, and he took her breath away.

She wasn't aware she was crying until they emerged into the watery sunlight outside, the rain having stopped and a feeble sun beginning to break through the clouds. And then it was Andreas who said very softly, 'Don't cry,' as he reached down and carefully wiped her eyes with a large handkerchief. 'I just needed to see you before you go, that's all. There are things I have to make clear. Things which it's necessary you understand.'

'What things?' They had just turned a corner of the building into a quiet area of reserved parking, and now he stopped, turning her into him and cupping her chin before taking her lips in a hungry kiss, a kiss that was charged with passion and incredibly sweet. It was heaven—and hell—to be in his arms again. Heaven because there was nowhere else she would rather be, and hell because she knew it couldn't last.

'What things?' As he raised his head, she saw his eyes

were very clear and shining silver. 'That I intend to go on doing this, for a start. England is not so very far away and the wonders of modern technology mean I can be with you most weekends.'

It wasn't what she had expected and she stared at him open-mouthed for a moment, before shutting her lips with a little snap. And then she found her voice and said dully, 'You can't.'

'I can.' His voice was exceedingly firm. 'And I'm going to.'

Sophy pushed at his hard chest and felt the steady beat of his heart, but he refused to let her go, even when she said, 'Andreas, this is crazy. I said all there was to say—'

'Exactly.' He reached out and traced the outline of her lips with one finger and she quivered at his touch before she could disguise the weakness. 'You talked, I listened. Now it is my turn. I don't intend to let you ruin both our lives because of a shadowy figure in the past who bears no relation to me,' he said with a touch of grimness. 'I appreciate it might take time to convince you, but we have time. Lots of time.'

'I can't go through all this again. I don't want to talk—'

'I'm talking, you're listening,' he reminded her steadily. 'I've done a lot of thinking while we've been apart, and I can see this has happened too quickly for you, with your childhood and all the baggage you've brought into adulthood. But that *is* how it happens sometimes. My father knew within seconds of meeting my mother that she was the person he wanted to spend the rest of his life with, and nothing could have dissuaded him. I have discovered I am my father's son in more ways than one. I don't intend to give up, Sophy, so face it.'

Sophy shook her head, panic at feeling she was being swept away by an unstoppable force uppermost again. 'Your parents were different,' she objected feverishly.

'That was them, a different situation. You can't relate it to us.'

'I thought there was no us?' And then, as she went to speak, he said softly, 'I am not going to take away your right to choose when you are ready for me, Sophy, not by physical force, or mental. You love me but now you have to get to know me. I understand this. It can be as slow as you want. But please accept this and save us both a lot of wasted time—*I am not going to give up.* Not now, not five or ten or fifteen years from now. You will grow to trust me as well as love me. I want you for my wife, the mother of my children. I want us to grow old together and watch our grandchildren play in the sunshine. Nothing else will do.'

The rush of love she felt was so intense, she had to take a steadying breath before she could say, 'And if it never happens, what then? What if I can't forget the past and learn to believe you, to trust you? What then?'

'You don't have to forget the past.' He touched her face gently, his fingers moving over her cheek, her jaw and the silky skin of her throat. 'You just have to conquer it, and we can do that together. That is your first lesson in trust, my love, to believe me when you can't believe yourself. There is such a thing as happy ever after, but you have to reach out for it.'

'You'll get tired of waiting for me.'

'Never.' He smiled his beautiful smile that made her heart melt.

'There are hundreds of lovely women out there,' Sophy said a trifle desperately. 'Women without any hang-ups, women who would fall into your arms if you so much as clicked your fingers.'

'No, there is only you.' He took her face in his hands, his eyes stroking her. 'For me, that is.' And then he grinned as he added, 'But I appreciate your faith in my prowess.'

She smiled reluctantly. 'This isn't funny, Andreas.'

'No, it is not,' he agreed, his eyes suddenly serious. 'I have discovered that for myself. You are such a fragile-looking, delicate little thing, but you have this incredible will which I never guessed at when I first saw you. I thought it would be easy. I would wine you and dine you and you would fall madly in love with me, and that would be that.'

'I did fall madly in love with you.'

'But that was only the beginning of my fight to win you.'

He saw her eyes darken as he spoke and felt the slight withdrawal of the slender body in his arms. 'What is it?' he said quickly. 'What have I just said?'

'Nothing.' She dropped her eyes from his, her face tense.

'No, none of that,' he said grimly. 'From now on you speak from the heart, whether I will like it or not, and I shall do the same. No secrets, no fencing, no pretence.'

She was such a mess inside, she thought helplessly. He would get fed up with her—he would. And then, when she saw he wasn't about to give in, she murmured, 'I have always thought the reason my father married my mother in the first place was because she represented something of a challenge to him. He was used to women adoring him, and she did, she certainly did, but she held out for marriage before she would sleep with him. He had met someone who didn't fall into his arms so readily as all the others, and that was why he wanted her. Once they were married and Jill and I were on the way…'

'Sophy, I cannot deny that there are men like your father,' Andreas said quietly, 'only that I am not one of them. But words are cheap and words will not provide the balm you need on what is still an open wound. If you were pregnant with my child—' he paused for an infinitesimal second and she felt his hands tighten on her waist '—I would be the proudest man on earth. I would want to wrap you up in cotton wool and be with you every minute to protect you and our child. That is the natural response of a normal man. Your father—' He stopped abruptly, and shook his head, swearing softly in his own language.

'But we only met a couple of weeks ago,' Sophy pointed out with undeniable logic. 'How could we know if we're compatible?'

His eyes answered that question and she blushed hotly. He bent down, kissing her long and hard again, for good measure.

'Okay, so we're compatible,' she murmured when she'd got her breath back. 'But—'

'I will deal with the buts.' He moulded her against the hot, hard length of him. 'Or my name is not Andreas Karydis.'

'I have to go.' His self-assurance was frightening.

He understood instantly. 'That's not a problem,' he said with silky emphasis. 'Because I will see you at the week-end. I will see you at every weekend. Okay?'

'Andreas, this is crazy.' Her voice quavered a little in spite of all her efforts to project the cool, calm image that had protected her in the past. 'This whole thing is crazy.'

'Love is crazy, sweetheart.'

It was the second endearment since they had been talking and the quality of his voice sent her heart soaring before she called it to heel. 'We're only prolonging the agony,' she insisted with a brittle emphasis that told him she was near the end of her tether. 'I can't do this, any of it. I'm not what you think I am. I haven't got the energy to keep scraping at the wound, which is what you're asking; neither could I bury my head in the sand when it all began to go wrong.'

'It won't go wrong, so that deals with that one,' he said with magnificent determination. 'And it is not energy that is required, only courage, and you have that in abundance.'

She stared at him for long seconds, and then for the first

time since she had set eyes on Andreas Karydis the nagging sense of apprehension eased a little. 'You are so Greek,' she said weakly.

'But our children will have English blood too,' he responded with a devastating smile, 'so that is good, eh? But now you must check in for your flight, so we will return to the others, who will be very tactful and circumspect of course.' He grinned again.

'What are you going to say to them?' Sophy couldn't smile.

'The truth,' he answered simply. 'Just the truth.'

'Which is?' she asked nervously.

He stared at her, drinking in her fair, fragile beauty and the vulnerability in her face. 'That we are seeing each other,' he said quietly. 'That I love you with all my heart and intend to make you my wife, whatever it takes. That a moment spent apart from you is like a hundred years. That sort of thing.'

Their coffee was cold by the time they walked back into the terminal, but no one pointed it out. Evangelos took the news of their relationship completely in his stride and although Jill's eyes widened slightly she recovered quickly. It was left to Michael to say, with typical childish tactlessness, 'What does that mean? Seeing each other? Are you going to get married?'

'One day.' Andreas's voice was low and smoky.

'When?' Michael was all impatience, but in the next instant Jill had whisked him off his seat and carted him—not without protest—to wash his hands.

Sophy and Andreas were married ten months later, on a sunny Greek day when the sky was as blue as English cornflowers and the April sunshine was pleasantly warm.

They had both wanted the wedding to be in Halkidiki, and the little white church was full to bursting with English friends and relatives whom Andreas had flown over, along with a whole host of Greek ones. It was all colour and hushed excitement.

Michael was Andreas's best man—an honour which had the small boy as stiff and correct as a sergeant major—and Jill was Sophy's matron of honour and looked lovely in pale lemon. Christos had flown out with Sophy's sister and nephew; he had been a tower of strength for Jill since Theodore's death, and it was clear to anyone with eyes to see that the two had begun to think a great deal of each other.

But Sophy wasn't thinking about her sister's burgeoning romance; she had eyes for no one but her fiancé as she walked slowly down the aisle on Evangelos's arm. He looked stunningly handsome as he waited for her, Michael at the side of him as proud as punch. And the soft murmur of awe, as the assembled congregation turned and saw the bride, spoke of how beautiful Sophy looked in her ivory wedding dress of crushed silk, her lace veil as delicate as butterfly wings.

Andreas had spent nearly as much time in England as he had in Greece until he had persuaded Sophy to agree to marry him. She had said yes at Christmas, which she and Jill and Michael had spent in Greece with Evangelos and Dimitra, but she had known within days of arriving back in England in June that she couldn't live without him. He'd been right; he was in her head and her heart.

But the intervening time until Christmas had been necessary. The long-buried fears and issues which Andreas had brought to the surface had had to be faced and dealt with, and it had been hard. Very hard. She didn't think she could have got through without Andreas. But together they had faced the demons of fear, hurt, bitterness, resentment and not least doubt, and one by one the release had come and ghosts had been laid to rest.

'My darling. My precious, beautiful darling.'

As she reached Andreas's side his whisper was for her ears only, his eyes adoring her as she smiled up at him, happy and confident in his love.

She said her vows in a clear, soft voice that brought tears to Jill's eyes and made Dimitra reach for her handkerchief; Andreas's voice so ringing with pride that Evangelos remarked afterwards he was sure it could be heard ten miles away.

And then the service was over and they emerged from the church's flower-filled interior to a hail of rice and confetti, driving back to Evangelos's villa where a huge marquee had been erected in the grounds and a small army of caterers provided a banquet fit for royalty.

It was a wonderful day, a magical day, and the party went on long after the sky had turned to black velvet pierced with diamonds, the small band playing and the champagne still flowing into the early hours. No one wanted to go home!

But Andreas had stolen away with his bride long before then. They were spending their wedding night at home before flying to the Caribbean the next day for a month, and when at last Andreas carried her over the threshold they found Alethea had strewn rose petals over the floor to greet them. The delicate perfume filled the house, and on impulse Sophy pulled him into the garden where soft shadows danced in the moonlit fairyland.

It was still warm as they made their way down to the beach through the scented vegetation. The light was silvery, the full moon creating its own sense of whispering enchantment, and the sea sighed gently as it caressed the sand which shone white and gleaming. Everything was clean and newly washed.

'I thought we would never be alone.' Andreas's voice was dark and smoky and Sophy shivered in anticipation.

She had kicked off her wedding shoes in the house and taken off her veil and delicate gold and crystal headdress, and now she looked part of the night, her hair and billowy pale dress silvered by the ethereal light.

'You are so beautiful, exquisite,' he murmured softly as he took her fully into his arms. 'I'm almost afraid you will break if I hold you too close.'

'I won't break,' she assured him firmly. 'I want you to make love to me here, in the open with the sky and stars above us and the air as sweet as honey. And afterwards we will swim in the sea.' She smiled at him, the words a declaration.

'Skinny-dipping?' he asked teasingly, his eyes looking into hers. 'You are throwing off all your inhibitions for real, aren't you?'

'Oh, yes.' She stared at him with huge eyes, her face serious. 'This is a new beginning. My real life starts from now.'

He undressed her slowly, not least because the silk dress had endless tiny buttons, but then she stepped out of the dress and petticoats and watched his face as his eyes ran over her tantalising French underwear. The transparent cream lace bikini pants and suspender belt, and uplift bra which gave her a cleavage she'd never had before, had cost a small fortune but they were worth every penny. And she didn't feel shy, just overwhelmingly, fiercely in love as she watched the passion darken his face.

Andreas's hands were shaking slightly as he knelt down in front of her and unclipped first one suspender and then the other, peeling the silk, lace-topped stockings from her almost reverently.

As she stepped out of the last one he caught her ankle in his hands, kissing her foot with tiny burning kisses before he began to work upwards. She was shivering with desire by the time he removed the last of her clothing and, as he took her breasts in his hands, rubbing their peaks to throbbing sensitive life with his thumbs, she was already moist and ready for him.

She felt awe when Andreas was naked in front of her, hugely aroused, but in spite of his desire he touched and tasted her for a long time before he lay her on the blanket of their clothing. Sophy was in a feverish agony of need, no room in her mind for anything but her husband, and she welcomed him into her body with little cries that she was unaware of but which sent rippling contractions across Andreas's taut frame, as he tried to control his own passion until he had brought her to the peak of desire.

This was so different to anything she had known with Matthew that Sophy felt she had never been made love to before, but still Andreas delayed the moment of full release, pleasing her, and himself, until she felt her body wasn't able to contain the pleasure she was feeling and that it would shatter into a million pieces.

And then the wild rhythmic undulations that had been causing her to arch and twist hit the explosive trigger of his own need, and they disappeared over the edge together into a soaring world of pure undiluted sensation where nothing existed but each other.

His heart was beating like a hammer above hers when Sophy came back from that parallel universe, and he held her close, stroking her hair with loving fingers, kissing her face with quick burning caresses as he whispered endearments against her hot skin. It was all she could have hoped for and more.

'All I care about is you,' he murmured after a little while, 'you know that, don't you? You are everything I need, everything I will ever need. No other woman will ever touch my heart. I will love you for eternity.'

'I know,' she said softly, his body stirring again as she caressed him with hungry fingers. 'I know, my love.'

And she did. At last.

0505/02

Live the emotion

THE ITALIAN'S RIGHTFUL BRIDE by Lucy Gordon

Joanna was head over heels in love with her fiancé, Gustavo Ferrara, but…he married someone else! Twelve years on, Gustavo – now single – is thrown into turmoil when he sees Joanna again. Will she give him another chance – or is she once bitten, twice shy?

HUSBAND BY REQUEST by Rebecca Winters

(Heart to Heart)

A year ago Dominique faced the hardest battle of her life. Everything suffered – especially her marriage. Now, she's determined to win back her handsome Greek husband. Will Andreas agree to her request: to live as man and wife for one month…?

CONTRACT TO MARRY by Nicola Marsh *(9 to 5)*

Darcy Howard hires Fleur to help motivate his staff – but then she insists that workaholic Darcy needs to have more fun! But when he starts to show Fleur the best time of her life she wishes her contract was permanent – and she's not thinking about business!

THE MIRRABROOK MARRIAGE by Barbara Hannay

(Southern Cross)

Sarah Rossiter has been in love with rugged, handsome Reid McKinnon for years. They were happy together until Reid discovered a secret from his past that made him swear never to be a husband or father. Now Sarah's leaving, and Reid knows he must act or risk losing her for ever…

On sale 3rd June 2005

Available at most branches of WHSmith, Tesco, ASDA, Martins, Borders, Eason, Sainsbury's and all good paperback bookshops.

Visit www.millsandboon.co.uk

MILLS & BOON®

Live the emotion

Modern
romance™

THE ITALIAN'S MARRIAGE DEMAND by *Diana Hamilton*

Millionaire Ettore Severini was ready to marry until he learned that Sophie Lang was a scheming thief! When he sees her again Sophie is living in poverty, with a baby... Now marriage will bring Ettore everything he wants: his son, revenge, and Sophie at his mercy!

THE ENGLISH ARISTOCRAT'S BRIDE by *Sandra Field*

Rafe Holden needs a bride who will agree to an arranged, loveless marriage. He has a candidate in mind but then discovers a twin sister who arouses in him the desire he'd hoped to avoid. Will he play safe – or choose the woman who promises pleasure?

THE SPANISH BILLIONAIRE'S MISTRESS by *Susan Stephens*

Zoë Chapman loathes arrogant men like Rico Cortes! The sexy Spaniard thinks she's being nice only to get access for the film she's making. And yet each time she pushes him away their mutual physical attraction just drags them back together...

THE SICILIAN DUKE'S DEMAND by *Madeleine Ker*

Alessandro, Duke of Mandalà is every inch the Sicilian playboy. His millions and his suave Sicilian heritage make him dangerously attractive... Isobel Roche knew all this before she met him – but nothing could have prepared her for his skilful seduction...

Don't miss out...
On sale 3rd June 2005

Available at most branches of WHSmith, Tesco, ASDA, Martins, Borders, Eason, Sainsbury's and all good paperback bookshops.

Visit www.millsandboon.co.uk

MILLS & BOON®

Volume 12 on sale from 4th June 2005

Lynne Graham

International Playboys

Tempestuous Reunion

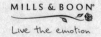

MILLS & BOON®

Live the emotion

0505/03b

Medical
romance™

THE HEART SURGEON'S PROPOSAL
by Meredith Webber *(Jimmie's Children's Unit)*

Paediatric anaesthetist Maggie Walsh fell in love with surgery fellow Phil Park when they both joined the elite Children's Cardiac Unit. But he never seemed to look her way – until the night they fell into bed! Now Maggie is pregnant! Phil will do the right thing – for the baby's sake – but Maggie won't consent to a loveless marriage…

EMERGENCY AT THE ROYAL **by Joanna Neil**

Dr Katie Sherbourn knows she shouldn't get too close to A&E consultant Drew Bradley. It would upset her ill father and alienate her from her beloved family. But memories of her relationship with Drew leave Katie yearning for his touch. And working closely with him at the Royal forces her to confront her feelings…

THE MEDICINE MAN **by Dianne Drake** *(24/7)*

Chayton Ducheneaux turned his back on his Sioux roots for life as a high-powered Chicago surgeon. He'd never give it up to return home. But then he meets the reservation doctor, Joanna Killian. She's dedicated, determined – and beautiful. And as the attraction between them grows Chay learns what being a doctor – and a man – is really about…

On sale 3rd June 2005